THE
LITTLEST
DOUBTS

CHRISTINA DUDLEY

Bellevue, Washington

The Littlest Doubts

VITA

Published by Bellavita Press
Bellevue, Washington 98004
www.bellavitapress.com

Author photo: Natalie Wallace, Platinum-Multimedia.com

Printed and bound in the United States of America

LCCN 2010904762

ISBN 978-0-615-36570-1

To my Readers.
Thank you for enthusiasm and support.
You make writing a joy.

. . .

Dear Susan —
How I treasure your friendship
and encouraging heart.

Christ

*W*here love is great, the littlest doubts are fear;
Where little fears grow great, great love grows there.

(*Hamlet*, III.ii)

CHAPTER 1:

Out of the Box

A banging on my bedroom door interrupted me.

I vaulted from the window seat, stuffing the book I was reading under the cushion and sitting on it a second before Joanie barged in. Her wavy red-gold hair was pulled back in a ponytail and she was armed with the lambswool duster.

"Whoa! I didn't know you were home," she said. "Why are you holed up in here? Not to be annoying, but I want to get all the cleaning done ASAP."

My best friend of many years and housemate for eleven months took in the state of the room: bed still unmade, trail of used Kleenexes from the bathroom to where I sat, my unshowered condition.

"Oh my God," said Joanie. "What is it? Is this the day Troy and Min died?"

"No," I sniffled.

"Then it's your wedding anniversary."

"No."

"Nadina had a miscarriage."

"No!"

"You met James' new girlfriend?"

"Definitely *No*." I smiled in spite of myself. "And that wouldn't make me cry, I don't think. I'm over him."

"I should say so," she agreed. "Dumping you just because you're adopting a baby. Not that I blame him. Fine, then. Don't make me play Twenty Questions—what on earth is wrong with you? Are you PMS?"

"Oh, for Pete's sake." I reached under the seat cushion and pulled out the book I'd been reading: *Parenting after the Loss of a Child*.

Taking it from me, her blue eyes rolled. "You have got to be kidding me—why do you do this to yourself? Like you need any more torture in your life."

"I thought it would be helpful."

"I see that." She flung it and the duster on my bed, coming to join me in the window seat. "What got you all morbid? Did you have another dream about Min?"

I nodded. "Yeah. This is—what—two weeks straight that it's been going on? Sometimes I dream it's the night she was born—how it was snowing and Troy had to put the chains on. Everything was white and soft and muffled. Then other times, it's her playing or talking to me. Last night it was when she saw the guy dressed up as Red Robin at the restaurant and cried till she was purple. And that's just at night, Joanie! Even during the day I find myself remembering all kinds of things now..." Things I hadn't thought of for a long time: the sound of my daughter's laugh, how she dragged herself around the house commando-style before she learned to crawl, how she didn't like stuffed animals with plastic eyes.

Joanie threw both arms around me and gave me a bracing hug. "I know it hurts, Cass, but it's probably not all bad that this is coming out now. You're always stuffing your feelings down. Everything you don't want to deal with just goes in the box, and now it's like the lid won't shut anymore." Having never stuffed a feeling down her whole life long, she shook her head as she said this, mystified.

"Great," I said, blotting my eyes with a fresh Kleenex. "Now I'm an emotional jack-in-the-box and no one knows when that clown is going to bust out and scare the pants off everybody."

"In my humble opinion, emotional jack-in-the-box sure beats emotional zombie," said Joanie, "which is what you were the first year."

True enough. After my husband's enlarged heart led to the car accident that took him and my little girl, I spent a solid four seasons lying in bed. Summer, fall, winter, spring. Not much to go on about. Picture Snow White in her glass casket and you have the general idea.

It was only in the second year, when Joanie's lawyer brother Daniel bought a giant house in Clyde Hill, that things started happening. Joanie and I and girlfriend Phyl Levert all moved in as housekeeping staff. We named the place the Palace, only half-jokingly, and Daniel's in-law apartment the Lean-To. I might have been stuffing my feelings down that second year, but at least I started functioning again, enough to keep up with household responsibilities, get a part-time job and even start dating. If I tried to avoid thinking about Min, it was only because I was afraid I'd get sucked back into that dark place. Better just not to go there mentally.

The second year also marked Nadina Stern's entrance into my quiet life. For reasons that shall ever be mysterious to me, I signed up to mentor a student at Camden School, the nearby alternative high school for kids kicked out of the public system. Never had I known anyone like her: 15-years-old at the time, abusing drugs and alcohol, foul-mouthed, living with her hopeless boyfriend Mike. We would hang out every Tuesday after school, talking, going for walks, training Phyl's dog Benny. Building trust with Nadina was a two-steps-forward-one-step-back process, but gradually she let me into her life. It was I who heard her breaking news first when she got fired or got robbed or got fired again or got pregnant, all of which did indeed happen in the span of a few months. It was I who convinced her to carry her baby to term, and it was I who would adopt that baby, when he was born.

Talking Nadina into having Baby Ned was no slam dunk. Her original plan was to tell no one and get an abortion, her second, as a matter of fact. She especially wanted to avoid the subject with me, fearing I would "go all friggin' religious and judgmental" on her. If I did get religious on her, it was her fault because—until Nadina entered my life—I had been keeping God at arm's length. After losing Troy and Min, I went to church, yes, but I didn't pray and I didn't trust and I really didn't want anything more to do with Him. It was Nadina's skeptical questions and crazy life that drove me back. She was too much for me to handle alone.

When I tried to persuade her that fateful afternoon that each one of us mattered to God, that each life mattered to God, I ended up convincing myself.

Nadina was still Nadina. She was minus the drugs and alcohol for the moment, and with Mike doing prison time at Coyote Ridge, she was minus the loser boyfriend, but she was still sixteen years old, mouthy and volatile. Always walking as far out on the cliff as she could and looking into the chasm.

From a worldly perspective, adopting Nadina's baby might not be the wisest choice I ever made, but I experienced peace like no other when I made the decision. I was no longer an unresolved cosmic plotline—I had a purpose.

Now, a few months later, I still had the resolve, and I needed it. Because my choice to adopt was making hash of my shaky self-possession. The tightness in my throat and gut was back; the tears were back. It was labor all over again, with its breathless constriction, but this time I was birthing loss and fearful hope. Could I love another baby like I loved Min? Did I really want to?

Joanie watched me for another minute, but apparently I had used up her daily allowance of empathy. Bouncing back to her feet she started picking up my used tissues between her fingernails. "My prescription for you, girl, is to stop with the depressing books. Clean up, get dressed and go do something. Or at least do your crying outside so you get some fresh air. Your eyes and nose are all red. Daniel's sure to notice, and then he's sure to say something, and then your jack-in-the-box is gonna come busting out again."

I didn't answer, turning my head quickly to hide my expression, but she saw anyhow. "What?"

"What what?" Grabbing a pillow off the floor, I threw it back on the bed and started straightening the covers.

"What was that look you got on your face when I mentioned Daniel?" Joanie flicked the used tissue wads in the wastebasket. "You know, you two have been weird lately—all friendly and polite and not needling each other. I was going to ask you what was going on, but you've been so dumpy that I left you alone."

"And I'm not dumpy today?"

"You are, but at this rate I don't know if you're ever gonna undump. What's the deal with you two? *Is* there something going on?"

If only I knew.

When I hesitated, Joanie sat right down on the covers I had in my hands and crossed her arms over her chest. "Spill it."

I spilled.

"Well—you remember that day when Daniel announced I wasn't going to move out?"

She nodded.

"He and I were talking on the deck, but we weren't…negotiating rent or anything. He—he told me that day that he…liked me. And I was trying to make it clear that I didn't want to go there. That's why we've been funny lately." I almost blushed as I said it, since, if Joanie had seen us that day, she might well have asked what I was doing making out with him if I "didn't want to go there."

Her mouth popped open. "He 'likes' you? I can't even picture those lame words coming out of his mouth! He told you, 'I like you, Cass'?"

Feeling my face get hotter, I said quickly, "Well, no. He put it more forcefully than that, you can imagine. But it doesn't matter. The end result is the same. I can't deal with it right now—the box is overflowing, remember?—and I'm sure he'll forget all about it in a couple weeks." I shooed her off the bed and handed her the duster.

"That's what you said about James," said Joanie, "and we all know how that went."

"Yes," I conceded. James' interest in me lasted more than a few weeks. In fact, for a time—that is, until I decided to take Nadina's baby—he even wanted to get married. But James was a good Christian boy, eager to make an honest woman of someone so he could have legal sex. Daniel, on the other hand… Daniel had already slept with most of the single women in the greater Puget Sound, so one more or less couldn't be a big deal.

"How long did my dear brother say he's been interested in you?" asked Joanie.

Squirming a little, I said, "Oh, I guess a few months."

"Months!" Joanie looked astonished. "Months! Crap almighty. Did you know this, Cass?"

"I suspected something… but I had plenty of other things on my mind. I didn't want to deal with it."

"So it went in the box," said Joanie. She frowned. "If he's been interested for months I'll bet he did more than just ask you on a date. Tell me everything. Stop holding out on me."

Throwing my hands up in surrender, I said, "Okay, okay. He said he's been trying to… win my respect and even going to the men's Bible study on Saturday mornings—" (Joanie gave a huge gasp at this) "—not that he's made any firm decisions in the religion department. And—and—he—uh… askedmetomarryhim."

Such was her amazement that she sank back onto my newly-made bed, mouthing my words to herself, looking like Helen Keller the instant before the Big Breakthrough.

At last she looked up. "And you said… no?"

"Of course I said no, you idiot!" I cried. "Haven't I had enough trouble in my life without marrying your somewhat-atheist brother who would have an affair every other week?"

"'If anyone is in Christ, he is a new creation,'" suggested Joanie.

I stared at her. "What are you doing? You sound like Phyl! Besides, Daniel isn't officially in Christ, as far as I know, so he's the same old creation he ever was."

Joanie gave herself a shake. "You're totally right. What am I saying? Living with Phyl for a year really does a number on you." She hopped up from the bed and started running the duster along the shelves, not really paying any attention to what she was doing. "Still, I cannot believe he even considered going to a Bible study for your sake. He must really like you. Ha! Serves him right. You're so practical and un-swoony that he must be frustrated as all get out." When I didn't answer, she got alert again, pausing. "Did he try to kiss you?"

"Ye-e-e-s," I said.

Her eyes got round. "And? Come on, Cass—dish! I tell you *everything*."

Seeing my chance to change the subject, I pounced on this. "That's not true. You don't tell me a thing about you and Perry." Perry, my recently-divorced younger brother, on whom Joanie had developed an ill-advised crush.

Sure enough, her lips compressed into a grim line. "That's because there's nothing to tell. Perry doesn't think about me that way at all, and you've already told me I'll break his tender heart and not to throw myself at him, so what's there to talk about? Now don't try to weasel out of this—what went on with Daniel?"

"Fine!" I griped. "He kissed me, and I liked it, but that doesn't change anything. I told him I could only live here if he laid off me because I have enough going on without him badgering me. So he agreed to leave me alone for at least six months, if not forever."

"Six months?" she repeated.

"He won't last that long, right?" I asked. "He'll be off on someone else way before then. I even told him he had to date a couple other people."

Joanie shook her head. "You're crazy! If you wanna keep a guy in reserve, why would you tell him to date other people?"

"I'm not keeping him in reserve. I'm encouraging him to know his own mind. I figure he'll move on, and if he's going to, he should do it sooner, rather than later."

"I don't know," she said slowly. "Ordinarily I'd say forget it—he'll be long gone in a couple weeks. But he also gets really set on things, and if he's already lasted months with no encouragement from you, what's a few more? Plus the fact that he's even willing to set foot in a church for you—!"

I righted a picture frame she had knocked over and then propelled her by the shoulders toward the windowsills.

"Well, if he sticks around, it's at his own risk. I need to deal with that baby first. Between meetings with the lawyer and obsessing over Min and keeping an eye on Nadina and getting everything ready, the adoption is turning into a full-time job. But even without all that, Joanie, I can't picture ever wanting to marry someone who has to beat off women wherever he goes. I'd always have to wonder if he was sleeping around. Can you honestly say you think Daniel could stick to just one woman—any woman—the rest of his natural life?"

She mulled this over. "Probably not, barring some sort of near-death, life-changing experience. But he always has liked you as a person. I think for you, Cass, he'd make an effort."

This made me smile. "Mm…what more could a wife ask for, than her husband 'make an effort'? I can picture me finding lipstick on his collar and him saying, 'Yeah, sorry about that. This monogamy business is rough, but I do give it the old college try.'"

Shrugging, she propped the duster in the wastebasket and headed for my bathroom. "Fine, then. You're determined not to be my sister.

You won't let me like Perry, and you won't let my brother like you. Just be nice to Daniel, okay, Cass? You can be so mean sometimes."

"Like you're such a sweetheart!" I said indignantly.

She waved this off with a rubber-gloved hand. "I just mean, if he really is this crazy about you, go easy on him. You might end up wanting him after all."

• • •

"I suspected there was something like that going on with him," Phyl said in her soft voice, when I took Joanie's advice and went outside for fresh air therapy. "Ever since you two went to the New Year's party, as a matter of fact. And of course he would like you."

"Bless you for that, Phyl," I said, remembering how she herself had a pretty severe crush on him last fall, a crush so evident that Daniel had wanted to kick her out. "I think my bra is at least two cup sizes smaller than his average, and I've never been offered a modeling contract, but I appreciate your sentiment."

We were in the front yard, replacing some of the spent flowers and pinching back the petunias in the hanging baskets. Or at least, Phyl was. I was sitting on the step, idly swinging the spade on its leather strap and handing her things when she asked for them.

"I meant you have similar minds," she explained, cramming one more fuchsia clump in with its fellows. "Not that you're not beautiful, Cass."

I grinned. "Naturally. My looks are a given. But back to our similarities: you're saying I think like a worldly, half-atheist, oversexed lawyer? Well, 'let me not to the marriage of true minds admit impediments.'"

Nodding, she smiled. "That's what I mean. Quoting people. Sometimes Joanie and I listen to you two talk, and it's like you're in your own little world."

"Not you too, Phyl," I complained. "Don't you think he would cheat on me, like Jason did on you?" Jason was Phyl's ex-husband, and a cheater, if ever there was one.

Sitting back on her heels, she slowly rotated the basket she was working on, checking for bald spots. "Daniel's a nicer guy than Jason, and he respects you more than Jason ever respected me. I think he probably would mess up a few times, especially since women always fling themselves at him, but he'd definitely be more sorry about it than Jason ever was."

Laughing, I pelted her with some of the petunia deadheads. "I thought you and Joanie loved me! Here you are, the two of you hoping I'll hook up with a guy you both admit will try very hard and very unsuccessfully to make a good husband, but at least he'll apologize nicely. Forgive me if I stick with my original plan and just try to ignore him till he snaps out of it. Which he may already be doing."

• • •

The subject of all this speculation emerged from the house shortly afterward, golf clubs in tow, chest indecently outlined by his polo shirt. Glancing around, he saw Phyl at the side of the Palace, rinsing out the empty plant start containers with the hose.

He paused beside me on the porch.

"It's the 19th of June," said Daniel, looking down at me.

I tilted my head back to squint at him. "Your point being?"

"One month," he said, continuing down the steps. "One down, five to go."

With that, he threw the clubs in the trunk of his car and drove away.

CHAPTER TWO:

Birth Pains

"There's a Preparation for Childbirth class at Overlake starting next week," I said, pulling the newspaper announcement from my purse.

Nadina barely glanced at it and certainly didn't reach for it. Instead she picked up Benny's chewy and sent it flying. Benny was the apricot Labradoodle shared by Phyl and her ex-husband. We were on our favorite bench at the lake on an unusually hot afternoon. Nadina's pale blonde spikes had wilted somewhat, giving her rather a boyish air, apart from the distinctly rounded bump that made it more comfortable for her to sit splay-legged. I was always surprised how much she did stick out at this point, given her long torso.

When it was clear she wasn't going to answer, I continued, "I thought I could go with you, or your mom could. It's only once a week for six weeks."

"What's the point? Doesn't the baby just come out when it's ready, while you lay there screaming your ass off?"

"Sort of, but not necessarily," I said patiently. "If you get an epidural, like I did, you can't even feel your ass, much less scream it off."

Nadina turned on me, laughing with delight. "You cussed! You said 'ass'!"

"Yeah," I said. "The Bible says 'bad company corrupts good character.'"

"Damned straight," said Nadina. "Look what you've done to me."

Waving the announcement to recapture her attention, I continued, "The class would probably be helpful so that you know what to expect—what exactly is going on inside your body to get the baby out—and what to do if you decide to go without the drugs, or you have your baby in a taxicab."

"No friggin' way!" declared Nadina. "I am getting all the drugs they offer me. Why can't you just tell me what's going to happen? It sucks enough that friggin' Lori Lincoln wants me to meet with that adoption counselor, like I don't have enough people telling me what to do. You had a baby—just tell me what I need to know."

"But I don't remember half of what went on," I objected. Never mind that my subconscious dwelt more and more on it. "It was years ago, and I took the epidural the first time the anesthesiologist offered. Some women don't have the option—by the time they decide they want drugs after all, the guy's nowhere to be found."

"Dude, I could've told you, you never pass up drugs when they're offered," she said incorrigibly. Retrieving Benny's chewy between two fingers, she wiped the slime off it onto the grass. "I woulda never let you talk me into having this baby if I knew all the crap I'd have to put up with. People nosing around in what isn't any of their friggin' business. Like, if I go with you to the class, they're gonna look at me and think things, right? 'Cause I'm there with you, instead of with Mike or something."

Personally, I thought people would find a lot more to stare at if Mike were there, he being half a foot shorter, wispy, and pale as death, but I kept this to myself.

"Oh, whatever," I said. "I bet half the people who show up aren't your standard husband-wife combo. They'll probably just think I'm your midwife or doula or something."

She grimaced. "What the hell is a doula?"

"A birthing coach."

Nadina gave a derisive snort. "That's even worse! I don't want people to think I can't push out a friggin' baby without my own personal cheerleader."

"Look, you," I said, laughing in spite of myself, "having a baby is a big deal. It's hard on your body, and it's emotional, even if you're just going to hand Ned to me. Maybe especially if you're going to hand Ned to me. Don't knock people for wanting some help with that. Are you in? Are we going to the class?"

. . .

To my chagrin, it turned out Nadina guessed right: with the exception of us, the class was entirely made up of your standard male-female pairings. *Lord, would one single mom or a lesbian couple have been too much to ask?* I wondered. Nadina's eyes narrowed and her shoulders hunched defensively, but we found chairs in the circle. Troy and I had taken one of these classes, in my past life, and if I wasn't mistaken, we had the same touchy-feely, wire-haired, middle-aged instructor. With Troy, her style had struck us as amusing—with Nadina I suspected it might be a dealbreaker.

"Childbirth," breathed the woman, who introduced herself as Pat and had apparently not gotten the memo that the sixties were over, "is both completely natural and completely miraculous, otherworldly." Pat turned her face upward like a sunflower, shut her eyes, let the miracle wash over her, and then turned to gaze at each of us. Beside me, I heard Nadina make a slow, nasally sound, like air escaping an inner tube. When I didn't look over, she poked me in the ribs. Frowning, I shook my head.

"In this class we will cover how your body changes in late pregnancy—" ("You get hella fat and your ankles get bigger than your neck," supplied Nadina in a low voice.) "—What to expect during the labor and birth process—" ("Sharp pains in the ass, and then a baby.") "—How to increase your confidence as you approach your baby's birth—" ("Don't look in any mirrors or wear any tube tops.") "—Skills for comfort and progress during labor—" ("They're called drugs.") "—When to come to the hospital—" ("Before the baby falls out.") "—And finally, how to care for your newborn—" ("Give it to Cass.") ("Would you shut up and listen?" I ordered.)

Pat described the stages of labor, including the nuttiness that is active labor, by which time she had all the pregnant women wide-eyed and the partners looking uneasy. "Because the behavior of the mother can change under duress—I have seen the most modest women rip all their clothes off, and I have heard the most mild-mannered women cuss at everyone around them at the top of their lungs—I think we should practice some trust-building exercises now."

"Dude," hissed Nadina, "if the modest women rip their clothes off and cuss everyone out, what do you think I'll do?" Despite myself, I snickered, and Pat gave us stink-eye.

Besides Nadina's stream of wisecracks, the thought of doing trust-building exercises with her *was* funny, given how I had spent the last ten months trying to earn her trust, and if I didn't have it now, a couple exercises were not going to do the trick. Especially exercises like these, where even the most gushy couple present was hard-put to keep a straight face. With one half of every pair seven months pregnant, Pat at least didn't force us to do the drill where one person has to fall and be caught by the other, but we had to do others equally corny: staring at each other to work on eye contact, one partner blindfolding the other and leading her through an obstacle course, and so on.

"It'll get better," I said bracingly, as we finished our first class.

But the following week we worked on breathing, which apparently a few couples mistook for a chakra meditation class, assuming enlightened poses that Pat praised. ("I feel the peace emanating from you! Take that mindset, that focus, with you into childbirth.")

Predictably, Nadina took one look at this and said, "I'm done. This is such bullshit. I'm not coming back next week, Cass. I could be getting more hours at Petco before I'm out of commission."

Ever since I had known her, Nadina worked at Petco off and on. When it was on, it was a good fit for her, given her extraordinary talent with dogs. When it was off, it was usually because Nadina blew herself up.

Sighing, I abandoned rubbing her back, the relaxation technique Pat had assigned. "Can't you just take what's useful and ignore the rest?" I asked. "Try to pretend everyone else isn't here." She scowled but didn't answer. This was an improvement, since ordinarily she loved to do exactly the opposite of what I told her. Pressing my advantage, I said, "We'll just take it one class at a time. Come next week, and we'll decide."

But that session turned out to be a blow-by-blow rundown of preeclampsia: what is was, what the symptoms were. When Pat mentioned it being more frequent in teenage and over-40 mothers, I looked sharply at Nadina to see if any of the symptoms alarmed her, but she was texting away on her cell phone and not paying the least attention.

So be it. It really was pointless. Maybe I could continue coming alone and try to download any nuggets into that girl's brain, but, truth be told, Pat was getting on my nerves too. As were the earnest couples. Call it sour grapes, but I did want to tell many of them to give it a rest. Give it a rest with the detailed birth plans and the yoga poses and the pre-class chatter over anti-stretch-mark creams. With my crazy Min dreams and the recurring lumps in my throat when I saw the tender couples goggling at each other, husband's hand on the wife's belly, I could see myself snapping one afternoon—completely losing it—shrieking and tearing around the room wild-eyed, my hair streaming behind me: "Beware! Death can strike at any moment! I too once had a husband's hand on my pregnant belly! Beware beware *beware*!!!"

"Fine," I said. "Never mind the class."

"Whoo hoo!" Nadina cheered. "Let's go get some ice cream."

. . .

The Baskin-Robbins at the mall was close enough to Pottery Barn Kids that Nadina wanted to take a look. For all her scathing comments about the preciousness and the prices, I could tell her scorn wasn't unmixed with envy. "Check this out!" she exclaimed, pointing dangerously at the airplane-appliquéd crib bedding with her gooey, half-eaten scoop of cookie dough ice cream. "The whole friggin' set only comes to $220, not including the stupid matching curtains. I want this for Ned."

"Not buying it," I said shortly. "What do babies care about bedding? I don't have the money or the inclination to give Ned the Pottery Barn life, so if that's what you want, you may want to check out an adoption agency after all."

"What about the airplane-shaped bed?"

"Not buying it."

"Dude, he could have his own kid-size farmers market stand set—on sale for $489! Oh, wait, that's just the friggin' apple cart. The awning is $215."

"Not buying it."

Nadina jammed the last of her cone in her mouth and wiped her hands off on her jeans while she chewed. Then she faced me, arms akimbo, trying to look threatening, but her hands couldn't get purchase on her hips because of her belly. "Cass, tell me straight up. You know I don't want any of this crap—not really, I mean. I mean, I wish it could be something I had the money for and decided not to get, instead of stuff I couldn't get even if I wanted. But aren't you going to get Ned anything? I mean, is he gonna be one of those kids who grows up having to wear clothes his mom sewed?"

Laughing, I said, "God help him if he were, because I can't sew.

Ned would have to wear pillowcases with arm and neck holes cut out of them." I tugged on her. "Come on. Why don't you come over and see what Phyl's been doing with the spare room? I may not be buying much, but there's plenty of stuff I got from church friends who are done having babies. And there'll even be new things when we have the baby shower. Don't worry—Ned'll have what he needs in life, and probably even some of what he wants."

• • •

It was odd to think that Nadina had finally only met Phyl and Joanie a few weeks ago, when they came to the Camden School graduation with me. Nadina didn't graduate, of course, being only sixteen, but Mark Henneman the director had a special moment of recognition for her, since she would be moving to Cleveland, Ohio, after the baby was born. In Cleveland her Great-Aunt Sylvia awaited, along with St. Helen's Institute for Girls. Having heard so much about Nadina, Joanie and Phyl were as eager to meet her as she was to meet them, and it didn't hurt that, with the girls along, conversation with my ex-boyfriend James wasn't too awkward.

Phyl was out front when we got there, thinning the carrot and beet sproutlings, and she cheerfully waved her trowel at us.

"Want to come show Nadina what you've done with Ned's room?" I asked.

"Be right there," Phyl said. "And Cass, I set up my interview time with that social worker for a week after our group interview."

All prospective adoptive parents had to undergo a home study, to my dismay, in which a social worker came out for several observations and interviewed all people living in the future home, at least once as a group and once individually. The Palace was no crack house, but neither were we a conventional living arrangement. Daniel's lawyer friend Lori Lincoln assured me the study was largely *pro forma*, but I still wasn't looking forward to it.

Coming inside abruptly from the glaring sunshine made it hard to make things out at first, and I didn't see Joanie until she sprung up from the couch, cell phone crammed to her ear. "Yeah, okay, that's great!" she muttered, whisking past Nadina and me into the kitchen. "Looking forward to it. See you soon. Bye."

She clicked her phone shut, swished her hair over her shoulder and greeted us too casually.

"Date?" I asked, following her into the kitchen.

"No, no," said Joanie hurriedly, turning faintly pink. "Just catching up. How are you, Nadina?"

Trying to recall a time I'd seen Joanie blush before, I drew a blank. Very suspicious. "Were you talking to Perry?" I asked accusingly.

"What are you, telepathic?" she demanded. Her chin jutted out. "I can talk to Perry if I want, if that even was Perry. It's a free country."

"I can't believe you, Joanie," I groaned. "Would you please, please go out with somebody else? And what did you mean, 'See you soon'? Is he coming down from Bellingham? Are you going up?"

"You know, Cass," Joanie said, firing up, "I would be more willing to open up with you if you weren't always so negative and trying to make me feel guilty. Maybe I should tell that social worker who wants to interview me what a paranoid tight-ass you are."

This would ordinarily be the time that Nadina would chime in, shrieking with laughter, since "tight-ass" was one of her favorite designations for me, but when I glanced at her, surprised by her silence, I saw her gaze was fixed on the view out the bay window: Daniel, scouring the grill with some fancy wire-bristle brush Joanie had gotten. Nadina's mouth had actually fallen open, no joke, and who could blame her? No one but Daniel could pick and whang at a grill rack and make it look like the June foldout of a Fireman-of-the-Month Calendar.

My distraction distracted Joanie, and we shared half-exasperated, half-amused looks.

"Dude," breathed Nadina, when she finally recovered the power of speech. "Is that Daniel? Oh my God, Cass, you forgot to tell me that he is fi—i—i—ine!" Each "i" in "fine" became its own word, the way she said it.

"Did I?" I asked dryly. "Well, now you know."

"Oh my God," she said again. "How did you ever even notice friggin' James? Forget stupid Ned's room—I'd rather just look at this dude the rest of the day!"

"For crying out loud, Nadina, he's almost old enough to be your father," I chided. "In fact, in your teen pregnancy book, he's almost too old."

"Shut up, Cass, he's coming in!" she hissed, straightening her t-shirt, which had ridden up her belly, and fluffing her blonde spikes.

Daniel took the scene in at a glance. Maybe it was Nadina's reaction rubbing off on me, but when his eyes met mine briefly, the hint of a smile lifting the corners of his mouth, I felt suspiciously rubber-kneed. For Pete's sake.

Without a word, he handed the Joanie the grill brush, the wire bristles now mangled and ineffective.

"Did it work, before you trashed it?" she asked.

"I think we can have our first barbecue this Thursday," he said easily, "without eating too much carbon from last summer." He turned toward Nadina, who was by now gripping my upper arm painfully. "You must be Cass's friend." He held out a hand to shake, and after another beat, she managed to unclench hers from me and offer it to him.

"I'm Daniel," he continued, "Cass's—Cass's—what am I now, Cass?" He gave me a look, as we both remembered full well a fight we'd had a few months ago when I introduced him as my "landlord."

Feeling my pulse quicken, I felt a wave of irritation with myself. What was wrong with me? "This is Daniel," I said shortly. "Joanie's brother and one of my employers."

The shot fell wide because he only grinned and went on into the garage to dump the grill scrapings in the trash. Thumping on Nadina's back, I hissed, "Breathe! The baby needs oxygen."

Thankfully, Phyl came in just then, or I might never have been able to haul Nadina away from the kitchen; as it was, she trailed regretfully after us up the stairs.

The pleasant, but age- and gender-neutral, spare room had been transformed under Joanie and Phyl's care. Joanie had given the walls a coat of cheerful blue paint and painstakingly stenciled gray-green turtles along the tops. Phyl contributed a hanging spider plant and a potted peace lily, both chosen for their air-filtering powers and non-toxic greenery.

Blinking, Nadina took in her surroundings, running her hand along the white crib rail. For the second time that afternoon I found her nonplussed, but at least Ned's future nursery was a more appropriate cause for awe than Daniel's shocking good looks.

"Someone—someone gave you all this furniture?" she managed after a minute, gesturing generally at the crib and changing table and glider and ottoman and dresser.

I nodded. "Uh-huh. Who needs Pottery Barn Kids when you already know people who have things just as nice? And look, Louella Murphy herself made the crib bedding. I told her to save it for the shower, but she said this was just extra."

"Your church must be like some giant swap meet," Nadina muttered. She put her hand on her belly, which was undulating just now under her snug t-shirt. Seeing where all eyes were drawn, she added diffidently, "You can feel, if you want to."

Phyl hesitated, but Joanie slapped a hand right on. "Is this his head?" Joanie asked. "It feels hard."

"Probably," said Nadina. "If it's huge and feels like it's made out of cement. He gets that from his dad."

From Mike, I thought. The original blockhead.

As if she heard my thoughts, Nadina looked warily at me. "Mike's been writing me lately. He has lots of questions about how I'm doing and the baby."

"Did you tell him you're better, now that he's gone? And why is he even writing you?" I asked sharply. I wondered if she had deliberately brought this up when Joanie and Phyl were here to act as a buffer. "I hope you don't answer him. Why taxpayers like us have to pay for prisoners' postal service is beyond me."

Nadina whipped away from Joanie's hands and flumped down in the glider. "I knew you wouldn't like it, but I only answered him the first couple times, and then I told him I didn't think I wanted to be 'pen pals' and to leave me the hell alone."

Joanie raised her eyebrows at me, but she and Phyl discreetly left the room so we could have it out.

"So you did write him back?" I demanded. "What did he ask, and what did you tell him? You know Lori Lincoln told us not to be in contact."

Nadina looked really squirrelly now, and I saw her brows contract defensively. "He just asked if I was okay, and if I would think about naming the baby after his dad and—and—not giving it to you right away. Maybe giving it to his dad, instead." Her voice dwindled over the course of this speech, making the last almost inaudible. Almost.

Feeling as if the wind had been punched out of me, I sank onto the ottoman. "Why didn't you tell me this, Nadina?" She didn't answer, and I fought to take a few deep breaths. "Well? Say something! Did that sound like a good idea to you?"

"Hell, no!" she said scornfully. "Like Mike's dad did such a great job raising Mike? I wrote back that, too bad, sucker, I was giving the baby to you, not that it was any of his business, and that you could name it whatever you wanted, and he should butt the hell out at this point."

Groaning, I put my head in my hands. "Please tell me that that was all you said, bad as it is to antagonize him. Tell me you didn't let him know Lori Lincoln wants us to keep him off the birth certificate."

Silence.

I groaned again. "You did! Oh, crap, Nadina. What did you say to him?"

She took as deep and huffy a breath as she could manage around the baby. "You don't get it, Cass! He was being so flipping fake! He was all, 'How are you? I've missed you. I've been thinking a lot about everything, and I want to try again,' and 'My conduct has been so good so far they might let me out way early,' and 'Don't go to Cleveland and give the baby to that church lady because we need to take care of our own.' So I thought you'd be proud of me because I told him he could just cut the crap, and I was done with the part of my life that had him in it, and this baby had nothing to do with him, and I wasn't even going to put him on the birth certificate because my lawyer told me it was my baby to do with what I want, so there, asshole!"

Even groans failed me at this point. How could she have been so foolish? Lori had recommended we leave the paternity section blank, so that we wouldn't require Mike's consent for the adoption and could get by with just Nadina's. It looked like that plan wasn't going to fly anymore. Whatever vague ideas Mike may have had about alternate futures for Ned, those ideas were, I'm sure, rapidly firming up now that Nadina had pissed him off.

"And what did he say?" I asked finally, when I thought I could control my voice.

Her voice wasn't quite ready for prime time either. "He said—oh, Cass, don't be too mad at me! He said, oh yeah, well he could get a lawyer too. He knew his rights. The state would pay for all the lawyers he wanted, and don't worry about him writing me anymore because from now on it was all gonna be through them. And the last bit of his letter was like all caps: I'M THE DAD AND I'VE GOT RIGHTS AND I'LL SEE YOUR ASSES IN COURT!"

I sighed.

And so he would, barring some unforeseen miracle.

CHAPTER THREE:

Wildebeests

Traffic on the I-90 bridge crept along. I kept shooting my dashboard clock pleading looks to slow it down, but, no, I was going to be late. Is there anything worse than being late for the lawyer? Hearing not only the clock tick, but the fatal clinking of money going down the drain?

To make matters worse, the parking garage at Lori Lincoln's building was almost completely full, and I circled around and around on floor after floor, sweating copiously, before finally squeaking into a space and making a mad dash for the elevator. I knew they had cameras in there, but I could hardly pull myself together in Lori's lobby, so I shamelessly dabbed at my face and brushed my hair and straightened my clothes before the doors opened again.

Lori's receptionist looked up, a warm, grandmotherly-looking woman. Perfect for an adoption attorney's office. "There you are, Ms. Ewan. Ms. Lincoln took another call when you were late, but I'll let her know you're here." The news perked me up a little—if Lori took another call, maybe she could bill that client the twelve minutes instead.

There was only one other person waiting in the reception area, a striking, dark man with long black hair pulled back in a ponytail. Part

Native American? His black eyes flicked up from his *National Geographic*. No, not Native American. Some kind of Middle Eastern.

Although his expression was decidedly cool, I nodded. Barely returning my nod, he went back to the magazine, the cover of which caught my eye.

"Topkapi Palace? Are you reading about Topkapi Palace?" I asked impulsively.

He shook his head. "Wildebeests." No accent, at any rate, although 'wildebeest' wasn't necessarily a shibboleth. He didn't seem inclined to say more, so I grabbed the closest magazine and feigned interest: *Family Fun*. Hardly appropriate at this point, considering Ned wasn't even born, but the only other nearby choice was *Motor Trend*.

To my relief, the door to Lori's office soon opened. "Come on in, Cass." She glanced at my lobby companion and added, "I'll be with you shortly, Mr. Saberi." If Mr. Saberi felt one way or another about this, he didn't show it.

Lori Lincoln was the kind of tidy, Lilliputian person who made average-sized women like me feel slightly ungainly. From her sleek, angled chestnut bob to the tips of her navy pumps, nothing was out of place. No last-minute freshening up in elevators for her. Her almond-shaped brown eyes were clear and penetrating, her eyebrows penciled in perfect arches, her hands delicate and still. While not being precisely pretty, there was something exotic about her, and I found myself wondering again why Daniel never slept with her in law school. Whatever touch-me-not air he claimed to find in me, she had in spades.

When I was seated on the edge of the leather armchair facing her desk, she folded her hands on the blotter and began abruptly. Fine with me. Chitchat cost money. "Two days ago," she said, "I was contacted by Gary Lansing, a state-appointed public defender. Mr. Lansing was recently retained by the State of Washington on behalf of a Michael Loftus, who claims to be the father of Nadina Stern's child."

After Nadina's confession last week, it was nothing I wasn't expecting, but my stomach sunk to hear Lori lay it out so calmly. "Yes," I said inadequately. Lori didn't ask if I was agreeing that such a lawyer existed or that Michael Loftus was the baby's father. I knew at any rate she wanted no declarations from me on the latter point, especially ones that supported Mike's case.

"It was my original recommendation," Lori continued, "that we leave the question of paternity open, so that Ms. Stern could then consent by herself to the adoption. However, Mr. Lansing has made it clear that Mr. Loftus intends to go forward with a DNA test when the child is born to establish paternity."

What was the point? I thought dismally. We all knew Mike was the dad. Maybe we should save everyone time and money and slap him on the certificate. Lori didn't look in the mood for any whining sagginess on my part, however, so I kept all this to myself. "And then what happens if he establishes paternity?"

"He then requests a custody hearing before a judge."

"Custody," I echoed flatly. "He's in jail. He abuses drugs."

"Gary Lansing claims he has been punctilious in meeting all the drug rehabilitation requirements at Coyote Ridge."

Yes, well Mike had crossed his t's and dotted his i's before, but who knew how long that would last this time?

"What about the jail part?" I tried again. "He's also a convicted felon, doing two to five years. Drug possession, vehicular assault, speeding, evading capture." I counted them off on my fingers. "How could he get custody? Do they have a locker for storing kids at Coyote Ridge?"

She suppressed a tiny sigh. I didn't know if it was over the weaknesses of the system or the weaknesses of my understanding. "I'm sorry to say, that a sentence of two to five years does not always translate to two to five years in time served. The prisons are overcrowded, Cass. Were Mr. Loftus halfway behaving himself and playing his cards right, he could be on the streets again in under a year. By the time our case crawled through the courts, he could very well be back at home with a place to 'store' the child."

Feeling suddenly lightheaded, I realized it was because my breathing had become rapid and shallow. Then a sharp pain in my palm alerted me that I was clutching the corner of the desk in a death grip. *Lord, all this doesn't matter, does it?* I asked. *Deep down I know that you intend me to have this baby, and surely no judge would just hand an innocent child to a convicted felon? And against the wishes of the mother? I know I've been telling you I maybe can't handle getting this baby, emotionally, but, come to think of it, I don't know if I can handle* not *getting this baby.*

My trip down the panic spiral was halted presently by a growing burst of electronic song: "'Forget your troubles, come on get happy, you better chase all your cares away..!'"

Not exactly the ringtone I would have guessed for Lori, but people are full of surprises. We looked at each other as the singing volume went up a notch.

"Did—did you need to take that?" I asked hesitantly.

"Why would I?" Lori exhaled irritably. "Cass, would you mind turning that off?"

"Me?" I squeaked. "That's not my phone. Isn't it your phone?"

"Nonsense. I forgot mine somewhere. Do I look like a woman who would have Judy Garland as her ringtone?"

"Do *I*?" I asked.

Lori blinked at me. "Hold on." She whisked open her top desk drawer just as Judy belted out, "'The Lord is waitin' to take your hand—'" Picking up the bright pink cell phone like it was a slug on the sidewalk, she quickly switched it off. "My admin's. I'd forgotten I borrowed it."

Anywho, I wanted to say, can we get back to the matter at hand? Me going down the panic spiral, I mean.

To Lori I said only, "Does he have a case? Are we talking about just a hassle or a legitimate cause for concern?"

She tapped her fingertips together. The minimum-two-carat

diamond on her left hand winked at me. "It sounds like a slam-dunk to rational people, but the law is designed to protect the rights of the vulnerable. Yes, Mr. Loftus is a convicted felon without a reliable employment history, but if he is indeed the father, the state takes his rights quite seriously. All the more so because he has neither your position nor education nor wealth to win favor for him. Who are you, after all? You bear no relation to the child."

My mouth dropped open at her bloodless tone. What the heck was I paying her for, if it wasn't to stick up for me? While she had never been warm and fuzzy in our previous meetings, I assumed she would unbend on longer acquaintance. Maybe she blamed me for the recent wrinkles in our case, but I didn't see how that tone was going to help. How could Daniel have paired me with this cold fish?

Noting my expression, she nodded and went on serenely, "I'm only trying to help you understand the state's point of view. It is a serious matter to take children from their biological parents, especially if the biological parents are eager to prove their fitness."

"Fitness?" I echoed incredulously. "How can behaving himself for a year in prison prove his fitness? This is ridiculous—I have to go through home studies and interviews and all sorts of legal hoops, but Mike just has to show up for drug counseling and make a few license plates, or whatever they do there, and suddenly he's got a case?"

"If he is the biological father, the state feels he deserves consideration," Lori said again. She frowned at the two silver pens lying next to the blotter, which had gotten slightly out of parallel, and lined them up again. Fine, obviously, if her client got out of whack, but for heaven's sake, let's keep those pens under control.

"What about the mother's rights?" I changed tacks. "If Nadina wants me to have this child, doesn't that outweigh Mike not wanting me to have the child?"

"It's a common perception that the mother's wishes outweigh the father's, but that isn't the case. If Ms. Stern herself wanted to keep the baby, that might be different." She tapped her fingertips together once more. "Cass, I'm not saying you're not going to win. I'm saying this could be long and expensive and difficult, and I want you to be aware. Do all you can to improve the strength of your position."

"Meaning…?" I prodded, "Don't blow the interviews and home study?"

"For starters."

"Starters."

Lori leaned forward precisely, her brown eyes locking candidly with mine. "Think about it, Cass. You may have the mother on your side, but you're single, underemployed, and you live in a potentially unstable household where people could be moving in and out at any time. You don't want the social worker doing the study to meet new housemates each time she comes by."

"Do you mean I should get a job and my own apartment?" I asked, feeling panicky. "You told me before not to worry about the home study—that it was more of a formality."

"With no one contesting the case, it was."

"So…so…" I floundered, "so you're saying…"

She shook her head, possibly dismayed by my thickness. "I'm saying, completely off the record, that it wouldn't do you a bit of harm to look more like the American Dream. Get a job, by all means. And while you're at it, get married if you can possibly help it, to a good earner. And lose the transient roommates."

Floored, I slumped back against the slick brown leather chair. Could Daniel have put her up to this? I hardly knew her, but that didn't stop me from hoping desperately she was going to smack the desk and shriek with laughter, "Kidding, kidding! Had you going there, for a second, didn't I?"

No such luck.

"Think about it," she said again, before turning to tidy the pages in my folder and drop me back in the file cabinet.

Session over.

. . .

Stumbling out of the office, I managed an unintelligible response to the receptionist's farewell, while the pony-tailed man darted past me, impatient for his own appointment and indifferent to my emotional state.

I punched the button for the elevator, but by the time it dinged and the doors opened, I had sunk onto a nearby bench, clutching my cell phone. Someone. I needed to talk to someone. Someone level-headed who could talk me down. Daniel popped into my head, only to be instantly vetoed—how could I tell him, of all people, that Lori thought I should get a new home, a real job, and, most of all, a husband?

At least this answered the question of why he'd never slept with the woman in law school: she appeared to be half-robot.

Call Joanie, then? She would fret with me while simultaneously dismissing Lori's advice. Phyl?

Just as I flipped open my phone to call Phyl, it began vibrating, and I saw in amazement that Phyl was calling me. Maybe God had nudged her: *Call Cass. She's going berserk.*

"Phyl?" I breathed tentatively.

"Cass!" came her excited voice. "I'm at the Palace—I rushed over because I wanted to tell you, but you weren't here!"

"Tell me what?" I asked, sidetracked.

"Wayne! He tried again—he took me to lunch at Seastar and asked me to marry him, and this time, I said yes!"

This could not be happening.

Lori Lincoln just finishes telling me my transient housemates are a drawback, and Phyl calls to announce she's getting married? To the man she's been dating and turning down for months? Getting married and moving out, presumably. Unless I could convince Wayne to take up residence with us. Heck, we could make space for his disabled mom out in the Lean-To, to sweeten the deal, and at this point I was willing to build her a wheelchair ramp with my bare hands.

I gave myself a shake. For Pete's sake, Cass, what planet are you on? This isn't about you! This is about something wonderful happening to one of your closest friends. Wake up!

Phyl had been rhapsodizing about lunch and the proposal, and I realized I hadn't heard a syllable of it. Guiltily I decided I would ply Joanie for the details later, rather than confess my utter self-absorption. "That is great, Phyl," I said earnestly, if vaguely. "I am so happy for you both. So happy. Tell Wayne congratulations for me. We can't wait. He's such a better man than Jason. Wayne is a good, solid guy, and he'll make the best of husbands."

Blissed-out people don't tend to notice if you feed them platitudes. Or, at least, Phyl didn't. "And you and Joanie will be bridesmaids with my sister Mary, won't you?" she asked.

"Of course, of course," I assured her, wondering if she'd already mentioned when the wedding would take place. "You sure you want to do the big production again?"

"Yes, I really do," Phyl gushed. "Jason didn't count. He was probably figuring out how he could hook up with my maid of honor the whole time. This is my first real wedding, Cass."

"You're the boss, Phyl. Just tell us what to wear and where to stand."

"Hurry up and come home," she urged. "I was so excited that I already got some fabric swatches. Joanie's going to try to cut out early. Let's have fun planning, okay?"

"Absolutely," I agreed, grinding my teeth together and making an effort. "I'm in Seattle right now, so give me some time."

Clapping the phone shut, I didn't move for a minute. So Phyl was a goner. How long would it take to plan a second wedding? A few months? Maybe a little longer, if it was going to be another big production. I was happy for Phyl—really truly I was—but it was impossible to sustain the appropriate response under the circumstances. Let me get all my self-absorption out now, the better to focus on her when I got home.

Lori had said they spaced out the home study visits, so they could catch you at different times. Could I have Phyl come back and pretend still to be living in the Palace? No, that wouldn't be honest, and if they caught me lying, well, so much for the moral high ground.

Okay, would it be evil to tell Daniel that, on second thought, I'd marry him after all, and pronto? He probably wouldn't begin the cycle of infidelity, betrayal and repentance for at least a year, and by then the home studies and court case might be wrapping up just in time for me to file for divorce. Maybe I could get a two-fer.

Faintly, from Lori's office, I heard a clock chiming. All I needed now was for her to emerge and ask me why I was still hanging around, instead of off improving my Strategic Position. She'd probably charge for the comment, too.

A lengthy sigh escaped me as I got to my feet. *Help me, God. I know Lori's plan, and I don't have one of my own, so I could use a clue as to yours.*

CHAPTER FOUR:

Small Detour

He wasn't helping. God, I mean.

Or else the help was going to begin right after I located my car. Which I had been searching for fruitlessly, for the past twenty minutes.

Where was my stupid car? Just another reason I took the bus whenever possible, but I had already been running behind when I left for my meeting with Lori, and who had time for the bus tunnel and a transfer? Okay...I already checked this floor, and it couldn't be higher up because those floors were full when I came.

Frustrated, I finally sank onto the bumper of the nearest vehicle to regroup. To my alarm, no sooner did my backside contact rubber and chrome than the Audi gave two loud beeps, and I sprang to my feet, putting on my best I-swear-I-was-not-trying-to-steal-this-car face. Hearing a low laugh, I whipped around to see the man from Lori's waiting room coming toward me, remote extended. Apparently he had triggered the beeping, and not my behind.

"Sorry," I muttered, making to walk past him.

"You were looking for something," he said. "Have you forgotten where you parked?"

"Yes," I confessed reluctantly, "but obviously the car's here somewhere, since it's almost ten years old, and I'm sure no one would steal it. Sorry to sit on your bumper—I was just taking a break."

"How was your meeting with Lori?" he asked unexpectedly. A grin broke on his face, rather at odds with his dark, remote looks. Weird, too, after his curtness in the reception area. Maybe he was bipolar.

He must have read my expression because he added, "I wasn't much for chatting earlier because I was anxious, but she had good news."

Ah ha, that explained his sudden friendliness: I was the first person he came upon, and he wanted to share. If only my news had been as good.

"I'm glad for you," I said. "Have a nice day."

"What does your car look like?" he asked my retreating back. "I could do a quick sweep of the garage and report back."

Turning, I protested, "That's all right—"

"Let me guess," he interrupted. "A Hummer. Real big and bad-ass."

I stared. Now Grimstock was joking with me? "Not even close."

"Hmm…a little condescension there. You must be one of those holier-than-thou Prius drivers."

"Too expensive, and I said it was ten years old," I responded. "It's just a beat-up old Civic sedan."

"Color?"

"It used to be blue, but really—I'll find it. I'm sure you have things to do, places to be." Hint: leave me alone, strange man. My eyes did drop to his ringless left hand. What would a single guy be doing in an adoption attorney's office?

He shrugged and, without another word, hopped in the Audi and started the engine. Hoping I hadn't offended him—he definitely had some Middle-Eastern blood, so maybe I had committed some cross-cultural faux pas—I continued my perfunctory search of the 3rd floor.

A few minutes later, when I emerged from the stairwell to re-investigate the 4th, headlights flashed as a car came zooming up to me. The Audi. The passenger-side window glided down, and when

I reluctantly bent to look in, the man said only, "I found it on Level Five. Want a lift?"

I paused. He could hardly be a stalker, since I was the one who had sat on his bumper in the first place, and surely a single guy with a heart for adopting children couldn't be too bad. Besides, I'd burned enough calories for the day.

"Who are you trying to adopt?" I asked, when I was belted in.

"My stepson."

Oh, I thought. Married then. Just not a ring-wearer.

As if I'd spoken aloud, he said, "I lost my wife several months ago, but we were married for five years. Bryson always lived with us because his father didn't want him. Or he didn't until Katherine … was gone. Katherine and I always planned that I would adopt Bryson. We just wanted to wait until he was a little older, so that it would be his choice."

A widower! Suddenly I felt terrible for the judgmental thoughts I'd been having about him. I was certain that everyone who came across me in that first year of grief found me far worse than moody. And I had called him Grimstock. Poor man. It would have been horrible to lose Troy and then be forced to fight for Min. Though at least she would have been there to fight for. My throat tightened. *Don't think about Min.*

"I'm sorry for your loss," I croaked conventionally. Beyond a curt nod, he didn't even respond to this, but I knew it had to be gotten over with. We pulled up in front of my car. "How old is Bryson now?"

"Six."

So Bryson probably didn't even remember a time without this man. "But you got good news from Lori today?" I ventured.

He nodded again, shutting off the engine. "Reiner—the biological father—he's showing signs of being persuadable." He shrugged. "What's your story? Who are you trying to adopt? A little girl from China, maybe."

"I hope you don't try to guess things for a living," I said.

To my surprise, he laughed. A rich, guttural sound. "Unfortunately,

I do. I'm an investment banker."

"Oh," I said lamely, feeling a stupid blush coming on. "Well, no offense. I'm trying to adopt the baby of a—a friend. She's all for it, but the estranged father…isn't. He's in pretty sorry shape—" not to mention prison "—so Lori thinks I would eventually win in court—" emphasis on the *eventually*, "—but it would be nice not to have to go to court." Nice also not to devote the next several years of my life and every available penny to it.

"You look harmless enough. Why is the father opposed to you, if you don't mind me asking?"

Good question. Why was Mike so dead set against me? Why had he always been?

"Several reasons, I think," I said. "For one, he's young, and I think he resents the mother making the choice for him. For another, I think he blames me for changes he sees in her—"

"Changes?"

"Getting off drugs," I muttered, adding quickly, "But it wasn't me—the mother went to a school with great teachers and counselors, and they're the ones who helped her clean up. That, and her best friend went to rehab and got sober. The father didn't like the school any better, but it was more convenient to charge everything to my account. And then, on top of all that, I think he doesn't like how I'm—I'm religious." A vague way of describing myself, but given this man's indeterminate ethnic background, I hesitated to say "Christian." So sue me.

I might have offended him anyhow because he fell silent, frowning at the Audi's tachometer. Maybe "religious" was too nebulous, and he was picturing some kind of weapons-stockpiling, artificially-flavored-beverage-swilling cult.

O-kay.

"Well," I said, reaching for the door handle as the silence stretched out, "thanks for finding my car—"

"My name's Skandar. It's Arabic for Alexander." He extended a long, narrow hand at me, as if we were across a table from each other, instead of side by side.

Awkwardly I shook it and responded, "My name's Cass. Short for Cassandra."

"Would you like to have coffee, Cass?" was his next unexpected question. Seeing my surprise, his face darkened, and he added, "Just coffee. I'm not coming on to you—Katherine only passed a few months ago. It would just be nice to trade adoption stories."

But I thought that was what we just did, sort of. Guiltily I realized I had indeed feared he was coming on to me. Hadn't I hated that, after I was widowed? Feeling like you couldn't talk to someone single of the opposite sex without everyone thinking you had something in mind? But he was a man, after all—by definition a champion rebounder.

I said gently, "Skandar—don't worry. I lost my own husband a couple years ago, and it makes it weird to talk to people, doesn't it?" Amazement at our shared experience appeared on his face. Then the curtain fell again.

"I'm sorry about Katherine," I repeated, wanting him to know I meant it. "And I'd love to have coffee and swap bad birth father stories, but I'm from the Eastside, and I'd better get back over the bridge before the traffic gets worse." Not to mention a jubilant Phyl was waiting.

The furrow in his brow deepened. "I'm headed back to Bellevue myself. How about just twenty minutes at the café on Main?"

Sheesh. It didn't seem the moment to mention that I had already promised to go straight home and rejoice with loved ones. And to be honest, I didn't mind having an excuse to put that off a little longer, since what I really wanted to do was sit and stew.

"Okay," I relented. "Meet you there."

• • •

My phone rang when I was approaching Mercer Island. Joanie. "Yeah? What is it, Joanie—I can't talk—I'm driving. And I already know about

Phyl and Wayne."

"Phyl's thinking mauve for the stupid bridesmaid dresses," Joanie complained without preamble. "You've got to talk to her. I told her I hate mauve, but she says you and Mary would look great in it and that it'd be fine with my hair, but you know it would be hideous. She says she's got the flipping swatch already, so get your butt home and tell her no way on the mauve. I told her I can't leave work yet."

"I'll be home in about forty-five minutes," I said, when I could break in. "I'll tell her then."

"Forty-five minutes! Where are you? Fife? I thought you had a lawyer appointment in Seattle."

"I did, but now I said I'd meet someone for a quick coffee," I said, "then I'll head home."

Joanie was too alert for that. "Someone for coffee? Who?"

"Another adoptive parent I met at Lori Lincoln's office."

"Why are you being gender-neutral? Are you meeting a *guy*, Cass?"

"Yes," I confessed, "but it's not like that—"

"You're running around on my brother?" she demanded. "You think he's the cheating type, but you're the one running around on him?"

"I'm not running around on your brother!" I huffed, having to hit the brakes hard since I was following the car in front of me too closely. "This isn't a date. And besides, Daniel and I aren't dating—"

"Oh, hogwash!" retorted Joanie. "You may not think you're dating, but Daniel is just behaving himself with one eye on the calendar, so you can't be running around on him, Cass."

"I'm not running around on him," I said again, more loudly. "And I've been really clear with Daniel that we're not dating, so I am not responsible for whatever he's doing or thinking. I'm just having a coffee with this guy Skandar I met so we can swap adoption war stories. It's nothing. He's a recent widower. I don't think he has anyone to talk to. It's not a date."

"*Skandar*? What the hell kind of name is Skandar?"

"He said it's Arabic for Alexander," I explained. "And Joanie, I really have to get off the phone because some cop is going to see me, and I'm a menace to society like this."

"How well do you know this guy? What if he's some kind of terrorist, with a name like that? At least tell me where you're meeting him, in case you never show up again and I have to call Homeland Security."

"I'm meeting him at the café on Main," I said. "Stop freaking out. You're so politically incorrect—he didn't have any kind of weaponry strapped to him. In fact, he may not be more than half Middle-Eastern—"

"Even worse because he probably identifies with his oppressed half—"

"I gotta go, Joanie. See you tonight."

"Is he cute?" came Joanie's parting shot, but I was already flipping the phone shut.

• • •

Parking can be tight on Main, so I was fortunate to find a spot a couple blocks away. Before I got out, I checked my reflection in the mirror and then felt a stab of guilt and embarrassment. Why should I check how I looked? Stupid Joanie, putting thoughts in my head.

Skandar was already in line, and to my relief, he didn't ask me to cut in with him or offer to buy mine. On the other hand, he barely glanced at me, and I wondered if he'd forgotten that he initiated this. A couple minutes later, dirty chai in hand, I joined him at a window table. Now that we were actually sitting face-to-face in a well-lit coffee shop, awkwardness descended. His demeanor, in particular, was shuttered, closed-off, as if he were regretting his momentary social impulse. Remembering how much of the first year of widowhood I spent prostrate, I was amazed he looked so well. Maybe it was the guy thing. He could bury himself in work and another romance; although, on second thought, he didn't look up for the romance part.

"So," I began, when it didn't look like he was going to say anything, "if Bryson is six now, did he go to kindergarten last year?"

Skandar nodded. "He was on the younger end, but tall like his father and verbal like—like his mother."

Crap.

I tried again. "Who watches him while you work?"

A deep breath. "Katherine's mother."

Stirring my chai, I watched the curls of steam rise from the surface. Skandar, for his part, seemed to have forgotten all about his cappuccino. "Bryson must be very attached to you, if you've been in his life for such a large part of it."

"I'm the only father he knows," he said, making an effort. "I met my wife when Bryson was only six months old, right after his father walked out, and up until…Katherine… passed, Reiner had no interest in Bryson. Saw him maybe once a year. Bryson could barely understand who Reiner was and always found it confusing if he asked him to call him Daddy."

"Does…Reiner live around here?" I asked.

He shook his head. "Los Angeles. He's trying to make a living as an actor. He doesn't know what he's asking for—what would he do with a kid, with that kind of lifestyle?"

"It's not ideal for child-rearing," I agreed. "My brother tried for a while to get into acting and writing in L.A. It didn't work out, of course, and his wife ended up divorcing him. I was thankful he didn't have kids yet."

More silence. I could only pretend to be so involved with stirring my chai to cool it off. Maybe I could start stirring his drink. This was a bad idea. I'm certain he agreed with me and was kicking himself for trying to be social. Reaching for my purse, I was about to plead Phyl's swatches and put us out of our misery when he spoke again. "What about you, Cass? What's your story? I'm sorry I'm so…scattered. The excitement of Lori's good news is wearing off, and now I just…"

"Oh, don't apologize," I said quickly, reaching out a hand and stopping short. "Those first few months...I remember..." I swallowed. "You're doing amazingly well." To my alarm, I saw his black eyes fill with tears, and I rushed into the long version of my story to give him time to recover. The very long version. I have no idea if he heard a word I said about Troy's heart condition, but he returned to the present enough to inhale sharply when I mentioned Min's death and to look mildly interested when I got to the whole Nadina part. "So anyhow," I wrapped up, "I think Mike has always disliked me for my supposed influence and...church affiliations. I'm not sure exactly how he thinks he's going to make a case for himself in court, when he's a convicted felon, but it looks like he's going to try. It may be a long time before baby Ned is officially mine."

"Katherine and I started going to church again, when she was diagnosed with cancer," muttered Skandar, finally taking a sip of his cappuccino. "She was raised Catholic. After she died, I stopped going." Understandable.

"Were you not...raised Catholic too?" I asked timidly.

A different expression flickered across his face. I only recognized it because of all the time I spent with Nadina: irritation at a dumb question. I suppose, post-9/11 and with his mysterious-but-Middle-Eastern-leaning ethnicity, he did get tired of answering questions about who he was and what he believed. I felt my own twinge of annoyance—at least I was asking, not assuming.

"My father is Persian," he said in a clipped voice. "Iranian, if that's what you're wondering. My mother was Chaldean Catholic. We've been in this country in California since the late '70s, before the Shah was overthrown. I think after seeing all that ideological upheaval, my father was done with religion. Of any kind. We only went to Mass once or twice a year growing up, always because my mother wanted to. Katherine stopped going to Mass after she and Reiner divorced, but when she got sick she wanted...comfort. I went for her sake."

"And—and did it comfort her?"

He shrugged. "Yes. It comforted her. It made me angry, but it comforted her."

Silence fell again. I thought about asking what Chaldean Catholicism was but decided religion was too touchy a topic. Not that there seemed to be any untouchy topic with him. I smothered a sigh. How did I get in these situations? What was I supposed to say? I wasn't sure anymore that my own grief experience gave me insight into his. Maybe I could describe my stages: Numbness, Functioning, Partial Relapse. Then again, maybe he didn't care.

Crud.

No, my own grief experience made me an expert only on my own grief experience. Period. But, for what it was worth, it was all I had to offer.

I dug my nails into my jeans, trying to whomp up my courage. "I… felt angry at God too, after Troy and Min died," I said cautiously. "I still went to church—I have no idea why. It wasn't about God, then. I guess I just thought if I threw out everything at that point—threw out my faith—there would be nothing left to me. So I kept going and, after a long time, I realized I wasn't just faking it. I could see it in my friends and family, and when Nadina asked me to take her baby, I knew it. I knew God still had something for my life. You already know that, though," I added gently, "because you have Bryson."

Skandar said nothing for a minute, and when he did finally speak, his voice was so low I had to lean forward to hear him. "That's nice for you. But I didn't have any faith to throw out. And I don't want to think about God. Losing Katherine was bad enough. If I lost Bryson, I would hate God."

I really sucked at this. Having no adequate response, I talked to God instead: *Look, Lord, I know you're not big on ultimatums, but if at all possible, could Skandar please keep Bryson? And put people in his life to help him through this awful time. Show yourself to him. How fortunate I was to have my family and friends. Forgive me for not recognizing it sooner.*

The café clock started chiming, and I shifted nervously. If I didn't watch out, Joanie was going to call again, and how would I explain that I was *still* having coffee with this strange man?

"You probably need to go," said Skandar abruptly.

"I do," I admitted.

"This has been … helpful … to talk to you. You understand, I think." Fishing in his wallet, he pulled out a business card and handed it to me. "Do you think we could we talk again? I don't have a lot of people at this point to do this with."

I gulped, feeling my cheeks turn pink. My heart sank at the thought of spending more time with him, but I didn't feel I could say no, given what I had just prayed. But it wasn't as if he wanted to go out with me—he just didn't have the support system I had when my own life fell apart. Maybe if I met with him again, I could direct him to his priest or my own church's Grief Recovery class. I nodded, looking at the card: Skandar Saberi, followed by the name of some investment firm.

"Maybe lunch some time?" he asked.

Lunch? Stuck in a restaurant for at least an hour? I took a deep breath.

"You could call my cell after you check your calendar or shoot me an email," he continued, "or I could contact you, if you have a card."

This, at least, made me want to smile. Hard to imagine me needing business cards for my Free Universe piecework or asking my ex-boyfriend James to print some up. Maybe Daniel could: Cassandra Ewan, Cook and Shower Scrubber, The Palace.

"Sure. I'll email you," I answered.

I left him still sitting there, staring out the window.

At least the painful encounter succeeded in distracting me from my own adoption woes. I was now overdue for home and wedding rejoicing, without another minute to spare on self-pity.

CHAPTER FIVE:

Week's Worth of Worries

Unburdening myself proved elusive.

As I pictured, when I tried to tell Joanie about my discouraging conversation with Lori Lincoln and her impossible advice, Joanie merely shrugged. "She's right, you know. You'll probably win in the end, but why not just marry Daniel and make it easy on yourself? Then—bonus—he can pick up the legal fees. But don't stress—when that social worker lady interviews me, I'll make it sound like I'm here for the long haul. You may be losing Phyl, but unless your brother gets a clue, I'm your go-to gal for lifetime spinsterhood."

I wouldn't bet on it. Not on her staying single and not on Perry staying clueless. But I knew better than to expect sympathy from Joanie.

As for Phyl, she was in her own universe, floating through the Palace trailing bridal magazines with folded pages, swatches of tulle and organza and organic silk, green alternatives to wedding favors. Even when Wayne wasn't over, which he almost constantly was now, she was too happy for me to unload on.

The days passed. I managed to keep it together through endless hours with Joanie and Phyl, talking colors and cuts and cake flavors. I managed to keep it together through the hours at Free Universe when I showed up. I managed to keep it together through my first meeting with the social worker: no, I wasn't married, but I had been and had loved it and being a mom to Min, and here I was, living with good church people (Daniel's men's Bible study attendance counted, in this case), plenty of insurance money in the bank, a part-time job to prove I was employable. What child wouldn't want to be adopted by me?

But things were falling through the cracks. I completely forgot the time I scheduled to hang out with Nadina and had to bear her guilt trip the rest of the week. I burned Sunday's dinner. I accidentally streaked Daniel's sheets blue-purple when I washed them with new towels. I didn't always notice when people were talking to me.

Friday I woke from yet another dream about Min—this one that both she and baby Ned were doing forced prison labor under Mike's supervision—and was in such a state that I didn't know whether to laugh or cry at the scenarios my subconscious invented. After a few minutes scanning unpromising job ads over breakfast, I decided something had to give. I had to talk to someone.

First I tried Louella Murphy, my former fellow mentor from Camden School. Louella did not do email and had no answering machine, but she did lead a life twice as full and busy as mine. Therefore no luck getting a hold of her.

Mom and Dad also didn't pick up, and I wimped out, leaving a vague "thinking of you, nothing urgent, call me when you get a chance" message.

Then I tried my brother. I knew better than to call Perry in the mornings, but I texted him. "Would love 2 C U. Really really miss U. Come down."

By Friday evening the silence was deafening.

So much for my community of family and friends, I thought sourly, as I sat down to leftover chicken fricassee.

No, that wasn't entirely true. Over the course of the week Daniel had twice asked me if anything was bothering me, only to be rebuffed. But people who were part and parcel of my problems didn't count as support.

Twiddling my fork over my half-finished plate, I rested my chin on my hand, daydreaming. What would Daniel do, if I simply threw myself at him and wailed, "I'm a grief-stricken mess who finds you very attractive, so would you mind marrying me, to help me adopt a baby who may or may not intensify my grieving?"

Hardly had I finished picturing this moving scene when I heard the garage door going up. A minute later the same master of the house walked in, and the sight of his bright blond hair and careless grace made my stomach do a somersault. What a disaster I was. I couldn't be too upset about Min and adoption obstacles if they dropped out of sight whenever Daniel crossed my path. This must be the attraction part. I felt fluttery, nervous. On the other hand, attraction was a welcome change from fretful self-pity. When was the last time he and I had been alone?

"No plans tonight, Cass?"

It took me a second to get a hold of my voice. Two throat clearings. For Pete's sake. Finally I gave up and shook my head. Then I addressed the salt and pepper shakers: "There's more chicken in the fridge."

"Tempting," he said, coming to sit across from me. "But what I'd really like to know is where I can get more of that pie you made yesterday."

"Oh, ha ha," I said sarcastically. In my spaced-out state I'd forgotten to put any sugar in yesterday's peach pie, leaving our suffering open house guests to sprinkle it liberally on top while they taxed themselves trying to be polite. "Even the garbage disposal didn't want it," I admitted.

He grinned at me, waiting for me to say more, but when I didn't he began again. "You know, Cass, you've been really out of it lately, if you don't mind me saying."

I did mind him saying. Unwillingly, I met his eyes. "Out of it" didn't begin to cover it. Why couldn't he just let me be distracted by his good looks?

"I know you haven't wanted to talk about it," he went on, "but I've got to say something because it's starting to affect your job performance. That pie is going to have to go in my files."

So much for distractions. My crazy emotions, skating wildly lately between crying and laughter, no longer fell into distinct categories. To my horror, I felt my eyes fill with tears.

Not just to my horror.

"Good Lord, Cass—I'm kidding!" Daniel exclaimed, reaching a hand across the table to me. Before I could whisk my own away, he had my wrist in a hard grip. "Uh-uh. Not a chance. Not till you tell me what the hell is going on with you. I've hardly ever seen you like this. Except—" Except the time he had, last December when a Christmas ornament for Min rolled into my lap and destroyed my self-composure.

That did it.

I burst into tears, reaching for a clean napkin with my free hand so I could hide my mortified face in it.

"Cass—"

"I don't want to talk about it," I said desperately, almost choking on an insane urge to ask him to marry me. Yanking my wrist from his grip, I used both hands to smear away my embarrassing outburst. "It's— it's—just don't worry about it. There's nothing you can do about it. I just—I miss my daughter!" A half-truth was better than an outright lie.

Daniel bought it, because he sat back suddenly. "I'm sorry." He took an uneven breath. "God—I'm so sorry I went digging."

Shaking my head in vague response, I dabbed at my eyes some more, so I wouldn't have to look at him. If he hadn't seen me cry over Min that other time, I doubt he would have been as easily fooled. One corner of my mind wondered absently if he felt that impatience people often do: *Get over it already. It's been six months. A year. Two years.* Did that same ruthless timeline apply to me, since I'd spent the two years stuffing my grief down?

To my relief, his phone rang. When he made no move to answer, I said hastily, "Please. You'd better get that."

"It can wait."

"*Please!*" I begged. And please stop looking at me. I vant to be alone.

Reluctantly he dug the phone out of his pocket and glanced at the number, a shadow crossing his face. To give him some privacy, I made a noisy business of taking my dishes to the sink, but it didn't stop me from hearing "yes—hello, Darla. Uh-huh. Yes, I'll be by shortly. No, I'm sure that's fine. It isn't too dressy. Okay. Yes. Okay, bye."

He had a date, the big giant Loser! Forgetting how I'd just been wishing he'd go away, I fought an irrational desire to hurl china and cutlery around the Palace kitchen. A date! A *date*?! He pretends to be so concerned about me, and then he goes out on a date? My own dismissive words to Joanie rose to reproach me: I guess I did care what Daniel was doing and thinking.

I slapped on the garbage disposal, only to fill the kitchen with a jarring, metallic, monster-chewing-on-wind-chimes racket. Damn it all! Smacking the switch again, I ruefully dug out the spoon I'd just destroyed. Deep breath, Cass. Breathe. B-r-e-a-t-h-e. Or else you really should have yourself committed. You're the one who told him to go on a couple dates, after all. But not on nights when I wanted him for myself! my irrational side protested.

"Oops," I said, tacking a smile on, and turning to display the battered spoon. "Will this go in the files with my pie?"

Hearing my joking tone, he gave me a long look.

"'...When I cry she laughes,'" Daniel murmured, "'and hardens evermore her hart.'"

Scowling, I tried unsuccessfully to place the verse. Sidney? Shakespeare? Wyatt? Wherever it came from, the sentiment wasn't good. I sniffed. Daniel wasn't crying, at any rate. Licking his chops, more like, at the thought of dinner and a hook-up. I took a slow, deep breath and was pleased by the sound of it. Nice and level. Not frantic. Not desperate. Not at all upset that I was going to spend the evening alone in my room with a book or tagging along with Phyl and Wayne if I could find them, while he traipsed off to feel Darla up. Darla, who, I'm guessing, probably wasn't Marked by Tragedy and experiencing mood swings like the PMS that Ate Pittsburgh.

"Where are you going for dinner?" I asked casually.

"Purple—in Kirkland," he said, his blue eyes continuing to x-ray me. "The timing seems bad. Would you like to come? It might take your mind off things."

Yeah—take my mind off 75% of my worries and plant them squarely on the remaining 25%. Considering how my blood pressure seemed to be rising, I might even be wrong about those ratios. "Thanks," I said, "but I did just eat." Not to mention I'd rather be deep-fried in a vat of boiling oil.

"You could just order a salad, and Darla would envy your birdlike appetite."

"In between being furious at you for bringing along a third wheel on your date," I scoffed.

He stood slowly, slipping his phone back in his pocket and coming to lean with his back to the counter. "Or I could cancel, you know. If you feel you need me."

"Need" him? I didn't "need" him! As soon as I thought it, I remembered the fire extinguisher weighing down the trunk of my car—somewhere down my priority list, I'd hoped for his help in installing it. But I was not about to ask him to make the ultimate sacrifice and give up an evening of action to hold my hand. Not as my confidant and not as my handyman. Resisting the urge to shake my fist at him, God, and the universe, I said merely, "Not a bit. You enjoy your date."

I shut the dishwasher with more vigor than strictly necessary and turned to wipe my hands on the dish cloth, only to find he had moved to stand in front of it. Well, I wasn't going to ask him to move, nor was I going to reach in the direction of his crotch, so I shrugged and wiped my hands on my jeans.

When Daniel spoke again, his voice was light, but there was a hard note underneath it. "You're right. Why let your troubles and moodiness spoil my evening? Especially when you'd always rather go it alone." Ignoring my indignant gasp, he added, "Tonight could be it. Darla could be the one, Cass. I've got a feeling."

Rallying, I said, "Well, that's the whole point of dating, isn't it? To find a spark and fan it to a flame." Not that he'd ever struggled with that. For most of the time I'd known him, Daniel had been more of a one-man forest fire where women were concerned. Total devastation. Scorched earth.

"Where did you meet this one?" I asked, striving again for casual, but even to my own ears I sounded a little off.

The blue eyes glinted wickedly. "Church."

What, at the men's Bible study? There always were those single women eager to volunteer at the men's events, decked out in high heels and low-cut tops that they strangely never wore for the women's. "How lovely," I croaked. "Do I know her?"

"Not yet, I imagine, but if things work out, I'll have her for open house next week."

I'm sure he would. Shooting him a glare, I caught his fleeting amusement, and swallowed my irritation as best I could. Beyond the irritation I felt a lowness: even if I wanted to marry him, was he already moving on?

"A week!" I said brightly. "I'm glad you found someone with such long-term potential."

Pushing off the counter, he walked away from me to reach down for his gym bag. "Oh, you'll see. Darla's got nothing if not … potential."

And on that mysterious note, he left me alone.

• • •

So added to absolutely everything else, I found myself worrying about Darla's potential. What if she succeeded with him, where so many women had failed? Was he going out with her because I'd told him to date around or because he wanted to go out with her?

Better for him to discover now that he didn't want me, I reminded myself sternly, rather than a few months into a marriage. Not that I had any intention of marrying him. Or, I shouldn't have any such intention, if my head was screwed on straight.

Daniel was gone a lot that weekend. Maybe off with Darla, maybe doing other things. I didn't ask. At least he didn't bring her back to the Lean-To. I wondered if his new potential religious leanings meant he wasn't going to sleep with his dates now, or only that he was newly considerate and wasn't going to inflict their company on us.

When it rains, it pours. On Monday, Nadina called me to say she was having so many contractions over the weekend that her mom had dragged her in to the hospital.

"Contractions? Hospital?" I gasped. "You're not even eight months along! Are you at Overlake now?"

"Nah," she said, "they sent me home, but I have to lie on the friggin' couch as much as possible or else they're going to give me some drug to plug me up or something. I don't want it, though, 'cause they say it makes you swell the hell up, and I'm already friggin' huge. No more Petco, and I could really use the money."

"Well, take it easy," I nagged. "Do everything they tell you, okay? Ned has to finish cooking in there."

"Yeah, yeah." She brushed this off in her usual teenage manner. Thankfully she was indeed getting huge, or I think she probably would have signed up for a racquetball tournament or something, just to irk me.

"Did the doctor say?" I persisted. "Are you officially on bed rest?"

"What? I don't know. I already told you everything I know. But who wants to lay around at home? The house is all stuffy and Mom is at work half the time, and I'm friggin' bored out of my gourd. It almost makes me want to write Mike because I'm all grouchy and pissy and fighting would feel good."

Thumping my forehead in frustration I said tightly, "Don't even think about it! You're going to get me chewed out by Lori Lincoln again, and she scares the crap out of me. You don't even know what trouble your last fight with Mike caused me."

"Oh, yeah?" Nadina shot back. "If I don't know, it's 'cause you friggin' *stood me up* last time we were supposed to meet. There I am sitting at Meydenbauer thinking I'm gonna dissolve in a sweat puddle or have heat stroke while I wait for you—"

"I told you, I'm sorry about that," I interrupted. "I've had a lot on my mind."

"But I'm supposed to be one of the things on your mind!" Nadina complained. "That adoption counselor told me I might experience emotional overload and shut down if I can't process everything. I thought she was full of shit, but if you're gonna start jerking me around, don't blame me if I lose it and freak out and decide I'm gonna keep Ned after all. I knew all you adoptive parents were the same—you just want Ned, and you're already forgetting about me—"

"Oh, for the love of God!" I burst out, at the end of my rope. "If you weren't pregnant and hormonal, and if it wouldn't bring on the baby, I'd come right over and whack you on the head with a brick, you idiot."

"Oh! Please come visit me, Cass," she urged, her tone changing instantly. "I know I'm being a crazy bitch—not that you're all together yourself—but I'd feel so much better if you came! Bring me a smoothie and some movies, but none of your books, okay?"

I hesitated, torn between guilt over having stood her up and reluctance to spend hours watching Nadina's favorite awful teen movies in the Sterns' admittedly stuffy house. Of course, if I dreaded being cooped up there, how much more the pregnant Nadina?

"If you don't want to come over, I could go there," Nadina prompted, reading my mind. "What time does Daniel usually get off work? If he's there, could I stay for dinner?"

"I'll be right over," I said.

CHAPTER 6:

The Knight and the Dragon

Thursday afternoon found me dragging back to the Palace after another visit to Nadina, where she lounged Jabba-the-Hut-style on the sofa while I fetched and carried like Princess Leia, only minus the dog collar and metal bikini. I wouldn't have put up with this long, except that Nadina genuinely was having contractions, her face and breathing getting tight whenever she moved around too much. When I did leave her, it was with a heartfelt prayer that God would keep that baby in just a little longer. Every day counted. The doctor thought if we could just get her to 36 weeks, all would be fine.

To my delight, Perry chose this day to show up unannounced. I'd been miffed all week that he hadn't responded to my pitiful text, but when I saw him draped on the glider out front, I forgave all. Hurtling up the steps with unwonted enthusiasm, I gave him a giant hug.

"Whoa!" he laughed, hugging me back. "Cass, it's me, Perry. What's up with you?"

"I'm so, so glad to see you, Perry," I cried. "I've had so much on my mind and no one to talk about it with—" Before he could even suggest we go inside, I was spilling my guts. "Perry, just when I thought

I was getting everything together again, it's all going to pieces! I miss Min like crazy all of a sudden, and I'm constantly dreaming of her and choking up—it's been two years! When will I get past this?"

Perry swallowed hard and crushed me to him again. There was nothing to say about Min, I knew. We both missed her. Perry was the only one besides my parents and in-laws who really understood what it felt like to have her gone, but with my parents we didn't go there, and with my in-laws we never went anywhere else. At least with Perry I didn't have to pretend that I was either on a smooth trajectory of healing or that I wasn't healing at all.

"Do you remember what she looked like?" When he didn't answer, I said, "I know, I know. Now when I think of her, I see her how she looks in the pictures I have of her. I don't know if I'm remembering, or if I wouldn't even be able to visualize her without the pictures. Isn't that awful? That's why I almost don't mind the dreams—they show me that somewhere in my brain I still have her."

"It's easier to remember things she said." He leaned his head back on the cushions and stared up at the beams above us. "Like when Gran died and we were all in Aunt Judy's van. Remember? Aunt Judy was driving, and we stopped at that light—"

"The light turned green—"

"And when the car in front didn't move, Min yells in her little voice, 'Less go, buddy! Get da lead out!'"

Perry and I laughed heartily. "That was awful!" I remembered. "Aunt Judy spent the rest of the drive telling me how children are like little sponges, and I had to be more careful what I said in front of Min."

"Yeah, I tuned that part out," said my brother. "You should've blamed it on Troy."

We sat for several minutes in silence, Perry rocking the glider with his foot.

"And that's not everything," I sniffled eventually, dashing at my eyes with the inside of my wrist. There was no stopping me now, and

I let it all out: Nadina provoking Mike, Mike getting a state-appointed public defender, Lori Lincoln telling me to give my life an Extreme Makeover and get married, Joanie being blasé about it all, Phyl getting married, Nadina having premature contractions, the social worker descending on us next week, Daniel dating for the first time in months, me working my piddly hours at Free Universe, which wouldn't be nearly enough money to cover all the future legal fees—

"Hang on a sec," Perry interrupted my verbal download. "How does Martin's dating life even rank on this list?"

I bit my lip, weighing my options. Perry had been one of the first to suspect Daniel had a thing for me and to warn me of it. I had put him off, then.

Better to feed my brother a line. "Well—er—if Daniel got married too, that'd be the end of Palace life as we know it." Perry raised his eyebrows, and I sighed. "Oh, all right. You were right about him … liking me, and I think I might be starting to—to—to care about him too, not that I mean to do anything about it right now because I have to deal with that baby first!"

"Why not kill two birds with one stone?" he suggested lightly. "I'm guessing you could persuade him. Get together with Daniel and streamline the adoption business."

"You sound like Joanie," I accused. "Maybe streamlining the adoption process isn't a good reason to marry someone. Especially someone I have such doubts about. Can you picture him being monogamous? And who even knows what that guy believes! Besides, even if I were such a user, Daniel's too smart to get used."

Perry laughed, kicking his long legs up on the porch railing. "Let me savor this moment—I was right about Martin liking you, and you were wrong, and now you're asking your little brother for advice."

"I am not asking for advice," I said. "I'm just venting. But … you do agree with me that he'd make a lousy husband? I mean, he'd cheat on me, most likely, and then we wouldn't even have a spiritual connection to hold us together?"

He groaned. "Cass, if you want to know what's going on there, you'd better just ask him."

"Has he—has Daniel said anything to you?" I asked hesitantly. The two of them were buddies, frequent emailers.

"He's told me what he's told me," said my unhelpful brother. "I'm staying out of it. And as for the monogamy thing, Cass, don't you believe people can change?"

"Theoretically." I frowned. "But how do I know? Everyone can act differently for a while, just through sheer willpower—look at dieting. How do you know when a change is bone-deep? Take—take Mike, for example. He managed to quit the drugs cold turkey for a while there, but the next time he hit a big stressor, he went back to the old behaviors, and worse!"

"I'd say it depends on what motivates the change," said Perry. "What causes people to change. Because if it's God, isn't that different from willpower? In Martin's case, if he's being changed from the inside out, wouldn't that be different?"

"Yes," I conceded. "But how can I tell? What if I got together with Daniel only to find out it was only willpower, after all, that kept him on track—or plain stubbornness—and he was the same old man he ever was?"

Perry shrugged. "Something you're going to have to figure out, Cass. I suggest you talk to him. But—just a warning—be careful you don't become a self-fulfilling prophecy."

"Meaning what, exactly?"

"Meaning, if you keep telling a guy he's gonna cheat on you, he might get fed up and cheat on you." Seeing my face, he put an arm around me and added, "Come on, Hon. Look, I'm not used to my big sister looking to me to solve her problems, though I feel an unexpected urge to rescue her rising up inside me!" He sprang to his feet and bellowed in his best regional theater voice, "Fear not, beloved Cassandra!

I myself will ride to thine aid! Herewith I offer thee, for thy protection, my Home, my Wealth, and mine Honor."

"Yeah, right," I scoffed, kicking at him. "Share your dumb apartment in Bellingham with your Craigslist roommate and live off your $200 a month, or whatever you're getting for *Waiters*."

He deflated in mock-hurt. "No, really, Cass—I've even gotten a second job with an office catering company. That's why I'm down here: to pick up special orders from Beecher's and Salumi. You really can make a guy feel small. Oh, well—at least you didn't disparage mine Honor."

Pulling on his hand, I laughed. He may have solved nothing, but I felt better for having dumped everything on him. "Come on, Sir Galahad. Let's surprise Joanie and get a jump on dinner. I think we'll have a busy open house tonight."

. . .

Kicking the door shut with her foot, Joanie stalked into the kitchen. "If she isn't leaving, I am!"

She flung open the refrigerator to retrieve a half cantaloupe, thumping it down on the cutting board and starting to whack at it with a cleaver.

I shook my head as I refilled the potato salad bowl. "You can't leave your own house and your own house party. Besides, would you leave Perry undefended?"

"Oh, what?" she snorted. "Now you're all right with me going after Perry?"

"It's all relative."

Phyl bustled in with the empty sangria pitcher, and even her brow was furrowed for the first time since she accepted Wayne.

"Fine if you make more sangria, but we're cutting Darla off," declared Joanie, drawing a finger across her throat. "She was okay until she got that first glass into her." Seeing my skeptical expression, she added, "Meaning, she only flirted with Daniel and left the other guys alone."

Unbidden, the three of us turned to look out the bay window. Sure enough, there was Darla, ducking her chin coyly and giving Wyatt Collins a playful poke. Whatever she said to him, the men nearby erupted in laughter: Perry, Wayne, Tom. Daniel.

"I wish you hadn't told Daniel to date around, Cass," said Phyl quietly, after she drew the cork from another bottle of Barberesco.

Caught off guard, I stared at her. I could have blown off such a comment, if Joanie had made it, but, coming from Phyl, this reproach had teeth. "Wait a second—how can I possibly get blamed for Darla? Yes, I told him to date around, but I didn't say to bring home Miss Maneater Northwest! And I don't even know if this has anything to do with me—he might just be dating because he's sick of waiting around, or he's over me."

Phyl didn't look convinced. Her mouth was still pressed in a thin line as she measured out the Triple Sec.

Joanie dumped the unevenly chopped melon into the bowl. "What is Daniel thinking?" she growled. "All these months he's had enough tarts through here to open his own bakery, so now he thinks he can get away with her?"

What was he thinking, indeed? I had spent the evening trying to determine that. He had shown up after most everyone else had gathered, Darla coming in with him through the garage door, giggling and prancing. She had curly, shoulder-length brown hair and round, Bambi eyes and a buxom little figure, accented by the heart pendant that dangled between her breasts like a road sign: **Curves Ahead**, maybe. Or it could have been **DIP**.

When she took Daniel's hand, he let her. Nor did he shrug her off the time the oven buzzer sounded, causing her to give a startled squeal and throw her arms around him. Darla also seemed possessed of two voices: a breathy, ripply one to use on men, and a matter-of-fact one for addressing women.

Joanie hadn't minded her at first, other than throwing me a can-you-believe-*this*-one glance, but as the evening wore on, Darla nursed her sangria and seemed to be casting a wider and wider net. While still nestling close to Daniel, she would coo and blink at any other man who happened to come in range, and they seemed happy enough to be tangled up like so much dolphin bycatch.

But what about Daniel?

Firstly, I knew it was uncharacteristic of him to let any girlfriend drape on him like Spanish moss. As far as I knew, only Joanie was allowed that privilege. Maybe the license would have extended to me, had I taken him up in May, but I wasn't sure. Secondly, he seemed more amused by Darla than anything else. Amused, not besotted. And while he found her attractive enough, he didn't, really. It was hard to explain. He most certainly was not in love with her. My glimpse had been brief, in May, but I think I knew what he looked like with love on his face, and this wasn't it.

He was enjoying himself, obviously, but part of that enjoyment, I suspected, came from getting my goat while he was at it. Well, he had it. And Joanie's and Phyl's goats, for good measure. Enough goats to start his own Alpine herd.

"You're the one who told me to marry him," I reminded Joanie innocently.

"Yeah, and I stand by that comment," said Joanie. "If you'd accepted him when he offered, he wouldn't have brought Bible Bimbo home to torture us."

"She is cute," put in Phyl, in spite of herself. In her desire to be just, she was relenting, and even gave me an apologetic smile. "And she's the first Christian girl he's ever dated."

"God," muttered Joanie, "give me a good heathen any day."

Her ears must have been burning because Darla popped into the kitchen the next moment. "How's that sangria coming? Can we get another round?"

Torn between hospitality and Joanie's command to cut off Darla's liquor supply, Phyl confusedly nodded and began stirring the pitcher at typhoon speed.

"Your voice is sounding stronger," said Joanie solicitously. "Not all breathy, like when you were talking to Daniel—were you having an asthma attack earlier?"

Darla looked puzzled, and I stepped firmly on Joanie's foot to shut her up.

"No, I'm great," responded Darla, clueless. "This is so much fun. Thanks for having me. I've never met so many cool people. You girls are so lucky. And, oh Lordy, is Daniel the handsomest thing ever, or what? I don't know how you can function, having him at close quarters all the time! I would just—aaah!" She made a swooning motion.

Apparently riddled with guilt for having mean thoughts about her, Phyl refilled Darla's glass over Joanie's loud throat-clearings.

"And your brother, too, Cass," Darla gushed, turning to me. "So creative! And engaging! And he has your beautiful brown eyes—I've always been a sucker for brown eyes—if I weren't going out with Daniel, I'd just love to—"

"Bang Wayne?" prompted Joanie under her breath, earning herself an elbow in the ribs.

"—Get to know him better," finished Darla, oblivious.

Everything reloaded, we headed back outside, Darla quickly relieving Phyl of the sangria pitcher so she could flit from man to man offering refreshment.

"Men love a good top-off," said Joanie.

I figured now was not the time to tell her that Darla had the same coloring and some of the same mannerisms as my ex-sister-in-law Betsy, and I wondered if that was part of the charm for Perry. For Perry did indeed seem charmed, even whipping out some of his theater tricks for her benefit: juggling peaches and balancing a spoon on the end of his nose.

"Would you stop already?" I hissed at him, when I could stand it no longer. "She isn't even your date, after all."

To my surprise, instead of looking miffed, he gave me a roguish grin. "Don't tell me I'm bugging you—and you say I can't act!"

"What are you talking about, you idiot?"

"You tell me you're desperate and unhappy, and I'm trying to help," he replied, reaching for another of Phyl's rocky road brownies. Leaning in, he murmured, "Just trying to make sure Daniel doesn't get too serious with her. Wanna keep my sister's options open."

"How thoughtful of you," I said dryly. "I doubt you'd be such a martyr to the cause if you didn't also think Darla was pretty cute. Can you say 'rebound'?"

The two of us watched the woman in question let loose a cascade of giggles, wagging a teasing finger in Daniel's face to make a point.

"Easy, Cass," soothed Perry. "Yeah, I'm on the rebound—can't a guy have a little fun? If you weren't my sister, I'd think you were jealous."

Jealous? Of Darla? As a matter of fact, I was. But not about Perry, unless it were for Joanie's sake. He and Joanie wouldn't be an ideal match, but I'd take Joanie over Darla any day. No, I was jealous of the way Darla was so at ease with herself—she liked men; she wanted men to like her, and that was that. No angst. No second-guessing. No am-I-doing-the-right-thing.

I didn't have to spare Joanie a glance to know she was breathing fire by this point, ignoring Perry completely and having a revenge flirtation with Tom. Darla would not be allowed to carry the day unanimously.

"Do you really think Darla is the most attractive woman here?" I asked curiously.

"You talk like there are a lot of options," muttered Perry. "I'm not into incest, and Phyl's engaged and Delia's married."

"What about…well, there's Joanie," I said.

"Joanie," said Perry flatly. "You do think pretty highly of me, Cass, so I hate to break it to you: Joanie's out of my league."

"Out of your league?" I echoed.

"Most definitely."

But that meant... "Do you mean you think she's attractive?" I squeaked.

My brother avoided my eyes. Took a sip of his sangria. "She'll do."

Well, then.

Here was a new development.

For Pete's sake—talk about self-fulfilling prophecies! All Lori Lincoln has to do is mention my unstable living situation, and the whole structure collapses in the next stiff breeze. If Perry decided he liked Joanie, the second she got wind of it, that would be that. Another housemate gone, barring one of Joanie's notorious last-minute broken engagements. Of course, maybe Perry didn't *like her* like her—he just thought she was hot. No big deal because everyone thought Joanie was hot.

"Yeah, Joanie is probably better looking than Darla," I ventured, "but looks aside, you think Darla has the advantage?"

Perry shook the ice loose in his glass and dug out an orange slice. "Let's just say I'm a realistic guy."

Which answered my question. Feeling defeated, I asked, "If your wildest dreams ever came true and you got together with Joanie, could Baby Ned and I live with you guys until the state takes him away from me?"

"Sure thing," he answered, recovering his easy tone. "If you're positive you wouldn't rather live with Daniel and Darla."

• • •

As it happened, apart from Daniel and Darla, no other couples fared well that evening. Delia put down her glass sharply at nine and fairly dragged Wyatt away. Joanie took this as her cue to disappear upstairs, leaving Phyl and me to clean up, after Phyl took a very cool leave of Wayne.

"Now Phyl, don't be mad at Wayne," I said when he was gone. "He didn't flirt a bit with Darla."

"He didn't discourage her," she pointed out unhappily.

"He wouldn't know how to," I countered. "He's as sweet as you are. You know you've never known how to drive anyone off."

Dumping the fruit cuttings in the yard waste bin, Phyl said tightly, "That's not it, Cass. If Troy had cheated on you, like Jason cheated on me, you would understand how even seeing any signs like that—the eye contact, the—the laughing together—how it just gets my back up. I don't want to go there again."

I stopped in my counter wiping. "Oh—I get it. I'm sorry, Phyl. Of course. I can understand you being sensitive. I just meant to say that Wayne did whatever he did innocently. It's not like he's someone with Daniel's history," I added darkly.

"Hmm…" said Phyl, evidently unconvinced.

"Remember when you liked Daniel?" I asked. "How would you have handled being engaged to someone like that?"

Sighing, she ran a hand through her wavy brown hair. "I guess I just wish men were different," she said. "That, when they committed to someone, they committed. That was that. No more looking around, no more shopping around, no more playing with fire."

"Really, Phyl, I don't think Wayne was playing with fire—it's more like he got sucked into Darla's backdraft." I gave her a hug. "He looked kind of down when he left. Why don't you give him a call?"

Carefully Phyl measured out a half scoop of dish detergent and poured it in the dispenser before she answered. "Maybe you're right. I overreacted. It's too late to call, but I could send a friendly text. Thanks, Cass."

After Phyl went upstairs, I looked around for Perry, but he must have headed for the Lean-To. Who knew where Daniel and Darla had gotten to, though if they wanted to make out they'd have to find another spot. It was still too hot upstairs to think of going to bed, so I ended up on the back deck, curled up on the chaise longue under an afghan. It was mid-July, and the days were getting shorter again, but the sky was still a little light, and here it was nearly ten o'clock. Good thing I wasn't an astrologer. There was no summer starlight to direct me in Bellevue, with the short nights and all the lights from the city. On the other hand, lately I felt almost equally rudderless.

What do you think about all this, Lord? I asked. *You and Troy and Min sitting up there happy as clams while I flounder around down here, missing them and trying to figure out what's going on. My housemates all pairing up, or about to. Mike getting his act together while mine falls apart. Ned no longer being my sure thing?* Where was that certainty I had in the spring, when Nadina asked me to take her baby, and I knew in my gut it would happen? It had cost me James, yes, but I knew I'd made the right choice. *Did you mean for me to take Ned until Mike gets out of jail? Was that all? Save the baby's life, so he can be handed over as a living sacrifice?*

Maybe I was being too hard on Mike. It was the same question again: how did you know when someone was really changed? Was he toeing the line to spite me, or because the gigantic mess he'd made of his life acted as a wake-up call? Heck, maybe I should go to Coyote Ridge and ask him myself, though I couldn't imagine Lori allowing that.

Watching the now-dim sky, I tried to silence my thoughts and wait. Last week's sermon had been on listening, how we all talk too much to God and fail to be still and listen, but tonight I heard only the occasional car passing and the neighbor's teenage son cranking his stereo. Maybe God and I were like one of those comic scenes in the movies: the instant one character began speaking, so did the other, so that, talk all they wanted, they never heard each other.

In my back pocket, my phone chirped. I saw with surprise that I had three new text messages. Maybe God was getting with the times. Or, like us, he resorted to texting when he didn't have the time or inclination for an actual conversation.

No dice.

The first was Nadina, reporting more contractions and whining about how boring bedrest was, and if Ned was this anxious to get out of her, she had no problem with getting rid of him because she hated feeling fat as a house. My terse response: "Stay horizontal."

The second, amazingly enough, was from James:

> Cass—if you can come in extra this wk, great.
> Kyle will too. Lots of testing needed.

I suppose that could go in the answer-to-prayer bucket. Additional work hours didn't fix my unstable living situation or net me a husband, but they did mean extra money. Additional paychecks I could sign right over to Lori. "Sure. See you," I keyed.

The last number was unfamiliar, and no wonder. Skandar. I had emailed him dutifully a few days after our coffee, making the perfunctory offer to get together for lunch, if he still wanted. I expected his social urge would have passed, but I was wrong, it would seem. Sigh. The last thing I felt like adding to my load was a morose widower, but so be it. Maybe I could scare him off with some rousing Jesus talk. Faith as anti-social weapon.

10:30. I had no idea when Daniel's long kiss goodnight with Darla would wrap up, but I didn't want him to catch me out here, as if I'd been lying in wait for him.

Casting one last, hopeful glance upward, I added a final prayer: *Lord, while I'm running down the laundry list, show me what on earth to do about Daniel.*

CHAPTER SEVEN:

Homeland Insecurity

Things got worse at the Palace over the weekend.

For one thing, Darla spent every waking minute there, which meant Perry spent every waking minute dangling after her, which meant the giggling and flirtation and shimmying went on incessantly, which meant Joanie and Phyl and I could hardly stand to be in our own home.

Even a forgiven Wayne couldn't resist warming to Darla's sunny advances, and by Saturday afternoon Phyl had to drag him away to hike the Talapus Loop, when I knew she'd rather be sitting with him in front of her computer, checking out reception sites.

As for Joanie, I had to admire her acting skills. Apart from the occasional verbal jab at Darla's expense (which Darla never noticed), Joanie was perfectly calm and civil in front of Perry. She saved her rage for late Saturday night, pacing furiously up and down my bedroom.

"Something has got to be done!" she exploded. "Tell your lame, puppy-dog-eyed brother to get the hell back up to Bellingham and take his stupid cheese and prosciutto with him!"

"*My* brother?" I said indignantly, slamming my book shut. "Why don't you tell *your* lame brother to keep Darla out in the Lean-To where she can't bother us?"

"Because he'll just tell me this is his house! And it is, damn it!" she snapped. "Why can't you just marry the guy as an act of public service?"

"Oh, right," I snorted. "You think I should just march right down there, pull her off of him and say, 'Daniel, I've been so blown away by your character these past few days that I can't hold out any longer. Take me! Take me now!'" Grabbing a cushion off my window seat, I clutched it to my chest and smothered it with kisses.

Despite herself, Joanie snickered. "Aaaaargh—this sucks. At least Perry's got rehearsals starting this week. He'll have to get out of here, even if he's got Darla clinging to his ankles as he tries to escape. And let's hope Daniel has an awful week at work. Then we might be free of her until next Thursday, and by then she'll be running up against his two-week limit."

"Some of his girlfriends lasted a month," I reminded her, sighing. "But something better happen. Our group interview with that social worker is Friday. If we're all like this next week, we'll flunk the home study."

On Sunday I fled to my usual early service at church, deeply needing the hour of worship and focus. Since I'd been up so late arguing with Joanie, I arrived later than usual and thought that working my way to Louella in front would be too conspicuous. Instead I took the balcony steps two at a time and squished into a back row.

The organ prelude was nearly over, but I closed my eyes in relief. Sanctuary. A still center in my spinning world.

"Oh, Lordy! Hello there, you handsome dog!"

My eyes flew open.

No.

Not here.

But it was. Several rows to the right and lower down, I saw dear Darla tapping on a man's shoulder, and waving for him to scoot in. A blond man's shoulder. The prelude rose to a crescendo, so I couldn't hear what they said to each other, but I'm fairly sure the micro-expression that flickered across Daniel's face was dismay.

Clearly, Darla's appearance at the service was unexpected. She must have found out he would be here and decided to surprise him. But what was Daniel doing here? Was this a one-time thing, or had he been coming, unbeknownst to me? Everyone knew I went to the early service. I'd never seen him there before, but the sanctuary held almost a thousand people, so even if he sat in the balcony regularly, decades could go by before our paths crossed.

Whatever the case, all I knew was their presence would only be a distraction. Slipping out of my row, I headed back downstairs and chose a new seat where I couldn't see them.

The pastor was preaching on Abraham that summer, a story long familiar to people like me who had grown up in church. Yes, yes, Abraham and his wife Sarah were old and decrepit, but God promised them a son against all odds, from whom multitudes of descendents would come. And then, when Abraham finally got Isaac many years and misadventures later, he very nearly had to sacrifice him—saved only by Isaac's last-minute reprieve.

As a kid, the story's main takeaway was that—horrors!—my grandparents might have a sex life. Other than that, like too many Bible stories, its shock value and plot twists were dulled by frequent repetition.

It was only when I saw Brunelleschi's baptistery door panel in Florence, on a weekend jaunt during my quarter abroad at Oxford, that the story came alive for me. The cheerful veil of children's Bible illustrations fell away, laying bare the stark terror of the situation. There was Abraham, knife held to his long-awaited son's throat, the angel urgently seizing his arm to stop him as Isaac twisted and cringed. Twice, the angel shouted the patriarch's name before his voice penetrated—Abraham having already begun to have bloody thoughts.

In the same way, when Pastor Jonathan read the day's passage from Genesis, it struck me as it never had before:

But Abram said, "O Lord God, what will you give me, for I continue childless, and the heir of my house is Eliezer of Damascus?...You have given me no offspring; and a slave born in my house will be my heir." And behold, the word of the Lord came to him, "This man shall not be your heir; your own son shall be your heir."...And Abram believed the Lord; and he reckoned it to him as righteousness.

Abraham believed—all evidence to the contrary, year after unfulfilled year to the contrary. How difficult it must have been for him and Sarah to plod along, having decades of sex with no reproductive results! Surely they must have wondered many times if Abraham had imagined it all—eaten some bad curds with his unleavened bread. Their forgivable doubts took them on many detours, into separations, stopgap measures, jealousy, fights—but through it all and underneath it all ran that slender thread of faith. And along, at last, came Isaac.

At present I was no longer sure I was meant to have Baby Ned, but once I had been. That afternoon with Nadina. Sure enough to make drastic life choices, whatever the consequences. Sure enough that Nadina had felt it too, the certainty of it all.

So now there were obstacles.

Well, okay.

Nothing worth anything came easy. Look at Isaac.

If I was meant to raise Ned as my own, I might have to spend years, spend money, fight in court, but there it was: the promise. Not that I was a hero of the faith—I was no Abraham—but I had my own tenuous thread to cling to. Knotted, fraying in places, but still holding.

Okay. God had spoken into my life back in February. Things had gotten pretty messy since then, but I guess I still had to go with that. If I was...off-base, He would just have to say something. Do something. Slam a door in my face. Otherwise, I was going to do my utmost to believe that someday Ned would be a done deal.

If God was still in, then so was I.

• • •

"Tell me you're not holding that drill in relation to my house."

Startled, I looked up from inside the pantry, DeWalt in one hand and instructions in the other, screw clamped in my lips. Gingerly I set down the drill and plucked out the screw. "Of course I am. I'm installing a fire extinguisher."

"Do you know what you're doing?" asked Daniel.

"Anyone can operate a drill," I answered evasively. "The hardest part is finding the stud." His eyes glinted in amusement, but I ignored him. "What a sexist comment, anyhow. Who says only men can handle power tools?" Granted, I hadn't handled one in years. With his engineering mind, Troy had always tackled the mechanical things in our marriage, and it had been easier to let him than to keep my own skills up.

"Actually, I meant it respectfully," he said, coming to lean against the door jamb. "I'm completely unhandy. One of the drawbacks of having no father."

"There you go again! Another sexist comment! Why couldn't it have been your mother who taught you?" The unlikely vision of Angela Martin wielding a jackhammer popped into my head, and Daniel must have imagined something similar because we looked at each other and laughed.

"Maybe I could help you?" he suggested. "I can't be the brains, but I can supply the brawn. That looks pretty heavy—" indicating the 2A10BC fire extinguisher I had wrestled out of my trunk.

"That would be wonderful," I said gratefully. "I was going to enlist Perry when he got back from church, but since you're offering…"

We worked in companionable silence. If you could feel companionable with someone who took up so much of the pantry's limited space and who I was being very careful not to touch. I thought of asking him what on earth he'd been doing at church that morning but couldn't come up with an opener that didn't make me look hopeful, lovelorn, confrontational, or all three. Daniel watched me install the bracket's top screw and then held the level for me so I could position the bottom one. When everything was even and tightened up, he hoisted the extinguisher and I fitted it into the bracket.

"Can I ask why you suddenly felt the Palace needed this behemoth?" he said then. "Are you planning lots of bananas flambé?"

"It's Christmas in July," I said dryly. "This whole adoption thing is kind of a money pit. I got this extinguisher and replaced that dead smoke alarm for the social worker's visit on Friday, in case she checks. And this week I have my medical exam to make sure I'm healthy enough to raise a child, and I'm also paying Lori Lincoln to run those background checks on all of us—just FYI, in case you need to flee the country and want a running start."

"I think I'm outside the statute of limitations," he smiled. He watched me carefully wind the drill cord and replace it in its case. "You know, though, Cass—since I am the landlord around here, why don't you let me reimburse you for the fire extinguisher and the smoke alarm?"

I stiffened. His friendly tone made my heart do a funny clenching move. What a good guy he was, when he wasn't being a bastard. His easy conversation—our first in who knew how long—and helpfulness with the task had lowered my guard. But I've just gotten an emotional hold of myself! I whined inwardly. I don't want Daniel mixing me up.

But he *was* a good guy. And sometimes a good friend. Feeling my put-upon heart thump in my chest, I looked up, unable to prevent a smile growing on my face. "You know, Daniel, tha—"

"Yoo hoo!" called a bubbly, breathy voice from the entry way, as we heard the front door thrown open.

"Look who I found at church," exclaimed Perry, leading dear Darla into the kitchen, their arms laden with bags from Whole Foods. "And we've brought lunch for everyone! Three kinds of soup, four kinds of salad, artisan bread…we ran into Phyl and Wayne there, so they're joining us, and hopefully Joanie will show up—she was doing something choir-related this morning."

Sliding her bag onto the counter, Darla clicked over to us on her little high heels. "My goodness, what are you two up to in there?"

"Just smothering any potential flames," said Daniel.

"Ooh!" wiggled Darla. She spared the fire extinguisher a glance but saved most of her admiration for Daniel. "Is there anything you can't do? Ladies are in good hands with you."

I rolled my eyes at the boxes of breakfast cereal. Yes, indeed. *Ladies* being the operative word. It was always plural with him. I didn't need to worry about anyone catching my expression: Daniel had his back to me as he emerged from the pantry, and with Darla, women always seemed to fade into invisibility when men were around.

I was not invisible to my brother, however, and I treated him to a ferocious glare. Perry trembled in mock fear. Under cover of Darla chattering at Daniel and the sound of my other housemates' arrival, he leaned in and whispered, "Have no fear, fair maiden. This very afternoon I will deliver your beloved from the clutches of the dragon!" Which only irked me more—I should never have told Perry that I liked Daniel.

"What does everyone feel like?" asked Perry loudly, throwing his arms out and rotating in the center of the floor like a showman. "Gazpacho? Corn chowder? Hot and sour soup?"

"Perry sampled everything, and he could guess all the ingredients," marveled Darla to the room in general, as if we hadn't all known him far longer than she had. "He's such a cooking whiz!"

"I suggested the corn chowder," volunteered Wayne. "Gazpacho and hot and sour were a little too fancy for my Midwestern tastes." Knowing Wayne's fondness for the King's Table Buffet, this came as no surprise, but when I tried to catch Phyl's eye to wink at her, I saw her mouth was set in a hard line.

"No excuses!" teased Darla, tapping on Wayne's hand. "You

shouldn't apologize for being a good, solid man with traditional tastes. Perry's a little too fancy for all of us, if you ask me."

"Perry has always been the gayest straight man I know," I said solemnly, earning myself a punch in the shoulder from the Faerie Queen.

"I didn't think we should buy so much food there," Phyl spoke up, her voice hard and tense. Most unlike her. "We can put the soup containers in the yard waste when we're done, but there are all those clamshells. And we really didn't need the plastic ware, when we were just going to come eat it at home!"

An awkward silence fell, but after a moment Wayne put a placating hand on her shoulder. "I'll help rinse out the clamshells and we'll recycle them, Sweetheart."

"You can't recycle them!" Phyl cried wildly. "You can't put clamshell containers in the recycle bin! You have to store them up for the special recycling event in October!" For a dreadful moment I thought she was going to burst into tears, but instead she took a deep raggedy breath and flung off Wayne's hand.

Joanie and I exchanged horrified looks—Phyl usually did all the conversational smoothing-over in our house—what were we supposed to do when she was the one making everyone uncomfortable? Darla clearly thought Phyl was both ungrateful and unhinged, and I could see pouty words rising to her lips, so I threw myself into the breach. "Well, in any case, we'd better eat the food—and thank you so much, Perry and Darla, for picking it up. Phyl, you know very well you never miss those special recycling events and that the Palace has room enough to store clamshell containers from here to eternity. Why don't you and Wayne go first, in honor of your *engagement*, and go *get some time to yourselves* out on the deck?"

"You go on out, Honey," Wayne said. "Go relax, and I'll bring you something."

"Yes!" chimed in Darla. "You go outside, and Wayne and I will pick the choicest things for you, with Perry's recommendations, of course."

"I'll get my own food, thank you," Phyl snapped.

"You can't," said Joanie, coming to grab Phyl's elbow and give her a warning squeeze. "Because it's your duty to mix us up some lovely summer cocktail. How about Blue Hawaiians, or mint juleps?"

"Perry and I were just talking about how we love mint juleps!" rejoiced Darla.

"My bad," said Joanie. "I forgot we're clean out of mint. Blue Hawaiians it is." Hissing something in Phyl's ear, she managed to drag her to the other side of the vast kitchen.

Wayne, to his credit, insisted on getting Phyl's food, so Darla was thrown back on hovering between Daniel and Perry, asking for their suggestions and critiquing their choices. "I'm glad you still have an appetite," she said to Daniel as he spooned the quinoa salad onto his plate. "I thought after you abandoned me this morning to go have coffee with those guys from your men's Bible study that you might be stuffed full of *pain au chocolat.*"

"Just coffee," he replied laconically.

Her kittycat pout returned, and she ran a finger down his arm. "I still don't see why I couldn't come along. I know plenty about the Bible."

"Not to mention men," I added cheerily, protected by my female invisibility.

Daniel heard me, however. Giving me a curious look, he held the back door open for Darla, for which she thanked him with a glowing face.

"Want me to wait for you, Phyl?" asked Wayne. He came to show her what he'd prepared for her. "Should I get you more of the Greek salad?"

Phyl drowned him out by hitting "Crush" on the blender, whirling the ingredients into a Blue Curaçao-colored slush. "Don't let me keep you," she sniffed, not even looking at him. This was terrible!

As a mystified Wayne moped his way outside, I scurried over to

Perry. "Get your butt out there, Galahad, and do something. The keep is going up in flames."

No sooner had the door closed behind him than I whipped the highball glass out of Phyl's hand and said, "Stop it, Phyl! You've got to stop acting like this. Wayne isn't doing anything wrong! If you're going to be angry at anyone, be angry at Daniel for bringing Darla into our lives—"

"And while you're at it," interrupted Joanie, "be angry at Perry for bringing that harpy home with him, when we thought we were rid of her for the rest of the weekend—"

"Perry is trying to help," I protested, turning on Joanie. "I mean, he shouldn't have invited her over—but I bet she didn't give him any choice. This whole mess is Daniel's fault."

"Don't you see?" wailed Phyl, wresting the highball glass back from me and jamming a pineapple slice on the rim, "What does it matter who brought her? Here she is, and I am NOT going to be married to another cheater! I am NOT!"

Joanie and I forgot our arguing in the face of Phyl's insanity. "Phyllida Rose Levert," I said, "what are you saying? Wayne is not Jason."

"Yeah," muttered Joanie. "God help us, if he were. It's almost too bad he isn't, then we could sic Darla on him and be rid of them both."

Frowning, I shook my head at Joanie. "Look, Phyl," I said soothingly, putting an arm around her. She was squashing the current slice of pineapple so viciously onto its highball glass that it broke into separate chunks and fell in. "Take a deep breath. You're not making any sense. I would gladly vouch for Wayne's character—"

"Cass, just stop," she moaned, putting her fists to her temples and twisting out of my grasp. "Stop already. I'm not Nadina. You can't tell me how to run my life." Over my indignant gasp she dumped more ice in the blender and ground it up. "If I say I need to break it off with Wayne and give myself some space, just stay out of it—please."

Before I could do more than shut my stunned mouth and then

open it again to defend myself, Joanie thrust the two glasses at me. "Take these out, Cass." She jerked her chin in the direction of the door and made a *she's-crazy* circle with her finger.

"I saw that!" shrieked Phyl. "And I don't need your advice either, Joanie."

Joanie fired up instantly. "Did I offer any, you nut job? I'm with Cass—you are out of your picking, paranoid, jealous mind—"

"Joanie—" I broke in, trying to shut her up.

"Don't bother, Cass," rejoined Phyl in clipped tones, "I know you two always gang up on me—at least Joanie's more honest about it and just says it to my face—"

"How did I become the focal point of these attacks?" I demanded, outraged. "I thought Darla was the problem here." I banged the Blue Hawaiians back on the granite counter, causing the slush to slop over the rims. "I'm only saying, can we all just calm down? Take a breather? For Pete's sake, what is that social worker going to think of us on Friday?"

"See! See! Can't you ever think about anything other than getting that baby?" accused Phyl. "You just want us to calm down and put on a happy face so that social worker thinks everything is peachy here."

I sank onto a barstool, defeated, laying my head across my arms. "Everything usually *is* peachy here," I sighed. "Other than the last wretched couple weeks."

Heartless Phyl was whipping off her apron and stuffing it in the drawer. "Tell Wayne I'm getting a migraine."

"Tell him your own self, you big chicken," yelled Joanie after her, as Phyl fled the room.

Perry's head popped in the door, his eyes taking in the Blue Hawaiian carnage, my slump and Joanie's narrowed eyes. "Hey, girls... everything all right in here? How are those drinks coming?"

"What does this look like—stinking *Cheers*?" snarled Joanie. "If you're thirsty, be our guest." With that she stomped out of the kitchen herself.

Perry whistled. "Mail not addressed to me. How's my timing, Cass?"

I smiled ruefully. "Impeccable."

"Need to do any more venting? I could listen for a minute, until Darla realizes I've slipped my bonds and made a bid for freedom."

Pulling a soup container toward me, I reached for a plastic spoon. With Phyl mad at me, there was a certain satisfaction in not getting up to get a real one. Straight into the landfill, along with my life. "Thanks but no thanks, Perry. If you ask me, there's been more than enough venting for one day."

CHAPTER EIGHT:

Bridge-Burning

"Keep up, Cass," urged Kyle. "You're falling too far behind again."

I was running through tangled underbrush, panting, my sword dragging clumsily from my limp hand. Peering ahead, I could just catch the rest of my party darting away, hot in pursuit of the stupid, glittering dwarf who served the Evil Emperor.

"Hang on a second, Kyle," I complained, heaving with effort and trying unsuccessfully to figure out which direction he'd gone. "You're always ditching me." Before I could continue my pursuit, however, I collapsed, my green-tights-encased spindly legs curling up to my chest. Then, scrunched in this too-familiar, we-who-are-about-to-die-salute-you position, I began spinning dramatically before evaporating with a slurpy sound.

"Crud!" I yelled.

Kyle's head appeared around the wall of my cube. "Did you die again, Cass?" he asked in his raspy voice. "How can we test all the features when you keep dying, and we don't get to the Castle?"

"Look, Mister," I retorted, "I wasn't born with a gamepad in my hand like you were. Come back and revive me."

"Can't," he answered. "That was your third death. And I need all my extra energy points if I have to kill Glitter Dwarf and do the Castle by myself."

Sighing, I uncoiled from the hard chair I'd occupied for the last two hours. "Fine. You finish the quest. I'm going to go check in with Riley."

Since Camden School got out, Kyle had been putting in more hours at Free Universe, whittling away at the $2000 he owed the state for last year's vandalism offenses. Interning had done him a world of good, giving him an outlet for his techie side that the school couldn't provide, and possibly prying open the college doors his earlier choices had slammed shut.

As for me, the Palace's weekend uproar provided ample incentive to hide out at work. Being around James regularly, distressing though it was, was preferable to the roiling tensions at home. It helped that I never saw any sign of a girlfriend, and if James spent any time on the phone with one, whispering sweet nothings, it wasn't when I was around. Despite Lori's advice to get a real job, I'd chosen to stall—I would work more hours at my inadequate pseudo-job instead, writing for video games, testing, and doing occasional voice work. After all, what was the point of getting a real job when I would have a newborn on my hands in a few weeks?

I found Riley the game developer rooted to his Aeron chair, mouth open, staring blindly out his fraction of a window. Since he was legendary for his absurd petrified candy display, I thought for one moment that, in an act of poetic justice, he himself had been turned to stone. Added to the exhibit, as it were.

"Hey, Riley. Are you okay?" I ventured, squeezing into his cube. I perched on the work surface, then grimaced and sprang up again, sweeping aside some miniature light sabers.

He didn't answer, but rotated as a single unit on his chair to face me, pushing off the ground with one tube-socked toe.

"What's wrong with you?" I asked again. "Did you have a stroke?"

"Oh, yeah, Cass," he said finally, "oh, yeah, I had a stroke. A stroke of *genius*."

Before I could reply, he shot to his feet and bawled, "Kittredge! Yo! Get over here."

The squeak of a rolling chair preceded Jeri's appearance around the neighboring cube wall. "Sheez, Riley, trying to get some work done here," she whined. "Oh, hey, Cass."

As the company's only full-time writer, Jeri viewed me with suspicion when I first started at Free Universe. But she warmed to me slowly, even venting to me once about the drawbacks of working in an all-guy office. "Sometimes they just *smell*, Cass," she groused. "I swear Riley only does his laundry once a month, and one time I even snuck Vil's sweatshirt home with me so I could wash it and bring it back, it was so nasty. Then he didn't even recognize it clean and kept saying it must be somebody else's. And Murray leaves his Chinese food leftovers in the fridge and keeps heating them up over and over till the place stinks like kung pao and popcorn or some other disgusting combo. Then, does he toss it? No, he leaves it there like some science experiment, so by the time I get hacked off enough to clean it out, its weight has, like, doubled, from all the mold and fungus it grew." She stopped to take a breath and a swig of her black coffee. "You know what? I think James is the only one who's always clean and never stinks or makes sexist remarks. I can see why you liked him there for a while."

This conversation came back to me when James appeared in response to Riley's summons, as clean and unstinky and gender-considerate as advertised. Nadina thought he couldn't hold a candle to Daniel, aesthetically speaking, but really, with his curling brown hair and gray eyes and cheerful demeanor, James wasn't lacking in charm. He paused momentarily when he caught sight of me, but before either one of us could say anything, Riley hollered, "Dude! I've figured out what we can do about that fifth path in *Ace Assassin*—check this out." Giving me a small smile, James leaned over to see what Riley had begun furiously diagramming.

With Jeri in mind and time to kill before the next event on my day's agenda, I decided to clean out the office fridge. Twenty minutes later the trash can was overflowing, and I was still at it. James came upon me chipping at some unidentifiable magenta substance in the back of the freezer. "Better just leave it," he advised, "or you might break all our sporks."

"What if that's some leaky refrigeration chemical that's slowly poisoning you all?" I countered, poking it a couple more times.

Leaning in over my shoulder to take a better look, he said lightly, "Nah. That's gotta be Otter Pop residue, circa Summer 2004. Riley has a weakness for them."

I scooted out sideways from the open freezer, feeling shy to have him so near. "You're probably right. It's hopeless."

"How have you been, Cass? Things going all right with Nadina?"

His question and manner surprised me, it having been a couple months since the last time we had a personal conversation. We had become permanent colleagues, I thought, able to meet at work and talk generally in groups without weirdness. While some women I knew insisted on becoming friends with men they broke up with, I had never had enough exes to warrant action plans or categorizations.

"Okay," I said vaguely. "I mean, I'm okay. Nadina seems to be doing fine, health-wise. Just another six weeks or so to go."

"How's it going with Mike and the adoption business? Has he come around?"

Despite wanting to keep things light, I felt my shoulders sag. "No such luck. It looks like I'm in for a long, drawn-out, bank-account-draining affair. Hence my extra appearances here. Hope it's okay—I don't know how long I'll have before baby Ned appears."

"It's fine," James said quickly. "You know we've always wanted as much of you as you're willing to give." There was an uncomfortable pause before he added, "I mean, in terms of hours."

"Yes."

"So...have you decided you're not going to move out before the baby?"

Inevitably, I blushed. Up to this point I'd been maintaining composure rather well, but now the spork in my hand snapped in my rigid grip. "No, no, I won't be moving. Daniel and I agreed it would be okay if I—if we—stayed."

He appeared to be weighing what he said next because the first couple options got nixed. Finally he came up with, "Still having your open houses?"

Not this week we weren't. Phyl had been avoiding everyone the last couple days, and Joanie and I were still too afraid of her wrath to press her. In any case, she left a curt note in the Palace kitchen cancelling the week's open house, with NO GUESTS in all caps. We assumed it was easier for Phyl to ban all guests than to ban Darla in particular and left it at that. If Daniel still wanted to fraternize with her, there was always the Lean-To.

I nodded. "Absolutely! Would you and Mira like to come sometime?" Disingenuous, I'll admit, since Joanie had told me weeks and weeks ago that James was making the dating rounds at Chaff again.

He was more straightforward than I. "Actually, Mira and I broke up."

"Whoever you're dating now, then," I amended, balancing the spork fragments on the heaped-up trash.

"And if I'm not dating anyone..?"

Because I couldn't come up with an immediate response, his words hung in the air, taking on significance.

What was going on? After breaking my heart a few months ago, was he really hinting that he wanted to see me again? If he wasn't, any assumption on my part could be embarrassing, but my life couldn't handle any more blurred lines. "What are you getting at, James?" I asked.

The self-deprecating smile I remembered. "I hardly know myself," he said. He took a tentative step closer, one hand reaching up toward me but stopping short.

Retreating hastily, I almost sat down in the box of dispenser napkins behind me. "James," I said bracingly, "what are you doing? Nothing has changed in my situation. I mean, I'm still adopting that baby—it's still not what you pictured for your life." I didn't mean to throw his own break-up words back at him, but he did have me cornered.

Seeing my predicament, he helpfully grasped my elbow and hefted me off of the napkins. "I know, Cass, I know. But I've had a lot more time to think. I mean, about the part you told me—where you felt like this was something God was asking you to do. I guess I'm getting more used to the idea. Maybe it would be worthwhile to explore it again. Could we—are you free for lunch today?"

"Lunch!" I almost shrieked. This unexpected encounter had completely driven my lunch appointment from my mind. Skandar and I had emailed back and forth after I'd finally replied to him—and today was the dreaded result.

"Or we could just start with coffee," said James quickly, misinterpreting my dismay.

I shook my head. "Yes—I mean, no—I mean okay to coffee, but I have to run right now because I'm meeting someone for lunch."

"Are you late?" he asked, as I pushed past him to head for the elevator, digging in my handbag for my Metro pass.

"Not yet," I called back. At least it was a straight shot on whichever bus came first over to the Transit Center.

Reading my mind, he hurried after me, "I'll bet you took the bus to work, like you always do. Let me give you a lift, at least."

Thinking of how moody Skandar was to begin with, I weighed whether it would be worse to accept James' offer or to show up late for lunch. Probably the latter. Which is how I found myself riding pillion on James' Ducati Monster a few minutes later, sporting the too-big and probably-illegal helmet Lewis used for his Segway. Even back when my husband Troy had his 750 I hadn't tagged along much, always feeling like I was going to slide off the back or inadvertently kicking up a foot peg whenever I stretched my legs, but riding with James was even worse because he noticed my fumbling efforts to grip the passenger handles—did Ducati test them on orangutans, or did I have unnaturally short arms? When we hit a stoplight, he finally reached back and put my hands on his waist. Fine.

We pulled up at the sushi place on Northeast 6th, and I climbed off as gracelessly as I'd climbed on, holding out Lewis's helmet without quite meeting James' eyes. To my chagrin, I spotted Skandar's long ponytail right away out front where he stood wrapping up a phone call, and instead of pretending not to know me, as I spinelessly hoped, he raised one black eyebrow and came forward to meet me.

Suppressing a sigh, I muttered, "Thanks for the ride, James. Um… Skandar, this is James Kittredge, one of my co-workers, and James, this is Skandar Sebari." No description for Skandar came readily to mind. My fellow sufferer in the widowhood and adoption process? My gloomy companion in grief recovery? James had removed his helmet, but between my low, embarrassed voice and the rumbling of the bike, it was no wonder he leaned forward, frowning.

"Skandar Sebari," repeated Skandar more clearly in his cool voice, "not 'Scandal Safari,' or whatever Cass just mumbled."

This drew a sheepish laugh from me. At least he didn't seem too mournful at present. Here's hoping his good mood lasted through lunch.

Speaking of good moods, James' had abruptly evaporated, and after nodding at the introduction, he quickly smashed his helmet back on and rolled the bike back into the street. The sigh escaped me now. This was nuts—was James really thinking he wanted to try again? What was the point? Nothing had changed, not our age difference, not the baby situation.

Nothing at all had changed except the fact that I no longer loved him, I realized with a start.

No longer loved him because—because I—well, because I was in love with Daniel.

In love with Daniel?

My mouth fell open. Had I really just thought that?

Yes.

In love with an overly handsome, partially-reformed-at-best, borderline-irreligious lothario. Talk about losing my mind. If I needed final confirmation that everything I'd been going through was more than I could handle, here it was. *Idiot!*

No time to dwell on it at present because Skandar was holding the restaurant door open for me. It was one of those little places where the sushi floats by on boats and the chefs holler at appropriate moments. They hollered now when we came in, and one pointed with his cleaver at two empty seats. I hadn't actually ever eaten here before, but—when she was still talking to me—Phyl had suggested it. "It's nice and noisy in there," she said, "and there's always plenty to watch, so you hardly even have to talk to each other, if you don't feel like it. Jason and I used to go toward the end, when we could hardly be in the same room together." I frowned. Now it would be the perfect place to eat with Phyl herself. Or I could come here with Daniel when we reached the fear-and-loathing stage. This could be my new favorite restaurant. Of course, me going for Daniel didn't necessarily mean he was still interested in going for me. There was Darla, Destroyer of Worlds, after all.

"So you came from work?" Skandar broke into my thoughts, eyeing the tuna nigiri bobbing by. I hadn't thought to ask him if he even liked sushi.

"Yes," I said, reaching for the California roll because I recognized it. "You?"

"Yes." With misgiving I noticed his face was closed off again. Far away.

This was going to be a long lunch.

After a few minutes where we each munched our cucumber-seaweed salads, I tried again. "How is work going?"

"It's going. They're being patient with me, since my mind isn't all there."

"I can't imagine how you do it," I said hesitantly. "I spent the first year after my family died doing almost nothing—hibernating. Conserving emotional energy."

"Men are different," Skandar said. "Besides, I have Bryson. I have to function—or, at least, appear to function." His face softened slightly. "You seem to be functioning now, at any rate. Working, dating. Maybe in a couple years..."

To cover my discomfiture, I reached for whatever was drifting in front of me: yellowtail. Not my favorite. "Oh, I'm not dating," I gabbled, pinching the sushi too enthusiastically with my chopsticks, so that it squirted back onto the dish. "But I'm certainly working. Lori suggested it would help my case if I tried to look as employed and stable as possible."

"Stable?" he repeated, puzzled. "Mentally?"

I laughed. "That probably wouldn't hurt either, but actually Lori meant stable socially. I guess a single woman living with a bunch of other singles doesn't cut much ice with the court. She even told me off the record that I should try to get married! You know, try to look like the American Dream—heighten the contrast between me and the convicted felon father."

A spark of humor lit up his face. "Seems to be her silver bullet for everything. Before Reiner backed down, Lori was telling me—off the record—that I should cut my hair and remarry some nice American girl—try to look less like a terrorist and more like your average citizen."

I gasped, half with incredulity and half because of all the wasabi the yellowtail had fallen in. "She is too much! She sits there looking so precise and collected, and then she says the most shocking things. If I weren't so intimidated by her, I might protest."

"She's got a point," he said simply. "If Reiner hadn't given up I would probably be sitting here with my hair cut off, wearing a flag pin and wondering who I could convince to marry me."

He was striking enough, intelligent, employed. I'm sure there were plenty of women who would overlook his tenuous emotional state, if it came to that. Darla, for one. I took a sip of my green tea, thinking. "Well, even if it would help my case, for women it's easier said than done."

"Aren't you dating anyone?" he asked. "What about that guy who dropped you off? He didn't look too happy to meet me."

"He's a co-worker," I explained. "He does happen to be my ex-boy-friend, but now he's just a co-worker."

Skandar shrugged. "He still looked interested, and if he's an ex you must have liked him once. It could probably work."

His cold-blooded analysis halted me as I reached for a cucumber roll, and I stared at him, frowning, until he grimaced and pulled my hand back. "You're making a log jam, Cass."

The little boats continued on their journey. "How can you talk like that?" I demanded. "I thought you were joking about cutting your hair off and wearing a flag pin—you mean you would really consider just marrying someone, anyone, to get Bryson from Reiner?"

Another shrug. "Sure. If the person was pleasant and intelligent and would be good to Bryson—why not?"

"Lucky girl," I muttered. It was his grief talking, I knew, but I felt annoyed. Heaven knew I hadn't felt much like dating after I lost Troy, but saddling another person with my burden hadn't entered my mind. On the other hand, maybe I was just being overly sensitive because, here it was, only two years later, and I'd already been in love with two different men. So much for poor Troy. Daniel popped back into my head, accompanied by a panicked feeling, and mentally I shoved him away.

"Why did Reiner back down, anyhow?" I changed the subject.

Skandar shook his head, pointing at the giant bite he was chewing. At least he was eating now, although I didn't think either one of us tasted anything we put in our mouths. Taking a swig of tea, he managed to swallow, and I noticed his eyes were watering with what was hopefully only wasabi. "Met a new girlfriend. Some actress. She already has two children from her previous marriage and didn't want any of his, so goodbye Bryson. I hope I can get the adoption wrapped up before she dumps Reiner and he changes his mind again."

"And if you don't?"

His black eyes met mine. Definitely wasabi, and not tears. "Then I'm going with Lori's plan."

For a moment we stared at each other—I incredulously hoping he wasn't finding me pleasant and intelligent—and then he gave a short bark of a laugh. "Relax, Cass."

Easy for him to say. A couple more minutes passed, while we each doggedly ate. There seemed to be nothing more to talk about, since he had his opinions and I had mine, but a niggling feeling grew in my gut. I hadn't completely had my say. And if there really was any divine purpose to today's lunch, I might as well hit him with the God talk now. He could always tell me to shut up, as Nadina did.

"My church offers a Grief Recovery class," I began, out of the blue.

Skandar didn't look at me. "No, thank you. I was planning on leaving my grief recovery to Time."

Not "shut up," exactly, but equally effective.

He seemed to sense he had been too quelling because he relented slightly. "Did you find it helpful?"

Did I? Truthfully, only vague memories of the class remained: stumbling in and noting listlessly that I was the youngest person in the room; crying a lot; taking a few mental notes that I thought might help later when I felt less numb. "I don't really remember much about it," I admitted slowly. "The healing process is so slow. Like silt building up in a riverbed. The class was probably a layer. After enough layers, you change the course of the river."

He didn't answer, and when I stole a glance I saw his face was set in hard lines. Fighting tears. My own jaw hurt with the remembered effort. "Skandar," I said, twisting my napkin in my lap, "one thing they did say was that it was okay to be angry at God."

"Then there's really no need for me to take the class," he said tightly, "because I've got that mastered."

"You...you have the anger mastered, maybe," I mumbled, "but not the what-to-do-with-it."

Skandar turned and met my eyes squarely. "All right, then. I wouldn't have taken you for the tiresome religious type, but why don't you give me the Cliff's Notes version."

Sheez. Having never been much of an evangelist, how did I get stuck with the hostile guy? Not to mention Nadina. Was God not catching on that I actually had no talent for this? I thought talking to Daniel about religious things was difficult, but now I realized what a cakewalk it was. Daniel had been indifferent, not furious, for one thing, and his natural intellectual curiosity made him more open. "Umm... well, I think the main message was to stick around. That is, take our anger at God...to God. Tell him about it. Keep talking."

"I've never met the guy," said Skandar. "And if this is how He runs the world, I'm not interested in meeting Him."

By now I was sweating. If only the fire alarm would go off or something. Anything to rescue me from this wretched situation. Maybe I could plunge my head into the sushi boat river and end it all. Headline: Woman Commits Suicide to Avoid Squirmy Conversation. Sigh.

Twiddling my disposable chopsticks, I cleared my throat. "I know," I said. "The world doesn't always make sense to me, either. Troy and Min dying didn't make any sense to me. Things only made sense after the fact—when I looked back on them months later. I could see God still loved me because of the people he put in my life. They helped me...feel God. I guess that's where—I guess that's why—umm...I guess I'm glad that there was Jesus, then."

"What?" he said. Apparently it wasn't only God's running of the world puzzling Skandar.

I tried again. "I mean, it's easier for me to relate to another person than to some big invisible deity. For God to become a … a person helps me. I can—umm—look at Jesus' life and understand better what God is like. And, at least, whatever terrible shape the world is in, and whatever terrible things happen to us, we—we—at least we know God went through them too."

"You mean Jesus," he said, his mouth twisting skeptically.

"Yes, Jesus. Jesus the—uh—the Son of God," I clarified, feeling like a total idiot. "God in human form." Skandar was looking at me like I'd lapsed into Martian or like I was, in fact, a total idiot. Maybe if I just nailed him now with a do-you-know-Jesus-Christ-as-your-Lord-and-Savior, we could wrap this up and be rid of each other forever.

As it happened, I didn't even need to whip out the off-putting phrase. Like magic, Skandar slapped his wallet on the counter while he caught the eye of one of the hollering chefs. Lunch over, apparently. I foraged in my own purse for my credit card so I wouldn't have to make eye contact.

"You've given me a lot to think about," he said at last, when the waitress took our cards to charge them. Yeah, right. Apparently what weighed heaviest on his mind at the moment was how quickly he could get away from me. And now that I'd botched my attempt to share with him what had comforted me, I felt unexpected regret that I wouldn't get to know him better. He would have to walk his path alone.

Outside the restaurant, he shook my hand. "Thanks for lunch, Cass. I'll see you around." If he remembered James had given me a lift there, he had no intention of doing the same. Turning on his heel, he walked swiftly off, leaving me to wonder exactly how many people in my life I could alienate in one week.

CHAPTER 9:

Lunch with a Conscience

"You talked religion with him, Dear. Is that really what you meant to tell him?" Louella leaned across the table to pat my hand.

We were sitting outside Gilbert's having brunch a couple days later. It was the Friday of the Social Worker—D-Day, Joanie and I had taken to calling it. Louella had on a huge pair of sunglasses against the late July sunshine that would have put Jackie O to shame, and the morning's warmth promised a hot day ahead.

Although I was no longer an official Camden School mentor and Louella still was, the two of us had developed a relationship outside the school doings and tried to get together at least once a month. In her late seventies and a widow herself, Louella Murphy was fearless, optimistic, faithful—she was who I wanted to be when I grew up.

I put down my ham and egg bagel without taking a bite. "What do you mean? I tried to tell Skandar about Jesus—what else am I supposed to tell him?"

"You said you told him that Jesus was the Son of God and God in human form," said Louella, shaking her head.

She had a smidgen of jam on her upper lip, and I pointed to my own to get her to wipe it off. "Well, he is," I said defensively.

"Oh, Cass, I know that!" she said impatiently. "But what did that have to do with anything? When you were still reeling after Troy and Minnie died, if anyone had said such stuff to you, what difference would it have made? That's theology—that's religion! You might as well have fed him some crock about God working in mysterious ways or joy cometh in the morning."

I winced. "Oh, crap—you're right, Louella. I didn't know what to say. He's such a hard man to talk to, and then I was afraid of making him sad—"

"Sad?" she scoffed. I think she was raising her eyebrows behind the Jackie O glasses, but I couldn't be sure. "He's already sad—his wife just died! He reached out to you because he wanted someone who understood what he was going through."

"That's what I tried to express," I said helplessly. "That because Jesus was human, he understood what we go through."

"He didn't want a referral, Cass. He wanted a live person on the phone."

Pondering this, I watched over Louella's shoulder a black Escalade trying to parallel park. After a few forwards and reverses, the driver glared into her rear view mirror and laid on the horn, causing all the sidewalk diners to jump. Louella turned with me to see a beat-up white sedan pull out suddenly behind the SUV and go zooming up Main. As the driver flashed past, he shot me a look: pale, guarded.

I frowned. Did I know him from somewhere?

Louella lowered her sunglasses to peer at me over the tops. "Were you listening to me, Cass?"

"Yes," I said, my mind snapping back to the issue at hand. "Skandar wanted a real live person to connect with, and I tried to palm him off on the church. I get it." I sighed. "I just don't think I can be that shoulder for him to cry on, Louella. I mean, I've got so much on my plate emotionally right now, and he *is* a single man, and I'm a single woman, and I don't know if it's appropriate."

She beamed at me. Even when Louella was straightening you out, you still felt loved. "No one said you had to marry him, dear. And you've never had any trouble expressing yourself. If you tell him you're not interested in him that way—"

"No, no, I'm not," I insisted. "And he's been clear that he's not thinking that either."

"Then what's the issue? I'm just saying, if God brought you into this young man's life at this juncture, maybe you should do a little more exploring. You don't have to be his lifeline—when I lost Frank there were times when I just wanted other people around. Didn't you? Think about Job's friends: when he lost everything, they sat with him in silence for days—before they wrecked everything by opening their mouths."

I grinned. "Hey! I wasn't bad as all that. I didn't tell Skandar the tragedy was his fault, that he must have done something wrong."

"Of course not."

"Yeah," I said, "because if that were the case, I must have done something really, really, really wrong, to lose a spouse and a child."

This comment bothered her enough that Louella wagged her fork at me reprovingly. "Just promise me you'll try to contact him one more time, okay? One more time, and no religion."

"Fine, fine. I'll call him one more time—just for you, Louella. And if he still turns and runs, we'll know it's just my naturally repellant personality."

"Good girl. Now let's hear about all these things on your emotional plate."

Where to begin? Surely with the most pressing. While my companion polished off her eggs and toast, I filled her in on the whole Mike thing. "Can you believe it, Louella?" I asked. "No judge in his right mind is going to give Mike that baby, but Mike still has the power to drag this process out for months, maybe years! And by then, if he's gotten out of prison and been a model citizen the whole time, maybe the judge might actually give Ned to him." But then again there was that feeling I'd gotten in church last Sunday, when I heard the Abraham passage. "I guess I'm trying not to give in to fear," I concluded. "Somewhere deep down I think I'm supposed to have this baby, and I've just got to go with that. Though if it's something God wants, I wish he would just do it already. Enough with all the obstacles."

"There is one obstacle you don't have—is Nadina positive *she* doesn't want the baby?" said Louella. "So many times these teenage girls think it's the greatest thing. For the attention it gets them. They never think through what it would mean—how hard it would be at times—how it would change their lives forever. How the baby gets older and isn't so cute anymore! They just think how exciting to be pregnant and have people make a big deal about it and give you gifts." We both thought back to Caslin, a girl who had dropped out of Camden School early on last year, after her baby was born and it became too difficult to find childcare. She thought she would come back later when things fell into place, but no one knew when that might be.

"I don't think Nadina for a second considered having the baby and keeping it," I said. "For all the crazy bad decisions she makes, she really is a practical girl. She had her thing with Mike, and he said he didn't want any babies, and she didn't want to rock that boat. I'm just glad they broke up. If she still wanted him and he wanted this baby, that would be the end of it."

Taking out a little notebook, Louella scribbled in it. I didn't have to ask to know it was her prayer list. "What else, Cass?"

I sighed. "One of my best friends is avoiding me. You know—my housemate Phyl? She's been having some trouble with her fiancé lately. She blew up at me the other day, and I don't think it was all aimed at me, but some of it was." Louella waited. "She said I was totally self-absorbed, basically, and that all I cared about was getting this baby."

"Mmmm…" said my companion. It was something I respected

about Louella: she wasn't going to leap to my defense just because she loved me. Joanie thought Phyl was totally out of line here, but I knew she wasn't.

"I have been, of course," I admitted. "Totally self-absorbed and Ned-obsessed, I mean. Look at our lunch today, for example. Me, me, me. Enough about you, let's talk about me. Blah blah blah. But still—she's usually so gentle! It really hurt."

Putting her pen down, Louella said, "I think you already know what to do about this one, Cass."

"Yes," I answered. "Apologize, I know. Phyl hasn't been around much, but when I get the chance, I'll talk to her."

"And if she doesn't give you a chance, you might have to make the opportunity yourself. I imagine this can be patched up easily. What else, now—while we're on the topic of you—" grinning at me.

I hesitated. "Well, my lawyer, Lori Lincoln—she said it might expedite things adoption-wise if I got married."

Louella laughed. "Did she have anyone particular in mind?"

Feeling the heat creep up my cheeks, I focused on cutting off precise bits of my bagel. Each slice should have a sliver of the ham and a wedge of the egg—a cross-section.

"I thought you and dear James called it quits," she added, when I didn't say anything.

"We did," I said. "Or he did." I went to take a drink of water, only to discover my glass was empty. Thunking it down on the table, I blurted, "This will make me sound flighty, but I'm actually…interested…in my housemate Daniel now." For Pete's sake, I hadn't even told Joanie or Phyl yet. Just Perry and now Louella. Everything was bass-ackwards.

Her face lit up, and she propped her sunglasses on her hair so she could look me right in the eye. "Cass! How wonderful! I'm so excited for you! If I had a son, I would have set him up with you long ago." She rubbed my arm affectionately. "How long have you been dating?"

"Uh…well…we aren't actually dating."

"Oh, you young people," she waved this off. "I can't keep up with your terminology. Whatever you call it—going steady—hanging out—"

"No, 'dating' is fine," I said quickly. "I just meant we're not. Because Daniel is dating somebody else."

That puzzled her. "But—but—does he know you're interested in him?"

Did he? He knew I wasn't indifferent to him. But not that I lov—I shied away from the word, even in my mind. "Not yet."

Louella's warm smile returned. "Then I'm sure you just have to let him know, and that'll take care of the other lady."

"What confidence you have in my charms, Louella," I snorted.

"I do," she said simply. "I consider it a done deal. So, if you like him, this housemate of yours must be quite the fellow. Does he love Jesus?"

I could really use that water refill about now. Out loud I stammered, "Uh… he… um… well—maybe. He might. Or not. I don't know. I haven't nailed that bit down."

This clearly wasn't the answer Louella had expected, and her next question came a little sharper. "Then it must be his character that attracts you. A man worthy of respect? Unimpeachable integrity?"

I gulped. What exactly did "unimpeachable" mean? I wasn't sure I could vouch for Daniel's integrity being unimpeachable. "I've learned to respect him," I began, before I realized that sounded bad. But it was true—it hadn't come automatically. "And I think his character is certainly, definitely *solid*." Whatever that meant. I suppose even your average Colombian drug lord might be described by his familiars as solid. *Sólido como una piedra.*

It suddenly seemed like a very bad idea to mention that Daniel's looks made my insides churn. Louella wanted character references, not read-outs on our sexual chemistry.

"He helped me install our fire extinguisher," I added lamely. Resisting the urge to smack myself on the forehead, I recalled the better examples I could have provided and blithered onward—"And of course he's letting the baby move in with us all and he got Mike that job before Mike imploded and went to jail—"

Louella stemmed the flow by placing a firm hand on mine. "It sounds like he has some real potential, Cass. You keep exploring that one. But no need to rush into anything, even if he weren't seeing someone else."

"Exactly what I thought," I said in a small voice, feeling unaccountably disappointed. It would have been nice to have someone, whose opinion I respected as much as Louella's, tell me just to drop everything and grab that man while the grabbing was good. Instead I was now obliged to call the man I didn't want to call and give additional breathing room to the one I wanted to smother.

The rest of our meal wound up uneventfully. "I'll be praying for you this afternoon when the social worker comes," she concluded, when we stood to hug each other good-bye.

If Abraham had Louella to pray for him, I'm sure God couldn't have held out so long on handing over Isaac. Her heartfelt petitions surely would take care of any issues in the spiritual realm, where this adoption was concerned.

Alas for the human obstacles.

CHAPTER 10:

Unnatural Habitat

Joanie flipped back the curtains. "She's here, Cass, if she's the woman parking across the street. Ooh! She almost side-swiped that other car. "

I wrung my hands together. "It's ten till! She's early! Where is Daniel? I told him three o'clock."

"So call him—is your phone charged?"

When I nodded, Joanie tossed me hers. "Get the number from mine, but call from yours because Daniel doesn't always answer if it's me. I'll run upstairs and get Phyl."

I took Joanie's post, peeking out between the gap in the drapes. The first thing I saw was a beat-up white sedan parked directly across from the Palace driveway. The very same piece of junk that had ticked off the Escalade driver on Main Street that morning, if I wasn't mistaken. Had the social worker been stalking me? But no, the social worker was a certain Barbara Dobbs, while the driver outside Gilbert's had been a pale man.

Sure enough, a sensibly-dressed woman clambered out of a car further down the street and scurried over to the sedan, presumably to apologize for almost hitting it, but even as she approached, the white car took off with a squeal of tires. Springing back like a deer, the woman stared after it a minute before shaking her head and going back to her car for her attaché case. I watched her organize herself while I dialed Daniel's number and waited for him to pick up. If he picked up.

"Well, hello there." It was noisy in the background, but I could hear the note of amusement in his voice.

"Hello," I said shyly. I wondered how many nagging phones calls from infatuated women he received. At least I wasn't calling to berate him for breaking up with me. What with the mysterious sedan and Barbara Dobbs outside and my new awareness about Daniel, my heart was hammering. "Umm...sorry to bother you—did you remember the social worker comes for the group interview today?"

"Uppermost in my mind," he said casually. "There's some road construction, but I'll cut over to 100th. Be there as soon as I can."

Two minutes later the social worker gave the doorbell a smart ring, and three minutes later the girls and I were gathered with her at the kitchen table. She was a short, plump woman with iron-gray hair and a maroon sweater which she kept tugging surreptitiously to make it cover the waistband of her gray trousers. "Hmm... what a very nice house you have here. Very nice."

"Thank you. Would you like something to drink?" I asked. Ordinarily Phyl would have been all over the beverages, and I noted her vacant expression and hollow eyes anxiously. At least she didn't look angry with me anymore.

"Maybe in a little while," said Barbara Dobbs. She took a seat on the cushioned bench directly across from Phyl and flipped through some of her papers. "I believe from my initial phone interviews, there is one more person in residence here?"

"Yes," I said quickly. "Daniel Martin."

"My brother," put in Joanie.

"He's on his way," I added, taking a seat next to Phyl.

Barbara Dobbs smiled. "Then perhaps we should start with the tour of the baby's future living area?"

Popping back up like a jack-in-the box I slammed my thigh on the table and uttered through gritted teeth, "Yes. That would be fine. It's all ready. Joanie, Phyl, did you want to come show her Ned's room with me?" At the sound of her name, Joanie also shot to her feet, discreetly kicking off her heels so as not to hulk over Barbara Dobbs.

Phyl, however, only shook her head slowly. "I'll stay here and get everyone drinks," she murmured, as if she were the ghost of her former self, doomed for a certain term to haunt the kitchen.

"Iced tea," I suggested, "or water." Under normal circumstances I wouldn't have felt it necessary to hint that the drinks be non-alcoholic, but Phyl was so out of it that I didn't want to risk coming back downstairs to a round of Kamikazes.

Joanie and I made anxious faces at each other before leading Barbara Dobbs through the Palace. Instead of pointing out artwork or architectural features, I stopped to highlight future baby-gate locations, smoke alarms, cabinets which would have locks, plants with edible greenery. Fortunately, the Dobbs seemed approving of all, and my spirits lifted when she complimented the nursery and how I'd "thought of just about everything."

Even Daniel turning up a few minutes late was a bonus. Barbara Dobbs was trailing after us down the stairs, remarking on the one fiddly smoke alarm on the vaulted ceiling, and did that require a ladder to change the batteries, when she caught sight of him, framed in the doorway from the Palace kitchen, looking up at her.

"You can reach it by leaning out from the landing? That's convenient—otherwise you might need a fourteen-foot lad—" Barbara cut off abruptly—"Oh!"—her clipboard dropping with a clatter over the railing onto the hardwood floor, the pen spinning away.

Was it my imagination, or did women seem to be reacting to Daniel's looks even more extremely? Nadina, Darla, the Dobbs. I would have to ask Joanie what she thought later. At this particular moment, she was staring up at the skylight to keep from laughing, and she muttered just loud enough for me to hear, "Cue: *Love Is in the Air*."

"It *is* convenient," agreed Daniel affably. "Because fourteen-foot lads are so hard to come by nowadays."

He bent to retrieve her dropped items while Barbara Dobbs blushed the maroon of her sweater, tugged on said item self-consciously, and fairly scampered down the remaining stairs, giggling.

"Good Lord," whispered Joanie. "He's like Polyjuice Potion. She's transforming into Darla."

So long as Darla-Barbara approved the home study, I didn't care.

And for a time, it looked like we would pass with flying colors.

We settled at the table again, each with our listlessly mint-sprigged iced tea, Phyl still staring out the bay window, while Barbara Dobbs tidied her now-crumpled papers. Our sensible social worker had been stricken with the hair equivalent of Phantom Limb Phenomenon, as she kept patting and flipping and even twirling on her finger imaginary locks that must have been cut off decades ago, each time she looked at Daniel.

"You all had clean background checks, I'm sure you know," Barbara said, eyes fluttering from the page to Daniel and back down.

"Oh, good," I said, squashing Joanie's foot under the table as I saw a joke forming on her lips. Who knew if home studies were like airline security, and we would be flunked instantly (if not arrested) for cracking jokes about the child-slavery ring rolling doobies in the garage?

"This is a somewhat unconventional household, you're probably aware," continued Barbara Dobbs. "No one married to anyone—no one even paired up with anyone. All…single…" another flustered glance at the man of the house.

"Phyl's engaged," corrected Joanie, earning herself a kick to the ankle. It was hardly necessary to remind the social worker that we were not only unconventional but also unstable.

"I'm not," said Phyl.

I stared at her. "It's okay, Phyl—to talk about, I mean."

Her normally mild blue eyes narrowed. "I know it's okay to talk about," she replied icily. "I wouldn't think of trying to hide anything. I only meant that I'm not engaged anymore."

There followed a measurable drop in the room's oxygen level as Joanie and I gasped, stupefied. Even Daniel might have sucked in his breath.

"When—"

"Why—"

"Since it just means that I'll be living here, the same as always, I don't think the details have any bearing on this discussion," Phyl interrupted.

The details didn't, but the same didn't go for the overall dampening effect of her attitude. A thick cold front of tension rolled over us— even the Dobbs noticed and made a few ominous notes.

"Well, whatever the reason, we'll be happy to have another woman around when that baby comes," declared Joanie, her voice a shade too hearty. "Cass and Phyl and I have been friends for years, and we fully support this decision of hers to adopt."

"Lack of women has never been a problem around here," said Phyl darkly.

Joanie kicked me so sharply that tears sprang to my eyes. "Not a bit," I agreed, "because the three of us have lived here the whole time. Plenty of women. Exactly."

Puzzled by this interchange, Barbara Dobbs opened her mouth to speak, so I hastened on. "We share the cooking and cleaning—not that we'd share raising Ned—he'd be my responsibility, absolutely, but I know Joanie and Phyl will be a great help with the little guy."

"Don't forget Darla," Phyl grumbled. "She loves men of all ages and sizes."

Barbara Dobbs' pencil hesitated. "Darla..?"

"How terrible to announce this like this," said Daniel, speaking up for the first time since laying his spell on Barbara Dobbs in the hallway. "It seems to be an ill-fated afternoon for relationships around here because Darla and I have broken up." He favored the Dobbs with quite the heartbroken-yet-deprecating smile. "Darla was a woman I dated briefly."

"Do you date any other way?" whispered Phyl.

Such a flurry of kicking each other under the table followed this that I'm amazed Barbara Dobbs wasn't caught in the crossfire. I knew very well Daniel was to blame for bringing Darla into our lives, but I hadn't meant for Phyl to get after him about it now.

"When did you break up?" Joanie couldn't help asking him.

"Recently."

"As in, *recently* recently?" I asked, willing him to look at me. As in, did Darla even know, or had he decided this on the spot? My heart felt like it was vibrating inside my chest. If he was free…

"Recently," Daniel said again.

His news sank in, with a salutary effect on us all. Phyl looked hopeful again—or maybe that was me; Joanie positively glowed and threw her arm around him, mischievously whistling a few bars of *Ding, Dong, the Witch is Dead*; the Dobbs smiled and doodled a little flower on her paper.

"Well, then," Barbara Dobbs began again, "as I was saying, you're all single. At such a stage in your lives, how do you feel about having a child in the house? Can we talk about some of your past experiences with children?"

We could, and did. Apart from my experience with Min, which I got through with a tolerably clear throat, no one else had much to add. I hoped that no experience with children at least outweighed bad experience with children, in a social worker's estimation.

This was followed by our families of origin, education levels, household routines, support systems. Most of it was aimed at me, but Ned would be coming into such an odd setting that the Dobbs showed almost equal interest in the others' responses.

Gradually I began to relax. Joanie was making a grand effort to control her loose cannon tendencies, Daniel had the full charm turned on, and the good news about Darla stemmed the flow of Phyl's sniping comments. Had Barbara Dobbs only wrapped it up ten minutes earlier, we might have scraped by with Most Promising Unconventional Household.

But, no. Just as I was winding up a moving speech about all the friends, including Louella, who had offered to help with childcare when Ned came, there was a banging on the front door, followed by a good lean on the doorbell. Only one person I knew announced herself in that fashion, and sure enough, before I was halfway out of my seat, we heard the door burst open.

"Cass—what the hell? Pregnant lady here," complained Nadina, lumbering into view. "Do you got money for the cab? I didn't want to wait for the bus and Mom had to cover someone's shift—oh! hey." She broke off upon seeing the group gathered at the table. Her glance barely took in the Dobbs before landing on Daniel, at which point her whole face brightened up.

"What are you doing here, Nadina?" I asked, hastening over and trying unsuccessfully to steer her back into the hallway. "You're supposed to be home lying on the couch."

"I'm sick of lying on the couch, and I haven't even had any contractions the last couple days—"

"—Meaning, you were doing the right thing by lying on the couch," I interjected.

"Meaning, since Mom was gone, I wanted to sneak out and do something for the first time in forever, but I couldn't get a hold of Sonya and Carly was busy, and you didn't answer my text—"

"Because I'm in the middle of something, *as you can see*," I hissed. Behind me I heard Daniel and Joanie launch into a determined discussion of the weather and everyone's summer plans, and even Phyl rallied and started bustling around, clinking the glasses and refilling the teas.

"—But I knew you didn't have any life, so you were sure to be home," said Nadina artlessly. With me tugging on her arm, she had no choice but to follow me back toward the front door where I dug my purse out of the closet.

"Listen to me, Nadina. I'm glad you're feeling a little better, and I get that you're bored and sick of staying home, but it isn't much longer. Just do this for me." I lowered my voice, adding, "That's the social worker in there interviewing us, for Pete's sake! What's she going to think if the baby's mom drops by unannounced?"

Nadina straightened up. "That was the social worker? I didn't even notice her 'cause I was checking out your hot housemate. No, hang on—" she pulled her arm away. "I'll go—fine—if you lend me some more of your DVDs—and do you have any more of Phyl's cookies?—but let me just put in a good word for you."

Before I could stop her, she waddled back into the kitchen, me right behind her, trying to look like this was all just dandy. "I'm Nadina Stern," she announced, looming over Barbara Dobbs. "The mom of the baby that Cass is going to adopt. I just want you to know that Cass is awesome. My mom and boyfriend wanted me to get an abortion, and my friends at school told me I should keep the baby, but I feel good about this. I mean, who wouldn't want to live here, right?" This, while pointing behind her hand in Daniel's direction and goggling her eyes at the Dobbs. "Cool people, lots of money, good schools Cass says. Hell, if I have any more babies, I'd feel good about giving every last one of them to Cass."

This prompted a shrieky giggle out of me. "Oh, Nadina. But there aren't going to be any more unplanned babies, right? She'll be too busy at her new all-girls, private, Catholic school in Ohio," I explained to Barbara Dobbs. ("Norplant," coughed Joanie into her hand.)

"If I stay there," said Nadina, shrugging. "I'm starting to think I'd miss my friends and the weather here. And it'd be kinda cool to see how Cass raises my baby."

Feeling like she had just punched me in the gut, I somehow managed to wheeze, "The cab, Nadina. That meter's running."

Having said her piece, Nadina docilely accepted a baggie of lemon snaps and waved her good-byes. Sweating now, I tore over to the media cabinet and grabbed the first ten movies that came to hand and then shoved her out to the waiting taxi.

"Thanks, Cass! I think I helped in there."

"You were something all right," I said, thrusting money at the driver. "Go home and lie down. Be good. I'll call you later."

The table fell silent when I rejoined it. Smiling apologetically at the Dobbs, I took my seat again.

"Does the birth mother drop by often?" asked Barbara Dobbs.

I sighed. "Honestly, that was the first time ever." But who knew if it would be the last. And what was with the "my baby" business? From the phone interview, the Dobbs knew how Nadina and I were connected, but I couldn't help adding, "When I was her mentor, Camden School provided pretty clear-cut boundaries to the relationship, but with the whole baby thing, things have gotten a little blurry."

"Yes," said Barbara Dobbs simply. Her pencil hovered over the clipboard, and she looked thoughtfully for a moment at Daniel. Probably trying to measure his Pervert Factor: would he ever take advantage of Nadina's attraction to him?

At least I knew the answer was No. For all his faults, Daniel did date women roughly his own age.

His face was a careful blank, though when the Dobbs finally returned her eyes to her notes he gave me roguish grin. I was still too upset by Nadina's surprise visit to muster more than a wobbly smile, and Daniel shook his head slightly. "It's fine," he mouthed.

Fine or not, it appeared to be over. "Well," said Barbara Dobbs, tapping her pencil decisively. "I think I have enough material here to begin writing up the study. Of course, I'll be visiting again after the baby arrives. Seeing how everyone is adjusting, checking once more on the home safety, making sure you are coping and that everyone gets the support he or she needs, Cass. I'll also need to schedule a phone interview with your brother Pericles, since you say he comes by frequently—"

As if on cue, the front door burst open again, and in walked that very brother Pericles, holes in his faded black t-shirt and his hair standing up in odd places, as if not one, but several cows had licked him. Clearly I had been teleported from my own life into some sort of Murphy's Law farce. "Am I late? Traffic was a bear." He stopped short, taking in the unusual sight of the entire household plus mystery woman gathered midafternoon in the Palace kitchen. "Whoops. What's going on?"

"This is Barbara Dobbs, a social worker," I said hastily. "She's doing a group interview for the home study. Barbara, this is, strangely enough, my brother Perry. I didn't know he was coming down from Bellingham today, but it seems to be the day for dropping by."

To my dismay, my brother's face was draining of color, and he shot a glance at the wall clock. "Man, I didn't mean to intrude—I'm just gonna wait out front, if you don't mind."

"Oh, no, no," spoke up Barbara Dobbs. "I was just telling your sister that we needed to schedule a phone interview—"

"Happy to, happy to," said Perry. "Do you have a card? I'll just give you a call." Even as he held out a hand for it, he was already looking over his shoulder and edging toward the door. What on earth was his problem? On the pretense of hugging him I growled in his ear, "Stop acting like a nervous freak. Sit down and say hello."

"Seriously," he murmured, grabbing me *Godfather*-style, "I'm getting out. You'll thank me." Slinging me off, he whisked Barbara Dobbs' proffered card from her fingertips. "Perfect…Barbara. I'll give you a call Monday. You all get back to your interviewing. I'm gonna get my bag out of the trunk—"

"I'll help you," offered Joanie at once. "We're done here, I think." She slid out of the booth after shaking Barbara Dobbs' hand, not noticing Perry's anxious expression.

The Dobbs was still taking a last sip of her tea and shaking the rest of our hands when we heard some kind of kerfuffle from the entry way. "Crap!" came Joanie's voice. "What the—what is *she* doing here?"

She who? Could we please stop with the unexpected encounters? Fairly shoving the Dobbs' clipboard into her chest, I demanded, "Would you like to see the backyard, on your way out? It's all fenced. Perfect for kids. We recently had the gate repaired. You can go out to your car from there."

Daniel cocked his head, hearing something I didn't, and he reached for the Dobbs' elbow. "Please, Barbara, I wish you would. I'm quite proud of Phyl's flourishing salal this year. Phyl, let's show Barbara what you've done."

Both Phyl and I blinked at him, caught off guard by this praise of the household flora. Biting back his impatience, Daniel gave me a sharp look reminiscent of his sister as he helped the Dobbs up. Snapping to, I pulled on Phyl. "Oh! Yes, Phyl. Give her a little tour. Of the salal and *the new latch we put on the gate.*" Our instant of mental denseness cost us, however, for Daniel no more than got the door open, than we heard the voice we thought ourselves rid of forever.

"You made it, clever boy!" gushed Darla. "I was listening to the traffic on I-5 and thought no way would we make the first pitch—hi, Joanie—but you made such good time we might actually catch the tail end of batting practice."

If Joanie returned Darla's greeting, I didn't hear it, drowned out as it was by the sound of her stalking back into the kitchen. She gave Daniel a look that should have incinerated him on the spot before remembering that Barbara Dobbs was still there and whirling on her heel to flee upstairs.

Phyl, too, came to a dead halt by the open door.

"The salal, Daniel?" I suggested dismally.

Mistake. Darla appeared in the doorway. "Daniel? What is going on—is Daniel here too? Were you all having a little party?" She sashayed over to him, wagging a reproachful finger. "Cruel, hard-hearted man. Don't any of you girls fall for this man because he is Trouble. *Trouble!*"

With a capital T and that rhymes with P and that stands for pool. Surely Barbara Dobbs would excuse me now if I went over and stuck my head in the oven.

"Good thing Perry agreed to go to the Mariners' game with me," continued Darla, oblivious. "He said we could drown our sorrows in beer."

Shut *up!* I screamed inwardly. At least, I hope I didn't scream it out loud, but my meaning must have been clear on my face. Perry rocketed over to put his arm around Darla and guide her back toward the front door. "Just speaking figuratively," he said to no one in particular. "One beer a night is about all I can hold. Let's hit the road, Darla."

"Darla?" echoed Barbara Dobbs.

"Darla," said Phyl. She gave Daniel a filthy look which I think the Dobbs must have seen unless she had conveniently been stricken blind. "Please, Barbara, let me show you the plants…"

Daniel understandably made no more motion to follow them out, only shutting the door firmly behind them.

He was wise enough to avoid Phyl's wrath, but not mine. When he spoke again, I could hear the laughter in his voice. "I'd say that went about as well as it could have."

"How can you even joke about it? That was probably a leading contender for worst home study in history."

"What gave us the edge, do you think? Was it Phyl seething at me, or Nadina saying she couldn't wait to come over and see how you raised her baby, or my ex-girlfriend inviting your brother to get hammered with her?"

"It's not funny, Daniel!" I almost wailed.

"Hey…" Closing the space between us, he tried to take me by the shoulders, but I stiffened immediately and wrenched away.

"Don't you touch me! This is all your fault!" All my pent-up rage and anxiety boiled over at that point. "You brought that dreadful woman into this house just to torture us, and now look what's happened: Phyl and Wayne broke up and Phyl fought with me for the first time ever and then, after doing your usual make-out-and-break-up routine you think you can just smile your way back into everyone's good graces?"

"Cass—"

"She's got her claws in my brother now, you loser!" I accused. "He'll probably end up marrying her and ruining every family holiday, and meanwhile the state will give Ned to stupid Mike because better for that baby to be living with a reformed felon than in this—this—this—*seraglio*!"

"'Seraglio'?" Daniel laughed incredulously, only making me angrier. "I know you've been under a lot of stress, Cass, but have you completely lost your mind? My dear, overeducated girl, 'if this be not love, it is madness, and then it is pardonable.'"

For some reason, this sent me over the edge, if I wasn't over it already. I didn't want to be told by Daniel that I was in love with him, even in jest, and it fried me that I was just another woman to be charmed. Another card in the mental Rolodex: for Barbara Dobbs he wheeled out the subdued smile and little jokes, for Cass the literary references, for Darla—well, in Darla's case, a Y chromosome seemed to be sufficient.

"Don't you try to pull one over on me," I steamed. "I'm having a hard enough time around here, Daniel, without having to deal with all the fallout from your dysfunctions."

That took care of the fake concern in his eyes. He slammed his hand down on the counter, and it probably would have been considerate to give him something to throw at me. As it was, he had only words.

"You're right, Cass. I won't take up any more of your time. Who needs my dysfunctions, when your own keep you so damned busy."

Turning on his heel, he left the field of battle.

Meaning, I won, I guess. Not that it helped. Like everything that had gone wrong that afternoon, lashing out at Daniel just felt like one more reason to hole up in my room for a good, long cry.

CHAPTER 11:

Booth Babe Saves the Day

"Yeah, so this pen doesn't write smoothly. Do you have another one I could swap for?"

I looked up to see the same Napoleon Dynamite who had been by the booth twice already. He was shorter than I and boasted a gut to rival Riley's, but I was going off the ginger-colored afro wig and "Vote for Pedro" t-shirt.

Not wanting to get into it, I fanned the *Tolt* floaty pens over the table surface. "I've been using this one myself," I said, holding one out to him. "It seems to write pretty well."

Napoleon grabbed my hand and turned it to see what was floating inside. "Nah. Not the Elf Archer. I wanted one with the … Snow Goddess."

For the tenth time that day I mentally cursed James Kittredge. He was the reason I was here at the Game Expo, after all, wearing this ridiculous Snow Goddess get-up that had been fitted on Vil's more buxom teenage cousin—the cousin who bailed at the last minute because she got concert tickets at the Gorge.

"C'mon, Cass," James had begged on the phone. "Riley and I will be at the Expo, too, and you can page us if you get in over your head. All you have to do is stand there and smile and hand out pens."

"For Pete's sake—why do I have to do it? Can't you and Riley swap off, then? Or get Kyle."

"That's not how it works, Cass. No one is gonna come by Free Universe's booth if we have a guy there. It's a girl or no traffic."

"Then make Jeri do it," I suggested. "She knows more about *Tolt* than I do anyhow."

"Jeri's great—she really is—but let's be honest: she's no booth babe. Please, Cass. We'll owe you big time and we'll pay you double time. All just to stand there looking beautiful."

I felt my resistance wavering in the face of money and flattery. "What would I wear?"

"Oh…uh…don't worry about that. Just come down. I'll explain later."

In retrospect, I could hardly blame him for not coming clean with me. Had he sent me a picture of the Snow Goddess costume I might have quit Free Universe on the spot. As it was, I found myself in the Convention Center's handicapped bathroom stall, wriggling and wrestling and scratching myself into a gauze and sequin and feather creation: Queen Frostina crossed with Tonya Harding and opening for Celine Dion.

Compared to some of the other costumes women were sporting at the Expo, the Snow Goddess fell on the modest side. Nevertheless I felt myself turning scarlet each time I had to hike up the diving bodice, and I didn't dare sit down any more, since I was already losing feathers like a leaky pillow.

"What time do you get off?" asked Napoleon.

"Here all day."

"You mind if I take a picture with you? My buddies aren't going to believe this."

Thank God my hair was pulled back under my plastic "ice" crown and that no one knew my name—otherwise these pictures, which I'm sure were being posted straight to the Internet, would doom any future attempts to gain real employment. On the other hand, maybe I should download a copy for Barbara Dobbs' expanding file on Reasons to Reject Cass.

To my relief, no sooner had Napoleon thrown his arm around my waist and hauled me against him to snap the photo than I saw James approaching the booth, rummaging happily through the latest swag bag he'd picked up.

"Hey, Ca—er—Snowy, need a bathroom break? I brought you a sandwich, too."

"Sweetheart!" I squeaked, giving him a sidearm hug. "How thoughtful of you!"

Napoleon slumped dejectedly and wandered away, Elf Archer pen in hand, and I turned to James with my first real smile of the day. "You owe me more than a sandwich for this, Mister. I can't imagine why that guy kept coming around—I tried to steer him toward the blonde Avenging Angels over there."

"Didn't I mention? Most nerds have a thing for brunettes, actually." He hesitated. "And you look pretty nice in that."

"In this?" I demanded. I pretended to read the label on my sandwich, so I wouldn't have to meet his eyes. "You should see my triple axel."

A few minutes passed in silence—if you didn't count the relentless din of the Expo itself—James handing out pens and answering a few questions, while I ate my turkey-cranberry, but the crowd was thinning a little as people went in search of food.

"So," he began again, in a lull, "if you aren't interested in Napoleon Dynamite, who are you seeing nowadays? That Skandar guy?"

With difficulty I swallowed my bite. "No, no. He's just a guy I met at the adoption attorney's office. We've gotten together a couple times because he lost his wife and just wants to talk. I even got him to sign up for the church's Grief Recovery class." Miracle of miracles.

Per Louella's instructions, I'd called Skandar again and apologized for being so pushy, only to have him say he had indeed given my words some thought and checked out the class online. I guess neither one of us was good at reading the other.

"Then what about Daniel?" persisted James.

I concentrated on brushing crumbs off my costume so I wouldn't blush. "What about him? He's back to his usual MO. Dating a lovely lady named Kristen." Kristen, who had put in her first appearance shortly after the home-study debacle and my most recent argument with him. She was lovely, of course—all Daniel's dates were—but Kristen was also quiet and only had eyes for him. She should have come as a relief after Darla, but, once I got done being angry at that man, all that remained was a muddle of chagrin and—yes—jealousy.

Not that Darla was history, by any means. The Mariners game with Perry was followed later that weekend by a picnic at Meydenbauer Park. Joanie couldn't wish Perry gone fast enough on Sunday, and she'd been in a towering bad mood for the past couple weeks. He hadn't come down again last weekend, but that didn't mean he wasn't with Darla.

James reached over to straighten my ice crown, and I sensed we were hovering uncomfortably close to the let's-revisit-our-relationship topic. "There's no time right now for dating anyway," I said, "because Ned could come any day. The doctor thinks she won't hold out till her due date."

His hand dropped. "How's that going? Will you take him the minute he's born?"

"Nadina's counselor has us working on an adoption birth plan, to make things less messy," I explained, "but I don't know if there's any avoiding that. I mean, they're having us map everything out—how much contact we have after the birth, like visits and even calls and emails, but Nadina will say one thing with the lawyer and another to me. She says she wants me there when Ned is born, and she says she wants me to take him home from the hospital, and that she'd want to stay out of it after that, but then she turns around later and says things like she wants to come over and hang out every day."

"Uh-oh."

I sighed. "Yeah. We'll see—that might be too much for both of us."

"It'd just be for a few weeks, though, right? Before she heads off to Ohio to her new school?"

"*If* she heads off to Ohio to her new school," I mused.

A middle-aged couple approached the booth then, the man scratching the belly of his wizard outfit while the woman and I sized up each other's Snow Goddess ensemble. "You look amazing," I told her. "You have twice as many sequins, and your outfit fits you better."

She gave a satisfied smirk. "And check this out." Squeezing some remote control in her feathery fanny pack, I heard a tinny version of my own voice holler, "Die, Varlet!"

"True fans," said James, the tremor of laughter in his voice almost undetectable. "Can I offer you a floaty pen?"

"Actually, what we really want," said the wizard, while his Snow Goddess scooped up the freebies, "is to know why you made it so that the Shadow Blade was too heavy to carry if you already had the mace and the crystal numchucks."

Sensing a lengthy nerdy analysis in the offing, I prodded James and mouthed "bathroom." He nodded, winking at me. Hiking up my heavy skirt, I made my escape.

After spending three straight hours in the confines of the Free Universe booth, I thought James would forgive me for taking a quick tour of the Expo before I returned. In such a setting my outrageous costume didn't attract too many stares, though several more Napoleon Dynamites and a few Anakin Skywalkers gave me the thumbs-up.

One quick circuit of the convention hall had me wondering why anyone would even wander by the obscure Free Universe booth, when companies like Nintendo and Microsoft had whole football-fields of interactive displays, live bands, free food, flashing goodies. And never mind my complaining about the Snow Goddess's low-cut bodice—at least I was wearing enough material to deserve the name of costume. One of the Grand Theft Auto girls, cavorting in her straining teeny tank top and short shorts, caught sight of me and elbowed her colleague, who I think would have doubled over laughing, had her microskirt not made such a reaction out of the question. Maybe I should get their business cards for Daniel, I thought grumpily. He'd clearly gone into the wrong profession.

"Excuse me—Miss Princess?"

Feeling a tug on my skirt that probably detached a few more feathers, I looked down to see a young boy staring up at me. He was small—maybe five or six—with red hair and hazel eyes and more freckles than your average boy. "Have you seen my dad?"

His dad! If his father took him to see the Grand Theft Auto girls, I wasn't sure I wanted to see the guy.

"Maybe," I said. I tried to crouch down in my giant gown. "What does he look like?"

"He's bigger than me."

That didn't exactly rule out many men here. "Where did you last see him?"

"By the cars." He couldn't make the 'r' sound, so it sounded like 'caws.'

"These cars?" I asked, pointing at the Mustang with its writhing ho hood ornament.

"No," the boy answered. "The cars with the faces. By the princesses. There were lots of princesses, but now you're the only one."

"Oh!" I exclaimed, relieved. "I'll bet you were in the Disney tent next door. I'll take you back there. What's your name?"

What with the background noise and his speech issues, I gave up on his name, but I took his hand firmly. We threaded our way through the crowd, me resisting the urge to cover his eyes as we passed various exhibits. Why didn't the Expo put all the family-friendly game companies in one area and all the sex and gore somewhere else?

"Here we go," I said, when we were standing in front of the animatronic Lightning McQueen. Belle floated by, offering me a teapot keychain. "Do you see your dad anywhere?"

He threw some cursory glances around, swinging my hand and now not looking the least bit concerned. "Nuh-uh. Guess he went somewhere else. Could we go see the Wii stuff now? I want to see if they have soccer. I play soccer."

"But your dad will be getting worried about you," I pointed out. "Plus, I'm actually working today, and I should get back to my job. I think I'd better take you over to Security. Your dad is probably already there."

Wherever Security happened to be. Although the boy was content to hold my hand as I led him hither and yon, progress was slow because he was also frequently distracted: "Princess, look! That guy has a light saber! Princess—did you see that pirate? Princess, stop! Over there!"

"Your dad?" I exclaimed hopefully.

"No! It's Super Mario!" The boy tore his hand free, the better to run after the guy in an enormous, puffy red suit below us on the grand staircase landing.

"Little boy! Kid!" I yelled after him. "Wait!" Panicked, I shoved aside Darth Maul and a Lego man, hitched up my skirts and charged after him.

Had I mentioned that Vil's cousin, besides being flaky and more buxom than I, also had bigger feet? If I didn't, it was because the thigh-length, sparkly boots worked just fine when I was standing still or even walking carefully, but running was another matter. As was running down concrete steps.

On about the fourth step down, I felt the boot heel twist treacherously under me while my foot kept going. Time slowed. Tumbling forward, the Snow Goddess gown blooming around me, half of my brain thought objectively, Oh—this is like that scene where Scarlett O'Hara pitches down the steps and has a miscarriage—I wonder if Vivien Leigh used a stunt double..? The other half of my brain thought, This is going to hurt! A multi-note, keening shriek filled my ears that I hoped—in vain—wasn't coming from me.

Yoda broke my fall.

I don't think he meant to be heroic, but after clutching desperately for whichever sleeves and pantlegs I passed on my way down, I finally crashed sideways into him, slamming him against the side wall. Because of him, by the time I actually hit the steps I only had the wind knocked out of me. The shrieking cut off abruptly, and I rolled down the three remaining steps to the landing, coming to a rest on my back, white feathers drifting down and my ice crown jerking free of its hairpins.

There was a brief interval of silence, save for the ringing in my ears, and then all at once everything rushed to swallow me. Unfamiliar heads closed in a tight circle: "Hey, are you okay?" "Can you move?" "Somebody call an ambulance!" "It's clumsy you are."

"No ambulance," I blurted. I would have liked to sit up, but I didn't think my body would cooperate yet. "Has anyone seen—there was a little boy—"

To my relief, a head of bright orange hair thrust itself through the circle. "Princess? I caught your crown before it rolled away."

Feebly I snaked a hand around his ankle. "Stay right there, Kid— You—stay right there." Some of the heads backed off, and Yoda helped heave me to a sitting position. "I'm fine, I'm fine. Thank you," I announced generally, with little effect. "Can you do that little trick?" I whispered in Yoda's pointy ear. "You know—" I waved my fingers. "'There's nothing to see here. These aren't the droids you're looking for...'?"

"Bryson?" a hard voice interrupted. "My God—there you are! I've been looking everywhere." I felt Bryson's ankle whipped from my grasp as his father pulled him into a rough embrace. "Where have you been, son?"

Bryson, then. No wonder I didn't catch it. Skandar had never mentioned that his son was a redhead. For Skandar it was—dark, brooding face, ponytail and all.

"I got lost, Daddy," explained Bryson cheerfully. "But the princess found me."

His father's black eyes flicked automatically over me. "Thank you, Miss, for—" Then he did a double-take. "*Cass?*"

I hauled myself up on Yoda's arm, giving him a grateful pat of dismissal on the shoulder and waving sheepishly so my crowd of rubberneckers would disperse. Wincing, I shifted my weight to my untwisted ankle. "Yes, it's me. I told you I had to work the Expo. I didn't expect to see you here."

"Well, when you mentioned it, I thought Bryson might enjoy it. He loves Super Mario and all those characters." As his anxiety for Bryson faded, Skandar's amusement seemed to be growing. "Who exactly are you supposed to be, Cass? And was falling down the stairs part of the act?"

"Oh, aren't you a funny guy," I said.

"Do you know the princess, Daddy?" asked Bryson. He wiggled out of his father's arms to run around scooping up feathers while I worked on pinning my crown back on.

"Sort of," said Skandar.

"She's pretty, isn't she?" volunteered Bryson, dumping the ball of feathers in my hands like a dead chick.

Turning bright red, I said loudly, "And she's on the clock. I have to get back to work." I thrust my hand at Bryson. "I'm so glad I met you today and that we found your dad. Have fun with him." To Skandar I added, "And watch out around here. There are a lot of adult-themed displays—the Expo isn't really aimed at kids."

Instantly his face closed up. "I can handle the parenting, thank you."

I smothered a sigh. "Of course." Turning, I went to gather my shreds of dignity and march back upstairs, but I'd forgotten about my twisted ankle. When I tried to put weight on it, I gave a squeal of pain and just managed to hop to the half-wall railing before collapsing.

"Are you okay?" asked Bryson solicitously.

"I think Princess Piety sprained her ankle," said Skandar, earning himself a dirty look.

"Help her, Daddy!" Bryson insisted, tugging on Skandar's arm.

"If you wouldn't mind," I said in the most pleasant tone I could muster, "you could really do me a favor by calling my co-worker James. My own phone is back at the booth."

"What's the point? You just need help getting back up the stairs, and I can do that." Before I could respond, Skandar had my arm around his shoulders and hoisted me against him. "You—" nodding at Bryson, "stick by me this time, if you know what's good for you."

Because Skandar was a good several inches taller than I, he hardly made a comfortable crutch, and my trailing Snow Goddess garb threatened to trip us both. "If you let me hold your arm, I can hop," I suggested, self-conscious.

He didn't answer me but instead addressed Bryson. "What do you think, Bry? Should I carry the princess like a bride or a sack of potatoes?"

"Sack of potatoes!" crowed Bryson.

"Don't you dare," I breathed, withdrawing my arm and teetering back from him.

"Don't worry," Skandar said. "I think if I tried to do the sack of potatoes, your Abominable Snowman dress would smother me. Bride it is."

At least my mortification was brief. At the top of the stairs Skandar dropped me none too gently onto my good leg, and we avoided looking at each other.

"What the hell, Cass? You look like you got run over by Power Wheels Bigfoot." It was Riley, decked out in a Roman centurion helmet and beer pong t-shirt.

"Long story."

"Jimbo's been paging me like crazy 'cause guess what—no gamer wants to come by our booth when all we've got are dorkwad pens and the frakkin' game producer standing there. He tried calling you, but your phone was in your purse under the frakkin' table, Cass."

"I know, I know," I said hastily. "I'm coming." Commandeering Riley's shoulder, I leaned hard on him. "Help me out—I twisted my ankle in these stupid boots."

"What's 'frakkin'?" asked Bryson. Although with him it came out 'fwakkin.' "Is that the F word?"

"See?" I accused, poking Skandar indignantly. "Inappropriate."

"Yeah, frakkin' is the F word," said Riley, unfazed. "But don't say stuff like that till you're a bad-ass grown-up like me."

Rolling my eyes, I elbowed Riley. "Thank you, Dr. Spock. Let's go."

"Bye, Princess!" called Bryson. "Daddy, can the Princess come to our house?"

To my surprise, Skandar put out a hand. "Wait, Cass." I did, looking at him questioningly. "I am…grateful…that you found Bryson and looked out for him. Without Katherine I'm kind of making this up as I go along. Would you like to…get dinner with us sometime?"

"Hot dogs!" hollered Bryson. "Pizza! Calamari! Falafel!"

"Calamari?" I echoed. "Falafel?" With Bryson's eager face beaming up at me, I could hardly say no. "Sure," I said. "That'd be great. Email me."

Nudging Riley into motion again, we were in sight of the Free Universe booth before he spoke again. "Dude, that dude had way better hair than me. Took a sly picture of him on my phone because he'd make a great Desert Warrior. Glad to see you're bouncing back after Jimbo trashed your heart."

"Thanks, Riley," I said tersely. "But I'm not dating that guy." How many times did I have to explain this?

"Dinner with single guy equals date, Cass," Riley answered imperturbably. "You women—oh, the little games you play."

Hobbling back into my booth prison, I unceremoniously shoved James and Riley out.

Enough men for the day, already.

CHAPTER 12:

An Affair to Remember

Given the choice of falafel or calamari, I went with falafel, thinking it sounded like the quicker, more casual meal.

"Perfect," said Skandar. "Why don't you come around 5:30 to help us?"

"Help you what?" I asked. "Won't we just go to Mediterranean Kitchen?"

"What for? We do the falafel that comes from a box. Bryson loves making the patties."

My heart sank. I really, really did not want to go over for a family dinner. "Well, how about calamari then?" I suggested. "I don't want you to bother having to cook."

"We do calamari at home too," he answered inexorably. "Katherine was a pescatorian. How do you think Bryson got to have such weird favorite foods?"

Sigh. One family dinner, coming right up. I hoped Bryson had an early bedtime. "Friday at 5:30," I agreed.

Thankfully no one was home the afternoon when I left. My couple attempts to patch it up with Phyl had been unsuccessful. Once she shrugged, "Everything's fine—don't make a mountain out of a mole-hill," and the other time she said coolly, "I really don't want to talk about this now." Any attempt to introduce Wayne as a topic met with freezing silence. After that Phyl made herself scarce again, except when she was home and accompanied by her sister Mary. I was also glad to avoid any awkward explanations with Joanie, and after Thursday's open house I wouldn't be sorry if I never saw Daniel with girlfriend Kristen again. The woman was truly the anti-Darla—she hardly had a word to say to anyone but him, and what she did have was uttered in so low a voice that even he had to lean forward to hear her. Only by assidu-ous eavesdropping on our parts did the girls and I piece together that she was annoyingly thrilling: Kristen golfed, snowboarded, sailed; she had worked for years at Lonely Planet, visiting exotic destinations and writing them up; hip local clothing stores gave her free samples so she could plug them when people complimented her (Phyl fell into this trap). But worst of all was the moment when I went to get the tongs out of the kitchen drawer and sent Phyl's tea infuser ball bouncing across the floor—down on all fours by the barstools to retrieve it, I spied Kristen's athletic, capable hand stroking Daniel's thigh under the table. Back and forth, back and forth—good thing we installed that fire extinguisher because, with all that friction, his pants might ignite at any moment. Though probably they already had, figuratively speaking.

I clutched the tea ball so viciously that the wire mesh dented inward.

Maybe, when all was said and done, I preferred Darla. At least she was up front with her manhandling. No covert operations under the table. Discovering Kristen's handiwork suddenly opened up new vistas to me: who really knew what Daniel was up to, right under my nose? Or, even worse, who knew what he was up to when he was off on his own?

"You did tell him to date other people," the objective part of my brain reminded me for the umpteenth time. I *know*, responded the rest of me. But when I told him to date other people, I didn't mean for him to get so into it!

It was my own fault. I had said something I thought I meant, only to discover shortly after that I didn't mean it at all. But I had meant it at the time, hadn't I? Hadn't I? Or was I passive-aggressive and manipulative? Was I playing games, as Riley accused all women of doing?

Glaring once more at Kristen's insistent hand, I clenched my own over the tea ball, wishing I could chuck it at them. I hated Daniel! No way would I have let anyone be rubbing me, if I were in love with someone else, but when I rose to my feet, there he was, giving stupid Kristen that lazy, heavy-lidded look. Get a room, already.

So—ahem. Where was I? Oh, yes. While I didn't want to do a family dinner with Skandar and Bryson, it sure beat having to stay home and potentially watch Daniel and Kristen paw each other.

• • •

The Sebaris lived in what looked like a Haussmann apartment building, plucked up from the streets of Paris and set down by the Bellevue Regional Library: cream-colored stone facing, balconies with iron grillwork, dark slate roof. The building also had a doorman—or woman, I should say—to whom I timidly gave my name and purpose. After calling up to make sure I was welcome, she pointed at the elevator. "Fourth floor. When you come out of the elevator, unit 425 will be down the hall to your left."

Thick carpet in the hallway hushed my footsteps, the only noise being the crunch of butcher paper as my nervous hands clutched the farmers-market flowers I'd bought, and small plaques on the wall indicated which direction to turn for which units. The overall effect was hotel-like, so I was surprised that no music was piped in. I wondered if Bryson felt like Eloise at the Park Plaza.

Pausing at the corner, I saw a bright red head peeking out from the open door at the end. "Princess!" shouted Bryson, tearing out to hug me around the waist. He certainly was not a shy boy, but I had no idea why he should be so happy to see me. Was this normal? "Come in, hurry," he urged, pulling on my arm. "Do you want to see my room? Daddy made me clean it for you."

Smiling weakly, I followed him. The condo was surprisingly spacious. Square-footagewise it probably equaled the house Troy and I had owned. Light poured in the floor-to-ceiling, west-facing windows of the great room, where dining, living, and informal eating areas flowed together, separated only by half-walls. On either side of this space were doors leading off to bedrooms and bathrooms, I imagined. And the décor could only be described as pescatorian: modern, earth-toned, glass and hemp and bamboo.

The brave souls who visited me in the early months after Troy and Min died had to step over heaps of clutter and thread their way through land mines of the life I had let fall. Min's toys, Troy's projects, mail, clothing, vases of dead flowers from sympathizers. I wouldn't let anyone touch anything save the kitchen, which was why I would end up sitting there with most people, if they didn't insist on getting me out of the house. Skandar's place, by contrast, was immaculate. Either it had awesome storage or he really didn't have many possessions. The lack of clutter fit the general hotel vibe of the place.

"Hi, Cass. How's the ankle?" He was in the kitchen, falafel mix box in hand, wearing an incongruous striped denim apron that would have made Riley eat his words about Skandar's Desert Warrior resemblance.

"Better, thanks," I said. Lamely I held out the flowers, and he froze for a minute before taking them from me.

"Sweet peas. They were Katherine's favorite."

Oh, crap. Couldn't I catch a break with this?

"My mommy died," announced Bryson, tapping me on the hip to regain my attention.

"I know," I winced. "And I am so, so sorry about that."

"Do you want to see a picture of her?"

"Bryson—" said Skandar, but I waved my hand at him before

answering, "Sure I would."

Taking me by the hand, Bryson led me through one of the closed doors off the living room and down a short hallway to his bedroom, which I was relieved to see was decorated in standard young-boy fashion. The walls were bright blue, apart from around the window, which featured an outer-space mural, complete with a red-headed boy in a bubble helmet astride a rocket. The words "Star light, star bright, first star I see tonight…" wove their way between ringed planets, the ellipses fading out just under the little astronaut's foot.

"How beautiful!" I exclaimed, wondering if Katherine had painted it. I knew I would never ask.

"And look," said Bryson, drawing my unwilling eyes from the mural to a photograph collage on the opposite wall behind me. Half the pictures were of a baby I assumed was Bryson: as a newborn, taking a bath, eating in his high chair, shaking a rattle, and so on. He was a baby of standard cuteness, no more, no less, but the woman whose pictures filled the rest of the frame, both with her son and without him, had a face to remember. Her eyes drew yours—large, amber-colored, liquid. The eyes of someone who died young.

"That's Mommy," Bryson said superfluously.

I gave myself a shake. *The eyes of someone who died young!* Enough with the melodrama, Cass, when there's real grief around. "She's very, very pretty, Bryson."

"She wasn't that pretty when she died," he said matter-of-factly. "'Cause she looked funny-colored and her hair was all short and her eyes were sad."

Dragging my fingernails across my palm, I made a vague sound in my throat which could have been agreement or pity or whatever. Briefly I debated mouthing some platitudes: hair grows back; now she wasn't sick anymore; now her eyes were happy again. But when a movement in the doorway caught my attention and I glanced over to see Skandar there, I knew I didn't have the nerve to utter them.

"Glass of wine?" His eyes had that hard, determined look.

"I'd love one."

. . .

After that rocky beginning, things improved for a time. For one thing, we stayed off the dead people topic, and for another, the falafel was messy and fun to make. Bryson's presence made things decidedly easier, certainly.

"Princess, did you know I can do the backstroke?" Backstwoke.

"The what?" I asked.

"Her name is Cass, Bryson," said Skandar. "The backstroke. He's in swim lessons."

"Oh! That's great, Bryson. That's my favorite stroke because you can breathe all you want." Skandar handed me a tomato to slice, while he supervised Bryson smashing the balls of falafel mix into patties.

"Except, you know what, Princess—?"

"Cass," interjected Skandar.

"'Princess' is fine," I assured him, hoping Daniel never got wind of this.

"Except I bangeed my head on the side of the pool because I didn't see where I was going," said Bryson. "That's what's not so good about backstroke. I cried but then the lifeguard let me pick out a candy, and I stopped crying."

"That usually works for me too," I said. I glanced over at Skandar, who was pouring oil in the skillet. "Do you...take him to the pool?" Hard to imagine him—shirtless, kicking back in one of the lounge chairs.

He shrugged. "My mother-in-law."

"My gramma," explained Bryson. "She used to have red hair like me, but now it's orange-pink."

"Oh."

Skandar looked at me then, amusement in his eyes. It was a good look for him. Better than stunned misery, I mean. "More Zinfandel, Cass?"

"I'm good until dinner." At the sink I washed the tomato juice from my hands. Drying them on a dishcloth, I added casually, "Your mother-in-law must be with him a lot this summer, since you work. Don't investment bankers have crazy hours?"

"I used to," he replied. He flipped on the fan and dropped in one of the falafel patties. ("Do 'em really crispy!" urged Bryson over the sizzling.) "When I started out. Seventy hours a week, lots of travel. It's how I met Katherine."

"Huh?"

His dark eyes met mine squarely. "She was my boss. When you work like that, you don't have much of an outside life. We...got together."

I gulped, picturing him and the liquid-eyed Katherine ripping off each other's Brooks Brothers suits in a deserted conference room, sweeping empty coffee cups from the vast table in their eagerness. Was this why she and Reiner got divorced? Who was watching infant Bryson—was it the pink-haired grandma even then? None of these were questions I could voice, but he anticipated me.

"Hey, Bry—why don't you go set the table?" He nudged him, but Bryson was already in motion, tuck-jumping his way across the great room toward the buffet. "I-banking isn't easy on marriages," Skandar continued. "She and Reiner were already on the rocks when Katherine was getting her MBA, since he didn't pull his weight. And he never wanted to leave L.A. to move to San Francisco. After a couple months of being a stay-at-home dad to Bryson, he was out of there. Katherine had to hire an *au pair*."

Yes, yes. But was this all before or after he and she "got together"? Without thinking, I blurted, "Are you sure you couldn't avoid the whole adoption hassle—maybe a DNA test—?" The instant the words were out of my mouth I wished them unsaid and turned away to stuff lettuce in the pitas.

His hand stopped me midway to the third pita. "Bryson doesn't like lettuce. What is the deal with you? You're all red."

Swallowing, I gave him an uncertain smile. "I'm sorry—I didn't mean to accuse you of—not that it's my business—I mean I'm sure—"

Mercilessly, head cocked to one side, he let me dither my way into silence. "You are the strangest creature," he said finally. "Are you apologizing for thinking I might be Bryson's biological father?"

Sort of. The boy in question was still bouncing his way around the table, laying placemats and napkins. I cleared my throat. "Well, if you were, it would mean that Katherine was still married when you—you—hooked up. So it would mean I was accusing you of—you know—having an affair with her. That's what I was apologizing for."

"I did."

"Did?"

"Did technically have an affair with her."

"Oh."

My continuing blushes appeared to mystify him. "She and Reiner were only separated at the time. But what Katherine and I had together—how we felt about each other—couldn't be denied."

Apparently not.

I couldn't help it—it made me less sympathetic to him to know he'd been a home-wrecker. He would probably say the home was already wrecked, but I imagine his appearance in her life convinced Katherine that it was beyond repair. Was that why he always had to speak of her and his marriage in larger-than-life terms? To justify its beginnings?

In his defense, he had stuck by her when she got cancer, not abandoning her for a more appealing colleague, or boss, as the case might be. And he truly did care for Bryson.

"I might have helped move things along," Skandar was saying, "but I'm most definitely post-Bryson. Do you really think I would have gone through the legal rigmarole if there were any chance he were mine in the first place?"

I didn't know what to think with him.

I was still blinking at him uncertainly when Bryson turned up at Skandar's elbow, reaching for the plate of falafel patties.

"Take it slow," Skandar cautioned, as Bryson spun on his heel and nearly slid the lot of them onto the floor.

"That's what Mrs. Poundstone said," said Bryson, now walking in measured paces, a page carrying a crown on a pillow.

Skandar frowned. "Nosy neighbor," he told me *sotto voce*, handing me the salad bowl, while he took the tahini and wineglasses. Then, louder, "What Mrs. Poundstone said about what? Were you running in the hallway?"

"No," said Bryson. "She asked if you were seeing anybody yet, and I said what did she mean seeing anybody, and she said like a girlfriend, and I said no, and she said good because you should take it slow."

I was distracted from renewed embarrassment by Skandar's expression. He looked like he might blow a gasket. "And did you tell her to mind her own damned business?"

"No...." breathed Bryson wonderingly. "You mean I could? I told her I thought you would get married again because Mommy told you to."

Shrinking down in my chair, I tried unobtrusively to assemble my falafel. I needn't have worried—Skandar had other things on his mind than my discomfiture. "You leave her to me," he answered. "God, what is it? She brings over one damned casserole and now she thinks she gets a vote?" He shoved the falafel fixings toward Bryson. "And, Bry, there's no need to tell Mrs. Poundstone things about our family. You didn't mean anything by it, but there isn't any need to do it, you understand?"

Bryson nodded, his eyes huge. "But when she asks me questions, what should I say?"

"Questions like what?"

"Like how come we don't go to Mass anymore, was one."

Skandar slammed the turned-wood salad bowl back on the table, causing the cutlery to rattle. I was beginning to understand why he'd gotten so irritated with me that day at the sushi place. To him I'd been just another Mrs. Poundstone. Though surely if I were, he would not have asked me to dinner, no matter what Bryson wanted.

"Tell her," Skandar ground out, "that we switched to a Satanic cult, so we could worship in the comfort of our own home, and could she please send over her cat when she's done with him."

"For Pete's sake, Skandar," I chided, unable to prevent my mouth from twitching. Bryson, thankfully, looked positively mystified. "That's the kind of thing that gets innocently repeated, and then you're in real trouble."

To my surprise he smiled back at me. "You're right. Bry—don't tell her I said that. Tell her I've been going to a class at Cass's church instead."

Having just taken an enormous bite of his falafel which pulled the tomato slice completely out and left tahini running down his chin, Bryson managed an "okey-doke."

At the risk of ticking him off again I asked hesitantly, "Has it been okay—the class?"

He shrugged. But at least he didn't look annoyed. "It's pretty much what you described. It's fine." End of subject, clearly.

With Bryson intent on his food, I cast about for another topic so we wouldn't all sit chewing in silence. "So...you were saying the hours used to be pretty long at work... are they better now?"

"My goal right now is to stay employed," he grimaced. "I'm not complaining about hours. But they did get better before... all that. Katherine and I made a conscious decision that, once we got together, we weren't going to live that life anymore."

Indeed. Especially since any change in the org chart might lead to changes in marital status.

"We quit and moved up here. She did some private consulting, and

I switched focus. Went downwardly mobile. No more big mergers and buyouts. Small stuff. Local stuff. When she first got sick I was at, maybe, sixty hours a week. By the end…" His voice broke off. Clearing his throat, he reached for his wineglass. After a bracing sip he began again. "Enough about me. What about you? How many hours are you putting in at that video game company?"

Eyeing Bryson's tahini-splattered face, I self-consciously dabbed at my own with my napkin. "Well, I've been about half-time lately, and some of that is working from home, but who knows what I'll manage after the baby is born."

"Baby?" hollered Bryson, a chunk of pita tumbling out. "You're having a baby?"

"*I'm* not," I said quickly. "A friend is. I'm adopting a baby, I hope."

"I'm gonna be adopted."

"Yes," I agreed. Should I add an *I hope* to that one, too, or would it irk Skandar? "So then I've told James and Riley that I'll have to play it by ear, but I'm going to try to keep going—I've got to make a dent in those legal fees somehow."

He pushed away his half-eaten food. "What's the point of paying for all that legal advice, if you're not going to follow it?"

"Excuse me?" I laid down my own fork.

"C'mon, Cass. I'm talking about Lori's silver bullet. She did say it would simplify things if you just got m—"

"I know what she suggested," I interrupted, glaring at him. "Did you have somebody you wanted to nominate, Mr. Poundstone?"

Bryson shrieked with laughter. "He's not Mr. Poundstone! He's Mr. Sebari."

Skandar neither laughed nor apologized, but he rubbed his chin musingly.

I folded my napkin in half, then in thirds. Add my own marital status to the list of *verboten* subjects. If I didn't think of something, we would be thrown back on politics and the weather to get us to 7:30, the time I'd decided was the earliest I could flee.

In desperation I turned to Bryson. "Hey—you never did say—did you find any soccer games at the Expo after I left you?"

Bingo. His hazel eyes lit up. "Oh, yeah, Princess! There was this place where I got to be the goalie and I looked at a screen and these pretend balls came at me and I had to jump and like dive and block them and stuff—and I got the high score of the day so far that day I mean…"

· · ·

At 7:30 on the dot I brought my hands down with finality on the balcony railing. We had been people-watching for the past half-hour, Bryson waving and calling to passersby strolling down below while Skandar and I looked on in what passed for amicable silence. "Thank you, Sebaris. This has been a very nice dinner."

"You're already going?" demanded Bryson. "Do you go to bed this early? Even I don't go to bed this early."

"I have some things I need to get done," I said vaguely. Things like catching up on the housework if Daniel weren't home, or killing time at the mall if he was. Or maybe I would go for a walk, since what I wanted most of all was to think and not see anyone.

It was all Bryson's soccer talk. I found myself wondering what Min would have gravitated toward, had she lived long enough to develop any kind of physical coordination. I was no jock—maybe her only chance would have been basketball, like her father. On the other hand, having half my genes, she may not have grown tall enough to make that feasible. I would never know. Never know her changing likes and dislikes, never know what meal she would want me to make when she came home on visits in college, never know her friends or boyfriends or spouse or children. At least, I wouldn't, this side of heaven. We would recognize each other when I got there, right? Though we had such little time.

I stifled a sigh—shouldn't I stop looking back and start wondering what Ned would be like? I should, but he still felt unreal to me, while Min was all too real. Not good. Focus on the future.

What I really ought to do was drop in on Nadina. She was probably climbing the walls again and plotting another contraction-inducing prison break.

"I wanted you to read a book to me when I went to bed," said Bryson. The pitiful note in his voice recalled me.

"I'll read you a story," said Skandar.

"You read me a story every night!" complained Bryson, stamping his foot. It was the first sign of childish temper I'd seen from him, and it took me by surprise.

"Then we'll call Gramma and ask her to read you one over the phone," Skandar suggested next, before I could speak.

"It's not the same over the phone," wailed Bryson, more loudly, his eyes filling with tears.

"I can stay five more minutes," I said. "If you have a really short book. No—really—it's okay."

"I try not to give in when he behaves like this," Skandar argued woodenly.

"Of course," I said, "but—"

One minute later I was in the hemp armchair, Bryson perched on the arm, reading *Harry the Dirty Dog*, while Skandar loaded the dishwasher. It seemed to do the trick. And five minutes later I was standing in the doorway, making my good-byes.

Bryson was hugging my legs—"Remember my soccer game—you promised!"—*had* I in fact promised?—when a door kitty-corner across the hallway cracked open wide enough to reveal one forehead and an eye.

"Good evening, Mrs. Poundstone," said Skandar loudly. The door slammed shut.

"I saw black hair," I whispered, even though she couldn't possibly hear me. "Is she actually a young lady?"

"Forty going on a hundred and forty." He shrugged. "But it might be I judged her too harshly."

"How so?"

"Her advice isn't all off," he replied. He tousled Bryson's red hair thoughtfully. "I tend to rush things I've decided on. There are times when you have to take it slow."

CHAPTER 13:

Ducks in a Row

Before Min was born, I nested by stockpiling baby things, getting a jump on her scrapbook, reading ratings of breast pumps and baby products. I tried to decide if I needed a diaper-wipe warmer, which color mobile would aid her brain development, or if I really was okay with dressing her in gender-neutral colors when the rubber met the road.

In contrast, with Ned's imminent arrival, my nesting instinct took a psychological form: I found myself wanting time away from home, even if I couldn't go far, and I wanted to get as many of my personal relationships in order before I was too busy and tired to do repair work. Fortunately for me, Louella's daughter and husband were spending the middle of August sailing in the San Juans, and I leapt at the chance to housesit their condo in West Seattle. Besides popping by every couple days to check on the cat, I had their permission to spend a few nights, which I did when the weather turned gray and drizzly. One evening, sitting on the floor in front of the picture window, watching beach-combers huddling in their windbreakers against the mist, I drew up a list of problems:

Phyl. She's avoiding me. Must corner her and apologize. Get on her calendar, if necessary.

James. Keeps hinting he wants to revisit our relationship. Nip this in the bud.

Nadina. Am I adopting one child or two? Wait and see how things play out. We might need joint counseling.

Min. ??? Quiet, focused time?

Perry. Still dating Darla but now avoiding the Palace. No idea what to do.

Skandar. Not sure getting together with him and Bryson is good for Bryson, but if I bring it up, do I look like I'm reading too much into it?

Daniel.

My pen paused over this last entry. Really, the Daniel problem called for a flow chart. But what would I even put in the Decision diamond? After a minute, I scratched another "No idea. Talk to Joanie and Phyl."

I could, after the last couple days, almost put a check mark after Min. Not that I was over her death by a long shot, but 72 solid hours of rest and solitude and long walks meant I could explore my feelings for her without witnesses—separate them from other issues, indulge them or hold them at arm's length, inspect them. And paradoxically, by focusing my attention on my daughter during the day, I finally managed to sleep without dreaming of her.

We had a few one-sided conversations—something that never happened when she was alive. From the moment Min learned to talk ("do-o-g! dog-uh!") she never really stopped. But this time I had the floor. So I told her again that I missed her, that I loved her, that I was sorry not to see her grow up, that no one could replace her.

It was because no one could replace Min that I think my former mother-in-law Raquel hadn't emailed me in weeks. As the day of Ned's birth drew closer, Raquel seemed to be closing off from me. Her message frequency had plummeted from the time she found me having lunch with Daniel and I admitted to dating James, but since I announced my adoption plans, even the trickle had dried up. A relief, on one hand, since Raquel and I grieved so differently, but a new source of pain on the other. Tapping my pen absently on the paper, I briefly considered adding Raquel to my list before I decided I wouldn't be able to check her off easily, and really, I was in the mood to check these puppies off.

The next morning, per my action plan, Joanie and Phyl showed up for a late breakfast. I'd already run down to the bakery for treats and put the kettle on, and as an added bonus, the dreary November-in-August weather cleared, unveiling a sparkling Sound, the Olympics rising sharply in the distance. Surely Phyl would forgive me on such a day.

She gave me a big hug, for starters. "Cass—we've missed you."

"You have?" I said, trying not to sound too eager. "I'm so excited you and Joanie took the day off so we could be together. Kind of a last hurrah before Baby Ned shows up. Have I missed anything at the Palace?"

They exchanged glances and Joanie threw down her marionberry scone. "Tell her, Phyl."

"Tell me what?"

Phyl bit her lip, but then a big smile spread over her face. "Wayne and I are back together."

This time my whoops and hollers were sincere, and I threw my arms around her. "Tell all! How did it happen?"

"I'll tell—but first I have to ask your forgiveness, Cass," Phyl blurted. "No, no—let me say this—I've been unlivable, I know. I was so freaked out by Darla flirting with Wayne—"

"And everyone else," put in Joanie.

"—And everyone else," repeated Phyl, "that I lashed out where I felt safe. Of course you were trying to help, and I got mad at you because I could never confront Darla or Daniel—"

"Except for taking potshots at him during the group interview," Joanie pointed out.

Groaning, Phyl covered her face with her hands. "I know, I know—it was terrible! And Cass, I so hope we don't flunk the home study because of me. When I had my individual follow-up with the Dobbs, I apologized for being out of sorts the other day, and I behaved as sanely as possible. I said I was out of line—"

I hugged her hard, resting my head against hers. "Thank you, thank you, Phyl, but it wasn't all you—"

"Wait!" she interrupted. "Don't forgive me yet—I'm not done confessing." At my questioning look, her mild blue eyes avoided mine, wandering instead to the brown and orange macramé wall hanging by the front door. Her voice dropped. "I'm sorry for being…jealous of you."

"Jealous of me?" I echoed, dumbfounded. "Jealous of *me*? *You* were the one getting married! What am I, except the cursed Tragedy Queen who can't even adopt a baby without the state thinking he might be better off raised by a convict?"

Phyl laughed, then, to my relief. "If the state thinks that, it's only because Barbara Dobbs told them you live with a madwoman. No, Cass—I mean I was happy to be getting married, but I think I hadn't even admitted to myself that I was jealous of you months ago, when I figured out that Daniel liked you instead of me." Seeing the words on my lips, she added, "Don't worry. I love Wayne, really truly. And I want to marry him. I'm just saying I was carrying baggage and didn't even realize it. Forgive me. I was so hurtful."

"Okay, I grant you—that was irrational," I smiled. "But I won't let you take credit for everything because I was out of line too. These past couple months I've been so wrapped up in me and my life that I could barely pull my head out to notice what anyone else was going through. You were absolutely right to point that out, and I'm so sorry. Can you forgive me too?"

We were wiping tears away now, while Joanie made headway on the pastries. To her credit, she did make us each a cup of tea, just how we liked it. "'How good and pleasant it is for brothers to dwell together in unity,'" she sang, sliding me my Earl Grey and Phyl her peppermint. "At least, it sure beats everyone yelling at each other."

It could only be a glorious morning after that. I'd checked another box off my list! We went for a long walk down the beach and up Harbor Avenue, dodging rollerbladers and people with multiple accessory dogs, getting the juicy details on how Wayne had "practically beaten down the door" to come and tell Phyl that he wasn't going to stand for being broken up with. "He said, 'I know you've been hurt, Phyl, but not by me and not ever by me. That's what I want to promise you, in front of our family and friends and God.'"

"That Wayne is the most secret romantic dog ever! If only I could have gotten my claws into him before he laid eyes on you, Phyl." I linked my arm through hers and gave it a squeeze. "I can't resist saying I told you so. But are you going to believe him this time, even if my idiot brother comes down again and we have to have Darla cooing and wiggling everywhere? Because Perry will come down, you know, after the baby is born."

"I'll try," Phyl said ruefully. "But I don't have to like it."

"Clearly," said Joanie. She swung the stick of driftwood in her hand so that it whistled through the air. "But we are done letting Darla trash our lives." Launching the stick like a javelin, she brushed her hands off. "I'm even going out this weekend. No more pining after Perry."

"With who?" Phyl and I asked in unison. Guiltily, I thought of my secret knowledge—that Perry figured he'd have no chance with Joanie—but I squelched it with the same rationale I applied to Daniel: better for them to know their minds sooner, rather than later, even if it meant they didn't choose us. Besides, any man who could date Darla for several weeks running deserved his fate.

"A guy named Craig Sloane," Joanie muttered.

Craig Sloane. Craig Sloane … "Wait a sec," I said. "Isn't he that guy who called you at the church a bunch of times after he saw you sing at that benefit concert? You were still with Roy then."

"You said he was creepy," Phyl observed timidly.

"I didn't say he was creepy," retorted Joanie. "I said he was sleazy."

"Creepy, sleazy—what's the difference?" I snorted.

"Creepy guys stalk you and pop up with these comments on Facebook, when you didn't even know they were lurking there, and then they give you nasty gifts, like pictures of themselves in their underwear."

"Sleazy guys don't do that?" I said doubtfully. Having reached a vacant bench on the point, we sat down to take a rest.

"Well, if they did, you wouldn't mind so much, because sleazy guys are better looking than creepy guys," she explained. "Craig wasn't creepy—just sleazy. He hit on me while his date was in the bathroom, plus he kept hinting that he was really rich."

"Yuck!" I protested. "What do you want with him?"

"I *want* that he's the first guy to ask me out in a month," scowled Joanie. "And he's cuter than your brother. I'm not gonna marry him."

"Good thing," said Phyl, "otherwise you'd be Joan Sloane."

"Yeah." I tried it out. "Craig and Joan Sloane. And in the society columns, Mr. and Mrs. Craig Sloane…Mr. and Mrs. Creep Sleaze."

"The Creepy Sleazies," said Joanie, brightening.

"The Sleazacreeps."

"Maybe I will marry him." We stared across at Queen Anne and Magnolia for a few minutes, appreciating the sunshine and lively breeze before Joanie started in again. "You're one to talk, Cass. Craig might be sleazy, but at least he makes attempts at humor and wants to have a good time. He'll be way more fun that that mopey Skandar guy you've latched onto. How many times have you seen him, and why does he never come by the Palace?"

I shifted uncomfortably. "I only went for dinner once at his house, and his son Bryson was there chaperoning, and then I dropped in on a game at Bryson's soccer camp. I haven't invited Skandar over because we're not together."

"You're so not together that you may end up together. Does he know you're not together?"

"With so many dead people between us, relationship comments are pretty taboo," I admitted, thinking of my Problem list. "Those two things just kind of happened, after they came to the Game Expo. But while I've been out here I've been thinking I probably shouldn't do stuff with him and Bryson—not for Skandar's sake, since I don't think he cares one way or the other—but for Bryson's. It would be... complicated... if he got attached to me." Frowning, I remembered how Bryson had come running over when I showed up at the soccer camp, his face lighting up. Maybe the damage was done. But it could be undone.

"There would be something sweet about it," said Phyl thoughtfully. "You know: you're a widow; Skandar's a widower. You're both trying to adopt sons; his son already likes you. And he carried you up those stairs in your big white gown."

"Because she twisted her stupid ankle!" Joanie pointed out. "No way. Forget 'sweet.' Like Cass hasn't had enough crap in her life without taking on the widower charity case. Cass: I forbid you to date anyone who's constantly on the verge of tears."

"He's not *constantly* on the verge of tears," I objected. "Just occasionally. Give the guy a break... He is pretty moody, though. Still—when he's not in tears or hostile, he can be kind of funny. Maybe even as funny as the Sleazacreep."

Joanie rolled her eyes heavenward. "God help you. You've got to dump him. Dump both of them. Kids are kids. Bryson will forget all about you."

I couldn't resist playing devil's advocate. "But Louella said—and I feel this way, too—that Skandar was reaching out for someone who understands. I can't think what that first year would have been like without you guys or my family, and he doesn't seem to have a lot of support."

"I suppose…" agreed Joanie reluctantly. "My guess is you'd still be in your PJs, in bed, with the covers pulled over your head and the power turned off because you never got around to paying your bill."

"Probably," I admitted. "See? Everyone needs somebody to kick them in the pants once in a while."

"Just so long as that's all you're doing—kicking him in the pants."

"Something like," I said. "So I think I'd better avoid family activities in the future but still look in on him from time to time." Mentally I made another check mark on my Problem list.

Joanie shrugged, shaking her head. "When do you ever listen to me anyhow? Fine. I'm just saying watch out: no guy invites single women to dinner just to please his son and mourn over woe is us."

Don't tell me Riley and Joanie were on the same page. "Meaning what?" I demanded.

"Meaning you're so dumb about these things, Cass! You may think the guy doesn't have anything in mind, but that doesn't mean squat because you're always the last person to figure these things out."

"Joanie…" soothed Phyl, "we just got done making peace."

"I'm not fighting," she responded. "I'm trying to get Cass to take the blinders off."

"I don't think there's anything going on," I insisted. "If you saw him with me, you'd believe me. It's always Katherine this and she-was-the-love-of-my-life that."

"So invite him to an open house."

I hesitated. Skandar might have nothing in mind, but I still didn't want him showing up at the Palace. Joanie's eyes were doing their usual x-ray thing, and I knew I was starting to blush.

"Ah ha!" she cried triumphantly. "See? You do think he likes you!"

"I don't. That's not it. I just don't want him coming over because I don't want to give him any ideas. And I don't want—I don't want—" I trailed off.

Phyl made to say something, but Joanie gave her arm such a ruthless squeeze that the comment died aborning, swallowed up in a pained yelp.

"You were saying…" she prompted.

"Nothing," I muttered. A seagull landed on the nearby trash can, eyeing us to see if we had any goodies to share.

"Say it. Say it say it say it say it," Joanie chanted. "You don't want *what*?"

"You're so bad," I grumbled. Picking up a paper cup littering the ground, I hucked it at the bird. Lazily, it gave a half-hearted flap to dodge the projectile and settled again on the grass. "I don't want Skandar coming over because I don't want Daniel thinking I'm dating the guy."

Boom. Joanie was all over me. "What do you care what my brother thinks?"

"I care, okay?" was my surly answer. "Happy now?"

She and Phyl seemed to be holding their breath. "What do you care if he thinks you're dating?" Joanie persisted, a slight taunting note creeping into her voice. "You don't want him yourself, you've told me a hundred times."

I huffed out a defeated sigh. "What? Do you want to put your triumphant foot on my neck? I admit it, okay? I like him. I—if he thinks—if after I get Ned and Daniel gets done dating around he still wants—well—I think I'd consider it."

Joanie leapt to her feet, flinging her arms wide and twirling around like some kind of lunatic Fräulein Maria. "Yipeeeeee!" she exulted. "You love him, you love him, you love him…Guess what?" she shouted at passing bikers, "Cass loves my brother!"

"Are we in junior high?" I asked Phyl disgustedly.

To my dismay, instead of smiling, Phyl looked grave, and I felt a stab of anxiety that my confession had resurrected her jealousies. "What is it?" I asked her unwillingly, wishing I had something to throw at the cavorting Joanie.

Phyl bit her lip, but before she could work up her reply, Joanie had hauled me to my feet. "Sing it with me—'We are fa-mi-ly! Da da da da da da…I got all my sisters with me…Uh-huh... We are fa-mi-ly— da da da da da da…get up everybody and sing!'"

"'A lady's imagination is very rapid,'" I said dryly, yanking my hand from Joanie's grasp and resuming my seat. "'It jumps from admiration to love, from love to matrimony in a moment.'"

Making a face, Joanie only crammed right next to me on the bench and started humming Lohengrin's *Wedding March*.

"I think he's moved on," said Phyl quietly.

My stomach took a dive and landed somewhere around my ankles. "Wh—what?"

"Daniel," she added unnecessarily.

"Bull—ballyhoo—!" sputtered Joanie. "Kristen hasn't been by for days."

Phyl studied her hands. The insides of them, at least. She wasn't the type to twiddle her engagement ring at you while she told you the man you loved didn't want you anymore.

"What makes you say so?" I asked, dreading the answer.

Another pause. And then, "He doesn't stare at you anymore, Cass. He used to all the time."

"She hasn't been home to stare at, you unbeliever," snapped Joanie.

Phyl shrugged. "But when she was home, too, the last couple weeks. He…he…spent a lot of time looking at Kristen, though."

"Because she's got those perfect, perky boobs," declared Joanie, dismissive. "I spend lots of time looking at them myself! They're Modern-Day Marvels. The Bobbsey Twins. You can barely pull your eyes away before they get sucked back by the gravitational pull of those things.

Talk about underwire."

"It's just what I think," said Phyl stubbornly. "I'm not trying to be a wet blanket. I only want Cass to be careful."

"Don't listen to her," commanded Joanie, flicking Phyl with an irritated finger. "She also thought Darla and Wayne were messing around."

"Well, who brought Darla home?" countered Phyl. "And Daniel *is* going out with Kristen—just because we haven't seen her for a few days doesn't mean anything. Or it means he's dumped her and already moved on to someone else, like he always does."

"Phyl!" huffed Joanie. She drummed her fists on the bench. "You go home now. Or go to work. I think something in Bellevue needs recycling. Let Cass and me handle this." When Phyl crossed her arms defensively over her chest, Joanie forged ahead. "I can't wait, Cass! Let's go drop by Daniel's office and tell him you love him—"

"In your dreams!" I gasped, appalled by the idea. "No way am I doing that."

"Oh, come on," she wheedled. "It's almost his birthday. We could pick up some shortbread from the bakery and bring it by. It's a really cool office—you should see it."

"No way. No. way."

"We're doing this."

"We're not doing this."

Now my arms were crossed over my chest as well. Phyl was butting out, keeping her eyes trained on the Bremerton ferry.

Joanie weighed her options.

"How about if we visit his office and bring him shortbread but don't mention the love part?" she suggested.

"Forget it," I said. "You know perfectly well you'll dance around and open your big mouth, and it'll be mortifying. I'm not doing a darned thing until Ned is born."

"Oh, you're so mean, Cass!" Joanie protested. "I promise I won't say a thing, and you won't either, you big chicken. Just do something nice for him, for a change, after all these months of being such a cold fish." When I made indignant sounds, she talked right over me. "We're doing this. I'll say it was my idea for his birthday. And we'll get some extra shortbread for the receptionist, for all the times she's had to page him for me."

I met Phyl's sympathetic glance, and she shook her head slightly, the beginnings of a smile lifting the corners of her mouth. She wouldn't come.

But apparently I would.

We were doing this.

CHAPTER 14:

Birthday Boys

Daniel worked in a high-rise near the Columbia Center in downtown Seattle. Joanie had only been there once herself, so it took a bit of driving around to jog her memory. And then, because it was so beautiful out, we had to take the elevator as high as we could to take in the view.

At last, however, we pushed open the door to Fields & Wyler Legal—as offices go, about the polar opposite of Free Universe: silence, space, walled offices, clean décor. No inflatable Hobbits to trip over; no *U.S.S. Enterprise* or Death Star models dangling from the ceiling to club the unwitting. No running monologue provided by Riley. Instead, one frosty receptionist behind a massive desk, giving us the evil eye.

Undaunted, Joanie tripped forward, plopping a paper bag of shortbread right on the desk. "Colette, right? I'm Joanie Martin, Daniel's sister. You've been kind enough to take my calls and hunt him down from time to time."

Before my very eyes the receptionist thawed like the Greenland Ice Shelf, yielding as ever to the Martin charm, and I wondered idly if Daniel had the same effect on her. Most likely. She popped up to shake Joanie's hand. "Oh! You're Joanie. So nice to meet you, finally—you look a lot like your brother." After Colette had oohed and aahed over the shortbread gift, Joanie introduced me and asked, "Can we pop in to see Daniel?"

Shooting a glance at the wall clock, Colette chewed and swallowed the wedge in her hand and then discreetly wiped her hands on a piece of Kleenex. "Mm-hmm. He should just be finishing up his meeting—yeah, I hear them coming. Just go right in."

Must have been quite the meeting because at least five other people filed past us, dressed to the business nines on such a warm day. Joanie sensed me digging in my heels and grabbed my hand again, bugging her eyes out at me. What was the point of this, again? I had no plans to make a declaration, and even if I had, I would hardly choose Daniel's workplace as the setting.

Daniel P. Martin read the little bronze plaque. What was the P for? Philip? Paul? Pythagoras? The door to his office was ajar, and before I could try any of these possibilities in combination, I felt Joanie give an almighty yank on my arm.

Stumbling forward, I unexpectedly crashed into her, since the crazy girl had suddenly pulled up short. "What—?" I began, as she backpedaled into me and my elbow flung the door wide.

"Go go go," she urged. "His meeting's not done."

Nor was it.

Tableau in a law office.

There was still a client in with him. Or, I should say, a client on him. One with lush, Catherine-Zeta-Jones hair and shapely legs. One who was perched on his lap, pulling on his tie with one hand and snaking a fingertip through the placket of his button-down shirt.

His hand lay lightly at her waist.

A fraction of a second was more than enough time for Daniel and his client to register our presence, and for me to feel the sickening swoop in my stomach.

Joanie was right: Kristen was history.

And so, apparently, was I.

He set the lovely lady quickly and firmly on her feet, rising himself, his sharpened gaze fixed on me, which might explain why the bag of shortbread Joanie launched at him caught him off guard, nailing him square in the chest.

"Oh, excuse me," she said loudly. "I thought you were the trash." If I was crushed, Joanie was furious. What with Perry and all, she'd been watching quite a few dreams crash and burn lately.

"What—what are you doing here?" Daniel asked, rubbing the point of impact.

Seeing a genuine Joanie-rant looming, I managed to step in front of her, babbling, "We—she—wanted to bring you some cookies for your birthday. Those," I added lamely, pointing.

"Hope you enjoy them, you stupid ass-for-brains!" his sister jeered over my shoulder. "You stupid, dickbrained, lame-excuse-for-a-human-being JERK!"

Good gracious—what was Daniel going to think, having her go nuts like that? It wasn't like she hadn't seen him entangled with one woman or another from the time she was in sixth grade. He might think—he might guess—she was upset on someone else's behalf. Choking with embarrassment, I tugged insistently on her hand, dragging her backward out of the office, while she offered as much help and volition as a totem pole.

When I had wrangled Joanie into the hallway, Catherine Zeta-Jones' bemused voice drifted back to us: "Your girlfriend, I gather?"

"Sister," was Daniel's laconic response, as I pulled the door shut.

· · ·

I heard the dog-on-roller-skates sound of Colette the receptionist scrambling back to her place, but, really, what she'd overheard was too juicy to resist, and I didn't blame her for trying to eavesdrop.

"Is there a bathroom we could use?" I asked, as she threw herself too enthusiastically into her rolling chair, sending it careening to the other end of the monolithic desk.

"Yes, yes," she replied nervously, keeping her head down and her eyes fixed on the drawers she started opening and closing.

"Is it in the desk?" said Joanie caustically.

Colette flushed. "Past the elevators, on your right."

It was one of those giant, posh restrooms, with separate mirrored sitting room. Deserted, thankfully. I sunk onto the velvet settee, leaning my head back against the gold-striped wallpaper. Joanie, meanwhile, was returning to a rolling boil, pacing back and forth in front of me.

Her rant had dropped to indistinct muttering, with the occasional epithet rising to the surface of intelligibility. Whenever one did, she shot me a look, but I only watched her blankly. I felt too weary for more. Too defeated.

"So that's it?" Joanie demanded finally. She halted in her pacing to stare me straight in the eye. "You're not even mad at the sleazebag— just depressed?"

"That woman must think you're totally nuts," I said, avoiding the question. "Whoever heard of a jealous sister? And what will Daniel think?"

"Whatever," said Joanie. "Answer the question."

"He's not a sleazebag," I said after a minute, pushing in one of the settee's fabric-covered buttons and watching it slowly pop out. "It's Kristen he's messing around on, if anyone."

Joanie groaned multi-syllabically. "Cass, stop it."

"Stop what?"

"Stop rolling over and playing dead. Get mad! Be mad!"

"What's the point?" I hollered, my voice breaking. "I told him to date around, so he's dating around! What do you want me to be mad about?"

"That's more like it," she sighed. Nudging me with her foot, she plopped down in the space I made for her. "I knew you were mad. I'm mad…Were you this mad about Darla and Kristen?"

I thought about this. "No…I mean, I couldn't stand Darla, but I knew he brought her home just to rile me. Kristen I was dumpy about, but at least he was dating her openly. No secrets. Who knows how many women he's been having on the side, or what he's been doing with them? For Pete's sake—in his office!—how cliché is that—at least we interrupted before he had her spread out on his desk." Daniel and his client. Skandar and Katherine. Maybe I should feel insulted that James never tried to jump me in his cubicle at Free Universe.

Over the noise of the maxed-out bathroom air conditioner, I heard a faint ringing sound building. My phone. Absently I began to rummage through my handbag, until I realized Daniel had my cell number now. Joanie had the same thought, and we looked at each other. I threw my purse aside: "Sleazebag."

She giggled. "Sleazacreep."

"Creepy sleazy."

After a minute the ringing cut off, and, sure enough, a few seconds later Joanie's phone burst into song. She pulled it out and grimaced at the number. "It's him. I should block his calls."

"What could he possibly want to say?" I wondered.

Before she could answer, I heard my own phone trilling again. Huh? Was he calling Joanie on his cell and me on his office phone? Curious, I dug mine out and checked. Jill Stern. Jill *Stern*? "Nadina!" I gasped. I flipped it open. "Hello?"

"Er—this Cassandra Ewan?" came the die-away voice of Nadina's mother.

"Yes—Mrs. Stern? Is everything okay with Nadina?"

"She wanted me to call you." Her voice was so soft that I had to plug my other ear, to hear her over the air conditioner.

"Yes?" I prompted again.

"They've just admitted her," said Mrs. Stern colorlessly. "Baby's coming."

. . .

Nine hours later I sat on a stiff plastic chair in the cafeteria, my tired head propped on one hand while the other curled around a cup of weak tea. Just a little shot of caffeine and I should be able to make the ten-minute drive home.

She had done it.

Brave girl.

I'd shown up at her birthing room just as the anesthesiologist was swabbing her back prior to sticking in the epidural needle. Mrs. Stern stood by the door, arms crossed, looking on edge. Nadina scowled at me. "About time, Cass! You'd think you'd be more interested in this—ow! Fuck! Dude, watch where you stick that needle or you're gonna paralyze me!"

The anesthesiologist merely made soothing clucking noises. He must have seen too many women out of their minds in this place to be offended by Nadina's mouth. Just as he went to stick her again, the woman in the room next door let loose a screech that raised the hairs on my neck. "God—make her shut up! She's making me all tense," complained Nadina. "Maybe you should be over there doing her up first."

"Too late for her," he replied calmly. He poised the needle once more, only to have Nadina turn to rock as another contraction started. It took her breath away, leaving her unable to swear aloud, but she mouthed up a storm until it loosened its hold.

This time he got the needle placed. We were in business.

"Bet you wish you'd paid attention to the breathing exercises in that birthing class," I teased after she was lying back, drugs flowing. She looked pale but was no longer sweating. Mrs. Stern and I pulled up chairs to one side, trying to keep clear of the monitors and cords and IV and whatnot.

Nadina didn't bother replying, merely rolling her eyes and scratching her forehead with her middle finger. I laughed.

For the next several hours we waited. Nadina channel-flipped, nurses popped in and out to measure her dilation, Mrs. Stern kept her cup of ice-chips full. Jill Stern was certainly no talker, and after numerous attempts to engage her I gave up.

"Was this the room where you had Min?" Nadina asked at one point, interrupting my unpleasant Daniel-reverie as I stared out the window.

I smiled. "I don't know. All the rooms look the same. I had other things on my mind."

"How long'd it take you?"

"Maybe four hours, from the time I was admitted. Min wasn't very big."

"I bet Ned is huge." Nadina glanced over at the monitor, and I followed her gaze. I could see from the squiggly lines that she must be having another contraction, but with the drugs it didn't seem to affect her more than to make her out of breath. "I was huge, wasn't I, Mom?"

Mrs. Stern nodded, patting the bedcovers. "Aunt Sylvia said you were the biggest baby she ever saw. Like a Thanksgiving turkey."

"Mom," gasped Nadina, "what if I move out there and Aunt Sylvia up and dies?"

Her mother snorted, fingers twitching for a cigarette. She'd excused herself a couple times already but was trying to limit her intake because it was a long haul to the smoking area outside. "That old bird? She'll probably live longer than I will."

Nadina exhaled slowly as the contraction released her. "Whew... she better. I've been thinking it would freak me out if I got up one morning and she was all stiff and cold." She looked over at me. "Did it freak you out, Cass, when you had to go identify Troy and Min?"

"Sheezus, Nadina," chided Mrs. Stern.

"Yes." I shuddered. "My father-in-law went with me." Raquel had waited outside, a blithering mess. Which was fine with me—if Raquel hadn't blithered, I would have.

159

"Father-in-law..." repeated Nadina pensively. "Cass, did I tell you Mike's dad called me a couple days ago?"

My mind snapped back to the present. "Not him too," I grumbled. "Is he filing his own separate lawsuit?"

Had she not been ponderous and drugged from the waist down, I think she would have squirmed. "God, Cass—way to hold a grudge. Having a baby here—think you'd loosen up."

I held up a placating hand. "Hey. Sorry. Mike would've kicked up a fuss about Ned anyhow. It wasn't like he was ever happy about it. You probably just...sped things up a little. Made it a little more...acrimonious." Seeing her eyebrows lower, I added hastily, "So what did Mike's dad have to say?"

"It was crazy because it's not like he's the talkative type," she said, swinging the on-demand button for her epidural by its cord. "And he was boring the crap out of me telling me stories about when Mike was a baby and how that was such a cool time and he didn't know where everything got off track and blah blah blah blah."

"Do you think he might have been...drunk?" I ventured.

"God, no. I mean Dale usually perks up after a beer or two. I kept trying to get rid of him—Dude, I don't care about how many bibs friggin' Mike used to drool through—so he kind of quit with the good-old-days stories and started asking me a million questions."

My stomach tensed. "Questions like what?"

She shrugged. "You know—how was I feeling and how much longer did I think it'd be...was I still going to Ohio...was I still thinking about giving the baby away...did I know how much Mike was shaping up over there in Prisonland..."

"Mike Loftus is no damned good," spoke up Mrs. Stern. She had her pack of Marlboro Menthols in hand by this point and crushed it in her vehemence.

I tried to shoot her a warning look—didn't she, after all these years, know better than to issue Nadina face-slapping challenges like that?

Sure enough, Nadina straggled up on her elbows, glowering. "Did I say he was any damned good? I'm telling Cass what Dale said, Mom. It's called an indirect quote. And for your information, I can make up my own mind about people." This rebuttal took it out of her, apparently, and she flopped back, giving her painkiller button several angry clicks.

"Whoa, there," I said, tugging on the cord and striving for a light tone. "It's for meds, not Morse code."

"Yeah, well if you two are gonna be such pains in the ass I gotta max this thing out."

How I got to be numbered with the transgressors was a mystery to me, but I chalked it up to pre-partum insanity. We all stared at the television and, after a decent interval, I tried again. "It was nice of… Dale…to be concerned, I guess. How are you feeling about everything, by the way?"

"Everything what?" she said maddeningly.

When I rolled my eyes, Mrs. Stern looked pleased and went so far as to smile around the cigarette in her mouth before Nadina yelled, "No fucking smoking, Mom!"

"Watch your language!" retorted Mrs. Stern. She whisked the cigarette out nonetheless and stuffed it back in the mashed pack.

"Everything everything," I rejoined. "The birthing plan we drew up. Do you still want me to take Ned home from the hospital when he's got the okay, or have you changed your mind?"

"How many times do I have to say, Cass?" Her voice rose into a whine. "Are you changing your mind—want me to give him to Mike? This was all your friggin' idea—me having this baby. I should keep him myself and make you pay child support—'cause it's all your friggin' fault—"

I shouldn't have asked. What was the point of the epidural, if not to spare Mrs. Stern and me this in-labor abuse?

"Don't come crying to me if you're gonna have Mike and his sorry-ass dad breathing down your neck the rest of your life," Nadina carried on. She seemed to be gaining in volume and energy, and I stole an anxious look at the monitor. "If I'd just gotten rid of it like Mike wanted, it woulda been hella easier on everyone. Especially me right now!"

"Yes," I conceded, finally goaded into responding. "But you'd still be stuck with Mike then, waiting for the other shoe to drop."

"What shoe?" demanded Nadina. "What shoe? We were doing fine—" But then, thanks be to God: "Crap!" she shrieked. "I think I just peed my pants!"

Her mother and I sprang up. "You can't pee your pants," I pointed out. "You're catheterized. Your water must have broken."

Things went very fast after that. In rushed the nurse, shortly followed by the birthing team. Mrs. Stern and I tried to stay out of the way, but whenever we backed up too far, Nadina bellowed at us to get our asses back over there, and where did we think we were going?

I had friends who were copacetic enough during birth to watch the process in a mirror, but when a nurse offered Nadina the option she squealed, "Are you fucking kidding me? Like I wanna see my body ripped in two—that's why my head is up on this end, dumb-ass—call the drug man—I think the epidural ran out—Aaaaahh!"

Heart hammering, I clutched my elbows, praying silently while Nadina sweated through each contraction. Mrs. Stern looked like she could really, really use that cigarette about now and had resorted to gnawing on her fingernails.

But once the doctor gave Nadina permission to push, it didn't take long. Four, five concentrated efforts, the last to the soundtrack of Nadina shouting every cuss word in the book ("Nobody—told me—about—the fucking—shoulders!"). Those same shoulders were the worst of it, and out, at last, slid Ned.

"A boy," announced the doctor, holding him up after the cord was cut, in all his slick, red, bawling splendor.

"You were expecting maybe a walrus?" demanded Nadina wearily, falling back against her pillows.

. . .

I slid my paper cup away and checked my watch. Midnight. Only one other person was still keeping vigil in the hospital cafeteria by this time, and we nodded at each other as I rose.

Time to go home.

But my feet, instead of heading for the elevator, took me back toward Nadina's recovery room. When I peeked in, she was snoozing away, mouth open, pale and exhausted. Her mother lay curled on the narrow futon against the wall, also passed out. For some reason, the sight of them choked me up. Maybe it was that Nadina looked so very young. Or that there was no anxious, hovering husband to pet her hair and tell her how well she'd done. Or that there was no newborn baby struggling against its swaddling beside her.

When the doctor asked if Nadina wanted to hold the baby before they washed him up, she burst into tears, shaking her head and mumbling incoherently. Mrs. Stern jabbed a finger at me: "That's the adoptive mom—you leave my girl alone now." She flew to cradle her daughter's head, and for once Nadina didn't rebuff her. Feeling out of place and emotional myself, I tried to hover unobtrusively, only to have one of the nurses deposit the newborn Ned in my arms, fresh from his wipe-down.

"Then you'll be the one wanting to bond with him," she murmured. "Sorry about that—we have the paperwork, but you know the doctors just come in and do the delivery—"

"Oh, it's all right," I said, not really hearing her—I was too distracted by the new bit of squirming humanity I held. Good heavens. I forgot how small they were—and Ned wasn't nearly so small as Min had been—how small and puffy and blind-seeming. Oh, Lord. What on earth was I doing?

The nurse beckoned me to follow her. The next part was blurry: a battery of tests, needle pricks, umbilical cord care, diapering, a swaddling demonstration, a bottle thrust in my hand. I held Ned for a couple hours. Bonding. We were supposed to be bonding. Because that was what parents did with babies.

Joanie texted me. I texted her back. She could do all the announcing.

It was only when the nurse on the next shift asked me if I wasn't tired or hungry that I realized I was, in fact, both. She took Ned from me, away to the nursery, and sent me down to the cafeteria. "He's in great shape. Mom better go take care of herself now."

So here I was, fed, if not rested. I would go home to my bed and come back for Ned in the morning.

"Sleep," I whispered to Nadina and Mrs. Stern now. "That was probably the easy part."

My steps took me one last time past the nursery, where I found Ned wriggling in his little acrylic bassinet. Not only was he a good two pounds heavier than my daughter had been at birth, but from the looks of it, most of that weight was in his head. He also had a cap of dark blond hair, where Min's had been black.

I swallowed against the lump in my throat. Poor little Minnie. What is your mother doing? How exactly did I get here?

This was so different.

I had kept Min with me from the get-go. No nursery for her. She had only gone as far away as the bedside bassinet when Troy insisted I try to get some sleep.

That was then, this was now.

A whole different reality.

"Good night, Neddy. See you tomorrow."

Turning slowly on my heel, I made my way out of the hospital.

CHAPTER 15:

Be My Guest

A soft "eh—eh—eh—" woke me. I'd been dreaming about Benny the dog chasing a squirrel round and round the towering cedar in the backyard. Finally he sat at the base, barking. A bark that gradually morphed into "eh—eh—eh—eh—"

A full five minutes passed where I didn't move a muscle, hoping against hope that Ned would go back to sleep. We'd already been up once that night, after all, for a goodly two hours, and I felt like I just succeeded in drifting off before the dreaded sound came again.

Really—this single mom thing—had I thought this through? A memory rushed in: Troy and me, sleep-deprived and at our wits' end, hissing at each other in the darkness—"You get her." "No, you." "Your turn." "What if we just let her cry?" "She only weighs seven pounds! We can't let her cry." "Then you get her." And so on. At least, as a single mom, I could drag myself out of bed without resentment. There was no one else to do it.

Throwing back the covers, I managed a sitting position on the edge of the mattress. Sure enough, there were Ned's little fists waving in the air, just visible over the side of the bassinet. He was only nine days old—could he help it if his body clock was still reversed? Snoozing all day and awake and hungry at night. Min had been awake around the clock, restless and fussy until she was three months old. Ned, on the other hand, was largely content. He either slept or was hungry. Two modes, two moods. Like a man, I supposed.

I glanced at the clock and saw it was only five in the morning. Rats. That meant, once Ned was fed and changed and started getting sleepy, the rest of the Palace would be waking up. And I mean the rest. We were stuffed to the gills with visitors, not even counting those who would probably put in an appearance once it was a decent hour. My parents, upon hearing of the birth, had flown up immediately and were camped in the nursery; Perry drove down from Bellingham having finagled something akin to family leave and was out in the Lean-To in Daniel's spare bedroom; and then, to everyone's astonishment, when Angela Martin called to wish Daniel a happy birthday and heard the baby sounds in the background, she booked a ticket on the Amtrak Cascades and squeezed herself into Joanie's bedroom. ("How can this be happening to me?" Joanie demanded of the universe. "My mother and Darla in the same weekend?")

It was the fear of Ned getting louder and waking everyone up that finally got me upright. Reason to be thankful number two: when you adopt a baby, there isn't any horrible recovery period after childbirth. Flicking on the light, I padded over. I might have been tired and irritable, but when I saw him I couldn't help but smile. He had completely unwound his blanket and was kicking energetically in his little cotton sleeper, both pleased and startled by the thumping noises he generated. Although his mouth was working, he was content enough until he caught sight of me, whereupon his little round face screwed up and he let out a hearty wail.

"Okay, okay, shhhh…" I soothed, taking him in my arms, fingers fanned out behind his heavy head. Joanie called him Baby Melonhead and thought he looked like the football-noggined kid on *South Park*, but I liked that Ned was a moose. Better that he take after Nadina than dainty little Mike.

An hour later I was kicking back in the glider, one leg tucked under me, a full, burped, changed Ned resting in the triangle of my knee. He did not appear to be the least bit sleepy, and I was fully awake myself now, singing softly to him as it grew lighter in the living room. "Your eyes aren't as dark today," I told him. "Though maybe that's because you never have them open when the sun is up." Those same eyes crossed slightly to have my face so near. "When your grammy gets up," I continued, "I'm going to take a shower. Be thankful for your blurry vision because I am a sight to behold this morning."

"I don't know—a little rumpled maybe, and not as much on as you usually have, but you'll do."

Muffling a shriek, I grabbed Ned to my chest, the better to cover the inadequate straps of my pajama tank top, and untucked my leg to cross it over the other. Ned was such a little hot lump that I hadn't bothered putting on a robe when I got up, and the threadbare shorts from my alma mater felt suddenly inadequate. "You're up early," I said tersely, aware of the hot blush washing over me. Could bare legs blush? If they could, I was sure mine did.

"Your siren song drew me," said Daniel. He was standing in the doorway leading to the kitchen, sipping the coffee I'd made. "I never can decide if my favorite verse is the horn on the bus or the mommies on the bus." Or the horndog ogling the mommies, in his case.

Outwardly I said nothing, fiddling instead with Ned's blanket and rocking nervously.

"And maybe you could explain," he continued, coming to sit leisurely on the arm of the sofa, "why Ned is practically mummified in clothes and blankets, while you barely have a stitch on."

"Babies can't maintain a steady body heat like adults," I choked. When I saw the amused twist of his mouth I wished I had chosen my words more carefully, but he let them lie. Daniel, for his part, didn't seem to have any problem putting out body heat. When he reached to rub Ned's blond hair I made a conscious effort not to shrink back.

"I'd ask to hold him for a minute," said Daniel, "but God forbid I should take him and expose your clavicles."

"Oh, shut up," I grumped.

This made him laugh. "You must have been up a lot last night—where's your witty repartee? It's one of the things I most enjoy about you, Cass." Yes, I could picture that on the Rolodex card he kept for me. Strengths: witty repartee, likes books, cleans up after me. Weaknesses: frequently grouchy, has a thing for monogamy and Jesus.

"Another thing being your generosity," he went on, seeing I wasn't going to answer. At my questioning look, he said, "What with Ned's arrival and all our visitors, I haven't had a chance to thank you and Joanie for that shortbread you brought me at the office."

"For crying out loud, Daniel," I burst out. "When most people have an embarrassing incident, they don't usually bring it up again later. We all politely pretend it didn't happen."

"Pretend *what* didn't happen?"

I glared at him. He really was going to do this. It hadn't been too hard, in the fullness of the last week and a half, to push my romantic woes to the back of my mind, but apparently it was time to drag them out and inspect them. I gritted my teeth. "Pretend that Joanie and I didn't interrupt you, mid-seduction."

"Oh. Is that what it was?" he asked innocently.

"Well," I said, feeling my blood pressure rising, "that would be my first guess. I suppose it could also have been some kind of physical therapy session. Or…she was the office ergonomic specialist and needed to check the pitch of your chair—with you in it. Or…maybe she was just a clumsy client—she tried to leave the room with her colleagues, but her foot caught on the plastic chair mat and she collapsed into your lap, clutching at your tie. What does it matter? It's none of our business. It's Kristen you should be explaining yourself to."

"As it happens, even if I had been doing something underhand at the office, I wouldn't have to explain myself to Kristen because we'd already called it quits."

Oh! So Joanie was right and Phyl was wrong. I guess Daniel would have to get his thigh massages elsewhere, then. I'm sure Catherine Zeta-Jones would be happy to lend a hand.

"I bring it up," Daniel continued, when I didn't say anything, "because you and Joanie were upset."

"Joanie. You mean Joanie was upset," I insisted. "If you recall, she was the one throwing things and yelling—not me—it's her feathers that need smoothing."

"I did try," he answered mildly. "And apart from telling me she'd had it with me for being such a player and that I was going to die alone, a dirty old man, that was all I could get out of her."

Thank goodness. I would have to thank Joanie later for keeping her mouth shut.

"All right then, Cass. Let's say you weren't upset—just Joanie. May I just say, for the record, that it wasn't what it looked like? You've met all my...girlfriends. That woman in the office was a potential client. When everyone else left after the meeting, she hung back, and the next thing I knew, she was on my lap. I hadn't asked for that—hadn't done anything to give her that idea—but given that I'd just spent the last two hours trying to get them on board, I had to be careful how I set her straight. And believe me, Cass, I was planning on setting her straight."

Unwillingly, I raised my eyes to his and something very much like hope fluttered in my breast. Why was he telling me this? Was Phyl wrong, and he still felt something for me? Or was this just his general tendency to work things through when they got out of kilter? He already tried to have it out with his sister, after all. You would think, with all the trouble women caused him, he would be more leery of them. Not that that would necessarily help. It was disconcerting that, everywhere he went, Daniel basically had to fight women off with a club. But did it matter, so long as he did, in fact, fight them off?

My blush returned under his steady gaze, and wild thoughts of laying Ned gently down on the rug and flinging myself at this man tempted me. He might send me packing as well, but maybe first he'd give me a real, world-exploding kiss for old time's sake. Daniel smiled slowly at me—my thoughts being perhaps too easily read—his eyes drifting downward from my face to my neck, shoulders, clavicles—until they stopped rather pointedly at my chest.

I expected more subtlety out of him, but given my mood I thought I could let it slide. When Daniel raised his finger and pointed toward that same chest, however, that was too much even for me. "Do you mind?" I asked, hunching my shoulders protectively. Bad move. I felt a warm trickle run down my sternum. "Euuurrgh!" I cried, pulling Ned off me. Bad move number two. Separating us only released his little pool of spit-up to run more freely down my shirt.

"Here—hold him while I get a towel," I ordered, thrusting the baby at Daniel.

When I returned from the kitchen adequately wiped down, I burst out laughing to see that he was still holding Ned exactly as he had received him—hanging straight down by the armpits like a foosball figure. It made Ned easier to wipe off, at any rate, and kept his big head from lolling around too much. "I could really use that shower now," I joked.

"You don't smell as pleasant as you normally do, I grant you," said Daniel, lowering Ned enough to rest him on his knee.

This was how my mother found us, grinning at each other, me leaning toward him in a tank top not only scanty but damp. "Good morning, C—good heavens! Oh, hello, Daniel. You're up early. Why don't I take Neddy, and Daniel you can go eat some breakfast, and Cass you can go get—get decent." She laughed nervously and whispered as she passed, "What were you thinking, running around like that?"

"I was thinking it was only six in the morning," I muttered, suddenly reminded of the time when I was eleven years old and phoned Brian Duarte so many times in one day that Mrs. Duarte "had a word" with my mother. Only when I was halfway up the stairs did I look back. Over my mother's shoulder, Daniel's eyes met my embarrassed ones.

He dropped me a wink.

• • •

Apart from the nights spent in his bassinet, I think Ned spent every other minute of the next few days in someone's arms.

When I came down from my shower, only Angela Martin and my mother were in the kitchen, Angela having wrested the snoozing Ned from Mom. Mrs. Martin was immaculate as ever in her white Capri pants and sleeveless ice blue tank top, and it went without saying that Ned would never think to spit up on her. "Fathers are overrated," she was telling Mom. They were deep in conversation and only nodded at me as I went to get my bowl of cereal. "Other than providing a paycheck—some of them—they generally do more harm than good. Cass will manage just fine. I did, after Karl left. I'm so proud of Daniel and Joan."

I knew Mom didn't agree in the least bit about the benefits of fatherlessness but was trying to be diplomatic, murmuring, "How old were the children when he left?"

"Daniel was in kindergarten and Joan just a baby. Karl loathed babies," Angela explained, as if babies were a variety of repugnant vegetable. "After Daniel was born he went on a real bender—I hardly saw him for months. And then little Joan was just the last straw. All that crying and mess and me losing my figure for a while."

"Oh! Yes. Well then, you probably were better off without such a person."

"My only regret," continued Mrs. Martin carelessly, "was not having him on hand when Joan went through her teenage rebellion. I can't say she's ever really come out of it. You know mothers and daughters—Daniel was fine, but Joan—!"

"Do you still have any contact with Karl?" asked Mom hastily, to cover my incredulous snort.

"Not a bit. I think the last time I heard from him was when Joan was engaged to her first fiancé. Somehow he'd gotten wind of it and had some crazy idea that he should give her away at her wedding, but fortunately she called it quits before I decided how to handle it. I sent Karl a two-word postcard: 'It's off.' He didn't bother with her next two engagements."

Good thing Joanie slept in. If she were to come down before this rehearsal of her misadventures in love ended, there would be fur flying.

"Has he remarried?" asked Mom.

"You mean to say, how many times has he remarried," said Angela dryly. "Joan must have inherited her misplaced faith in the institution from him. Karl may be on his third, fourth wife now, and God knows how many children that man has spawned. It never ceases to amaze me how some women persist in thinking they can change a man."

When Mom and Mrs. Martin headed out for a morning walk, Ned did a stint napping in Dad's arms, then on to Phyl. Daniel reappeared with Perry, and the sound of their banter eventually drew Joanie downstairs. She darted quick glances around but visibly relaxed when she saw neither her mother nor Darla. "Lemme hold him, Phyl," she said, prodding her.

Phyl raised an eyebrow but handed Ned over, Joanie fumbling with the burp cloth and letting his head roll down while she maladroitly tried to tuck him in the crook of her arm. Ned, true to form, kept on sleeping, but Perry let out a guffaw. "Whoa, Nurse Joanie! What's a baby gotta do to get some neck support?"

Joanie might claim to be over my brother and have gone out twice with Craig Sloane to prove it, but she colored up nonetheless. "With a head this size, he's gonna need flying buttresses."

Ned made one of those funny baby grimaces, and Perry shook his head, tsk-tsking. "Look, you hurt his feelings. Better hand him over, you cruel amateur."

For his part, having grown up as we did with many younger cousins, Perry was no baby neophyte, and he expertly whisked Ned away. "Show-off," I scoffed, watching him flip Ned onto his forearm, chest-down, head in his palm. "Watch out—you're gonna make him barf on your foot."

"You think he still has some in there?" asked Daniel.

"Plenty more—it's a loaves and fishes thing with babies," I said. "Two ounces in, four ounces out. I estimate Ned only nailed me with an ounce, max."

"Maybe it was the curved surface that made it look like so much more," said Daniel.

My reaction to this outrageous comment escaped notice, fortunately, because Dad spoke up. "What's the latest news from the lawyer, Hon? Did the little guy have to have a blood draw for the paternity test?"

"Oh, they stuck Neddy with all kinds of needles in the hospital," I answered. "At least Mike's was just lost in the crowd. Lori Lincoln said that we should hear any day that Mike has filed his paternity affidavit with the court, which means we would have sixty days from then to convince him to terminate his parental rights. After that, we have to go to court to make the judge do it."

"And?" prodded Dad. "Has she made any effort to convince them that taking you to court would be pointless?"

"They don't see it that way," I said grimly. "Lori said she got nowhere with Mike's defender. He went on about how Mike's felony convictions don't even play into it, since they weren't for crimes against Nadina or Ned, and how Mike probably won't have to serve the high end of his sentence because of his good behavior, blah blah blah-duh-dee-dah."

Dad frowned. "No judge in his right mind is going to give a baby to Mike, Cass. This is a stressful situation, but it isn't a hopeless one."

The subject of all this scrutiny gave an exaggerated yawn while Perry rubbed his back. It was after nine now. I should probably start heating another bottle.

"Certainly the burden is on Mike," said Daniel. "He has to convince the judge that the child would be better off with him, convicted felon that he is, albeit reformed. Not only that, but he also has to prove that he could support a child financially."

"I don't know how he'd manage to do that," I admitted, feeling slightly cheered by their confidence. "After all, the only job I've known him to hold for any length of time was the one you and Ray Snow got him." Ray Snow—Daniel's aging, recording-studio-owning, rocker client. With Daniel's help, I had persuaded Ray to take Mike on as the studio lackey, a job he managed to hold and enjoy for four months before he imploded. "Even that was for minimum wage. Coming fresh out of prison I don't think anyone's going to offer Mike six figures."

Opening the fridge, I stared absently at the shelf of condiments. "I sure wish Lori thought everything was going to come up roses. Every time I talk to her it's like a cold water bath. Like, hmmm, Cass sounds borderline cheerful today—let's turn the Reality hose on her, make her feel dumb and depressed and then bill her for it."

Phyl, clearly worried about the energy I was wasting staring at an open refrigerator, pulled out one of the last bottles of prepared formula the hospital gave me and shut the door for me. "I'll do it," she said. "You sit down."

Daniel drew one of the barstools out for me with his foot. "Cass, it's Lori's job to think hard and objectively about your case. That's what you're paying her for—to anticipate all the possible moves on the board and make you aware of them. She's not there to coddle you."

"You can say that again." I bit my lip. Lori Lincoln was one intimidating lady, but she'd come to me on Daniel's referral, after all, and I didn't want to sound ungrateful. "I'm sure she's a brilliant lawyer, bedside manner aside. But are you absolutely positive she isn't holding a secret grudge against you and taking it out on me?"

"Grudge for what?" Daniel asked, amused.

It seemed like every eye in the room was on us. And why not? Apart from Dad and Daniel himself, everyone else knew I had a thing for my dear landlord. From Joanie's calculating expression I knew she was wondering if I'd decided to forgive and forget the office lap-dance incident.

"Oh…I don't know," I said evasively. "Maybe she suffered unrequited love for you…? You did say you two were never an item."

"Have you seen that rock on her finger?" he laughed. "I imagine that would have helped her get over anyone, much less me."

"Besides, Daniel never lets any love for him go unrequited," put in Joanie. Apparently she was still sore about Catherine Zeta-Jones. "Tit for tat—that's his motto."

Daniel's eyes flicked over to his snotty sister—a warning in them—and then back to me. "If Lori was ever in love with me she wouldn't have made a secret of it. She's not shy, as you can imagine, and pretty in touch with her feelings."

"That's because she doesn't have many to keep track of," I grumbled.

"Well, what ones she does possess don't frighten her, at least," he returned evenly.

My fingers curled around one of the barstool's forged-steel back spindles. Frightened? My feelings didn't frighten me! Certainly not my feelings for the likes of him. I guess I had miscounted, however. It appeared that, of everyone in the room, my father was the only one who didn't suspect me of having a thing for Daniel. Even Daniel thought I had a thing for Daniel. Which I did. But curse his enormous ego for detecting it! This sucked. He needed some deflating.

"I'm perfectly happy to join Lori Lincoln's fan club," I rejoined in a cool voice, rising to take the warmed bottle from Phyl and handing it to my brother. "So long as she can get me Ned. If that happens, my faith in you and your recommendations will be completely restored."

Daniel rapped his coffee mug down on the counter. "Fair enough." He reached for his car keys. "Cheer up, though. If Lori and I turn out to be worthless, Ned will survive. Remember *Great Expectations*? Think how well Pip did, having a convict for a benefactor."

Glaring, I sputtered, "Oh! I see. So if Mike is Magwitch, am I some kind of Miss Havisham?"

("There they go again," murmured Phyl.)

That mocking smile. "You are rather...loony," he conceded, "but given that you haven't worn the same outfit for decades, plotted baroque revenge and set yourself on fire, I admit the analogy starts to break down."

"Give her a few more years," spoke up my worthless brother.

"If I set anyone on fire, it'll be Darla," I retorted under my breath, but I think Daniel must have heard me because the twist of his mouth grew more pronounced. Men!

"Only a male writer would have a woman go berserk because she didn't get married," I returned scornfully. "Considering what a low-down, double-crossing fiancé she had, Miss Havisham should have spent the rest of her life rejoicing over her narrow escape!"

"Hmm..." Daniel pretended to ponder this as he patted his pockets for his wallet and phone, the smug beast. "Well, an interesting possibility. But, rejoicing or embittered, that still means she spent the rest of her long and sad little life obsessing over the One That Got Away."

With which annoying comment, he headed out for his day's activities.

CHAPTER 16:

Too Close for Comfort

"Mmmm…jasmine. Unorthodox, but my favorite." Drawing in one more luxurious breath, I set the potted plant beside its more conventional fellows on the counter. There were roses from Free Universe (or just James, I imagined—I'm not sure Riley even knew flowers existed), carnations from Louella, a sunflower from Camden School, hydrangeas from Phyl's sister Mary.

"And Bryson chose these for you," said Skandar, whipping a straggly handful of tiny yellow daisies from behind his back. "He was upset that I was going to visit without him, but I told him he might be too much for a newborn at this point."

"Thank you." Relief flooded me as I took the proffered bouquet. It was bad enough that I would have to explain Skandar's presence to my family and Angela Martin, without having his overly-fond adoptive son clinging to me. "Skandar, these are my parents, Larry and Margaret McKean, and my brother Perry there. And this is Angela Martin, my housemates' mother. Umm…everyone, this is Skandar Sebari, a friend from the whole adoption process."

Having never mentioned him to anyone but Joanie or Phyl, I wasn't surprised to see the uncurious looks and polite handshakes Skandar received, although my mother did twitch slightly over the ponytail. They assumed he was only an acquaintance. At least it was lunchtime on a weekday. No arch looks from Joanie to combat or worries over what Daniel might think.

I hoped this was one of those courtesy visits, and seeing that, before he rang the doorbell, we were just sitting down to eat, I hastened to do the whole Ned dog-and-pony show so Skandar could be on his way.

Clearly, he had other expectations.

"Very handsome," he said, after looking Ned over. "Good set of lungs?"

"I don't know, actually," I admitted. "He doesn't cry very often—more of the strong, silent type, I guess."

"And you? Are you getting any sleep?"

"I can't complain. He only gets me up once or twice a night—for an hour at a time, unfortunately, but not too bad, considering how young he is."

Skandar leaned toward me, resting his fingertips for an instant on my wrist. "You look tired, though." It was a gesture of misleading intimacy, I thought in amazement, and I only made it more suspect by blushing.

"We were just about to eat, Mr. Se—Mr.—" said my mother faintly. She was clutching my father's hand in surprise. Her face read plainly: Who is this unknown man touching my daughter's wrist? "Cass, why don't you get a plate for him?"

Now I was in for it. I waited a beat, giving Skandar an opportunity to excuse himself, but when he didn't I hinted, "Of course—but I bet you need to get back to the office. You probably have a few errands to run, not just this one."

He shrugged. "Actually, just this one."

Taking the plate I handed him, he nodded his thanks to Perry, who moved down the bench seat, and joined us as if he belonged there.

In my lifetime ranking of uncomfortable meals, Skandar figured in several of them, and this one held its own. With my mother raising her eyebrows at me, I felt compelled to explain who on earth Skandar was and how we knew each other. Katherine's death I glossed over with almost disrespectful haste, but the murmured expressions of sympathy poured out nonetheless—Skandar's least favorite topic, of course—and I saw his jaw set in a hard line. Argh. Then the downhill slide really picked up speed because, when Perry heard about Katherine's ex Reiner and his acting aspirations, my brother tactlessly let his enthusiasm show, peppering Skandar with questions (all answered monosyllabically) about mutual connections, agents, auditions, and Reiner's actress girlfriend.

"Perry!" I broke in, finally, seeing that Skandar had stopped eating altogether and now sat back with his arms folded stiffly. "This salad could use a little more dressing. Any chance you could whip up some of your vinaigrette?"

The blockhead glanced in puzzlement at his perfectly-dressed salad, but before he could frame a protest, my mother blurted, "Oh, yes— too dry altogether," and he was forced to get up.

For once I was grateful for Angela Martin's presence: when she discovered Skandar's background she took us on a lengthy excursus into Persian history to which only he had anything to contribute. That was fine, and so was the discussion of Iranian cuisine and the place she knew about in Portland where you could get rosewater ice cream. Then followed politics—my father worked in one comment about the Shah—and religion. Apparently Mrs. Martin had dabbled in Zoroastrianism before becoming a born-right-the-first-time atheist.

"And you?" Angela asked. Skandar was eating again, finding religious dilettantism a more agreeable topic than his dead wife's ex-husband.

He paused, his eyes sliding my direction but stopping short. "I have no objection to religion."

This was news to me. I didn't think 'hostile' was too strong a word to apply to him.

Angela looked surprised for a different reason. "Oh! I thought that, as a friend of Cass, you were the religious type. Cass is *very* religious." She bestowed a deprecating smile on me, as if she had just pointed out a beloved pet dog who, sad to say, suffered from bouts of mange.

I bit the inside of my lip. Without Joanie there to rail at her mother, or Daniel to deflect her gently, I was on my own.

Skandar was unfazed. "She is. To say the least. I found it…off-putting…at first, but since she's stopped brandishing religion like a weapon I've decided it's not so terrible." I made strangling sounds. What wasn't so terrible? Religion? Me? Nor did I appreciate his word choice—"brandishing"! My indignation didn't seem to register because he continued calmly, "I've started to think that, if you don't go overboard, there's no harm in religion. And probably much comfort."

Another silence. Should I make some comment about how faith was not the same thing for me as religion? Or would this be considered weapons re-armament? I was sure to botch it anyhow. That, and I now discovered a heretofore unknown desire rearing its head: I wanted Angela Martin to like me. Because she was Daniel's mother.

"Hmm…" she smiled. "One might as easily take comfort in Greek mythology or the Saturday morning cartoons."

I suppose this barb didn't qualify as a conversation-killer, since this particular conversation always had one foot in the grave, but it certainly caused a relapse.

I cleared my throat. "I'm sorry if I came across…aggressive," I said to Skandar. "I meant it out of concern—not zealotry."

He shrugged. It was hard to get beyond the thought that, no matter what he did or said, he didn't give a damn anymore about most things. Bryson aside. And sure enough, his next words were, "But I took Bryson to church last weekend—for the hell of it." He nodded at me. "Maybe to get a busybody neighbor off my back. Bry had a great time at the Sunday school. I don't know how I feel about that."

"Yes, tell us about your son," urged my father, throwing out a conversational float ring. He laid a hand on my shoulder.

That topic got us through the rest of lunch, thank God. And Neddy woke up and had to be fed and dealt with. And Skandar finally, finally, headed back to his office or to sit at his desk and stare at the wall. It didn't matter which—I just wanted him to leave.

After lunch, Dad took one look at Mom's face and suggested he and Perry go outside to tinker with Perry's car. My mother and Angela for once didn't have their usual polite tussle over who got to hold Ned, my mother practically thrusting him in Angela's arms. And though I tried to escape detection by going to clean the Lean-To, Mom was right on my heels.

"Sweetheart," she began, taking an extra dustcloth from me so she could work alongside, "You're an adult, of course, and I generally stay out of your dating life—"

"I don't have a dating life," I interrupted preemptively. "I haven't been on a date since James broke up with me in March."

"But I hope you might share with me a little," she went on, right over the top of me. "That man today—I wouldn't have thought you were interested in him—especially after how I saw you looking at Daniel the other morning—"

"Mother!" I protested.

"Am I right? You care for Daniel now? I always did think more highly of him than you did, but are you sure about this? It worries me a little that he doesn't share your faith, though he seems to be genuine in his concern for you, and open to—"

"I'm sorry to keep interrupting," I said, "but I don't think I'm ready to talk about this. Yes, I like Daniel more than I used to, but like a friend—like a brother," I lied. To my amazement, she didn't look relieved. "It's moot anyhow, Mom, because he's making the dating rounds again. Just—please—don't bring this up with anyone. Like Angela, I mean."

"Why would I mention it to Angela?" Mom replied. "It's just that, now that you have Ned—it would be so nice if you married again. Maybe not to Daniel, but to another nice man. It would be like Skandar coming into Bryson's life—Ned would never remember a time when that person was not around."

As if I hadn't thought of all these things already! I got it, I got it—everyone in the whole stinking world thought I should get married, on the double. Snatching her dustcloth, I wadded it up and threw it with mine into the laundry room. Then I headed upstairs to strip the bed. Mom followed.

"You would at least say you prefer Daniel to this Skandar, wouldn't you?" she persisted.

I gave her a pillow to uncover. "Yes…" More true than I wanted to admit. I felt a twitch of rebellion in my gut. A desire to needle her for meddling. "Though, if I were considering Skandar in that light, he has some definite advantages over Daniel. For one thing, he has a track record of commitment—" (with an asterisk by his score for homewrecking, but no need to go into that here) "—and he's good with kids, and he's even fine with the whole church thing!" Not that Daniel wasn't.

"Mmm…"

"He's also been through a tragedy of his own," I continued, giving the fresh pillowcase a snap and holding it out to her. "We have a kind of shared experience. It was part of what made James and me incompatible—nothing awful had ever happened to James. And look at Daniel! What a golden life he's led. I don't think he's ever had a moment of inconvenience, much less suffering! Maybe the occasional toothache or—possibly, a Charley horse when he got too carried away humping someone."

"Cassandra Judith McKean!"

But I was on a tear. "Am I wrong?" I stomped into the bathroom to fetch the cleaning supplies bucket. Phyl made us use some non-sudsing, eco-friendly scouring powder, and taking the can in both hands, I shook it vigorously over the shower stall as if it were the neck of every well-wisher in my life.

"There are no easy solutions to my situation, Mom. Certainly none with a particular man's name on it."

"Did I say there was?"

"Not in so many words. You heavily implied it." The cleaning powder settled in drifts which I began to attack furiously. Mom was silent then, and, without turning around, I could picture her face: tentative, concerned. Fighting was uncharacteristic for us. And really, I was punishing her because she was unwise enough to be the fifth or so person to say the same thing to me.

Sighing, I threw down the scouring pad and turned to face her. "I'm sorry, Mom. I'm biting your head off. Believe me—I'm not opposed to getting married again and Ned having a father, but I don't just want to force someone into that slot, even if I could. How would you feel if I told you I *was* going to marry Daniel?"

She took refuge in cleaning the mirror. "I—I—I think your father and I would be glad for you, on the whole."

I shut my eyes against the temptation to roll them. "Oh, Mom. If I'd brought someone like Daniel home in college, you would have disowned me. Admit it. An atheist playboy? But now he'll do—desperate times calling for desperate measures and all. Pulse? Check. Solid marriage material."

Flustered, Mom was squirting the homemade Windex over every surface in sight. Daniel's bathroom would certainly be the cleaner for our distracted state. "Be fair, Cass. Daniel has more than a pulse. He's intelligent, educated, respects you and your decisions. I'm not sure the atheist label still holds—I heard him crack some Bible-related joke with your dad—"

"What—so now that makes him Martin Luther?" I muttered.

"I thought you liked him, Honey. I was trying to tell you that I would be okay with that. I have no idea how this discussion went so off-track. And it's unfair of you to say I think just any warm body would do. If you told me you were going to marry this Skandar person, who I never even met or heard of until today, I would have plenty of misgivings."

"Whatever for?" I demanded contrarily. "You don't even know him."

"He seems…hardened. Inflexible."

Exactly what I thought, but I had abandoned rationality this afternoon. "He's grieving! He just lost his wife! Can you blame him for getting all stiff when he has to talk about it? And when Perry has to go on and on with all kinds of excited questions about his dead wife's ex?"

"Yes, well," Mom didn't try to debate Perry's mistakes. "But that's not it, exactly. I sense he was probably like that even before all these things happened to him. Skandar would be fine as a friend, but if you were ever to marry him, I'm not sure you would find yourself on equal footing. Look at the dismissive way he talked about your faith."

The fact that Mom wasn't saying anything I didn't think myself didn't help matters. If anything, it was more annoying—like sitting in an echo chamber of my own anxieties. Two opposing facts were becoming clearer and clearer to me, however: firstly, that, outlandish as it might seem, Skandar wanted something from me, relationship-wise; and secondly, that even though he wanted something from me, he deep down didn't give a damn about me.

I unhooked the flexible shower head to rinse the remaining grit down the drain, but my mind was elsewhere. (Daniel must have wondered the next morning whether I'd tried to convert his shower stall into a sandbox for Ned.) If Skandar had cared about me, I would have felt obligated to avoid him and tell him I didn't share his feelings. But since he didn't, it would be odd to bring it up. What would I say? "I know you're not in love with me, but—just FYI—I'm not in love with you either"? Or, "I have a sinking feeling you're considering me as a stepmom for your son, even though you barely know me or like me"? Ugh.

Though we finished cleaning the Lean-To in silence, our minds must have continued down their parallel tracks because, as I finished folding the linens and moved the second load to the dryer, Mom dropped one last rock in the pond. "I think, Cass, he's had his share of 'inconveniences,' if not outright unhappiness."

No need to ask her who she was referring to.

When I didn't respond, she added, "It's not easy for a boy to grow up without a father. Don't give me that look, Cass! I'm not talking about Baby Ned this time. I meant Daniel. Having your father abandon the family makes a mark on a person. It's no wonder he and Joanie haven't gotten married yet."

I considered this. Joanie mentioned her father only as an absence in her life, and, apart from the one time when he admitted cluelessness with power tools, Daniel had never, ever referred to Karl Martin. Abandonment was a death, of sorts.

Out loud I said only, "Hmmph," prodding Mom out the door and locking it behind us. So, okay, I would grant him some suffering credit. But thank heavens there were plenty of women interested in helping Daniel Martin heal.

Angela burst in the front door just as we came in the back, and I heard the thuds and clunks of her wrestling the stroller back inside. She had succeeded by the time Mom and I hurried over, and all the jostling had its usual effect on the sleeping Ned: that is, none.

"Would you believe it? The nerve!" declared Mrs. Martin. A lock of her sleek white hair had detached from her chignon, and to my surprise, she appeared flushed.

"Oh, what is it, Angela? Did Larry or my son say something to upset you?"

"What? No, no. They're not even out there—they went to the auto parts store, I think." She whipped around and pointed a beautifully-manicured finger at me. "Cass, have you received any notices for sex offenders living in the neighborhood?"

Her question was so unexpected I could only stare.

"Were you—harassed by someone on your walk, Angela?" Mom asked.

"Yes, I was! And I'm going to call the police this instant. Ned and I were taking a little stroll through the neighborhood, but after a few blocks I noticed this car driving really slowly behind me. I turned and looked straight at the driver, so he sped off. But not ten minutes later I saw him go by slowly again. Well, that was enough for me. I wasn't going to stand for this creeping and lurking. When he pulled up at the stop sign, I parked the stroller and ran over to go get a hard look at him for a police description, but before I could reach the car, he took off through the stop. This other driver had to slam on his brakes! Not only is that man a menace and a predator—he's also dangerous behind the wheel."

"We haven't received any notices," I put in, when she paused for breath. I was fighting an urge to giggle. "Maybe he just found you attractive, Angela. You beautiful people. It would be the highlight of my day if a car slowed down to check me out."

The two women eyed me disapprovingly.

"This is no joking matter, Cass," Angela rebuked me. "You have a child to think of now. You can't have people like that running around your neighborhood. Why they let these sex offenders live next to perfectly normal people is beyond me! When one tried to move in where I live, the neighbors and I got together and took care of him!"

"Well, we haven't received any notices," I said again firmly. "So we don't know that this is the case."

So much for Daniel's mother liking me. Angela pursed her lips. "I can see you're determined not to take me seriously, Cass. Whether or not you think that person out there was a sex offender, he was still guilty of stalking me, and I intend to report him."

"Did you get a good look at the car?" Mom asked, trailing after Angela into the kitchen while I wheeled the stroller into the living room so Ned could continue his nap.

"Not the license plate, unfortunately," I heard Mrs. Martin reply. "It was bent and had some dirt on it, but the car itself was this piece of junk, beat-up white sedan. A Sentra, maybe."

Beat-up white sedan! My hand dropped from where it had been arranging Ned's blanket.

Had she given me that detail first, my whole response might have been different.

White cars were a dime a dozen. One of the most popular car colors in America, I think I'd read somewhere. But beat-up white sedans weren't a dime a dozen—at least not in Clyde Hill, where we lived. Could it be the same beat-up white sedan that was parked opposite the Palace on the day the social worker visited? Which was the same beat-up white sedan that passed Louella and me outside Gilbert's on Main Street, the pale, familiar driver looking straight at me as he passed.

Maybe Angela Martin wasn't overreacting.

The last thing I needed in life, on the other hand, besides a mysterious neighborhood stalker, was my mother worrying about me having a mysterious neighborhood stalker.

I decided to keep my own encounters with the beat-up white sedan to myself. They were so trivial, after all, and possibly chance.

It's those moment-by-moment decisions we make, I think, that surprise us with their repercussions. Decisions made without debate, consulting loved ones, prayer, to say the least.

As I sat there that afternoon, listening to Angela's frustrated "no, Officer, I didn't get a good look at him or the license plate, but you just need to be aware that this person is out there! Send some extra patrol cars to this neighborhood! We've got a baby here," I had no idea my small choice would end up being, when the pieces fell, one of my rather larger ones.

CHAPTER 17:

Departure

The second week of September. Summer was truly over, as the heavy freeway traffic had proven. After the solid forty minutes it took to get to the airport, I was glad I allowed so much time.

Ned's placid eyes considered me while I wrestled the car seat out and snapped it into the stroller. "Don't get hungry yet, okay?" I said, as we headed for the concourse entrance. "But I'm glad you'll be awake for this."

A bottle could wait a half hour. I would not have Nadina reproaching me for missing her departure—one that, even ten days ago, I wasn't sure would happen.

. . .

"So you take my kid and then you don't even call me?"

Nadina loomed over me as I sat on a park bench, Ned at my feet in his car seat. She looked strangely deflated, now that she was no longer pregnant, a state she was flaunting in an unusually—for her—body-hugging t-shirt. Her hair was much longer than when I had first met her, almost brushing her chin at this point, and I noticed the white-blonde highlights were newly brightened. "And what the hell? You never come to this park. It's like the third one I've checked."

Leaping to my feet, I went to hug her, but she anticipated me and backed up a step. I contented myself with giving her shoulders a good squeeze. "How did you find me? I came here for variety—if you knew how many times in the last few weeks I've walked to Clyde Hill or Meydenbauer...Ned and I needed a new angle on the lake." Not only that, but with the possible sedan stalker on my mind, I was trying to be less predictable in my movements.

"I showed up at your place, and that Phyl was all shocked to see me 'cause she was just home from work to grab something, but I said I wasn't going away until I talked to you, so she's been driving me all over. This park is not easy to find, Dude. If we hadn't come here that one time with Benny, I never woulda remembered it. And the parking lot is way the hell up there—I thought I was gonna rip out a stitch coming down all those stairs."

"How are you feeling? I take it you're recovering," I said, thinking I would buy Phyl flowers on the way home. Thank heavens it wasn't Daniel who happened to be there. On the other hand, would he ever have let Nadina coerce him into being her chauffeur? "I wanted to call, Nadina—a hundred times—but we agreed in the birthing plan that we wouldn't have contact for two weeks, remember? And then at that point you were supposed to call me, if you wanted to check in. When you didn't, I didn't know if that meant you wanted your space, or what." No response. Except to cross her arms over her chest and scowl at me. "If you didn't want to talk, I didn't think I should call you, much less drop by. But how are you? I know the recovery period is pretty awful—at least mine was."

She grimaced. "Yeah. It sucked. It took me like two weeks just to get off my ass and go to the bathroom without hurting. And this is the first time I've been out because I didn't want to haul that friggin' donut pillow with me. Embarrassing. But, Dude, you should've seen how *huge* my boobs got. Not to be believed. I was like a friggin' mad cow. Darigold. It woulda been awesome except they hurt like hell. Good thing I gave Ned to you 'cause I don't know how he coulda handled one of those puppies—" nodding in his direction.

"You should have called me," I said again. "I would have come over if you'd asked."

She snorted. "Yeah—don't do me any favors, Cass." Seeing me swallow my retort, she added, "And I didn't call you today 'cause I wanted to get out. Out of the friggin' cave."

Now my guilt was rising, birth plan or no birth plan. "Haven't you seen anyone since you came home from the hospital?"

"Some. Sonya. Carly. Mom, Mom, Mom. Aunt Sylvia kept calling till we stopped picking up. That Louella even came by—hell if I know how she found me. A few of the teachers from school and...other folks."

"Oh! Did Camden School already start again? I know you said the St. Helen's orientation isn't till after Labor Day." St. Helen's being the private, all-girls Catholic school in Cleveland that Aunt Sylvia had lined up for Nadina.

"Camden starts next week. I went there first this morning, but hardly anyone was there." She nodded at the bench, and I resisted the urge to help her, watching her gingerly take a seat on the side away from Ned. I wondered if it was lack of curiosity about him or deliberate avoidance. "But I had a pretty interesting conversation with who I did run into."

"Okay, I'll bite. Who did you run into?"

"Henneman." Camden School's Director. "I...asked him what he'd think if I didn't go to Cleveland after all."

She let that sink in while she watched some teenagers jumping off the dock, a girl about her age, bikini-clad and screaming between two guys. They were the only other people at Chism Beach that day, apart from a family with two toddlers who had come over earlier to investigate Ned. Shiny, happy people. Not for the first time I wondered why some were given so much to bear in life and others so little. Until I lost Troy and Min, I would have put myself in the latter category, but now it seemed like my life was making up for lost time, burden-wise. Or maybe God gave everyone a uniform misery allotment, but the delivery schedules varied. In some lives, the misery was doled out regularly, but in such bitty amounts that there was no cumulative effect: a paper cut here, a long line at the grocery store there. Like James' life. While others had fewer shipments, but the misery came in truckloads. If this were the case, Nadina and I should be in the clear fairly soon. But what if it wasn't?

I knew she was waffling about St. Helen's. When Lori Lincoln drew up the birth plan, we all assumed Nadina would be in Ohio after school began, not that Nadina seemed particularly keen on the birth plan anymore. My own feelings were mixed: on the one hand her absence would make the adoption process cleaner, but on the other she had been an important part of my life for the past year, and I would miss her. "What did Henneman say?" I murmured.

She shrugged. "That I could come back, of course, if I stayed, but that maybe I might want to at least try Cleveland." The bikini girl climbed back onto the dock, a dripping mermaid. Nadina sucked in her stomach.

"And?" I prompted. "What do you think?"

She exhaled loudly. "I don't know what to think! I wanna do something new, but that doesn't mean Cleveland. How'm I ever gonna get another boyfriend if I'm at a friggin' all-girls school with a bunch of nuns? But if I stay here what am I gonna do? You're not gonna hang out with me—"

"I'll hang out with you," I interjected. Forget the stinking birth plan. It would be messy, but it wasn't like anything other than an open adoption was even possible in this case.

"—And I'm even kinda starting to miss Mike," Nadina went on, hardly hearing me. Her voice broke ominously. "I was telling Dale—"

"Mike's dad?" I broke in. "You spoke to him again?"

Nadina broke off. Blanched. Cringed, even.

Standing up abruptly and then wincing, she pointed in the direction of the car seat. "Is he always like this?"

Ned was…being Ned. Meaning, he was fast asleep. Gradually his body clock was synching up with the waking universe, but his most awake times still fell at midnight and again before dawn. And when he was awake and fed, he seemed content to lie on his back on a blanket for as long as I wanted to leave him there, wiggling and watching the blurry world. Shortly before she left, I overheard Angela Martin whispering to Joanie, "Do you think everything's all right with that baby?" and Joanie tactlessly responding, "Are you trying to ask me if he's retarded, Mom? His dad sure was, so he's got a 50/50 chance."

"He sleeps a lot," I answered shortly. "He's a newborn. When did you talk to Mike's dad?"

Nadina silently mouthed one of her favorite words. "He came by. Couple weeks ago."

"To tell you more stories about Mike as a baby? Or to pass on messages from him?" I adjusted the sunshade on the car seat to avoid letting Nadina see my frustration. "Remember how Lori Lincoln told us not to have any more contact with Mike unless a lawyer—"

"I *know*, Cass. You don't gotta remind me. But what was I supposed to do? Mom was at work, and he shows up at the house, and I'm laying there with my friggin' mega maxi pads and boob bindings and donut pillow—it's not like I could run off or even kick him out."

If Dale Loftus were as petite as his son, I'd lay odds on Nadina, donut pillow or no donut pillow. "What did he want?" I ground out.

"He cared about my fucking *welfare*, okay, Cass? Which is more than I can say for you—*he* wanted to know how I was doing!"

Fine. If we were going to have a fight, let me at least go down swinging. I whirled on her. "What is the deal with you, Nadina? Do you remember a single one of those hours we spent in Lori's office, coming up with if we were going to visit, when we were going to visit, who was going to visit whom, who would call, who would email and when? We went the two no-contact weeks. Then the ball was in your court to call me. Like I said, when you didn't, I didn't know what would be the best way to handle this—visit you, don't visit you, call you, don't call you. If you already felt like crap physically, I didn't want to send you into…emotional overload. I've never done this before, okay? Cut me some slack. We had a house full of guests, and I haven't been getting tons of sleep, and everyone doesn't get along all the time, and my brother's girlfriend was driving us up the wall, and I only just got rid of them all. I was going to give you another couple days, and then I was going to call you. Promise."

"Whatever," she returned maddeningly. "Alls I know is, ever since I met you, I don't think that long of a time has gone by without you at least sending me a friggin' email. And now I go through this huge emotional *thing* and you, like, disappear. If you were still my mentor I'd tell Henneman that you lack commitment."

I closed my eyes. She just had a baby, Cass. Teenage girl + postpartum hormones = complete breakdown in rational thought. When I spoke, my voice wasn't entirely acid-free. "Seeing that I'm trying to adopt your baby and we'll be connected for life through him, I can hardly see how I lack commitment."

"To *me*!" Nadina shrieked. "Commitment to *me*!" Her hands balled up in fists as she towered over me, and I saw heads turning our direction.

Sheesh—was I ever this nuts after Min was born? I held up my hands in surrender. "Look. I apologize abjectly and yet again for not being in contact. I was not trying to hurt you. I was not trying to ignore you. I was not thinking I'd gotten what I wanted out of you and it was time to scrape you off. As I've told you before, you *psycho*, I love you."

At least the lunk's ears still worked. Her tense posture drooped and she sagged back onto the bench. "I am psycho, huh? Mom said so too 'cause I was watching TV and getting so friggin' mad at how many commercials there were—throwing things—and then this corny one for friggin' life insurance came on and I started bawling."

Relieved, I smiled. "If you'd been paying attention in that childbirth class we flunked out of, you'd remember Pat told us that your estrogen and progesterone levels go up during pregnancy and then plummet after the baby is born. It's like the mother of all PMS."

"Word."

Word, indeed. And then on top of spaghetti there was giving away the child you'd been carrying for nine months. I couldn't imagine. When I had been a teenager myself, my parents told me very clearly that, should I ever forget their training and God's best for my life and find myself pregnant, I would carry that baby to term and bless some family with it. How did that work? I could no more have handed Min over after she was born, than I could have lopped off my arm and adopted it out. Was it all about the mindset, going in? Maybe I would know all too well myself, if I had to hand Ned over at some future date.

My eyes dropped to him, stirring now. Even to myself I avoided calling him my son. He was The Baby or Ned or Neddy. Stop it, Cass. Remember Abraham and Isaac. Ned is yours. Or will be. Have faith. What faith? Who was I kidding?

"You'd care, then?" Nadina said after a minute. "Care if I went away to Cleveland?"

I sighed. "I would care. Lots. And miss you. Lots. But I want you to get back on your feet. You have a clean start now. You've been sober for months, and now's your chance. It's not like I'm dying for you to go to Cleveland, but look what happens if you stay here: you're dragged into this legal…morass, Mike will be out of jail sooner than we think, and Mike's dad feels free to stop by unannounced. Is this what you want?"

She didn't answer, and I followed her gaze to where it rested on the two toddlers. The little girl was clutching a plastic shovel to her chest while her brother stamped his feet and hollered, trying unsuccessfully to swipe it.

"We'll always be connected, Nadina," I said again. "Near or far. You've given me Ned—our lives will always be tied together."

"Unless…" she muttered.

"Unless what?"

The little girl hauled off and whacked her brother on the head, bringing the mom running.

"Unless Mike gets him away from you."

My stomach sunk and I felt my breathing quicken. I grabbed her arm to make her look at me. "What makes you say that? What did Mike's dad tell you?"

Her pale blue eyes met mine briefly, then faltered. "Dale said… Dale said that Mike's first hearing with the parole board is end of the month."

"*What?*" I squealed. "He's been in prison—what—three, four months? How does that work?" Without conscious thought, I reached for the diaper bag and started scrabbling through it for my phone. I needed to call Lori. Or Daniel. Some lawyer person. Lori would be cool and condescending, as always—she had warned me, after all—but at least I could comfort myself with picturing all her hard weaponry of contempt turned on the Loftus family. And Daniel—since our last tiff he had been on his best behavior in front of everyone. It remained to be seen what tack he would take with all our guests gone, but I imagined if I called in genuine crisis mode he would rise to the occasion.

"Dale said that, since the low end of Mike's sentence is two years, and since he had all kinds of 'mitigating circumstances' and since he's been doing all the right things there, they're willing to see him after he's only served a quarter of the time."

"Four months is not a quarter of two years," I protested, clutching the diaper bag to my chest like there was a mugger trying to rip it away.

Angry tears welled up. "What's wrong with everyone's math?"

"Dude," said Nadina bracingly. "You think I'm a mess. No, the hearing is after four months because they have to decide if they're gonna let him out at the quarter point, plus he gets some kinda 'good conduct' credit."

"Good conduct," I repeated. Really. It was too ridiculous. Rubbing my temples, I said, "Okay. So Mike the Eagle Scout gets out as early as November. What makes you think the court will award Ned to him? You've got to be straight with me, Nadina—do you think Ned would be better off with Mike?"

She flared up. "I'm not stupid, Cass. And I've known Mike a helluva lot longer and better than you have. I don't know what's going on with him. I mean, maybe he really is getting his shit together this time. But that still doesn't mean Ned wouldn't have a way better life with you. Dog, you should see some of the total skank hoes that Mike has for ex-girlfriends. If you did, you would not even have to ask me who I want to take this baby. No way is any kid of mine gonna grow up with some fugly bitch of a stepmother—"

"Whoa," I interrupted. "Tell me how you really feel."

An uncharacteristically girlish giggle escaped her. "I'm just saying that Dale makes it sound like Mike thinks he's got a chance. That's it. I'm not saying anyone else thinks that. I just get freaked out about it sometimes. I want you to have Ned. How many times do I gotta say it?"

Reaching out, I gave her shoulder a shake. "I don't get tired of hearing it. Too bad you're not a judge. What am I going to do if you go to Cleveland? Who's going to make my ears ring with their bad language?"

"You and Mike could be pen pals."

"Now there's a thought." Ned was starting to make preliminary mewing and smacking sounds, and I gave the car seat a rock with my foot. "So what's it going to be? Are you going to stick around and enroll at Camden again or do the clean-slate thing in Cleveland? What do Aunt Sylvia and your mom vote?"

"They're at it again," replied Nadina blithely. "Aunt Sylvia says she's gonna come out here and handcuff me to her to get me on that plane, and Mom says why doesn't Aunt Sylvia just stick to her bingo, or whatever it is old ladies do, and Aunt Sylvia says, well, at least she minds her business, instead of letting everything go to wrack and ruin. And Mom says what the hell do you call wrack and ruin—life is great, and then Aunt Sylvia starts in with the, if-you've-got-everything-so-under-control-why-is-it-you-haven't-laid-down-the-law-with-that-daughter-of-yours speech, and then Mom hangs up the phone again."

I considered. "Sounds like Aunt Sylvia is still in favor of Cleveland and your mom is on the fence."

"Pretty much." The advice of her elders interesting her as little as usual, she shrugged the subject off.

Ned picked up volume as he worked his way back to consciousness, and, having calmed down somewhat, I tossed my phone back in the diaper bag and ferreted out his bottle and powdered formula. "Do you want to feed him?" I asked.

"That has got to taste so sick," she answered, avoiding my question. Nonetheless, I saw her straighten up and rub her hands nervously on her thighs as I pulled him out of the car seat.

"It does the trick, though. The doctor says he's doing great—thriving. Here—at least hold him while I shake the bottle." I thrust the little guy at her, and she surprised me by remembering to support his head. After that she was at a loss, however, balancing him awkwardly upright on her knees.

"How come his legs don't uncurl? And is that dandruff? Friggin' Mike!"

"It's called cradle cap and it'll go away," I said, bending and arranging Nadina's arms like an artist's articulated doll to cradle Ned. I handed her the bottle. "Give it a try."

It turned out she wasn't bad at it, having a latent natural instinct. Not the pro Perry was, with his advanced holds, but not a bungler like

Joanie, who handled Ned like he were spun glass that she might drop at any moment. "Dang! Look at him chug it," Nadina said appreciatively. "I once went on a field trip in fourth grade to this farm, and we got to feed a baby goat a bottle, and it went after it, just like Ned's doing. Its mom wouldn't let it nurse 'cause it was runty, but he was such a good little sucker that I bet he caught up in no time."

I smiled. "See? Even then you noticed animals. It probably ate well because it was you feeding it. I'm telling you—one day you could be a great veterinarian."

Handing me back the now-empty bottle, Nadina gingerly sat Ned up and jiggled him on her knee. "Yeah...I totally forgot—Aunt Sylvia said that in Medina County there are all these alpaca farms that I could take the bus to. Isn't that crazy? Who wants an alpaca? But maybe I could get a job shoveling alpaca shit."

Ah...so she had given some thought to what a new life out there would look like. "Well," I said, "I'd warn you that they kick and spit, but knowing your gift with animals I doubt they'd ever try it with you. Not like—"

"Eeeeewww!" yelled Nadina, as her jiggling knee caused a predictable response in Ned. I just caught him under the arms when she threw her feet out wide to avoid the cascade. "Take him, Cass! I'll stick with the alpacas—that was hella nasty."

· · ·

"There she is," I murmured to Ned, wheeling his stroller up to the security checkpoint. Nadina was leaning with her back against the wall, earbuds in, chin jerking to some inaudible beat. When she saw me, she yanked them out. "Sheezus—it's about time. I gotta go through security, and they're boarding in like thirty minutes."

"Where's your mom?"

"Smoking in the loser lounge. She's gone through a pack since lunch, even though she's flying out in two weeks to visit." Mrs. Stern hadn't yet set a firm date to move to Ohio, and I hardly blamed her. Better to wait and see how the dust settled.

Nadina gave Ned's kicking foot a squeeze. "Later, Dude. Try not to barf on Cass too much." She endured a hug from me, but when I asked if I could pray for her, she drew the line. "God, Cass—do whatever, but can you do it in your head?"

It was no more than I had expected, so I pulled out the card I'd pre-written. "Fine, then, you hopeless heathen. Here it is. You can read it on the plane."

Her mouth worked for a moment, and then she grabbed the card and stuffed it in her backpack pocket. "You're gonna email me, right?" Her voice was low.

For probably the twentieth time I answered, "I'm going to email you."

"And if I actually start to like it out there and decide to stay, you'll come out and see me?"

Trying not to imagine sitting at the dinner table with Aunt Sylvia and Mrs. Stern and Nadina all hollering at each other, I nodded. "I'll come visit if you stay."

There didn't seem to be anything more to say. I found myself blinking rapidly and trying to relax my tight throat, and maybe Nadina was similarly occupied. Eventually she croaked, "Here comes Mom."

"Okay. Have a good flight. Don't get smart when you go through security." I threw my arms around her one more time, squeezing until I felt her squeeze back. In her ear I whispered, "I love you, and I'm proud of you, Nadina Stern. You hear me?"

She nodded, not meeting my eyes and swallowing again.

"I hear you."

CHAPTER 18:

WTH

My inbox was full.

Apart from Nadina, the senders' names weren't exactly lighting a fire under me. And I even half-dreaded hers.

> Hi Cass.
>
> What the hell? So UR never gonna write me? Place is a effing prison. No phones allowed on campus. No talking btw classes. Mandatory sport or job or volunteer crap after school. Who would of thought hanging out with crabby Aunt S at end of the day would be the highlight! Other girls suck.
>
> How is Ned? Tell Henneman to hold my spot. Gotta go— stupid Lorman coming to bust my ass.
>
> N

This was only my second message from her since she left—the first was a brief text to let me know she arrived, to which I had responded with a lengthy email. No credit for that here or answers to any of my questions. My fingers hovered over the keyboard while I considered a reply, but then I clicked over to the next message.

cass—

what the hell? [WTH, indeed. What were the odds of two
consecutive emails to me opening with "What the hell"?]
it's been four weeks that you've been sitting on your *ace
ass.* i say time to get back to work. if you've done anything,
shoot it to me, or i'm gonna have to go with jeri. thought
you needed money.

riley

I did need money, but I hadn't done a lick of work on *Ace Assassin.*
Tomorrow. Absolutely, I promised Riley. What was the point of all
Ned's snoozing, if I wasn't going to make use of it?

Speaking of needing money...

Cass:

The public defender cc'ed me on a copy of Mr. Loftus'
paternity affidavit. As of today we have 47 more days to
terminate it, if possible. Barbara Dobbs informs me that
she has contacted you twice but been unable to schedule
a post-birth follow-up visit. ["What the hell?" I whispered.
Surely that was what Lori's tone implied.] Considering
the time constraints, you should do this ASAP. By having a
complete and approved home study on file we may avoid
a far more expensive and drawn-out Bonding Assessment
down the line. Call if questions.

L. Lincoln

Pretty straightforward. I hoped she only charged me six minutes
for the message and not twelve. Add the Dobbs to my to-do list. I
wouldn't reply to Lori until it was done, however, lest she start the
clock again.

The final three messages fell in the Fully-Dreading category:

Hello, Cass.

Long time no see. Don't worry—this isn't a work email.
Ri tells me he already hounded you about *Ace*. I'd love
to come by and see you and Ned when it's convenient.
Didn't want to call in case I woke up the baby. How about
this Thurs for your open house? You said I could bring a
friend. I'd like to introduce Violette to you all.

James

Yippee! James had a new girlfriend. I could read between the lines: *Cass, you can stop avoiding me now because I took the hint and moved on. Let's be friends.* With pleasure. Smiling, I tapped back a quick confirmation.

If only the next one could turn out so happily:

Cass—

I know your hands are full with a newborn, but would
you feel up to a visit (with Bryson tagging along this
time)? We can keep it short. Bry has been asking
repeatedly when he will see you again. He's been wanting
to show you the Bible they gave him because I tell him
we go to "your church." Saturday?

Skandar

Stumped, I stood up to pace about the room. Was there any graceful way out? Not any obvious one. I was just going to have to initiate the exceedingly awkward conversation: there was not, had never been, nor would ever be a possible relationship for us.

I groaned. And Saturday—when all my housemates were likely to be home—! No way. Sinking back into my chair I typed my reply: the play structure at Clyde Hill Elementary. Neutral territory. Where I could plead Ned's needs the second I got the conversation over with and then spring into my own getaway car.

And finally, the *coup de grace,* a message from my former mother-in-law Raquel, dated four days ago.

> Hello, Cass.
>
> Forgive me for not calling or writing in some time. My heart has been very, very full, and you have been on it. I know you will understand how difficult it has been to see you move on with your life, although that is exactly what you should be doing. Max and I want to assure you that we will always love you because you're like a daughter to us. You ARE a daughter to us.
>
> We would like to meet your new baby. If we don't hear from you, I think we will take a chance and just drop by. I have a little gift for him. Although you've never specifically invited us to your home, we have the address from your Christmas card.
>
> Raquel

Nice little twist of the knife there, at the end. Anyone who saw what invariably happened whenever Raquel and I got together—crying—buckets and buckets—would surely understand my reluctance to have her over at the Palace. But I had better bite the bullet and do it now. If I didn't hurry and schedule the Ewans for a time when no one else would be home, I couldn't control the number of witnesses.

Hardly had I hit Send on my friendly invitation for lunch tomorrow or Thursday than the doorbell rang. Springing up, I twitched the drapes aside to peer out at the pearl gray Buick LaCrosse in the driveway. Clearly, procrastination had cost me the chance to do this on my own terms or with any emotional prep. At least it was only four o'clock. With any luck the Ewans would be on their way before any of my housemates came home, and I might even have time to repair some of the crying damage.

The doorbell rang again. A glance at the bassinet showed me Ned was stirring. Ordinarily I would have given him another fifteen minutes to drag himself to consciousness, but in this case he might prove an effective human shield.

"Hello, Sweetie Boy. How was your afternoon nap? Mmm…you smell like warm baby." And then, louder, "Coming!"

. . .

"I tried to get Raquel to wait until you got back to us," Max whispered over Ned's head. His wife had excused herself to the bathroom, since the two of us made quick work of the Kleenex box in the living room.

Dabbing my nose with my tissue wad, I nodded. "Thanks, Max." I could picture his feeble attempts and Raquel railroading him. "I've been lax—not keeping up. How are you? Were you still thinking of retiring soon?"

He ran a hand through his salt-and-pepper hair. I had always thought Troy would be a handsome older man if he took after his father—his temples growing more defined as his hairline retreated up and up, the black seasoned more liberally with silver and white each passing year. When Troy and I dated in high school, Max was the first to unbend to me, Raquel maintaining a chilly distance for a few months as she mourned the loss of the cheerleader and daughter-of-a-good-friend girlfriend who preceded me. I swallowed the treacherous lump rising once more in my throat—really, the pitiful Kleenex remnant couldn't take any more and was already biodegrading in my clutch.

"I've put off retirement a while longer," Max sighed. "It's…hard to be home alone together. Even the kids have been begging off from seeing us lately." No kidding. If I couldn't handle the emotional overload more than once every couple months— "Good news, though: Stu and Vanessa are expecting their first in February."

My delight was genuine. "Hooray! They always swore they weren't going to have kids. That's wonderful! Do they know yet if it's a boy or a girl?"

"Girl," sniffled Raquel, re-emerging. She tossed the bathroom box of tissue onto the coffee table. "So we'll have two grandsons and two granddaughters—one living—God willing."

Deep breath. Vanessa had always been a die-hard career girl, so I was itching to know what brought about her change of heart, but I didn't dare ask, in case it had something to do with Min's death. Despite my own sadness I felt a twinge of pity for my erstwhile sister-in-law. I'm sure the imminent birth of another granddaughter had turned the brunt of Raquel's emotional fire hose on her.

"Wonderful," I repeated, more faintly.

"My counselor says the birth of a new baby will help heal up the wounds," Raquel added with a touch of defiance. "I told her I would never forget little Minnie—never never!"

"She didn't say 'forget' Minnie," Max interjected impatiently. I suspected they were not canvassing this topic for the first time. "She said 'heal.'"

Raquel held out her hands for Ned. "Better let me do that. You're jostling him."

"I can burp a baby," Max retorted, continuing to thump Ned rhythmically on the back. He did cease jiggling his knee, however.

"Ned spits up pretty easily," I said apologetically. On cue, a bead formed on his lips and ran down his chin, and Raquel instantly engulfed him in fresh Kleenex. "No—here, here—I have a cloth for that."

"What do you think?" Raquel turned on me, once we had Ned's effusions under control.

"Of what?"

"Has a new baby helped you heal?"

"Raquel—" Max protested.

"No, it's okay," I said, feeling the heat rise in my cheeks. "Umm... I can only speak for myself, of course. But I think the whole anticipation before Ned was born actually made it worse. I missed Min more. Felt... worse... about her than I had since early on—"

"See, Max!"

Her husband grunted noncommittally, and I hurried on. "But it really has gotten better since Ned came. He's so different—his own person. And I'm so busy with him, and tired, physically. I guess I would have to say it's been healing."

"Healing or *distracting*?"

It's hard to get over wanting your mother-in-law's approval. "Both, I guess. I don't like to forget, but I have to confess that I am forgetting and that I am distracted. And because I am, I've been healing. I can't help it."

"You don't have to apologize for healing," Max declared, shooting another glare at his wife.

Raquel left off arranging Ned's cloud of hair and sat back on the sofa with a tiny "hmmph!" Her eyelids were blinking rapidly again and I took refuge in staring at Phyl's Ficus benjamina. Weeping Fig. The thing looked all right to me. What would a Ficus plant have to weep about, anyhow? The clock was chiming five—not only would more crying be inadvisable on my part, but I also had to figure out how to send Max and Raquel on their way.

"I can't say I blame you for moving on, Cass," Raquel began again, her voice almost managing not to be reproachful. "If I were young like you, with my life ahead of me: new children, probably a new husband—"

"Oh! That person I was dating a few months ago—he—it didn't work out," I put in, seeing an opportunity to earn back some brownie points. Sure enough, Raquel looked relieved, although she made the appropriate sympathetic sounds. "He was no Troy, I'm afraid," I added cravenly. It worked, though, and Raquel gave me a watery smile.

Hearing the door from the garage to the kitchen open I relaxed a little. "That'll be Phyl. Tuesday is her night to cook." I took a fresh tissue and blew my nose with finality.

Taking my hint, Max leaned forward to hand Ned back to me.

"We'll just say hello to her, then, and be on our way. C'mon, Raquel."

"Ah, but it's...the Ewans, isn't it?"

In the doorway stood not Phyl but Daniel. His blue glance took in my puffy red eyes and my in-laws' surprised recognition before he came forward. Seeing his late summer highlights and golden tan and panther grace through my mother-in-law's eyes, I panicked. No, no, no! He was going to cost me hard-won ground in Raquel's estimation, and I ventured a small shake of my head.

"What are you doing home so early?" I asked in an off-putting tone.

"I forgot the gym was closed for semi-annual deep cleaning," Daniel said. "Frightening to think it only happens that often."

He beamed down at us.

I heard myself say grudgingly, "Max...Raquel...you remember Daniel Martin. He owns this house."

He shook hands with Max and barely grasped Raquel's stunned fingers. Ignoring my scowl, he gestured at me to scoot over on the loveseat. "How's our boy?"

Our boy? Or, to borrow a phrase from Nadina and Riley—What the hell? "You mean, how is *my* boy," I corrected.

"It takes a village."

"*My* boy is doing fine."

Here, Max's fifteen minutes of back-thumping came to fruition, and Ned let out a resounding "br-a-a-a-a-a-ach!"

"Heavens!" exclaimed Raquel. Her head had barely turned in Ned's direction, so she might actually have been marveling at Daniel.

Daniel whistled. "One day that boy will be the pride of his fraternity."

"You would know all about that," I muttered. Why must he torture me by joining us, when he must know I wished him miles away?

Raquel rallied. "It's been so kind of you to let Cass live here with a new baby, too."

"No kindness at all," he replied smoothly. "I'm sure you know—Cass manages to endear herself to everyone, and she can dust like there's no tomorrow."

Turning faintly pink, I didn't know whether to kiss him or hit him.

"Oh," uttered Raquel. I'm sure she was remembering the constant state of disaster my house used to be in when she would visit. The dishes. The piles of laundry. Min's toys scattered like land mines. At least living with housemates forced me into a semblance of neatness.

For the first time that afternoon, I felt the urge to giggle. But it evaporated when Raquel squeezed my hand, tears filling her eyes again. "Yes, Cass is certainly very, very dear to us. We've known her a long time. She's family."

Max was done. "We're going," he announced, getting to his feet.

Hitching Ned to my shoulder, I sprang up as well, as did Daniel. Raquel had no choice but to follow suit. Max dragged his wife to the car while she trailed invitations, advice, and parting shots, each of which I tried to respond to appropriately.

The instant I shut the door behind them I sighed and leaned my forehead against it. "Is it that you can't read my nonverbal signals, Daniel, or that you *won't*?" I asked mildly.

"Don't forget your verbal signals—you were sending those too. It's not that. But if I humored you every time you wished I would go away, I'd probably have to move out, and this is my house, after all."

Turning my head, I felt a grin tugging at the corners of my mouth. "So it is. But you're wrong—I don't wish you gone that often. Just when my suspicious former in-laws come by."

"Ah. And for that kindness, I'll do you one: I could watch Ned, while you go get some ibuprofen or lie down for a minute."

"Watch him?" I laughed. "How sacrificial of you. He doesn't move yet. I can just lay him down." My temples were pounding, though, and I rubbed them ruefully. "Thank you, though. I should probably go change him, actually."

"It can wait a minute, can't it?"

It could. I needed to regroup.

I lay Ned on his play mat, jiggling it to make the dangling toys dance before throwing myself across the sofa the Ewans so recently vacated.

"Long visit?"

"Long enough."

"Always the same?"

I peered at him under my arm. He was kicking back in the loveseat, his hand to his own temple. Maybe I wasn't the only one who had a trying afternoon. The thought roused me, and I rolled up on my elbow. "Honestly, no. I mean, it was a lot the same—reminiscing and crying and all that—but something was missing. Max wasn't in the mood to go along this time, for starters. And even Raquel—there was something perfunctory about it. Like it bugged her but also relieved her that I might be moving on."

"Are you?"

"Moving on?" We looked at each other for a minute. "I…guess I am. Call me shallow."

"I think it's all right," Daniel said. He grinned. "Call me callous."

I laughed. "We sound like Shakespearean sidekicks. Or maybe Bunyan characters. Shallow would never get bogged down in the Slough of Despond because she's light enough to skate right over the surface."

"I would say you've actually spent a decent amount of time down there. But no *Pilgrim's Progress*—otherwise you'll have worse names for me than Callous."

Contrariwise, I thought. It turns out I wasn't the only endearing person at the Palace. Not that I was brave enough to say so yet. "No—no bad names for you. In fact, I appreciate you being so agreeable. We've had so many houseguests and visitors because of Ned. It must be…irritating…to come home from work to so many people."

"I think they're more draining on you than me. And with what's been going on at work and on other fronts, distractions are welcome."

On "other fronts"? What other fronts? He had his eyes closed at this point, his head tilted back, resting.

"Work's been rough, then?" I ventured. "Too many potential clients leaping on you, wearing out the shocks in your chair?"

"Careful—your claws are showing."

"I'm afraid they're non-retractable."

This drew a smile.

"The clients are behaving, for the most part."

Oh. "Then it's the 'other fronts' that are stressing you out?"

"You could say so," he answered evasively. Opening his eyes, he noted my dissatisfied expression. It seemed to amuse him. "Let's just say, sometimes people's moral and ethical scruples can complicate things—slow everyone down."

"Especially people like you, who are used to traveling at top speed?" I asked suspiciously. The maddening creature could be referring to any number of things—seducing a reluctant girlfriend, seducing *me*—but I knew from the twitch of his lips that he didn't intend to clarify.

"I'm up against a deadline," he said. "A trip I have coming up. But everything will get done and everyone will come around. I won't settle for less."

If "everyone" included me, I was sure I would.

The sound of a key in the door persuaded me that my recouping time was up. Phyl for sure, this time. Daniel had the same thought because, when I had Ned in my arms again and turned to go, I nearly collided with him.

He handed me Ned's burp cloth. "There was another reason I wanted to say hello to the Ewans, however."

"What would that be?"

"I want them to get used to the idea of me being in your life."

CHAPTER 19:

Plague of Frogs

To say I was walking on clouds for a day would not be an exaggeration.

Daniel and I didn't get another chance to talk alone, but what could his words mean but that he still cared for me? And if he did, then all the pieces of my life would fall into place. Despite what I had told my mother, I was more and more inclined to overlook my doubts about him. If he didn't share my faith yet—and I wasn't sure if he did or not, given the evidence—he was at least supportive. And if he continued to bring home girlfriend after girlfriend, well, maybe he was just biding his time, as Joanie said. We would get married, my life would look like the American Dream, the court would award me Ned, I would live happily ever after.

In my optimistic state, even the anxieties of the week didn't completely derail me.

"Have you heard from Nadina?" It was Mark Henneman, the Camden School director, whose phone call surprised me the next day as I scribbled away on *Ace Assassin*.

In my experience, those words were never followed by anything good.

"Just a couple very brief emails. I meant to call her today because I wanted to find out what's really going on. Have you heard something?"

"She's left a few messages for her old counselor here, mostly about everything she hates at her new school, but really that doesn't worry us much. We were expecting one or the other: messages about how she hated her new school and wanted to come back, or messages about how she loved her new school and thought Camden did everything wrong."

"Then you think this might just be part of the adjustment process?" I asked.

"We hope. Why don't you give her a call and let me know your take on it, Cass? And how's it going with that baby..?"

· · ·

"About time," sniffed Nadina, when I got a hold of her a few hours later. "I've been putting up all kinds of red flags, not that you give a shit."

Smiling, I shut my laptop and dragged my mug of tea closer. "Nice to talk to you, too. Hey—before you lay into me, let me lay into you: you are a lousy correspondent. I wrote you that long email and asked dozens of questions and wanted very much to know what's going on, so don't blame me if I'm not totally up on your life."

"I don't got time for emails, Cass," she retorted, unfazed. "You would not believe this place. They're all about how, if they work your ass off, you won't have time to get into trouble. Plus there's this crazy lady they assigned to me who checks on me *every day* and then the stupid 'Prefect' girl who thinks she's all that—"

"Is the crazy lady 'Lorman'? You said in your message that 'Lorman' was coming to bug you."

"That's her. Cass—she's like 150 years old and smells like prune juice and baby powder, and she's got eyes in the back of her head, and she's always trying to be my friend, but like the friend who is secretly trying to get something out of you."

"What is she trying to get out of you?"

"Hell if I know. But she caught this other girl giving me cigarettes—"

"You don't smoke!" I broke in. "You promised your grandfather you would never smoke!"

I could almost hear the click of Nadina's eyes rolling. "Duh—I know I don't smoke, Cass. The chick was handing me the cigarettes, not the other way 'round, and I was trying to say that, thanks-but-no-thanks, I don't smoke, when here comes Lorman like a bat out of hell and hauls me into her office and gives me the I-have-high-expec-tations-of-you and don't-you-know-you've-been-given-this-second-chance lecture. God, if she'da had a pack on her desk, I woulda lit up right there, just to piss her off."

That, I believed. "Okay...so St. Helen's is a little heavy on the su-pervision. What do you think of the other girls? Have you met any you liked?"

She exhaled sharply. "I hate going to school with all girls. All they do is talk about each other."

"Is it clique-y? Have you found anyone to hang out with at lunch?"

I pictured her shrugging. "There's this one girl Chelsea. She's new too. She doesn't talk a whole lot. Kinda reminds me of Sonya. But everyone else! Cass, you should see them. We're all wearing the same friggin' uniform—and I look like some kind of plaid, drag-queen line-backer—not my best look— so they all pick every other way to sit and judge on each other. The black kids don't hang out with the white kids; the girls who are there 'cause they got pregnant stay away from the ones that did drugs; the boarders don't like the day kids. It is *messed up*. Camden was so small that, even if you totally hated someone, you still had to hang out with them, pretty much."

"Oh...I'm sorry about that. You could be someone who brings people together, though, don't you think? Since you did the pregnancy *and* the drugs, and you grew up on the West Coast, where people are more relaxed about the race thing."

"Gimme a break, Cass. You are so corny," Nadina scoffed. "I'm not here to unite the friggin' world. I just wanna get my flippin' diploma and get out."

I sat up straighter. "Then, you think you might stay? Why would you, if you hate Lorman and the other kids, mostly—not to mention looking freakish in the uniform."

She didn't answer for a minute, but I didn't press her, instead filling up a measuring cup of bird seed to top off the feeder. I swung open one side of the casement window over the sink, scaring off the family of house finches which ever loitered nearby, chasing away all comers.

"Well," said Nadina slowly. "It's not that it doesn't suck—but I've got some stuff going on outside of school that's kind of okay."

Instantly, alarm bells started going off in my head, and I pulled the window shut with a pane-jarring yank. "What?" I demanded recklessly. "Tell me it's not a boy—"

Her shriek of laughter did nothing to allay my fears.

"For Pete's sake, Nadina—if you're going to be an idiot, use some birth control this time. Go on the pill. I can't afford to take any more of your kids."

"You could always give Ned to Mike and Dale, and then just keep my next one," she shot back. "I promise this time I'll get the guy to sign off."

"That is not funny. Not at all."

"Chill, Cass. You never did have a sense of humor. Must be the mom in you. No, it's not a boy, really, and I'm not out dealing on the corner. Guess again!" Her voice rose in excitement.

"You got me," I said, trying to keep the relief out of my voice. "Umm... Aunt Sylvia's buying you a car?"

"What the hell would I do with a car? Aunt Sylvia and the school and Case are all on the same bus line."

"Case?"

Now she outright squealed. "Case! Case Friggin' Western University! Lorman got me an after-school internship, Cass. I'm the grunt in her goddaughter's biology lab, so I get to clean the frog buckets and rat cages. Which is fine—nothing worse than the crap I had to do at Petco, but the professor said if I do a good job she can introduce me to one of the Animal Behavior profs. Cass! Those guys even work with the friggin' Cleveland Metroparks Zoo—can you see me at the zoo?"

"Nadina!" I breathed. "That's wonderful. That's perfect. It couldn't be more perfect. I am so excited for you." My mind raced ahead to her future possibilities: possibly college—certainly some impressive people who could write her recommendations—maybe they would recognize her gift with animals and love her so much that they would insist she attend Case Western on a scholarship. Thank God Nadina had always proven the reliable sort, showing up for work. If she could just control her mouthiness and her tendency to explode under the least provocation...

"Yeah, I'm pretty excited for me, too. I've only been to the lab twice so far, but I go again tomorrow."

I lay down my phone for a brief second to flap my hands. I had to get this right. Okay. "This is a great opportunity, Nadina. I know I've told you a hundred times, but you are the best person with animals I've ever seen. Just please promise me one thing. That you'll bite your tongue and count to twenty whenever someone in the lab ticks you off."

"Ye-e-e-s, Cass," she groaned. "I knew you were gonna say that. Is it totally impossible to have just one real short moment of celebration without the wet-blanket crap? I know, okay? And I'm gonna try, but you can't blame me if I lose it occasionally. There's this one post-doc there—*Jean-Luc*—who's prob'ly gonna drive me up the friggin' wall. He's like super OCD and kept following me the first day and straightening everything I touched and telling me that I can't touch his friggin' precious lab bench because he has everything just how he likes it and that he wished Diane the professor wouldn't hire inexperienced people like yours truly because I was sure to eff everything up and put tap water in the frog buckets, blah blah blah—"

"That's exactly it. Promise me you won't blow up at Jean-Luc."

She sighed. "I'll *try*. No promises. Even you would want to grab his teeny little smarty-pants glasses and stomp on them if he told you that frogs are 'amfeebeeans,' so I can't let them dry out. No shit, Sherlock. But—hey—I have a good idea: what if you came out to Cleveland and took a look around? You could give me all kinds of tips on how to live my life, and I might even listen to some of them."

"I don't know…"

"Oh, come on, Cass. You don't want me to get super lonely, so lonely I hook up with the wrong crowd or another Mike."

"You're terrible! Terrible and manipulative."

"Well, you're nagging and uptight, but I'm still *your* friend. Please, please, please? Aunt Sylvia wants to meet you and to see Ned, even though I know she'd never say so. You could stay with us, and it'd be a super cheap trip."

"No way. I'm staying in a hotel."

"Yay!" Nadina cheered. "You're coming, then! When? How soon?"

"I've got to work that out, you pain in the backside. I'll email you. Which means, if you want this to happen, you've got to read my messages and write me back."

• • •

Nadina wasn't the only person making new acquaintances and having new experiences.

Thursday's open house marked the entrance of Violette Bellamy into our lives, courtesy of James, and I had the dubious pleasure of seeing her fall in love at first sight. Only, it wasn't with James, of course, since she'd seen him before. It was with Daniel.

Having one's ex-boyfriend over for the first time since you broke up months prior is never something to look forward to, especially when he's bringing a girlfriend, but I figured that at least I would have Daniel, in an unspoken way.

Phyl and Wayne were the first to show up, inseparable again and nearly purring with mutual contentment. Ever since the whole Darla debacle, Wayne could hardly be brought to make eye contact with another woman if Phyl was around, so there wasn't much conversation to be got out of him, and he wasn't talkative to begin with. He was good with babies, though, and we gave him Ned to dandle.

Next came Craig Sloane, whom Joanie and I continued to call Creep Sleaze behind his back. Poor Creep was rich and descended from what amounted to Seattle royalty, but Joanie remained unmoved. "The guy could bore paint off a wall," she grumbled. "I think we'd break up, but we're too busy using each other. He wants someone to look good in all the society pictures that get taken of him, and I want a man around." After taking the roses Creep held out and tossing them to Phyl, Joanie posted him at the stove, where the roar of the exhaust fan and hiss of stir-frying would make conversation unnecessary.

Between the sweet nothings (Phyl and Wayne), the baby gurgling (Ned), the sautéing (Creep), and the vegetable chopping (Joanie and me), no one heard James and Violette come in. Only when I went to dump the cucumber slices on the platter did I notice them standing uncertainly in the doorway. Scratch that. James looked uncertain. Violette—for it had to be her—was surveying the Palace kitchen appraisingly, her nostrils twitching slightly as the smell of twice-cooked pork wafted her way.

Were I still in love with James, Violette would have come as something of a shocker, she being completely out of his normal style. Not so Meg Ryan and much more Carolyn Bessette-Kennedy. The silky blonde hair flowing down her back, the elegant lines of her figure, the haughty Gallic features. She was taller than he by a couple inches, which meant that James had to look slightly upward at her, a circumstance which only added to his air of puppyish adoration. On second thought, I'm not sure it actually did help that I was no longer in love with the guy. Violette surely knew our history and was making her own, probably unflattering, comparisons.

All this took place in two seconds, tops, and then James was saying, "Cass, I'd like you to meet Violette." He pronounced it the French way, not the Charlie-Brown way, and sure enough, when she murmured her greeting, I detected a faint accent. Where had he found her? It wasn't like the church singles group was overrun with exotic celebrity doppelgängers. Her thin mouth curved upward politely, and she presented me with a potted orchid, as striking and graceful as herself.

Like paparazzi, everyone in the kitchen was inexorably drawn to her, impelled by curiosity and the lure of the foreign. Only Wayne kept his eyes fixed on the Singapore Slings Phyl handed around; the rest of us frankly stared at her. Creep even drifted over, zombie-style, spatula still in hand. Uh-oh. Looked like he was considering other companion options for the society pics.

When I glanced at Joanie to see what she thought of this defection, I found her at my shoulder. "Wow," she whispered. "See Creep creep. What did I tell you? Right now he's planning how he can hit on her without me noticing because he thinks I'm as dumb as he is."

"We met at the driver's license place," explained Violette some minutes later, when all the introductions were complete. Despite all indicators, her accent was not French. She was looking doubtfully at the scarlet Singapore Sling in her hand. "James helped me with the computer."

James grinned, but before he could respond, Creep busted out with, "I'm something of a computer whiz myself—I'm always having to help my admin and my direct reports with their technology questions, even though we have plenty of qualified IT staff."

Violette nodded.

Creep turned to James. "And if you've got the skills, why don't I give you my card? We're always looking for talent and a way to offload some of my responsibility. So many balls in the air, you know, and everyone seems to think they need my personal say-so." The guy even did the move where he pointed both his index fingers at James.

A faint line appeared between Violette's brows, marring her serene countenance.

James cleared his throat, throwing me an incredulous look. "Er—thanks, Craig. I'm in the employed category, at present, but I'll keep that in mind."

"Great, great." In a pure sleazoid move, Creep proceeded to turn his back on James and focus instead on James' date. "So, Violette—that's sure a pretty name. I like it better than Violet. You don't sound like you're from around here."

"I'm from Buenos Aires."

"Buenos—*Buenos Aires?* Isn't that in Argentina? I thought your name sounded French."

"My name is French," Violette answered patiently, though the line between her brows deepened. "I am French-Argentine. You have perhaps heard of Paul Groussac?"

Creep, of course, looked blank but accommodating, and I saw Violette's lip curl. I suspect she threw out the name knowing not a one of us had heard of him. "Paul Groussac was a famous French-Argentine writer. He was my great-great uncle."

"That is amazing!" declared Creep. "I've always wanted to read more Argentine writers. In college I read some Pablo Neruda and really got into it."

"Neruda is Chilean," said Violette. With that, she stalked away on the pretense of looking out the bay window.

"God help me," Joanie muttered in my ear again. "It's like having your dog pee on someone. I feel responsible. Like I should apologize to her for Creep. I guess he won't be breaking up with me yet."

"What is that, out there?" demanded Violette. She was pointing to the Lean-To.

"The—the Lean-To," replied Phyl, who was closest to her. "It's a little—kind of separate apartment."

"It's charming. Does one of you live out there?"

"It's for our pet ogre," replied Joanie. "My brother. He owns the whole place, actually, and we just rent from him."

"Hmm! Imagine living with three women—and a baby," she added, turning her gaze on me. Clearly, James had filled her in on my background, at least. Feeling self-conscious, I retreated into the pantry to get more paper napkins. Violette's voice drifted in nonetheless. "He must be a very patient man."

"Judge for yourself," said Joanie, as the door from the garage opened.

Maybe because I was in love with Daniel it seemed that his entrance changed the whole chemistry of the room. I had a moment to observe it, all unseen, since the napkins were on a bottom shelf behind various small appliances, and I had gotten down on my knees to wrangle them out.

James tensed perceptibly. Creep straightened and scowled as he sized up the competition. Phyl and Wayne offered a muted greeting, Wayne putting his free arm around her. Slowly, deliberately, Joanie waltzed over to her brother. She slung an arm around his neck and pulled his cheek against the top of her red-gold head, the way she would whenever there was a woman present whom she particularly wanted to irritate. In this case it could only be Violette.

And Violette? Let me just say I never saw a person so instantaneously transformed. The haughtiness of her features melted. She dropped her chin and her gaze as if to control herself, but then, too quickly, looked up again, the expression in her pale blue eyes suddenly girlish, hesitant.

Now heaven knew I'd seen women respond to him before—the Dobbs and the lap client and Kristen being only the most recent examples—but in those cases I witnessed strong attraction, flirtatiousness. Lust maybe. This was different. In Violette's changed countenance, in the very line of her posture I detected symptoms of a fellow sufferer. I knew how her stomach was fluttering and her heart speeding up. I saw the color come and go in her cheeks as it did in mine when I was near him.

No sooner did I feel that jolt of recognition than resentment surged through me. What did she know of him? What right did she have to fall in love with him? Who was he to her, besides a remarkably handsome stranger who just walked in the door?

Clutching the package of napkins to my chest, I struggled to my feet, but the welter of emotion made me awkward, and I ended up knocking the coffee percolator off the shelf. It hit the floor with a resounding clang and then bounced off my foot. "Flying leap!" I hissed.

"Let me help with that," said Daniel, disentangling himself from his sister. The next second he had me by the elbow, propelling me aside while he reached for the stupid percolator. Replacing it on the shelf, he straightened up. His back was to everyone else, and in a moment he released me, but not before his fingertips brushed the length of my forearm to my wrist. He smiled. "Careful, Clumsy."

The addled gulping sound I made in response seemed to amuse him. Surreptitiously I wiped my arm across my aproned front to make the hairs lie back down and followed him out.

If Daniel suspected the furor his appearance had evoked in Violette's trembling bosom, he didn't let on, coming forward calmly to be introduced.

"Violette Bellamy, James' friend," said Joanie. "'Violette'—pronounced like 'virulent,' not like 'vile.' She's a great-great-grandniece of the famous Paul Groussac—perhaps you've heard of him?"

Thankfully Violette was too distracted to notice Joanie's tone. She extended one elegant, unsteady hand to Daniel.

"Groussac…he and Borges knew each other, didn't they?" Daniel asked.

Violette gasped. That had clinched it, I presumed. Not only was her newfound love to-die-for gorgeous, he'd also heard of Great-Great-Uncle Paul!

· · ·

All in all, not one of our better open houses. Was it my imagination, or were they frequently unpleasant now? At any rate, I didn't think we would invite this particular combination of people over at the same time again. It did not require my jealous vision to perceive the change in Violette. James noticed, for one, growing increasingly quiet over the course of the evening. When he finally moved to go, he couldn't hide a start of surprise when Violette rose to leave with him. Maybe she figured it would be cleaner to break it off tonight, leaving her free to pursue other options.

Speaking of breaking it off, the lamentable Creep might have burned through any of his remaining capital with Joanie. After his failure with Violette, he tried to cozy up again and met with stony indifference. When the clock struck half past nine, Joanie stood, yawned elaborately, and announced, "I'm going to brush my teeth and go to bed. You know the way out, Cree—aig. Craig."

Before Cree-aig could bound over to plant a smacker on her, she was halfway up the stairs, leaving me to see him out.

"I should probably get Ned settled for the night—or at least the next four hours of it," I said to the room in general as I gathered up the discarded mugs.

Phyl and Wayne waved without looking up from the movie they were watching, but Daniel—he followed me to the kitchen.

At the sink, I felt his arms steal around my waist, and he gave a low laugh when he felt me shiver. His heavy-lidded eyes met my alarmed ones in the window reflection. "You can't spend the whole evening gawking at me and not expect me to do something about it."

I suppose I couldn't. Managing a shrug, I didn't protest, reaching instead for the dish soap. "I wasn't the only one gawking at you, if that's what you want to call it."

His arms tightened, and he dropped the lightest of kisses on the side of my neck. "I know," he conceded amiably. "That's why I made out with Violette when you went to get her a coffee refill."

"You jerk!" I grinned, elbowing him away and swatting him with the bottle brush.

"Temper, temper…What would you say, Cass, to putting Ned to bed and coming back down for a little while?"

"I heard you telling Joanie you were tired and had a hellish day at work."

"All true, but I'm also opportunistic. It looks like things are shaping up for my trip next week, and you're not always this…amenable."

No. I wasn't.

We studied each other. Honestly, I couldn't think of a more tempting way to spend another hour or so tonight, but that didn't mean it was a good idea. Just to fall into this with him—thoughtlessly, perhaps meaninglessly on his part. No. If it was real, it could wait. Wait for day time. Wait for a conversation.

I walked away to dry my hands. "I'm glad your trip is coming together. I take it you got everything lined up and everyone overcame his…moral scruples." Or, more likely, *her* moral scruples. Whoever the overscrupulous person was, it wasn't me, since he called me "amenable." Who, then? "Where're you headed?"

To my surprise, the familiar evasiveness returned and his eyes slid away. "I shouldn't have said that. It's just a trip. Around and about. Business…clients, colleagues." He ran his hands through his hair and exhaled before waving the whole matter off. "You're right, though. It's been a long day. Good night to you and Ned."

Before I could react to this about-face, he had escaped to the Lean-To, the door clicking shut behind him. Puzzled, I lifted my hand to my cheek, where the warmth of his quick, parting kiss lingered.

Then I heard Ned give a tired wail, and I walked slowly out of the kitchen.

CHAPTER 20:

A Modest Proposal

The play structure at the elementary school was deserted on a Saturday morning.

"I know it's chilly this early," I apologized to Ned, pulling his little fleece hood out where it was caught on one side. "But believe me, we want to get this over with." We had walked, me casting the occasional leery glance over my shoulder, in case Angela Martin's car stalker was a morning lark. Apart from the few times when I was completely alone, the beat-up white sedan had been largely out of sight, out of mind, but this morning's low fog made me a little jumpy.

"Pwi-i-i-i-ncess!" came Bryson's delighted greeting from somewhere among the evergreens bordering the field. The voice was followed seconds later by its owner, clad in a long-sleeve shirt and shorts, by golly, the only concession to the temperature being the knit cap extinguishing his bright hair. He was accompanied by a friend kicking a soccer ball, and behind them both, at a distance, I recognized Skandar. He raised a hand in greeting.

"Princess, this is Fostah," said Bryson, giving me an abbreviated version of his customary hug.

"Hi, Bryson. Hello…Foster...?" Bingo.

In contrast to Bryson, Foster was bundled head to toe, and I worried contrarily that he might overheat. His black eyes peered at me from between the wool cap and muffler, but he quickly lost interest and tugged on Bryson. "C'mon. Let's go play."

"Wait, Foster. I want to see the baby."

Obligingly I put back the hood, and Bryson inspected Ned curiously. "He's got a big head."

"All babies do."

"His is real big."

"Yeah, that's big," agreed Foster. He wedged his foot under the soccer ball and tossed it Bryson's way.

"It means he's smart," I said, although I had a vague memory of reading somewhere that it was the number of folds in the brain that correlated to intelligence, so presumably the smaller the head, the more the brain had to fold and squish. Whatever.

Examination complete, off they went, passing the ball back and forth between them. At least, I thought with relief, Skandar and I would have privacy for our dreaded conversation.

He took his time strolling over, but when he reached me he held out a double-sleeved coffee cup. "Dirty chai, right? Extra hot."

"Mmm…thanks."

"Want to sit?" He looked around for a bench, but there wasn't any, so he pointed at the raised lip of the bark area.

"No, let's walk. It's cold." I said this rather pointedly, my eyes on Bryson. In contrast to his son, Skandar had a leather jacket on and jeans.

"Is that a nag, Cass? When Ned gets older you'll realize you can't always make kids wear what you want. Even if I wanted to. I knew Bry was going to run all over creation this morning. If I forced a jacket on him, I was going to end up carrying it."

"You forget I've had a child," I said indignantly.

"I don't," he returned evenly, turning his dark eyes on me. "But you lost Minnie when she was still pretty young."

"She was old enough to have opinions on her clothes," I retorted. I bit my lip, remembering the one ladybug outfit her Aunt Vanessa had given her. Min insisted on wearing it multiple times per week, clean or dirty, to my dismay, since I worried people would think she owned no other outfits.

Maybe Skandar was right. Who cared what they wore.

Feeling my throat tighten, I hastened to sip my chai and only succeeded in scalding my tongue.

"This must be why kids ideally have two parents," said Skandar, causing me to choke on my second sip. He considerately looked elsewhere while I coughed and hacked. "When we picked up Foster this morning, I couldn't believe how his mom had dressed him. This is late September in Washington, not January at the North Pole."

"Well, then," I gasped when my esophagus permitted, "why would anyone need a mother, if they're only good for being too anxious and overdressing children?"

"It's about balance. You know, Cass, when you offer your parenting opinions—like at the Game Expo, or this morning—it may annoy me, but I always do end up thinking about it."

"Do you? I'm sure your neighbor Mrs. Poundstone could provide you with plenty of food for thought."

"She probably could," he agreed, "but not in any way that would be palatable for me. What do you think for Ned? Do you think he'd be better off with a father or that you'll do just fine yourself?"

"We'll survive."

"Survive, yes. But, Cass, you could probably also do better."

I took a deep breath. Time to get this over with. "What are you getting at, Skandar?"

He halted abruptly, forcing me to stop as well. I couldn't read his expression. There was the grimness, as always, but on top of it—determination? Resignation? "I think you already know, Cass, judging from how uncomfortable you've been with me." He waited, but I said nothing. I was holding my breath. "Look. You're a reasonable, practical woman, and I'm going to be reasonable and practical with you—"

Another cough surprised me when I inhaled sharply. I couldn't help it—it made me want to laugh to be called "reasonable and practical." Were I really reasonable and practical I would never have decided to adopt Ned, or be, even now, trying to figure out how to work things out with a man like Daniel.

"You and I have both suffered…losses…recently," he went on. "Don't worry—I don't want to talk about them, and you don't either— but here we are. We both have sons to raise. We both would benefit from having a partner. The kids would benefit." I raised a hand to cut him off, but he held up his own. "No—let me get this out. I wasn't even going to bring this up for another few months or so, but I got the feeling you were wanting to pull back. I'm not trying to rush this. I just want you to consider it."

"Skandar—" I shook my head helplessly. "I don't know what to say, except that you've got to put this out of your head completely. This is not possible. Not possible."

"Why?" He threw the word at me.

Provoked, I snapped, "Because people aren't business deals! You don't sit down and weigh the pros and cons! Even if you did, I don't know how you'd come up with a green light on us—yes, getting together might help with the adoptions, and Bryson and Ned would get a traditional family, but we would still have to have a marriage. We would still be promising to spend the rest of our lives together, and we don't even love each other!"

I could feel the flush of stress burning my face, and I took refuge in rearranging Ned's blankets around him. The sounds of Bryson and Foster panting and running and laughing carried over the distance.

When Skandar spoke again, his voice was calm. "We don't love each other…now. But we could come to love each other. I find you intelligent and—"

"Don't say 'pleasant'!" I shrilled. This was exactly what I had feared that day in the sushi restaurant.

Plainly he didn't remember that particular exchange because he looked at me like I had sprouted antennae. "—Kind-hearted—?" he suggested, testing the waters to see if this, too, was on the no-fly list. When I didn't explode, he continued, "And all in all, not unattractive. I think if we decided to try this, we would have enough to build a loving relationship on."

Had no one ever told him that calling a woman "not unattractive" did not melt her heart? Thankfully, I wasn't in love with him, or that could have been a death blow.

"Surely," I said, in my best, we're-all-adults-and-we-can-be-sensible-about-this tone, "this was not how you approached your relationship with Katherine—'do we have enough raw materials to make a finished product?'"

"Katherine was Katherine." There went the hard set to his jaw. I didn't mean to wound him and dredge things up, but *really*. He swallowed. "There are different kinds of love. We could find our own version."

"It's not just that," I went on. It looked like I was going to have the raise the incompatibility stakes. "You know very well that I'm too religious for you. We're not a good match that way."

"I don't know about that. I admit it was a little much for me at first, but, like I told your family, I can see more of your point of view now. If you don't go too nuts with religion, I recognize the benefits."

By the end of his speech I was shaking my head vehemently. "That's just it, Skandar. If you knew me, you would think I was too nuts about religion! I'm adopting Ned because I think God told me to—how crazy is that? It's not just a—a—sideline hobby for me. I actually think of God rather personally—talk to him about my life—try to figure out how to do it together."

Skandar's pace didn't even slow. "And I tell you, Cass, that I'm okay with it. Your faith is a comfort to you—great. I like your church—the pastor's a decent speaker, Bryson has fun in Sunday school. There's no obstacle here."

For Pete's sake. The man was more stubborn than Daniel.

I was going to have to speak in a language he could understand. Which meant baring my heart to yet another third party.

I took a deep breath. "I'm sorry, Skandar, but it's out of the question. I—I care about someone else."

This, finally, caught him up short. Then he relaxed. "Oh—I understand. You mean Troy. You haven't gotten over the loss of your husband."

My cheeks flamed scarlet now. "Actually, no. I didn't mean Troy. I meant…I meant another person."

Skandar frowned. "Another person? Ah—your ex-boyfriend, possibly—the one I met that day."

For crying out loud.

I rubbed my forehead. "No, no. I didn't mean him either. I meant another guy."

"*Another* guy?" he repeated. I imagined he was only with difficulty repressing a whistle. "Then this is completely moot, I gather. I'm sorry. I didn't know you were dating someone."

"Hmm," I grunted. Technically, I wasn't, since Daniel and I hadn't defined anything. Did being kissed once on the neck and once on the cheek two days ago count as dating?

Skandar made as if to start walking again but stopped after a few steps. "Well, if you're quick about it, that should solve your adoption problems."

"Hmm."

We watched Bryson and Foster scrabble over the ball. Foster's muffler had come completely off and lay in the wet grass some way away, as had Bryson's cap, leaving his hair to glow like a torch. "Tell me, though—what would you say then to just keeping this in the back of your head for a while, in case that other guy doesn't work out?"

"Why?" I countered, mystified. "Why would you want me to do that? There are plenty of other intelligent…kind-hearted…non-repulsive women out there you could start working on."

Skandar burst out with his rare, unexpected laugh. "So there are. You're not turning me down just because I called you 'not unattractive,' are you? Which isn't the same as non-repulsive, by the way."

"I'm not," I said, smiling now. "But I would advise you to pick a different descriptor, next time you try this."

He shrugged. "Nah. I won't be trying this again anytime soon. It's not fair to Bryson to have different women popping in and out of his life."

"I guess not. Probably, considering our decision, it's not fair to Bryson to keep seeing me."

"I don't know about that. He's already fond of you. There's no reason I can't explain to him that we're friends…Don't look so doubtful, Cass—do you think your boyfriend would mind?"

The mere thought of referring to Daniel as my *boyfriend* made me cringe. "Uh…I guess he'd be okay with it. But really, Skandar, is that what you want? You could find some other friends who come with fewer complications."

"I could. But then, those friends wouldn't be you. Since we're on the business analogies today, you could say I'm swayed by all the sunk costs in our relationship. It's been a hell of a year for me. You can't blame me for being a little loss-averse."

• • •

Ned was fully awake and protesting with hunger by the time I got home. Leaving the stroller in the garage, I took him in my arms and hurried inside to get a bottle going.

Joanie and Phyl were sitting at the table, dirty dishes pushed to the side while they pored over a list. Random equipment lay scattered over the floor and countertops: sleeping bags, water bottles, a dinged-up mess kit.

"What's going on?" I asked, flipping on the faucet to heat some water. I grabbed a bottle from the drawer and dumped a scoop of formula in it.

"Chaff retreat next weekend," Joanie replied, referring to the singles group. "The stupid steering committee got it in their head that they want to do something rustic, so we're out somewhere east of nowhere in late September in unheated cabins. Unbelievable."

"It's supposed to be pretty there," put in Phyl. "Fall color and all that…"

"If you two are gone next weekend, it sounds like Ned and I are on our own," I said, thinking again of Mrs. Martin's sex-offending car stalker. Normally I didn't mind a little solitude, and I resented her planting the fear in my head, but there it was. "Daniel's off on some mystery business trip—maybe I can get Perry to come down."

"But that would mean Darla, Cass. I'd rather be alone than have her around," said Joanie. She folded the list into thirds and pressed the creases. "Of course, if she does come over, give Creep a call. She could steal him and kill two birds with one stone."

I rolled my eyes. "If you dislike him so much, why don't you just end it? I thought for sure it was the last straw when he tried to get friendly with Violette."

Joanie made a face. "I've told you: this is a purely utilitarian relationship. He wants me on his arm for the grand opening of that new retail complex in October, and I want him as a date to Phyl's wedding in November. Then there are the holiday parties, so most likely we won't get around to breaking up until January."

Shaking Ned's bottle vigorously, I reverted to the original subject.

"Maybe Jason would let me borrow Benny for the weekend. Do you think I could call him, Phyl?"

"You could try." Phyl wrinkled her nose as she always did if you mentioned her ex-husband. "His new wife Jessica *loves* Benny, though. Haven't you noticed we hardly ever get him anymore?"

"Well, one thing we know for sure," said Joanie. "You won't be having the Sebaris over. How'd it go this morning?"

"All cleared up," I answered, searching through the diaper bag for the cleanest burp cloth. "We're friends."

Joanie groaned. "Unbelievable, Cass. You *still* didn't manage to shake that guy! Did you at least have a real discussion, or are you just assuming that it's all cleared up?"

"It's all cleared up," I repeated firmly. "He told me that he saw some benefits to getting together, and I nixed it. Said it would be impossible."

Phyl laid down the water purification tablets she was counting. "Oh…I actually feel kind of sorry for him, all grief-stricken and lonely—"

"Well, quit already!" complained Joanie, chucking a packet of wet wipes at her. "The man will just have to find some other path back to wellness."

"I think Skandar will be fine," I assured Phyl. "It's not like he fell in love with me, or anything. He just said we could make something work, since I was—*quote*—'not unattractive.'"

Joanie laughed at this, and even Phyl's mouth twitched. "Poor man."

Nudging Joanie down the bench with my foot, I took a seat and shook a few drops from the bottle onto my wrist. Close enough. I hadn't found Ned especially picky about the temperature of his formula, but I still tried to get it somewhat consistent. Residual guilt from Min, probably, who was 100% breastfed.

"No, really—I think we'll get along better now, since we'll be on the same page. He even said he would tell Bryson we were all just friends."

"Yeah, right," said Joanie.

Absently, we watched Ned chugging away at his late-morning meal. I was going to have to up the amount I gave him pretty soon.

Phyl started stacking the dirty dishes to clear them. "Would you have been more open to Skandar, Cass, if you didn't already like Daniel?—Don't worry—he's off somewhere and won't hear us—I remember how you once said that, out of three billion men in the world, there were probably 100,000 that you could make a marriage work with."

"That's moot," I insisted. Heck, I'd already let Skandar call Daniel my boyfriend. Now I was getting rather reckless. "I even told Skandar I liked someone else. I like Daniel."

The girls were wide-eyed.

"Whoa…does this mean you're finally going to say something to him?" Joanie asked.

"I suspect he already knows. But, yes. Yes, when I get a chance."

Phyl looked concerned. "You think he still likes you, then—even after that office incident?"

I shifted uncomfortably. "He said she was a client and that he was about to get rid of her. And yes, I do think he still likes me."

"But what about the being afraid he would cheat on you?" persisted Phyl.

"Shut up, Phyl," Joanie ordered, exasperated.

I thought of Darla hanging all over him, Kristen stroking his leg under the table, Violette hovering about him at the open house, pink-cheeked and aflutter. But that was *before.* B.C. Before Cass. "Well, he hasn't yet," I answered stoutly, "since we weren't together. I guess I'll have to see how it plays out."

The next thing I knew, Joanie had crawled under the table to get out around me, and she and Phyl were running into each other in their haste to load the dishes and scoop the camping equipment into neater piles.

"What are you doing?" I demanded. "Aren't you going to sit and talk to me some more?"

"No way. We're getting out of here so that you can talk to Daniel the second he comes home."

"But you don't even know where he is! He might be out all day."

"We'll hit REI, Joanie," said Phyl, undeterred. "And then Nordstrom, so I can show you the dress I picked out for my mom."

"Perfect. And then we can go to Creep's cousin's restaurant and try to bum a free lunch."

"I didn't necessarily say I was going to tell Daniel today," I protested, not that anyone was listening.

Three minutes later, Ned and I had the kitchen to ourselves.

CHAPTER 21:

Taking the Plunge

Joanie and Phyl needn't have gone tearing off like that because Daniel didn't turn up the rest of the morning.

There were things I could have been doing: running errands, catching up on email, reading Riley's feedback on my *Ace Assassin* drafts. Instead I dawdled around, waiting, waiting, starting to lose my nerve. Why on earth had I bragged to everyone about Daniel?

After lunch and some laundry-folding and ten minutes of staring blindly at the same page of my library book, however, my sleep debt overcame my anticipation. I stretched out on the blanket beside Ned and passed out.

I dreamed.

I was Benny, leaning against the couch while someone petted my head, running his hand from my crown to the nape of my neck in long strokes. I luxuriated in the sensation, wishing I were a cat so I could purr. When the hand slowed, I turned, nudging it so that it would stroke my face. Which it did. But a funny thing happened: as it stroked, my apricot fur fell away in tufts, leaving bare skin. It's the mange, I thought. I must have it after all.

I opened my eyes.

And met blue ones.

Daniel lay on the blanket next to me, propped up on his elbow, his hand cradling my head as he rubbed his thumb along the base of my ear.

Gasping in shock, I would have scrambled away, had I not been afraid of landing on Ned.

"Shhhh…." Gently, he pulled me toward him again.

For a second I yielded, but then, just as his lips pressed against mine, I struggled free and sat up. "Wait. Wait, Daniel. What does it mean? What are you doing?"

A slow, electric smile. "What does it look like I'm doing? I'm seducing you."

"Oh." I tried to slow my breathing.

He reached for me again. "This house is always so damned full of people that I have to take my chances when I can find them. C'mere."

I closed my eyes with a sigh and let him draw me back down. But wait, I thought, as his lips brushed my chin, my neck. There was something we needed to do first, right? Right? *Right.*

Pushing off his chest, I sat up again. "Wait," I panted.

Daniel rolled onto his back, laughing softly. "'Had we but world enough, and time—'"

I cut him off. "No. No poetry. I'm going to sit here, and you sit… over there… and we're going to talk first."

Obediently he moved to the armchair.

"And wipe that wicked expression off your face."

"After you, my dear."

I put my hands to my cheeks to try to calm them. I needed to think. He waited.

"Daniel…" my voice came out pleading. Clamping my mouth shut, I swallowed a couple times and then tried again. "Daniel, I know this is all second nature to you—instinct—but have you thought about this?"

"To be frank, I haven't thought about much else."

"But—but—" Given that I hadn't thought about much else, either, it occurred to me that I should have prepared a set speech. Come with notecards in hand. Not that it mattered. With him so close and looking at me like that, I seemed to have regressed to a pre-verbal stage.

He helped me. "Let me guess…you want to know, like all women, whether I mean anything by this, or if I'm just gratifying some physical urge."

Experience did have its benefits, I supposed. "Well—umm—yes," I nodded. "Uh-huh—I guess that's exactly what I want to know."

He beckoned to me with one finger. "Then the answer is Yes and Yes."

I shook my head. To clear it, really. "'Yes and yes'?"

"Yes, I mean something by it, and yes, it's pretty damned physical by this point."

My grip on the couch cushions tightened, since my rebellious body threatened to set a land-speed record launching itself at him.

"So…I suppose that usually does the trick," I said unsteadily. "A little 'this means something to me' and a little 'I want you,' and the next thing you know, she's yours."

"It may astound you to hear this, Cass," replied Daniel with mock gravity, "but I usually leave out the first part."

"Oh! I see. With a man as charming as you, 'I want you' is sufficient." I crossed my arms defensively. "Seriously—'I want you' and your good looks have gotten you all those hordes of women?"

He made an impatient move. "You really want to talk about this now? All right, then—no. No. I guess I say more than that. If you must know, I probably tell the so-called hordes that I find them beautiful, irresistible."

I felt my face scrooging into a pout. "And you didn't think it was necessary, in my case, to say you found me beautiful—irresistible?" Sheesh, even Skandar bothered to tell me I was "not unattractive"!

"As a matter of fact, you little cat, I meant to pay you the greater compliment of not feeding you a line."

Oh.

Still— "You do, though, don't you?"

"Do?"

"Find me…attractive?"

He pinched the bridge of his nose. I could almost hear him counting to ten.

"You may find this hard to believe, Cass, but I do try to avoid getting involved with women I find revolting."

That was comforting. In my case, at least. And as much as he was going to say about it, apparently.

In my peripheral vision I caught movement. Ned, stirring from his midday snooze. That gave us fifteen minutes, at best, to get through my List of Concerns. Daniel saw it, too, and he raised his eyebrows at me questioningly. "You have more, I take it."

"Yes." It was getting easier to think now, but not easier to speak those thoughts aloud. I stared down at my palms. "I'm sorry—I know that you're…ready for anything…after you've gone through the I-want-you-you're-beautiful routine—"

"Which, I repeat, I was not doing here."

"Not at all!" I assured him. "With me you went straight to the ready-for-anything stage—no! Shhh—let me say this." Finding nothing more to inspect with my hands, I sat on them. "I mean, I know you probably don't have these kinds of conversations until the woman can't stand not knowing any longer, and then she probably brings it up, and you dump her for her pains, but I would—I would rather talk about this now. And then, if you feel that urge to…flee, it'll be cleaner this way."

He was silent, forcing me to meet his level gaze. "Cass, I promise to listen to every last item on your agenda, but you have to do something for me."

"What?"

"Get over here."

"It would be more…coherent and efficient if I stay over here."

"Screw coherence and efficiency."

Okay.

Puppet-like I found myself getting to my feet and crossing over to him. Reaching for my hand, he pulled me down on his knee, twining my fingers in his. "Shoot."

I took a deep breath. Made a half-hearted attempt to free my fingers. Stared at the fireplace. "Okay…well… umm, I'd say my first concern is that you're—you're a very physical guy. I don't think you…place the same value on things that I do, so even…doing things like this—this is a big deal for me. I don't do it lightly."

He tugged gently on my hand, and I turned to see him smiling at me. Not derisively, but with genuine warmth. "I know." His voice was low, caressing. "I know, Cass. I'm not doing it lightly either."

Coherence and efficiency took some hits. I found myself leaning—melting, more like—his direction, but Ned chose that moment to force one pudgy fist free of his swaddling, and he waved it jerkily, as if to get my attention. I straightened back up.

"Ahem. Good. All right, then. And—er—it still pertains—what we talked about months ago—I'm not into sleeping with men I'm not married to, so you'll have to go elsewhere for sex."

His eyes gleamed. "Okay."

Okay, what? That was a joke! Okay, he'd be going elsewhere? I assumed, by the twist of his mouth, that he was laughing at me, not with me. But no more time to explore that one. I'd have to be content.

"And then," I went on, in as business-like tone as I could muster, "I notice that your relationships generally don't last beyond two to four weeks, after which the girl is usually never seen again—unless, of course, you foist her on my brother—so if we…start something—"

"You mean 'continue' something," he interrupted. "I consider this relationship 'started.'" His transferred my hand to his right, that his left might be free to trace its way up the length of my spine.

"Please," I squirmed away. "I need to say all this now, before Ned decides he's ready to eat again. Especially if you say the clock is already ticking! Look, Daniel—I need some kind of pre-nup out of you—not that we're getting married, but more of a pre-relationship agreement: if this doesn't work out, after whatever length of time, you promise you won't kick me out of the Palace? No matter whether the sight of me turns your stomach or you're angry or you just wish I'd go away?" Daniel looked thoroughly insulted and about to tell me off, but I hurried on. "Because I can promise you in return that—when you're done—I can behave like nothing ever happened. No tears, no recriminations, no boiled rabbits. We'll just go back to being friends again. I'll make it as easy on you as possible—"

By this point, Daniel had shoved me unceremoniously from his knee, the better to leap up and hulk over me, his eyes narrow with displeasure. "Just what the hell do you think I'm doing here, Cass? You think you're just the latest pants I'm trying to get into, and when I've had my way, I'm kicking you and Ned to the curb?"

"Well, no—I mean, yes—kind of—" I floundered. Wasn't that what he did with everyone else? Was I way off base here? "I mean, that's what I want to avoid. And stop bullying me by getting in my face like that! If you had a different track record, I wouldn't have to be saying this, so don't get all ticked at me. I was just trying to reassure you that this needn't be messy. We're both adults. I won't make you uncomfortable when it's over—mooning around after you, like Phyl did. You wanted *her* to move out—remember?"

"For God's sake, Cass," fumed Daniel, "I'd like to point out to you that I didn't throw you out after I asked you to *marry me* and got turned down, so what makes you think I'd do that after you've adopted a baby, just because you decide you can't love me—"

"No, no! I mean if *you* decide it's not working," I corrected him.

Our raised voices succeeded in rushing Ned back to consciousness, and he let out a wail of irritation here. Hurrying over to pick him up, I cradled him to my chest and made soothing sounds. "He's hungry— it's been almost four hours."

Daniel followed me into the kitchen, his face still darkened. I wondered how on earth people did ask for actual pre-nuptial agreements, since my direct method wasn't going over very well, and I wasn't even asking for money, just civility. Sweeping aside a mess kit and sleeping pad, he perched on one of the barstools, his eyes tracking my progress from sink to drawer to cabinet.

When at last the bottle was ready and I settled with Ned at the table, he rotated around. "All right then, Cass. My 'track record' being what it is—did you want this agreement in writing?"

At least he'd calmed down.

I blushed. "Of course not. I believe you. I didn't mean to offend you—I just—with everything so uncertain in my life right now, I had to make sure."

The barstool squeaked as he rose from it to come sit opposite me. "Then be sure of this—look at me, Cass—I've waited a long time for you. I can see that you have pretty low expectations for us. We can't guarantee that it'll work out—I guess life has no guarantees—but, whatever you may think, I'm not going into this on a whim."

His sober expression relaxed into a grin, as if he could see my heart speeding up in my chest. On the other hand, maybe he could hear it, since its pounding filled my own ears. "Some girls you mess around with, and other girls you marry. You most likely fall in the latter bucket."

"Hooray."

"The question is, which bucket do I fall in for you? Did you have any more items on that agenda?"

"One more." I felt the heat creeping back up my cheeks. If I thought the pre-nup was awkward, this was downright thorny. Would he understand me any better than Skandar? "And I probably should have mentioned it first, if I had my head on straight and you didn't wake me up in the manner you did."

"Let's have it."

"It's about—about the whole religion thing," I said reluctantly. "You…know where I'm at—I just wondered where you're at. I saw you at church one morning…"

"Are you saying that sharing your faith is a prerequisite even to kissing you?"

"No…no, I'm not saying that." My color came and went again as I remembered the atheist Oxford tutor I'd dumped Troy for in college. Clive and I had done our fair share of *that*. "But…I wouldn't want to get too far down this road, no matter how well I—liked you—if you'd already decided you couldn't go there."

Daniel sat back, his eyes wandering to the bay window and the cedars outside. For a few minutes there were no sounds apart from Ned's greedy smackings and the whirring of the refrigerator.

I felt my heart sinking, inch by inch, somewhere down into my gut as the silence stretched. Oh, why did you have to ask right away, a foolish part of my brain spoke up. You could at least have made out with him a few times! It's not too late, another irrational voice insisted. Say something about how, on reflection, you could still have a lovely fling.

"Cass." Daniel cut short my second-guessing.

I jumped slightly. "…Yes?"

"I haven't brought it up because, at this point, I wouldn't know exactly what to say. I'm still…exploring." He smiled ruefully. "It's hard to overcome a lifetime of thinking about the world in such a different way. I wouldn't want to—to commit to something I wasn't at peace with. That I couldn't get behind. Even for you. Especially for you."

If I weren't already in love with him, this would have done it. Maybe it was the contrast with Skandar's unshakable indifference. I lowered my eyes, not wanting him to read them. Saw that Ned had emptied his bottle and was dozing a little. Gingerly, I sat him up and started tapping on his back, hoping he wouldn't choose this moment to spit up.

"Say something, Cass."

"I—it—I don't know what to say."

"Say it's enough for now."

And then some.

I smiled tentatively at him. "It's enough for now…"

He moved so fast I could barely follow him. "Aaak! Daniel—be careful! If you squish Ned when he's full of formula, it's going to end up all over us."

"Then let's go where we have more room to maneuver."

"I've got to change him first—he's falling asleep."

"Shall I come up to your room with you?"

Not bloody likely. Imagine if Joanie and Phyl came home to find Daniel in my bedroom—I was not ready to deal with the fallout from that. "No. No. You stay down here. I'll be right back."

"So will Joanie and Phyl, I imagine. If we've only got two weeks before I throw you out on your ass, and Ned with you, we've got to make the most of it."

• • •

I wondered, as I was upstairs cleaning Ned up, if Daniel was this hands-on in all his relationships. I didn't have much to go on, since, apart from the time I had caught him and Kelly in the Lean-To, he behaved circumspectly when others were around. But that time… I let the memory replay. Yes, I'd have to say his hands had been pretty much everywhere that afternoon. Or, more accurately, everywhere his mouth wasn't.

I spread a baby blanket on my bed, folded down a corner and lay Ned across it. He was growing quickly; swaddling had become more difficult.

But, in all or nearly all of Daniel's past relationships, all that physicality led straight to sleeping together—would he be content for long if it didn't? Nor had he mentioned getting married again. Premature, I suppose. Just that reference to their being "no guarantees," which sounded, on the whole, as if he didn't expect things to work out any more than I did.

Laying Ned in the corner of his bassinet I tucked a rolled-up blanket along his other side to keep him in place. Then, instead of going back downstairs, I threw myself across my bed and stared up at the ceiling. Joanie would tell me I was over-analyzing. But Joanie under-analyzed—look at her dragging it out with Creep because it was mutually convenient! Still, a little under-analysis might come in handy here. After dreaming about what it would be like to be close to Daniel, I could actually experience it, for however long it lasted. And I had his promise that, if things went south, Ned and I wouldn't have to start over someplace new.

"Cass?" I heard him call up the stairs, a note of exasperation tingeing his voice. "Are you putting Ned down or waiting till he's ready to leave for college?"

I didn't answer. But after another minute I sat up and flicked on the baby monitor. The glimpse I caught of my hair in the mirror sent me to the bathroom for my brush, where I splashed water on my cheeks. Just look at me! Face flushed, eyes unnaturally bright, hands gripping the countertop for dear life.

I turned in profile to one side and then the other. Sighed. No, those breasts were just going to have to do. I could get one of those push-up bras, but I wouldn't want to be accused of false advertising, and, with all the wire and machinery in those things, they smacked more of contraption than lingerie.

"Here goes nothing," I murmured. "You can do this, Cass. It can't be any worse than everything else you've gone through. And, if Daniel breaks your heart—well—there are always those 99,999 other men."

CHAPTER 22:

Call, Girl

"Don't call me," I told Daniel, before he left on his trip Wednesday morning. "I forbid you to call me."

He parked his rolling suitcase at the end of the kitchen island and came over to wrap his arms around me. "Mmm…good morning to you, too. What makes you think I would want to call you?"

"That's just it," I said breathlessly, when he left off kissing my mouth, moving down my jawline to my throat. "I don't want to spend how-ever many days trying to keep my phone charged because I'm hoping you'll call me."

I felt, rather than heard, him laugh. "Will you be calling me, then?"

"No. Not unless there's a real emergency, like I accidentally set the Palace on fire." Now that we were "together," I was trying to stretch out my two-to-four weeks by being as little like his past girlfriends as possible. No clinging, no asking how he felt about me, no wanting to know where he was at all times. "You just come home whenever you come home, Daniel, and we can talk then, if you like."

He paused in his attentions, to my mingled disappointment and relief, taking a step back. "And here I was, beginning to think you gave a damn about me."

My gaze met his warily, as I tried to gauge the percentage of teasing in his tone. "I do…a little." I put a hesitant hand on his chest. "You're easy on the eyes. In fact, I'll be sorry if this trip of yours counts as part of my time because I'd like my whole two weeks, please."

"You'll get it," he growled, jerking me back against him.

That was it for the heart-to-heart, conversation-wise, at least. When he left ten minutes later I sagged onto the cushioned bench at the table, limp as a rag doll. Looked over at Ned, who was trying to find his thumb, but gave up after a while and sucked on his fist instead. "Between the two of you, there won't be anything left of me, physically," I muttered.

It had been a crazy few days. No need to tell Joanie and Phyl the upshot of my talk with Daniel—it was there for all to see. Not that he touched me, if you didn't count grabbing me whenever we happened to be alone and kissing me within an inch of my life. (This didn't happen nearly as often as I would like, however, because, as he had pointed out, the Palace had its fair share of visitors—Wayne, Creep, the Dobbs—besides the ubiquitous Joanie and Phyl.) There was also that troublesome full-time job of his and Ned's periodic care. But other than all that, we were nearly inseparable. If we couldn't make out, we could still sit near each other and talk and talk and talk. I got to hear about the partner driving him crazy at work; he listened to the latest on Nadina and the anxiety-inducing Mike; we compared books we loved, plays we'd seen, places we had traveled. There were some topics we avoided, naturally: Religion, all Significant Others, Us, the Future—but if you only had a few weeks together, what did those matter? Or, if it turned out you had longer, then tomorrow was soon enough for such things.

As it happened, Daniel and I only had those three days.

• • •

On Thursday the doorbell rang, and I opened to a delivery man holding a potted rosemary plant. Bewildered, I inspected the card: "'There's rosemary, that's for remembrance.'"

On Friday came the pansies. The card read only: "'That's for thoughts.'"

My hand itched to call him. Surely he didn't mean to keep up with the *Hamlet* references. If so, a quick review of my dog-eared copy predicted fennel for Saturday and columbines for Sunday, unless he made it a combined shipment. In either case, the symbolism boded ill, as my edition noted that fennel stood for "flattery" and columbines for "male infidelity." That left Ophelia's bitter rue of regret for Monday. So was he remembering me and thinking of me, or did he know I would look up the reference and be provoked into responding?

After turning my phone over and over in my hand, then scrolling through my contacts to stare at his number, I put it down. I would not respond.

I gave the plants to Phyl.

• • •

Joanie and Phyl left Friday afternoon for their rustic camping retreat, rejoicing in the sunshine and clear skies. I felt optimistic myself, having managed to inveigle Benny from Jason and Jessica for a visit. An entire weekend to myself at the Palace was a rare thing, and I was fully prepared to enjoy it.

Saturday began with morning tea for me and a bottle for Ned, reading the newspaper while Ned lay on his back, blissfully sucking his fist or waving at the toys dangling above him. I read him sections of the movie reviews and the Mariners wrap, flipped him occasionally back to stomach like a sunbather, asked him for help on the crossword puzzle.

It wasn't till we were outside, having returned from walking Benny, that I noticed it.

The beat-up white sedan.

Ned was in his bouncy seat and Benny stretched out on the walkway sunbathing while I watered Phyl's hanging baskets. Being occupied, I might never have noticed the parked car, except that, when I climbed the step stool for a better reach, the neighbor's teenage son drove by, stereo pounding. I glanced up as he went by, smiling at the volume, and there it was. All its windows were rolled down, for air circulation I presumed, save the driver's side. And through that tinted window I could just make out the outline of a head. Feeling my heart give a uncomfortable lurch, my grip tightened on the spray nozzle, and I blew the heads off several of the Million Bells before I realized what I was doing and consciously tried to relax.

After all, the car's mere presence might not necessarily be threatening. We didn't live in a neighborhood with much house-to-house socializing, so it could easily belong to someone who moved in in the last few months, unbeknownst to us. But why, then, would the owner be sitting out in his parked car, instead of going inside? Why would he zoom off, rather than talk to Angela Martin, if she came from a neighboring house?

Slowly I climbed down from the step-stool, keeping my movements calm. The white-sedan driver might just be the reclusive sort. Clyde Hill's own Boo Radley. If you ran at him, he took off. But he watched you behind windows and yearned to give you chewing gum.

I thought briefly of dashing back inside and calling the couple who lived across the street to see if they knew who was parked in front of their house, before I realized I didn't know their number. That, and I couldn't remember their names. Or faces. I doubted I could even pick them out of a line-up if they weren't actually standing in their driveway with their house in the background.

Should I pretend I wanted to chat with the neighbors—march across and ring the doorbell, meanwhile fixing Boo with a beady eye? Too chicken. I was no Angela Martin, taking on stalkers and sex-offenders single-handed. Call the police? What would I say— "My boyfriend's [*yeesh!*] mother spotted a creepy white sedan trolling the neighborhood a few weeks ago, and I too would like to report a sighting"? I'm sure the officer would placate me—talk me down while he perused a take-out menu and made a teeny little mark by the sub sandwich he wanted for lunch. Sigh. Besides, Boo wasn't doing anything illegal, was he? I was just being paranoid.

If only the girls were home, and we could check it out together. Or, better yet, if only I could just go inside and send Daniel out to investigate.

Daniel.

This hardly qualified as an emergency. But still—

I could at least call him and see if he thought I was nuts to be concerned. Joanie and Phyl were off in some cell-phone-free hinterland, but maybe wherever he was lay in a telco satellite's path. And I wouldn't be terribly, terribly sorry just to hear his voice.

Digging my phone out, I scrolled through the contacts till I hit his name. What would he make of this, considering I'd declared calls off-limits? Probably what it was—an admission of trust and dependence on him. Ugh. But it beat facing Mr. Sedan Man alone. I dialed.

Before the phone even rang on my end, he picked up. There were some stifled rustling sounds. Some heavy breathing, and then— "Uhhh…?"

"Uh—" I echoed, taken aback. He was an unconventional man, and I only had one groan to go on, but I would bet that wasn't him.

The voice exhaled gustily. "What?"

What, indeed! Not only was the moaner-groaner not Daniel—it wasn't even a man. This must be the wrong number. But no, it couldn't be—it was the same number I'd gotten from Joanie's phone and the same number I reached him at the only other time I ever called him. Maybe he had gotten a new number. Too many enraged ex-girlfriends leaving him messages on the old one. Good thing this wasn't a real *emergency* emergency!

"I'm so sorry," I said quickly. "I think I must have the wrong number—this isn't Daniel Martin's phone, is it?"

"Dan-Daniel," the decidedly female voice repeated. She was *panting* now, for Pete's sake. I was about to ignore manners and just hang up when I heard her say stumblingly, "Yes! Yes, Daniel—mmm…yes, Daniel. Mmmm…(pant)…hmm…huh…aaaaaaahhhh…my chest…" More heavy breathing. Flumping and flopping and indistinct sounds. Good gracious!

Snapping my phone shut, I stood there for a long minute, gaping at Phyl's now-drowned flowers, Stalker Boo completely forgotten.

What was going on?

Who did I just call? *Had* Daniel changed his number, leaving his old one to be taken over by a phone-sex company or a studio that did porn soundtracks? Or—and unfortunately more likely—if that was Daniel's number, who answered the phone? And, if it was Daniel's phone, why would he let someone else answer it? And, if he let someone else answer it, why would she answer while she was getting it on, for heaven's sake? Because that was unmistakably what I seem to have interrupted. And if she was getting it on with Daniel, wouldn't he object to her picking up? Maybe he was so…occupied… that he didn't even realize his girlfriend was taking calls. Still—who took calls while she was going for what sounded like the ride of her life?

Ned made some gurgly, chortly sounds, and I glanced over to see that, in my dazed hands, the hose was even now sprinkling him. Quickly, I shut off the faucet and used a corner of his blanket to wipe his face.

Sinking onto the step, I thought briefly of calling back but quickly nixed the idea. If the woman answered again, I would have nothing to say. And if she didn't answer, it proved nothing. As I tapped the phone against my head, thinking hard, a disturbing explanation came to mind: maybe the woman hadn't answered the phone. Maybe she—or Daniel himself—had inadvertently picked up while otherwise engaged. It wouldn't be the first time someone's behind or someone's purse spoke to me—Joanie and I had a running joke about the number of times her rear end reached out and touched someone, usually me. I would end up hollering, "Joanie? Joanie! *Joanie!*" to no response, sometimes hearing her muffled voice placing a complicated latté order.

That had to be it.

Daniel or the girlfriend had unintentionally hit the Talk button on the phone just as I dialed him. Maybe he'd been ripping his pants off at the time. Or she was grabbing his butt and the phone slipped out—God forbid anyone had heard me squawking into indifferent space. Or maybe he'd hit something while digging in his pocket for a condom. Mercy me.

Mercy, mercy me.

Who knows how long I would have sat there, lost to the world, struggling to catch my breath as wave after wave of emotion knocked me senseless.

The *jerk*!

The two-timing, two-faced, slimy, sleazy, deceitful, no-good, hypocritical, lousy, worthless, poetry-spouting, symbolic-plant-mailing, roving-handed, sex-addicted *jerk*! I hated him! I *knew* getting involved with him was a bad idea, but I was so stupid stupid stupid!

Barely had the rage struck me than the jealousy swallowed it whole. Who was she? Violette. Kristen. The lap-dancing client. Any number of ex-girlfriends. Someone entirely new he'd met on his little business jaunt. The mysterious person whose moral qualms had to be overcome before the trip could happen. Darla. Kelly. Michelle. Missy. And those were only the women I knew of from the last year, for heaven's sake.

Rage took a turn again, and then jealousy once more, and then both emotions lost out entirely to heartbreak.

Three days. We only lasted three days. I couldn't even hold his interest for the minimum two weeks! Maybe I should have gotten the push-up bra. Maybe it had been completely unrealistic to expect a guy like him to be satisfied with no sex, but if he couldn't go six stinking days without it—!

If I were a reasonable and practical woman like Skandar thought, I would wash my hands of Daniel right now. Good riddance to bad rubbish.

And I would, I vowed to myself, be reasonable and practical from now on. Falling for Daniel was completely uncharacteristic of me, and that nonsense was going to stop instantly. Or very, very soon. Absolutely, positively, the very second after I got done crying.

• • •

A car door slammed.

My head flew up.

There was a man now standing outside the driver-side door of the beat-up sedan, and, in my overwrought state, all my earlier fears rushed back full-force to choke me. He paused, squinting across the sunny street to where I sat slumped on the porch step, draped around Benny, whom I had called over, in order to blubber into his soft fur. The man was not very big—I could see that from here—skinny and gaunt. His faded Huskies sweatshirt and jeans hung on him half-heartedly, and straw-colored hair poked out underneath a baseball cap.

In the two seconds before he took his first step, a dozen competing thoughts swarmed my head: oh! he's pale like Boo Radley—sic Benny on him—turn the hose on him—call 9-1-1—scream—run inside and slam the door—at least throw Neddy inside—tackle him myself—he doesn't look armed—what could I use as a weapon?—at least *stand up*, Cass!

My muscles, confused by the mental jumble, refused to do anything, but thank God for Benny. The Labradoodle must have absorbed the tension coursing through me—or he was tired of being cried on—because he burst from my stiff arms, charging to the base of the driveway to bark his head off at the stranger.

The man halted. Held up his hands. Waited.

Benny did his best rabid beast impression, complete with ears laid back and body crouched to spring while growls and snarls ripped from him. I'd never seen anything like it. I guess living with Jason did that to you.

"You gonna call off your dog?" Stalker Boo hollered, after a few more moments of the stand-off.

Slowly, as if I were rickety and had to re-assemble myself piece by piece to move, I got to my feet. I didn't especially want to come down off the porch, but I took a step closer to the walkway, angling myself so that I blocked Ned from view. "Can I help you with something?"

"Just walking by, enjoying the sunshine."

"No, you weren't," I responded. Too fervent. I tried again. "I saw your car parked there for some time, and you were sitting in it. In fact, we've seen you in this neighborhood before. Do you live around here?"

"Can't hear you," he called back, cupping his ear. "Can you come closer?"

Instead I raised my voice. "I said we've seen you around here before, and you've been sitting in your car there for a while—do you live—"

He took a tentative step my direction, but when Benny crouched even lower and let loose another volley of barks, he froze. "Oh…I'm from nearby. This a new dog for you? I'm used to seeing lots of people going in and out of that house, but not a dog."

I felt my blood congeal in my veins. He *had* been watching, then. Angela Martin was right—he was some kind of stalker pervert freak. I edged closer to Ned. "No—it's not a new dog. He doesn't always listen to me, though—so you'd better get back in your car."

"Well, hang on right there…no need to be unfriendly. I'd just like a word with you."

One thing was certain: I didn't want a word with him when I was by myself, even with Benny there to keep him at bay. My cell phone lay on the doormat where I had flung it after calling Daniel's ho—if I drifted backward up the steps I could reach it.

Barely had I taken my eyes from the stranger to get the exact bearings of the phone, than Benny came tearing back to me, his Doberman-act forgotten as he lolloped excitedly in a circle around me. "What are you doing, you idiot?" I hissed. "Get back out there and terrorize that guy!"

The reason for his cavorting became clear the next instant as a car swung around Stalker Boo and pulled into the Palace driveway. An Audi. Skandar!

Elation was too weak a word to describe my feelings. Pushing Benny aside, I dashed out to greet my unexpected visitor, whose appearance obviously threw a wrench in Boo's plans. That gentleman, after one startled hesitation, spun on his heel and headed back toward his car.

"No, wait!" I cried, brave enough now. "I need to talk to you!"

Boo ignored me.

As for Skandar, he didn't even get a chance to unbuckle before I was over hammering on his window and pulling the door latch. "That man!" I gasped, wrenching the door open and pointing. "Please—you've got to stop him—I have to find out who he is."

"What the hell—?" But one look at my desperate expression and the sound of Boo scrabbling for his keys lit a fire under him. Skandar launched himself from his bucket seat and sprinted across the road. "Hey! Guy! The lady wants a word with you."

Boo yanked his car door open, only to have Skandar slam it shut again. "One second."

"I haven't done anything," the man insisted, trying to push Skandar out of the way. "Get away from my car."

I was across the street by now, Benny at my heels. "Please—I don't know who you are or why you've been watching this house, but I'm warning you to stop. I'm going to have to call the police if I see you again—"

"You're calling them now," said Skandar sternly. He put out a hand to draw me behind him, keeping the other pressed against the car door.

Boo and I stared at each other around Skandar's rigid shoulder for a long minute. I wanted to be as detailed as possible for the police report. The man stood only a couple inches taller than me. He looked to be in his 40s. Lanky—almost bony—and a touch haggard up close. I scanned his faded white-blond hair, pallid skin, narrow jaw, my scrutiny hanging up when I reached his eyes. Light green. Something about the flatness of their expression struck a chord.

My mouth fell open.

"You're—are you—are you *Mike's dad*?"

The narrow jaw jerked in recognition. "It's a free country," he mumbled.

So not a pervert or a stalker, then. A grandfather. "You want to see Ned," I said slowly.

"Cass—" Skandar's voice held a warning note.

"I think … Mr. Loftus … you should have tried to contact me or my lawyer—not skulk around like this."

"What?" he demanded, suddenly aggressive. I felt Skandar's arm stiffen under my hand. "Like you would've let me come by and see the baby? You, who're taking him from us?"

My cheeks reddened. "I think … yes, probably I would have let you. I can understand you wanting to see him. But it can't be this way. You scared me, Mr. Loftus."

"What do you got to be scared of? You've got your big house and your rich friends—" this, with a sneer at Skandar. "I've seen you all going in and out. You think you can take my son's child and hire you a fancy lawyer and that makes it okay? Makes it legal?"

Hot tears formed at the back of my eyes, but they were half from anger. "Mr. Loftus—when Nadina got pregnant with Ned, nobody wanted him. Mike wanted her to get rid of it. It's only because I begged her that she agreed to have the baby. And it's Nadina who wanted me to take him. We didn't ever expect, given how Mike reacted, that you two would decide you wanted him after all."

"Well, we do. He does. What chance you think my son's got starting over? Here's you with everything, and it's not enough. You gotta have somebody else's baby, too."

"But let's be fair! I'm not trying to adopt Ned to—to round out my perfect life, Mr. Loftus! No—it's okay, Skandar—but here Ned is, and I feel—called—to take care of him. I wish Mike all the best in getting back on his feet—"

"Bullshit!"

"Watch your mouth," snapped Skandar.

"Really, I do, Mr. Loftus, but I don't think it's in Mike's best interests or in Ned's for Mike to be raising him! When he gets…done…serving his sentence, he has a chance to start over. Let him start fresh, not… embroiled in a legal battle for a child who might just be a burden at this stage in his life."

To my amazement, Dale Loftus deflated before my eyes, the fire draining away as quickly as it had flared up. "You got a lot of things in life, you do," he said again. "What's my boy got? Who's gonna give him a job now? How's he gonna stay off the drugs? What's he got to fight for?"

"Cass," spoke up Skandar again. "I think you should be going inside."

"I can't see the baby?" asked Mr. Loftus dully.

"I would feel better about it another time," I answered honestly. Like when everyone was home and after talking to Lori.

"You're just saying that to get rid of me."

"No—I will consider it. Really. But you'd better go now."

"You gonna call the police?"

"Yes," said Skandar, before I could speak. Taking his hand off the car door, he pulled it open. Mr. Loftus had no choice but to climb in, though he yanked it shut resentfully.

With infinite relief I watched him drive away.

Not that Skandar looked any easier to deal with, at this point. "How did you get in this situation, Cass? Where are all your housemates?"

"Retreats, business trips. Skandar, thank you ever, ever so much for dropping by. I don't even know why you're here, but your timing couldn't have been better."

His face was grim. "I'm here because I haven't heard from you since we talked last weekend...*friend*. If you're not going to call me I have no choice but to check up on you." He looked in the direction Mr. Loftus had driven. "I don't know if you and Ned really ought to be alone with him running around—not till you can get a restraining order."

"Surely you don't think I need one!"

"Talk to Lori, but I'm all in favor." He paused. "Where's the boyfriend?"

Memory came flooding back. I made a business of calling Benny over and patting him, so Skandar wouldn't see my blush or the tears starting to my eyes. "Oh. Actually—he's out of town too. And, umm, he's not my boyfriend—anymore."

"What? Are you tired of him? I thought you just started dating."

We were at the porch, and I squatted down to unbuckle Ned. "We did," I replied in a low voice. "...He...cheated on me."

Skandar was silent for a long time. I fiddled with Ned. Wound the hose back up.

"What would you think, then," he said finally, "of coming to stay with Bryson and me until your housemates get back?"

"Oh! I don't think that's necessary. I have Benny with me."

Skandar looked doubtful. "Or, if you prefer, Bry and I could also spend the night here."

Even worse—imagine Joanie and Phyl coming home to Skandar as an overnight guest! I shook my head. "No, thank you. I'll be fine. Do you want to come in for iced tea?"

He glanced at his watch. "Sorry—have to pick Bryson up. Cornering your adversary took all my spare time. But if you won't come over,

Cass, will you at least call me tonight and again tomorrow, to let me know you're okay?"

Ironic. Heaven knew I wouldn't talk to Daniel now. But I wasn't sorry to have someone who would notice if I was murdered in my bed.

I nodded. "Yes. I promise. I'll call you."

CHAPTER 23:

Ghosts of Cheaters Past

"What happened to my rosemary plant and my pansies?" Phyl asked. She stood at the sink rinsing out the mess kits and canteens from the camping retreat. Joanie lay stretched across one bench, gripping her forehead and moaning.

"I threw them away."

Her mild blue eyes wondered. "But you gave them to me."

"I decided I couldn't stand to look at them." Grumpily I prodded Joanie with a socked toe. "What's wrong with you, Whimpers?"

"My head," she complained. "It's bursting open. I'm all congested. Stupid Creep gave me this." She was so stuffed up it sounded more like Stoobid Creeb.

"You got Creep to go on a church retreat with you?"

"No way. Not Mr. My-Faith-Is-Private-But-I'm-Super-Spiritual. I'm just saying he gave me this before I left."

"It might not have been Creep," said Phyl. "It seemed like half the singles were coming down with it or getting over it. Kind of early in the season to get sick, but there you go."

"Well, I didn't kiss any of them, did I? It was Creep."

"Was it worth it, at least?" I asked. "A good kiss?" I would trade a head cold in a heartbeat, if I could kiss Daniel again without knowing what a rogue he was.

"For a dumb lunk, he isn't bad." Normally Joanie erred on the TMI side, so she must really feel terrible.

I changed the subject. "Other than the cold epidemic, was it a good retreat?"

Joanie merely grunted, but Phyl gave a satisfactory run-down of the setting, speaker, and sideline activities. "Wayne and I found it refreshing, too, to go a couple days without thinking or talking wedding 24/7. Be reminded of the big picture, and all that. How was your weekend, Cass?"

"Oh, not a dull moment, but unfortunately most of the moments sucked." I threw a wadded-up napkin at Joanie. "I got to meet your mom's car stalker."

Joanie shot to a sitting position before groaning and sinking back. "You're kidding. I thought Mom really lost it when she told me about that guy. The witch hunt she started over the sex offender in her neighborhood probably still has the guy on the run. Don't tell me she's right about all this. What happened?"

"Tell us everything, Cass," said Phyl.

I did, beginning with the very first time on Main Street with Louella when I saw Dale's car and ending with our mid-street confrontation.

"Oh my gosh," said Phyl. "I'm so thankful nothing worse happened." She inspected Ned as he snoozed in the sling against me, as if to assure herself that he had not, in fact, been kidnapped.

"That's freaky that he's been parked outside spying on us," said Joanie. "And how come you didn't tell us that mom's stalker was the same guy Barbara Dobbs nearly hit when she came for the home study?"

"Yes, Cass," breathed Phyl. "We never would have left you all alone if we knew there was anything to it. I would have had my sister Mary come stay with you. Or Wayne's mom. I'm amazed Daniel didn't think you should have someone with you."

"He didn't know either," I said curtly. "I didn't mention it to anyone because I didn't want anyone getting worked up about it, including me." I wasn't in the mood to make excuses for Daniel, but even I couldn't charge the stalker to him.

"What did the police say?" pursued Joanie from her prone position.

"To go into the county on Monday and file a restraining order."

"And you're going to, right?"

I made an impatient movement. "I haven't decided positively. I want to talk to Lori first. It wasn't as if Dale was trying to harm me or Ned. He just wanted to see Ned. Who is his biological grandson, after all."

Joanie scoffed. "Excuse me? Like the Loftuses wanting to keep him isn't evidence of intent to harm? You're out of your mind, Cass. File the flipping order."

"But it's an antagonistic move, and they're already hostile. A stinking restraining order could make things even worse."

"It was a good thing Skandar dropped by just then," put in Phyl. "I know you're not interested in him, but that's twice he's been helpful to you: once at the Expo when you twisted your ankle and then yesterday running Dale off."

"I know it. I'm grateful to him. And it's not that I don't like him. In fact..."

When I trailed off, Joanie bolted upright again, forgetting even to groan. "In fact *what*? Don't even be thinking in that direction, Cass. You're dating my brother now, remember?"

"Oh, yeah?" I countered. "Well, that was the other miserable part of my weekend! I did try to call Daniel first when I saw Dale parked out there, and instead of getting him, I got some—some *hooch* he was in the middle of *screwing*!"

"You didn't."

"I did."

"He wasn't!"

"He was."

I didn't have Joanie's talent for mimicry, but I gave it my best shot, relating the phone conversation, such as it was. At the end, Joanie flopped back once more, her arm thrown over her face while she kicked her feet in impotent disgust.

Phyl came over to hug me. "I'm so sorry, Cass," she said. "You know I'd rather have been wrong in this case."

Nodding wordlessly, I fiddled with the screw-top lid of Joanie's water bottle. The threads weren't lining up. Then I realized it might be covered in germs. I wouldn't necessarily have minded lying in bed nursing depression and illness for a couple days, but it would make caring for Ned difficult, and I shouldn't risk passing something to him.

Phyl must have read my mind because she fished an antibacterial wipe from the front pocket of her half-emptied backpack and slid it toward me. "I guess that explains my plants in the trash. Did Daniel… send anything yesterday or today?"

"He did." A fit of remembered pique surged through me.

. . .

Saturday's delivery man showed up not half an hour after the whole Daniel-and-Dale Debacle.

When I had assured myself it wasn't Mike's dad at the door, I opened it. "Yes?"

"I have a delivery for Cassandra Ewan." He held out a long white box.

"She's not here," I said for no reason, "but I can sign for it."

I waited until the man got back in his truck and drove away before flipping off the lid.

Not fennel and columbines, after all. No matter how appropriate they would have been under the circumstances.

Instead, nestled in forest green tissue paper lay a dozen long-stemmed red roses. No literary allusions necessary to interpret them.

He had one, nonetheless: "'And I will come again, my love,/ Thou' it were ten thousand mile.'"

. . .

"That's kind of romantic," ventured Phyl.

"Yes—he tends toward the sappy," I said viciously. "But don't you see? That makes it worse. For some reason he wants me *and* he wants to mess around."

"I don't know," Joanie sniffed. "'My love' is just an expression. There's an English guy at Starbucks who calls me that all the time. Maybe Daniel met this girl and got swept away—I'm not saying he's not an idiot—and he's gonna let you down gently."

"It's the rest of the poem," I grumbled. "*A Red, Red Rose.* It's kind of a mushy one." I knew. I had looked it up and not known whether to throw my poetry anthology across the room or go inhale a quart of chocolate ice cream. "Who sends that stuff to someone he's going to break up with?"

She grimaced. "Yeah, okay. Maybe he's gonna play you."

"Well, I'm not planning on being played. It's finished with him. I was willing to overlook all the women who came before we got together, and I'll overlook all the women who come afterwards, but I don't see how I'm supposed to overlook the ones who come *during*."

Taking a dishrag, I started helping Phyl dry the cleaned equipment.

"It's exactly what you both predicted," I said when we were nearly done. "He likes me well enough, but that's no reason to deny himself other people."

"What did you do with the roses?" Phyl asked. "Are they in the trash too?"

A sudden urge to laugh convulsed me. Really, when things got so awful, there was nothing else to do. "No—before I could pitch them, Violette showed up. I gave them to her."

"Virulent?" blurted Joanie, cracking her eyes open again. "What did she want?"

"You saw how she was looking at Daniel the other night! What else—she said something lame about wanting to get your stir-fry recipe, Joanie, but what she really wanted was to see if he was home. I mean, she was all done up and had her hair just so. The whole time I was flipping through your recipe folder she kept peeking around, checking the Lean-To, the living room, the hall. I finally asked her flat-out if she was looking for Daniel."

"What did she say?"

"Oh, she turned all red and said was it so obvious? And did I know if he had a 'special someone' in his life? I was so ticked by then that I said that, with him, the question wasn't if, but *how many*. Then I told her he was out of town, but gave her his number…" Scowling, I added, "I hope she called and got her own little audio peep show."

Phyl's brow furrowed. "Do you really think you should encourage her, knowing what you know about him? He might need time to… work out his issues."

"Like another 35 years?"

"'Don't cry for me, French-Argentina…!'" came Joanie's stuffed-up soprano.

"Believe me, I won't."

Phyl and I joined her at the table, keeping a safe distance on the other bench seat while we doctored our mugs of tea. I slid one toward Sickie. "To your health."

She dragged herself to a sitting position and raised her mug. "To stalkers and unfaithful men everywhere."

"Here, here."

"Speaking of unfaithful men," I began again, after a minute, "if you don't mind me asking, Phyl, when Jason cheated on you, how did find out?"

She sighed. "I found out because I actually caught him—twice. But when I finally decided to open my eyes, I had to admit those probably weren't the only times. They were just the ones I knew about."

"You caught him sleeping with someone?" I marveled.

"The first time I found a bracelet in our bed that wasn't mine. I know—he was doing it in our own bed! It was so gross."

"And you confronted him?"

"After about a week of being positively miserable and waiting to see if he would confess first."

"You showed him the bracelet? What did he say?"

Phyl made a face, remembering. "Oh...it turned out Jason had three techniques for me, when I accused him of cheating. That was the first time he tried them out, but after a while they got pretty familiar." Joanie and I waited while she got her thoughts together. "First there was just flat-out denial: he said he'd never seen that bracelet before and was I sure it wasn't mine and he had no idea why I would get an idea in my head like that. Then, when I kept pressing, he moved on to accusation: he said I actually planted the thing because I was jealous."

"What a loser," Joanie said inadequately.

"It was always, 'Phyl, you're making a mountain out of a molehill' or 'Phyl, I can't help if she likes me—it's just harmless good fun, you've got to stop being so jealous and insecure.'" Another sigh. She started turning her engagement ring round and round on her finger as if it were a talisman to ward off her ex-husband's memory. "Finally, if denial and accusation didn't get me off his back, he'd go into assurances: 'Come on, Phyl, you know you're my one and only,' and 'I married *you*, didn't I? What more proof do you need?' And each time I would forgive him because I didn't want to get a divorce, but even I had to give up when I actually came home from work to grab this poster I forgot, and there they were..."

We all tried unsuccessfully to avoid the visual of Jason going at it hammer-and-tongs. However unpleasant that was, in my mind the scene quickly shifted to the even-more-unpleasant visual of Daniel going at it with some woman, any woman. My own experience eavesdropping on infidelity, I would guess, was marginally less painful than stumbling upon it in the literal flesh. And surely, it hurt less to have a three-day boyfriend cheat on you than a three-year husband. Of course, if I ever wanted to make absolutely certain, I could just marry Daniel and find out.

See—I thought. Better that this happened now.

Phyl gave my arm a squeeze. "At least your cheater sent you flowers. I don't think I ever got anything except some carnations Jason picked up at the grocery store."

"What'd Cheater send today?" Joanie rallied some, now that her Tylenol was kicking in.

I glanced at the clock. "Nothing yet. Not that I'm waiting."

"Uh-huh."

"But I'd better call Skandar—he asked me to check in with him."

"Why are you going upstairs?" Joanie demanded. "You can talk in front of us. Cass, wait—! I know you have to dump Daniel, but promise me you still won't marry that guy—"

"My phone's in my room," I threw over my shoulder, ignoring her. "And I'm going to transfer Ned to his bassinet for the rest of his nap so you don't cough on him."

Unhooking the sling, I let it drop away from Mr. Sleepyhead and tucked him up with a kiss and a blanket. I stretched my chest and shoulders, glad to be free of the weight, before grabbing my phone and settling into the window seat.

Where I froze.

There was a text message from Mr. Cheater himself. From the number I'd dialed yesterday—which answered that question.

Cautiously I opened it.

> Probably breaking your rules here. Messages allowed? Sorry no botanical greeting—nonstop all day but a great day. Not that my offerings got a response from you, heartless.

> Send me a scolding reply? Home soon, but not soon
> enough.

Yes, I'll bet his activities were nonstop. And nice touch, calling me heartless.

How to respond? A text could not do justice to all I wanted to say to him. If it could, he would get more than a scolding. A disemboweling, more like.

It took me four tries of painstaking keying and deleting, but I answered.

> No messages either. Definitely cheating. Plants not
> necessary. See you when I see you. Talk to you when I
> talk to you. Enjoy your nonstop action.

Deleting his text, I dialed Skandar.

CHAPTER 24:

Mr. Ned's Wild Ride

First thing Monday morning I left Lori a message, but I was already leaning away from the restraining order. Really, I wanted to avoid adding fuel to the fire. And if Lori approved, maybe it would be all right to let Dale Loftus come have a look at Ned, in the safety of the Palace with housemates and friends around me. It might calm him down. Reassure him of my good intentions.

"You're playing with fire," Skandar said coolly. "You judge everyone by your own naïve standards. You've already got a lawsuit on your hands, and you need to press every advantage. Erratic, borderline-criminal behavior on the grandfather's part counts as an advantage."

"Would you try to get a court order against Reiner's parents, if they just wanted to see Bryson?" I demanded.

A pause. "Thank God they're dead. But I've already told you—I would do what it takes."

By ten I still hadn't heard from Lori, and I was growing antsy. Not to mention, the whole mess was having a snowball effect—with my scattered wits, I wasn't getting much work done on Riley's edits. I checked on Joanie several times, but she was drugged up and sleeping off her illness, so there wasn't much use for me there. That left the night's meal in the crock pot to be assembled and chopping up all the salad ingredients. Then I mopped the kitchen floor and vacuumed, toting Ned in the baby sling when he got a little fussy.

By 11:30 I dialed Lori's office again. Better to be reprimanded (and charged for two blocks of time) than to wait any longer.

Her grandmotherly receptionist answered. "Law Offices of Lincoln and Clark."

"Yes, hello, Dorothy. It's me—Cassandra Ewan. I called earlier this morning—I don't even think the office was open yet—to try to reach Lori. It's kind of urgent. Is there any possibility of getting her on the phone or squeezing in to see her today?"

"Oh, Ms. Ewan, I'm afraid not. She called in sick today, but I'll give her your message as soon as she's back in the office."

My stomach turned over. "But—but—is she so sick that she won't be checking in for messages? Or possibly you could call or text her personal phone..?"

"Mmm..." Dorothy sounded uncomfortable. "I'm afraid not, unless it's an absolute emergency."

"Oh... I see. Well, I guess I can't say it's an *emergency*. It could wait till tomorrow. It's more a matter of my peace of mind."

"Yes, all right," she said briskly now. "You're in good hands with Lori, and whatever it is can be handled expertly by her tomorrow. I'll be sure to push your message to the urgent list. You have a nice day, Ms. Ewan."

Yeah, right.

"That's it—we're outta here." I picked up Neddy and swung him around. "No more moping and hiding for us. It's a beautiful day, and we're going out. What do you think, little boy? Alki? A ferry ride?" His wide blue eyes blinked at me sleepily. Five weeks old now and starting to hold up his head for brief periods. It seemed like Min had done it sooner, but, then again, Ned's head was significantly larger. He was also far quieter. He hardly ever cried, and since he still slept so much,

I was apt to forget him at times. Min was so darned restless and noisy that forgetting wasn't an option. She constantly had to be held, sang to, rocked, pacified.

"Or we could just try out that bike trailer Phyl got at the garage sale," I suggested. "That way we won't get stuck in traffic. I'm only going to pack you one extra outfit, so promise you won't barf on it, okay?"

· · ·

I'd had better ideas. For one thing, I hadn't been on a bicycle for months, possibly years. And for another, Bellevue is rather hilly and not for the faint of heart. And for still another, the added weight of the bike trailer and Ned (9 lbs, 2 oz. at his last weigh-in) threatened to finish me off.

We only made it as far as Fire Station #5 on Clyde Hill before I pulled up for a breather and was seriously considering calling it quits and heading home. Peering through the vinyl cover, I saw Ned had passed out again, so it wasn't like he was loving this to death and I had to continue for his sake.

After sucking down half the contents of my water bottle, I reluctantly climbed back on, wincing to think how sore I would be the next day, despite Phyl's deluxe cruiser saddle. Then I procrastinated another minute by twiddling with the rear-view mirror on the end of the handlebars. When I finally decided I would actually have to pedal to get back home again, I gave the mirror one last tweak, just in time to see a car appear in it.

Not just any car—the battered white Sentra belonging to the erratic, borderline-criminal and completely non-restrained Dale Loftus.

My hand froze. How did that work again, with convex mirrors? Were things closer than they appeared or farther? "Who cares, idiot?" I fretted to myself. "We're talking a difference of a few yards, give or take. Get out of here—now!"

Without looking back, I clumsily jammed my feet on the pedals and heaved us into motion. Forget the rosy visions of grandpa dropping by the Palace to see the baby, while my housemates and I looked on smiling. Skandar was right—I was naïve and Dale Loftus was a freak. Pedaling furiously, my mind wheeled in rhythm: where to go where to go where to go—not home not home not home. A comatose Joanie could hardly help me fend off a crazy man. I wanted people around me—lots of them. Bombing down the hill, I headed for Bellevue Way. If Mike's dad wanted to do something extreme, there were going to be as many witnesses as possible.

I couldn't say afterwards what I hoped to accomplish. Or how I, on a bicycle and towing a trailer, hoped to outrun a car, but in my panic no alternate plans sprang to mind.

Forgotten was my fatigue in the surge of adrenaline. At the intersection I throttled the brakes, careening around the corner and feeling the trailer tip onto its left wheel. Ned! Thank God there were no passing cars. I'd forgotten there was no bike lane. *Please God—where to go where to go where to go.* And where the heck were all the Bellevue police who were usually tucked into alternating cross-streets, radar guns pointed at the unwitting?

I considered dashing down one of these side streets to shake my pursuer, but I didn't know the neighborhoods and feared getting trapped in a cul-de-sac. Maybe if I went through the light at Northeast 12th, and he had to stop—? That is, if I didn't manage to get Ned and myself killed before I got anywhere near there.

Over the drumming in my ears I heard shouting. "Cassandra—Ms. Ewan—stop a second! I just want to talk to you! Stop!"

"This is…not…appropriate!" I screeched breathlessly, bumping up onto the sidewalk to get out of traffic and put another few feet between us.

I heard the squeal of brakes as I whizzed toward the condos at 17th, scaring the daylights out of a car pulling out. My pursuer tried to draw alongside me again as another driver veered around him, honking.

Dale's passenger-side window was rolled down, and I glimpsed the baseball cap and set jaw and a pair of reflecting sunglasses he must have borrowed from the Unabomber. "You're crazy!" he yelled. "You're gonna get yourself killed!"

"Whose fault would that be?" I panted, trying to accelerate. I was coming up on a burly woman walking her dog. "Watch out! Move over!" I shrieked at her back. "And call the police! This man is following me!"

The woman leapt out of my path, yanking her little pet airborne. I saw the blur of her uncomprehending brown eyes and heard her curse me in a language I couldn't identify before I flashed by.

It was only when I was almost upon it that I realized she wasn't calling fire and brimstone down on me, after all. She was screaming, "Curb! Curb! Vatch outta da curb!"

Not a curb, technically, but a big drop in the sidewalk where repair work was being done. Had I not been more focused on the car chasing me than on what lay ahead I might have noticed the prominent orange sign. As it was, it only came to my attention when I smashed into it and then jolted down the six-inch drop.

The next thing I knew, I no longer had a bicycle beneath me—I was sailing free.

Floomph! I landed sprawling in a bed of English ivy, face-down, and, though I didn't see it, I heard every bounce and crash and rattle as the bike trailer followed me into the gap.

"Ned!" I hollered, rocketing to my feet so quickly that I almost fell straight over again. I staggered over to the toppled trailer, one scraped-up hand reaching automatically to stop the wheel from spinning. His neck—his head support—I'd surely killed him myself.

"Vat you doing? You crazy!" chided the woman from the edge of the sidewalk. I could hardly hear her over all the honking, which some part of me dimly realized was caused by Dale Loftus pulling over and blocking the right lane.

I didn't care. I fumbled with the zipper on the compartment and wrenched it open. Looked in. Sank to the ground with relief.

The accident had succeeded in waking Ned up, but there didn't appear to be any worse damage. He was still strapped in, though he was half-suspended on his side, his blanket hanging off and his eyes wide. As I stared at him, he negotiated one fat fist sideways to his mouth and began sucking on his knuckles.

"Is he okay?" demanded Dale Loftus, standing opposite the accusing woman on the other end of the sidewalk gap. He whipped off the Unabomber sunglasses.

"I…think so." I unbuckled my helmet and put it on the ground beside me, the better to rub my dizziness away.

"God almighty—I know I scared you on Saturday. I been going about this all wrong, but you're out of your mind!"

"Call police?" asked the woman, glancing from him to me and holding her hand up like a phone receiver.

"No police," insisted Dale. Eyeing me warily, in case I was about to endanger us all in another hare-brained move, he dropped into the breach and hauled Phyl's bike and trailer back upright.

The woman turned to me. "No police?"

I looked at Dale. "I would feel better not talking to you by myself, under the circumstances."

"Look—I know it freaks you out when I pull up like that, but I couldn't think of any way of getting in touch with you that wouldn't freak you out."

"How about through my lawyer like I asked?" I shot back.

"Matter of fact, I called her to give you a message today, but she's out sick, and I really have stuff I gotta say now. You can call a friend—that guy that was there on Saturday—if it'll make you feel safer. Show this is all…on the up and up."

"I will then." Smiling apologetically at the woman and clasping my hands together to indicate I begged her to stay a little longer, I got my phone out.

"Cass?" Skandar sounded astonished.

"I'm sorry to bother you—I know you're probably at work, but could you possibly, possibly come down to Bellevue Way and just south of 17th? It's kind of an emergency."

"Are you okay?"

"Yes, yes. But I have Mike's dad here—uh-huh, he found me again— and he says he wants to talk to me, and I would feel so much more comfortable if someone I knew was with me." Someone male and slightly menacing, I might have added.

"Give me a minute. I'll be there. You say you're on the street?"

I shut my phone. "He's coming."

Dale held up his hands and backed up. "Okay. So just so's to show you my good faith, I'm gonna go park the car and stay back till he gets here. That sound good?"

I nodded.

As I watched him walk away, the woman reached out to tap me. "I go now? No police?"

"Yes—no police." I squeezed her hand. "And thank you."

She clucked to her dog and shuffled off, but I could hear her still muttering, "You crazy."

• • •

"What the hell—? Cass, is that *blood* on you?" Skandar stepped down into my pit and grabbed my hands to inspect them.

Grimacing, I tugged them away. "Yeah. It's no big deal—I mean he didn't do it exactly. I went over the handlebars."

"This must be a long story. Where is the guy, and where's Ned?"

The guy was over Skandar's shoulder, coming toward us. As for Ned, I thought it best to leave him buckled up, zipped away and inaccessible. "You're just here as a bodyguard, all right?" I urged Skandar under my breath. "I want to hear what he has to say this time."

"Cass, think about this—you're standing in a dirt trench with scraped-up hands and scratches on your face after crashing your bike—this isn't really the time for parleying about the adoption."

I shook my head mutely at him. He didn't understand—for whatever reason, this had to be settled now. I couldn't have Mike's dad lurking about or chasing me around until he got to say his piece.

Dale Loftus stopped a cautious distance away. He and Skandar gave each other curt nods.

"What did you want to say to me, Mr. Loftus?" I began. "Or was this just about really wanting to see Ned and not wanting to wait?"

"I want to see my grandson, but that's not it." To my surprise, he fished in his jeans pocket and pulled out a folded note. We waited as he painstakingly smoothed it out. "I got a few things you need to know, if you're wanting to take this baby away from us."

"She isn't *taking* the baby from you," interrupted Skandar. "You don't *have* the baby."

"Shhh…" I nudged him. "Go on, Mr. Loftus."

Dale cleared his throat. "Okay, then. Here's what I got: you need to know that my boy's a good kid. He's made some bad choices, but he's a good kid."

"Mr. Loftus—" it was me interrupting now. "I never said Mike was a bad—"

"You maybe haven't said it to my face or put it out there, but that's what you think by trying to take his kid away from him."

Skandar made an angry movement. "This is bullshit," he snapped, apparently forgetting he had reprimanded Mike's dad for bad language last time, "and she's not going to listen to this. Face it, Man, your son is in prison. He's a convicted felon. That's true whether or not you can admit it to yourself—"

The paper rattled in Dale's hands. I thought he might rip it in two. I was thumping Skandar on the shoulder with my fist to shut him up.

"All's I'm saying," insisted Mike's dad, "is that she pretends to be all religious with her church and God-loves-you business—I know it! Nadina told me about it!—and then she goes and sits in judgment on my son like she knows the least little bit what his life is like!" He turned his glare on me. "If you'da been through half of what Mike and me's been through, you wouldn't be sitting there looking down on us."

"What the hell would you know about what she's gone through?" Skandar countered, his voice going up in volume. "What would you know about what anyone has gone through?"

I thought I was going to have to clap a hand over his mouth. I really, really did not want him rehearsing my woes at the top of his lungs on Bellevue Way.

Angling myself between them, I gave Skandar a shove backward. "I mean it," I hissed at him. "Now, Mr. Loftus, how about if we all agree that there's been some pre-judging on both sides? I'm sorry for it. I want to be a fair person. I'm sure Mike's been through a lot. Please—go on. What else do you have on that list?"

He wadded it up and smoothed it out again. Gave Skandar another dirty look. "What you need to know is that my Mike is getting his act together."

"Yes," I said eagerly, relieved to have something to agree on. "I hear he's…complying with all the drug rehabilitation programs. That's great."

Skandar made a sound in his throat—I'm sure warning me not to give any ground.

"It's real this time," insisted Dale. "He's going clean. He told me. And that's not all—you know his parole hearing is this week?"

I nodded. How could I forget?

"Well, we think he'll be coming home pretty early because he's been doing so well. As early as beginning of November, could be."

Also nothing I hadn't heard, and it didn't help to hear it again. My knees felt suddenly wobbly. Mike's dad appeared to be waiting for my acknowledgement. "Uh…that would be very nice for him," I said in a small voice. Then, taking a deep breath: "Is this what you wanted to tell me? What you chased me all over town to tell me? I already knew these things."

His gaze wandered to the bike trailer. "Nah…that wasn't all. Turns out there's a kind of program they're gonna offer Mike: it's a job and a chance to get some college credit over the computer if he keeps at it. I guess what I really wanted to say was that you may want to reconsider."

My throat closed over this information. So much for my confidence that, meager though my employment was, I could support a child financially better than Mike. I clenched my hands in fists so that Dale Loftus wouldn't see them trembling. Not that I fooled anyone. When he spoke again, I detected an odd, triumphant note. "You see, Ms. Ewan, it's not like you'll have everything on your side anymore. My son'll have a job—and far as I can tell, that's more than I can say for you. Mike'll have a job and a place to live, and that baby will have two of us to take care of him, instead of just one like yourself."

In the silence that followed this speech, Ned's vocalizing carried to our ears. I interpreted it as, "Where are you? Why am I still strapped in here? I'm starting to get hungry." Stumbling slightly, I went to put my face to the vinyl window. "You've said what you wanted to say, Mr. Loftus. I'd better go. He needs to eat soon."

"I said it, but did you hear me? I said Mike and I can support that baby and care for it better than some lone woman."

"She's not a lone woman." Skandar spoke up again. I turned to see that he'd thrust himself between Dale Loftus and me. "She has me. As a matter of fact, we're getting married."

This outrageous statement penetrated my fog. Had Mike's dad not been so clearly rattled by the bombshell himself, he might have registered my dumbstruck expression and stammering sounds. Sounds which Skandar cut off by clamping my upper arm in a death grip.

"Yes, getting married," he repeated. "So, actually, the baby will have two parents and financial security and a stable home. Not only that, he'll also have a sibling."

Ridiculous! This was turning into the adoptional equivalent of a poker hand. I'll see your two-caregivers-and-a-job and raise you one sibling. Except that Skandar was bluffing. Seeing his narrowed dark eyes, I knew better than to call that bluff publicly.

"I'd better be on my way," I said for the second time. "Please don't follow me, Mr. Loftus. If you need to get in contact again, I would appreciate if you went through my lawyer Lori Lincoln."

He stood uncertainly. Took off his baseball cap to scratch his head and then replaced it. Skandar's news had definitely thrown him.

"You…you mind if I just look in that little window at him for a second?"

I couldn't see that it made a difference either way, and heaven knew I didn't want any more surprise visits. "Go ahead."

Dale Loftus removed his cap again and waited for me to scoot aside so he could peer in. "Cute," he said, after a minute. His voice sounded thick. "Got his father's face and eyes."

"No he doesn't! He's the spitting image of his mother."

"Well, he doesn't look like you, at any rate."

Swallowing my indignation, I grabbed the bicycle's handlebars to pull it from the breach, and Mike's dad obligingly guided the trailer up.

• • •

"Have we set a date yet, for our wedding?" I asked dryly, after we watched Dale Loftus drive away.

"From the looks of it, I'd say the sooner the better," Skandar answered, unperturbed.

"Arrrgh! For Pete's sake—I appreciate you trying to help, but frankly I don't see what good lying will do in the long run."

He shrugged. "You already know my opinion on the whole business. You have to decide what you're willing to do, to get what you want."

I knew it. I swung my leg over the bicycle.

"Look—" said Skandar, "can I ask you something, Cass?"

"Ask away." Tucking my hair behind my ears, I slid my helmet back on.

"You don't owe me anything, of course. I don't mind running off your antagonists or picking you up after you wreck on your bike, but maybe you could help me too..?"

I stared. "Well, of course I'll help you! And not because I owe you but because we're friends. What do you need?"

"Tomorrow…it's…" His sentence petered out. He cleared his throat. Avoided my eyes. Uh-oh.

"It's what?" I prompted tentatively. Maybe I spoke too soon. He wanted me to take Bryson on a mother-son camping trip. He wanted me to pose as his wife for six months to fool his parents who were moving in with him. He wanted one of my kidneys.

"Tomorrow it's—my wedding anniversary. Could we possibly…do something? Thank God Bryson is too young to make a big deal about it or even remember. I—I got a sitter. I'd rather not spend the evening at home just—" He cleared his throat a second time, adding hastily, "If you can't that's fine—I'll go see a couple movies or something."

"Sure I can," I said, relief making me enthusiastic. "And if we were keeping track, that wouldn't begin to make up for how you've been saving my bacon lately. We could do a movie—at least, we could do one movie—and eat something beforehand."

One of his rare smiles lit his face. "Great, Cass. It's a date—or non-date. I'll swing by after work. You pick the movie." He thumped me on the top of the helmet. "You can make it home, right? No more crises?"

"I'll be fine. No more crises." Nudging my foot under the pedal, I rotated it into position. "If you could just straighten out the trailer—thanks."

Skandar complied, but when he turned back to me, he was frowning. In his hand he held a crumpled piece of paper—Dale Loftus's note. "You want this? Probably ought to keep it as evidence for Lori."

Evidence of my diminished superiority as an adoptive parent? If I must.

I took it.

• • •

It wasn't till I got home, an arduous fifteen uphill minutes later, that I smoothed the note out and inspected it.

Sure enough, there was the list in a chicken-scratch scrawl, obsessively numbered:

1. A good kid

2. She doesn't understand anything

3. Off drugs

4. Parole hearing

5. Early Nov.

6. Job

7. College

8. $

9. Two of us

But there was one more point which Mike's dad neglected to mention, sidetracked as we were by Skandar's wild one-upsmanship.

I read that unspoken tenth item three or four times, as if, by doing so, I might make it say something different than it did.

But, no. There it was, messy, but unmistakable:

10. Mike got religion too.

CHAPTER 25:

Not So Clear Cut

Despite having biked my own mini *Tour de France* earlier, I was restless that night.

In my mind I turned it over and over: Mike got religion too. Mike got religion too.

Could it mean what I thought it meant? I clutched my hair with my hands, staring up in the darkness. Or should the question be, Could it possibly mean anything else?

How little Dale Loftus understood how I ticked. If his intention was to throw me, to make me reconsider my efforts, he could have come with only that last item, the throwaway that he forgot to mention once he heard about my purported engagement.

Craziness. Had Nadina given me such news only a year ago, my rejoicing would have known no limits. What better outcome than that someone so lost as Mike would find his way back? Now the possibility only filled me with dread. Or, say, 95% dread and 5% guilt. Because I felt not the slightest urge to rejoice. Mike, the new creation? What possible advantage would I have to him as a parent, if that were the case? His past a thing of the past. The ground level at the foot of the cross.

Mike got religion too.

• • •

It was after one in the morning when I finally dropped to sleep, and Ned woke me at three and six, with the result that I looked and felt like re-warmed haggis by the time I finally admitted I had to start the day.

Somewhere in the night I decided I would speak to Mike's dad again. There was no use tearing myself up unless I was absolutely certain. Which meant I could either wait to catch him lurking about whenever he next had something to tell me, or I could take the initiative and contact him. A quick look through the phone book showed me the Loftuses were unlisted, or at least the ones I wanted. I would have to call Nadina and get his number.

She called back around lunchtime. "Hey, Cass."

"Hey. School out?"

"Uh-huh. I'm on the bus, headed out to clean frog shit."

"Well, keep 'em alive. I'm looking forward to seeing them. Did you get the itinerary I sent you?"

"Yeah, but why would you come all the way out here and only spend three nights? I know Cleveland's not like a huge tourist attraction, but there's stuff to see. And if I'm gonna be in school for one of the days, when are we gonna hang out?"

"Well, you'll be back here at Thanksgiving, you know, to help your mom get ready to move. We can hang out then, too. I can't be gone long stretches right now. There's stuff going on. Which is another reason I called."

"What's another reason?"

I took a deep breath. "Can I get Mike's dad's phone number from you? I need to ask him something."

"Whoa—no way…you wanna talk to Dale?"

"I've actually already…run into him." (Understatement.) "Nadina— he kind of mentioned in passing that Mike 'got religion' out there at

Coyote Ridge. What do you think he meant by that? Mike and Dale aren't religious, right?"

She snorted. "Hell no, unless you count worshiping the Seahawks. Who knows what the hell he was talking about. If he meant Mike went all friggin' born-again, that'd be something I'd like to see. Mike said something in one of his letters way back, before we got in that big fight, about some scary-big pastor guy who was always visiting the place, inviting people to the little Bible studies and 'prayer meetings'—the dude was right up your alley, Cass—but it's not like Mike was wanting to go or anything."

That was several months ago, however, and I didn't feel reassured. "So…that was the only religious thing Mike ever mentioned? A Christian thing. It wasn't like he was being invited to Buddhist meditations or any kind of…I don't know…toga-wearing sex cult?"

"What?" She laughed. "I thought you're always getting excited about people wanting to go to church. Why would you want Mike to join a sex cult?"

"…It's complicated. Look—just text me his number. And have fun with the frogs. I'll catch you later, Nadina."

A few minutes afterward, Dale's number appeared in my inbox. Hardly had I begun the internal debate over whether to call him now or procrastinate when my phone rang. Lori.

After trying so anxiously to reach her yesterday, I now found myself reluctant to pick up. Of course, if I didn't, Lori would only keep trying to reach me. Best to get it over with.

"Hello, Lori. Thank you for getting back to me."

"Of course." Her usual brisk tone, if a little huskier than usual.

"I hope you're feeling better…"

"Much. I could hardly feel worse than I did. Dorothy tells me you needed to speak with me?"

"Umm…actually, I think things are under control now. I didn't mean to get everyone worked up. It was just that—well—over the weekend, Dale Loftus turned up—Mike's dad—I mean the father of the father—"

"What?" I had her attention now. "I know who he is, thank you. What do you mean 'turned up'?"

"Uh—he...*turned up* outside my house, wanting to speak with me. My housemates were all gone this weekend—"

"Yes, yes," she interrupted. "Go on. What did he say? Had he been in contact with Mike?"

"Huh?" I asked, confused. "I...suppose. I mean, he's his father, and they communicate." I didn't really see what bearing Dale's contact with Mike had on this discussion. "I was more concerned with the fact that he was harassing me and accusing me, basically, of wanting to adopt the baby out of spite. I mean, he really shouldn't be showing up at my house, should he? We should be trying to avoid all contact with the Loftuses, you said."

"Yes," Lori returned curtly. "That's what I advised."

Truly, she was a hard enough woman to read when I sat with her face to face. Over the phone I couldn't get her at all. "Well, I was calling because I was trying to figure out if I should get a restraining order—"

Here I expected her to interrupt again, to pepper me with questions about the incident, but she was silent. Mystified, I stumbled on. "But, I decided that Mike's dad didn't mean me any physical harm, and that I didn't want to antagonize either of the Loftuses by taking them to court over a restraining order. It seems like we've got enough going on..."

I trailed off into silence, but, to my relief, Lori found her voice. "You say you were not physically harmed and don't perceive any ongoing threat to you or the child from Mr. Dale Loftus?"

"Er—no..."

"Then, good. I agree with you. It wouldn't do to antagonize them at this point in time. I think we're at a crossroads here, with just a few weeks left for Mike Loftus to rescind the paternity affidavit. I would recommend we let them entirely alone. Wait on the results of the parole hearing. Show only our good intentions and let them mull that over. Yes. Okay. Well, I have a lot of work to catch up on, since I was out of the office. Was there anything else Mr. Dale Loftus had to say to you that has a bearing on this decision?"

Now, okay— *not* filing a restraining order was entirely my idea, but Lori's cold-blooded indifference to my emotional welfare continued to amaze. I supposed that, as long as I was physically well enough to sign her paychecks, we were good.

"No," I answered, when I regained the power of speech. "No, that was all." Or, at least, all I intended to share at this point with Her Unsympatheticness. God only knew what Lori Lincoln would have to say, if I mentioned my agitation over Mike "getting religion."

"Very well, then. I'll sign off. Have a good day."

"Okay. G—" was all that I got out before she'd hung up.

$$\bullet \quad \bullet \quad \bullet$$

My internal debate continued all afternoon. Here I had Lori's renewed recommendation that I leave the Loftuses "entirely alone," but if I couldn't figure out what Dale meant by item #10 on his list, I might never have another moment's peace.

I worked hard to justify my disobedience. Yes, it would be sneaking around behind my lawyer's back and effectively flushing my paid legal counsel down the toilet, but that was exactly it: I only paid Lori for legal counsel, not spiritual counsel. If Mike, of all people on earth, had "gone all friggin' born-again," I needed to know.

But I'd already lied by omission to Lori, only telling her about the harassment (and not even all of it) and not half of what Dale had actually said to me. What if Lori later discovered my sneakiness, or it sabotaged her work? Would she be so irate with me that she would quit?

Twice I began keying in Dale's phone number, and twice I stopped a few digits shy. I would call. I wouldn't call. I should tell Lori first.

Nonsense.

I might have gone on like that for another couple hours, had a more immediate crisis not presented itself. From the vantage point of the window seat in my room, I saw a taxi pull up, and I froze in my dithering.

Daniel was home.

. . .

Despite having been furious at him for days now, my first impulse was cowardly: I dove out of the window seat and crept around on all fours to peek out of the very corner of the window, safely hidden, I hoped, behind the curtains.

Crap. He was looking directly up at my room, his eye probably arrested by the sudden movement.

I couldn't help it—I stared back, unseen now at least. How very handsome he was, the scoundrel! His hair, the corded muscles of his arm as he dug out his wallet to pay the driver, the grin that flashed across his face as he glanced once more at my window. What could *that* mean— was he looking forward to pulling one over on me? Or did he honestly like me, but didn't think he'd done anything reprehensible?

The front door opened, closed. I heard him wheel his suitcase in. Tiptoeing to my door, I pictured him pausing in the entry way. C'mon, Cass. Get it over with. You have bigger things to worry about.

Flicking on the baby monitor, I went down to meet him.

"Hey—there you are! I thought I was going to have to go up and get you." He leaned against the banister at the bottom of the stairs, smiling up at me, for all the world like he was thrilled to see me. "Cruel mistress of mine. How do you explain your behavior?"

"*My* behavior?" I stopped on the landing.

"I'm gone a week, I send you rosemary and pansies and roses, I woo you with poetry—when I can't bear the silence any longer I send you a humble plea for a word—any word—" His mocking tone belied this purple speech. "And for what? A verbal slap. Two lines, maybe. Curt, cold, crushing."

"You survived, apparently."

"Only the thought of revenge kept me going. Come down here so I can punish you."

As if he hadn't already.

When I didn't move, he straightened. "Should I have brought the flowers now? You can be a difficult read, Cass."

As could he. Having been as distracted as I was, and not knowing when to expect his return, I hadn't yet given thought to how I would confront him. It would have made things easier, in a way, had he flung open the door and announced he was sick of me. As it was, I would have to bring it up. And without a bracelet or something tangible to hurl at him.

"I don't want flowers," was all I managed to say.

He came up the bottom step, pausing when I retreated slightly. "Am I...in the doghouse, Cass? Is this one of those situations where you told me not to call and I didn't call, so now I'm in trouble for not calling?"

"No!" I said roundly. "No, I didn't want you to call."

He gave me another measured look. "All right. But I *am* in the doghouse, for some reason. Well, so be it—let's go out for dinner, and you can tell me all about how angry you are." He held out a hand to me as he said this.

"Dinner!" I gasped. "What time is it? Phyl told me to throw her casserole in the oven at five."

"It's nearly 5:30."

Dashing down the remaining steps, I gave Daniel a wide berth. "You can't go out for dinner—who will eat the casserole?"

"I'll eat some for lunch tomorrow," he said shortly, following me. "And what do you mean 'I' can't go out for dinner? Are *you* going out for dinner?"

In went the chicken divan. I set the oven temperature and wound the timer without looking at him. After all, we were breaking up not because of me going out with Skandar but because of Daniel's inability to keep his fly zipped.

I felt a firm grip on my upper arm, and he spun me to face him. "If the two of us can't go for dinner tonight, you'll just have to tell me now what's going on."

"I can't." Yanking my arm away.

"What do you mean 'you can't'?"

"I mean I didn't realize it was so late, and I need to change."

"I want to talk to you. What do you have to go to—one of Joanie and Craig's stupid events? Just wear what you've got on—"

"I'm wearing sweatpants, you idiot!"

We were in the entry way again, but Daniel darted between me and the stairs. He was grinning again. "So you are. I confess I didn't even notice—too busy looking at that face of yours."

Yeah, right.

That face of mine must have been sending him mixed messages because he drew closer, his eyes dropping to my lips. I felt my heart accelerate in response. Must move away, I thought confusedly. He's playing you, Cass—playing you like a fiddle!

Well, one little concert never hurt anyone.

"Go if you have to," he murmured, "but what would you say if we kiss now and make up later?"

Something was not right with this situation, but for the life of me, I couldn't remember what it was. Hypnotized, I thought. I must be hypnotized. I hope he doesn't tell me to bark like a dog.

Di-i-ing dong! The sound of the doorbell roused me from my trance, and I shook my head vigorously to clear it. Ding dong was right. What on earth was I thinking, about to kiss this Judas?

Turning on my heel, I went to get the door.

• • •

Skandar looked like hell.

I knew, after the night I'd passed, that I wasn't looking so gorgeous myself, but he was an outright mess. His clothes were rumpled—certainly a first for him—his eyes red, serious five o'clock shadow. Could he possibly have shown up for work in this condition? He didn't even move when I cracked the door.

"Ready?"

"Uh…I was going to change first," I said. That is, if I had any sackcloth and ashes in the closet. Wow. This was going to be a dismal evening. But if the alternative was staying home with Daniel, sign me up. Besides—what sort of friend was I, if I would consider begging out when he so clearly needed company? "And Phyl isn't home yet, to watch Ned. You're earlier than I expected. Want to come in?"

He shrugged, but before I could step back to let him enter, I felt the door whisked from my grasp. "Ah, your date, Cass," said Daniel coolly. "You were going to introduce me, of course."

"Of course," I answered, my voice tight. "Daniel, this is my friend Skandar Sebari. We met in Lori Lincoln's—Aaaaaak! Skandar, what have you done to your hair?" The ponytail was gone—as if it had never been. Farewell, Desert Warrior.

The shorn man shambled past me, barely nodding in Daniel's direction. "You don't care for it, Cass? Me neither."

"Then why—" I followed him, plucking at his sleeve. To my dismay, his eyes filled, and I quickly blurted, "Never mind, never mind. Tell me later." Good heavens, I thought, dashing up the stairs as if a fiend pursued me, I hadn't seen Skandar this bad since the first afternoon I met him. He'd been so relatively collected for weeks that the grief caught me off guard. Not that just about everything in my life wasn't catching me off guard, for Pete's sake.

Ned was awake and wiggling away. I dropped a hurried kiss on his forehead before thrusting my arms into the laundry hamper to find the most presentable pair of jeans. Why, in all my time spent hand-wringing today, had I not bothered to do a load?

The low rumble of voices carried up the stairs to me, and I wondered what they could possibly be talking about. Lori, most likely. Connections. I hoped Skandar wasn't crying. It would have been pleasant to flaunt someone more eat-your-heart-out at my ex-true-love, but a disheveled weeper was going to have to do.

I scrambled under my bed for my boots, re-emerging with my hair full of lint and fuzz, like some kind of knit Christmas tree. In his current mood Skandar probably wouldn't even notice, but Daniel would, and I was vain enough to care, scurrying to the bathroom to brush it out and pinch some color into my cheeks.

By the time I hoisted Neddy into my arms and headed back down, silence had fallen. Skandar was staring out the window—dry-eyed, thank God—and Daniel was watching me. The nerve of that guy! From his expression you would suppose he thought himself more sinned against than sinning.

"Ah, Phyl," I cried with relief, hearing the door to the kitchen open. "You're home." Before the poor woman could even put her purse down, I was shoving Ned at her and hissing, "Be an absolute darling—I've got to get out of here right now. Daniel's home and Skandar's a mess." And then, in a normal voice I said, "The casserole's in the oven. It's got another twenty minutes. We'll see you later, okay? Say hi to Wayne and thank you so, so much for watching Ned tonight." Leaning in again to kiss her cheek, I added, "I owe you. Big time. Bye."

I wasn't the only one delivering private messages.

As I pushed my zombie-like companion into motion, I found Daniel at my own ear.

"Do enjoy yourself. I'll be waiting."

CHAPTER 26:

Let Me Ask You Something

We never made it to the movie.

We never would have made it even to a restaurant, had I not insisted on driving. "What do you feel like, Skandar? Indian? Mexican? Burgers?"

"You choose."

"Ooh, look—those guys are having fajitas. Would you want to share some?"

"You choose."

"Okay…chicken or beef?"

"You choose."

How spicy? Black beans or pinto? Margarita or mojito? I chose, I chose, I chose.

At first I thought it would help just to get the whole Katherine business on the table, so the second I thought the waiter wouldn't be back for a while, I plunged in. I was sorry his day was so crappy, and the anniversaries were always hard, and did he and Katherine have particular traditions on this day, and had he and Bryson talked about it. One-sentence answers. One word, if he could get away with it.

The mojitos came (I chose), and I was alarmed to see him down the thing in two, maybe three, long gulps. Yikes. The only thing worse than having dinner with a despondent mute would be having dinner with a drunken, despondent mute.

I pushed the basket of chips his way, hoping to offset the rum flooding his stomach. "So…you want to tell me about the haircut?"

His eyes met mine for the first time that evening, and he favored me with a humorless smile. Without answering, he slowly removed his leather jacket. Straightened his collar. In the dim light of the strings of plastic chiles draped around us, I caught a gleam of metal.

A flag pin.

"Good Lord!" I cried, almost jumping out of my skin. "Reiner's girlfriend's dumped him!"

"On his ass."

Then all this wasn't just about Katherine. "Oh, no, Skandar—and now he's after Bryson again?" I felt the tears start in my eyes. And they weren't just about Bryson. "This is ridiculous. You can't treat children like possessions, saying you want them, don't want them, want them, depending on your mood. You can't want children out of spite. You have to want what's best for them—! It has to be not about you! Oh— why can't people just take up hobbies?"

My not-completely-coherent outburst seemed to rouse him from his funk. He frowned at me. "There's no call for total panic, yet."

"No call? It looks to me like you went ahead and panicked! Where's your hair?"

He ran a hand ruefully through its remnants. "Yeah, maybe I did. Lori didn't say Reiner was gearing up again—she just said he called her and asked where we were in the process. We'll have to wait and see if we hear from his lawyer again. Thank God the guy has no money. The haircut…was more prophylactic."

"And the pin?"

"That, Cass, was my weak attempt at a joke." He sat back as the waiter served up our sizzling meal. It was a ton of food. Since Skandar hardly ate when he was upset, I imagined I would be boxing up most of it to take home.

"It's been a lousy day," he continued, watching me assemble my fajita. "I should have cancelled. Thought about it. But then I thought you'd help get my mind off things."

"Oh." I guess my choice of conversation topics hadn't helped so far. We seemed to have this problem frequently. Giving up, I took a big bite.

A few minutes passed. I chewed; he sat. Finally, to my relief, he reached for the fajita ingredients. "Sorry…"

"No—please—it's okay."

"Maybe we should have stayed at your place so you'd have people to talk to."

Yeah, like the man I wanted to strangle. "No, this is fine," I said, completely sincere this time. I smiled. "What's not to like—I got to pick everything."

He shook his head. Rallied. "So—how's it going in your neck of the woods? Has Mike's dad gotten you to reconsider?"

Now it was my turn to be reticent. I hoped my blush wasn't visible in the chile light.

"What? Tell me."

Suddenly an idea took hold of me. What if—? I put my food down. "Actually, Skandar, I need to ask Mike's dad something. You remember that note he dropped yesterday." My words came tumbling out. "—Well, when I got home I saw that there was one more thing Dale forgot to mention, since you had to go and tell him we were engaged, and everyone lost their train of thought. It said that Mike 'got religion.' Mike! It kept me up all night. I need to know what he meant by that. Do you think—do you think you could call Dale and ask?"

I succeeded, finally, in distracting Skandar from his own unhappiness. "What? Have you lost your mind, Cass? I was kidding. You need to stay away from those two—quit giving them more ammo to use against you. What do you care if Mike found religion or not? That has no bearing on anything."

"But it does—for me," I insisted. "I care. Please, Skandar! I need to know." Rifling through my purse, I pulled out my phone. "Please—just ask him what it meant. Use any excuse—ask him if he wants the note back."

"We're not giving the note back."

"*Please!*"

He sighed. "You act like you want to lose this adoption case. Like you want to give Ned to a criminal and his nearly-criminal father. Don't give me that look—I'll call. And, no—you stay here. If I'm stupid enough to do this for you, I'm not stupid enough to let you play backseat driver."

. . .

I had drained my own mojito by the time he returned—was even absently chewing a soggy mint leaf while I watched Skandar pace back and forth outside the restaurant window.

He took his seat, handed me my phone, shook his napkin over his lap. I studied his face anxiously, amazed to detect amusement. He was enjoying himself.

"No need to worry, Cass. It's nothing. He says Mike has been going to some Bible study. The pastor agreed to represent him at the parole hearing. It's clearly a ploy. Part of his good-boy act."

"That wasn't what Mike's dad said, was it? He wouldn't say it was fake."

A dismissive wave of the hand. "Of course not. But he sounded uncomfortable about the whole thing. He just said, 'She's not the only one who thinks she's got God on her side.'"

. . .

If I had any manners I would have invited Skandar in when we returned, but I wanted to do some hard thinking about Mike. And besides, I remembered Daniel's threat.

Skandar followed me up the steps to the porch. One of the lights was out and another obscured by an overgrown shrub, making it hard to see his face.

"Everything all right?" he murmured. "You got pretty quiet."

"Sorry—I keep thinking about what Mike's dad said."

"Cass, I told you it was nothing."

"I know you did, but—" but he thought religion was a comforting crock, after all. Not something deserving serious consideration. "—But I still need to do some thinking."

"Thanks for keeping me company tonight. You're crazy, but you always do snap me out of things. Listen to me a second." Without knowing how it happened, he took my hands in his. "We're good for each other, Cass. We can help each other."

Yes, yes, I knew. He didn't have to keep harping on it. Go away, already.

Then—for heaven's sake—the thought hurtled through my head as Skandar leaned in toward me—the man is going to kiss me!

He did.

Nothing earth-shattering, nothing frightening, just his lips, warm on mine. Gentle and rather pleasant. He pulled back a hairsbreadth, to study my response. When I said nothing, he made a thoughtful sound in the back of his throat—kissed me again. Yes. Decidedly pleasant.

"Think about it, Cass," he said, his voice low. "We can do this together: solve the adoption problems, raise Bryson and Ned, grow to love each other. You choose."

Dazed, fingers to my lips, I watched him go. The man was hopelessly thick. He just could not get new ideas through his head. Or was that me?

It was after nine. I didn't see Wayne's car anywhere, so he must have gone home already. If only I had some kind of trellis I could climb to my bedroom window. Then I could just sneak upstairs and deal with Daniel tomorrow because it wasn't like I needed another emotional scene.

As it was, I decided to creep around the side of the house and see if the lights were on in the Lean-To. If they were, I could make a run for it before he realized I was back.

Taking off my boots so the heels wouldn't clop, I padded the length of the wraparound porch that fronted the driveway. But as I turned the corner of it—"Ooof!"—I collided with something solid in the darkness. Something? Some*one.*

Given my recent encounters, I would have screamed to raise the dead the next second, had a firm hand not clamped down over my mouth, cutting off my air.

"Good evening, my dear Cass," came Daniel's voice in the darkness, as he threw his other arm tight around me when I tried to hit at him. "You weren't trying to sneak inside, by chance?"

He released me the next instant, and I staggered with the surprise of it, grabbing at the porch railing to steady myself. "You're one to talk," I retorted. "What are you doing hiding out here?"

"Lying in wait for you," he answered shamelessly. "And I'm glad I did. I wouldn't have missed that little scene between you and your date for the world. Come with me—I mean it, Cass. Talk to me of your own free will or be kidnapped. *You choose.*"

So much for wondering what Daniel had heard, in addition to what he had seen. Sighing, I pulled my boots back on and followed him to the Lean-To.

It was disorienting to be there in the evening with him, my visits being largely confined to daylight cleaning hours. While he went around flicking on lights, I stalked ahead of him into the living room, coming to a halt before the wall of built-in bookcases. His library of come-on lines for me.

"Now…" I heard him say, cool and collected, "did you want to explain to me exactly what the hell you think you're doing?"

"Excuse me?" Before I even turned to face him I felt myself reddening with anger.

"You heard me," returned Daniel. "How long have you known that guy?" His eyes were fairly throwing sparks, and I imagine mine were none too friendly either. The man actually thought he occupied some kind of moral high ground!

"A while. Maybe a few months."

"A few *months*? Were you ever planning on mentioning to me that you were involved with someone else?"

"So what if I am?" I threw back at him, defiantly. What? I was supposed to wait at home, tending my baby and playing dumb while he took off for a week and did whatever he wanted with whomever he pleased? I didn't think so.

"So what if you are?" Daniel echoed again. He ran his hands through his hair. Paced away from me. Came back.

"Why do you keep repeating what I say?"

"Because you're not making any sense! Are you the same woman I've been living with for over a year—the one who told me she didn't do things lightly? The one I've been tiptoeing around, so I wouldn't scare her off? The one I was making out with a week ago? You might have told me it was an act—that all I had to do was take a number!"

This was beyond belief.

For a minute I could barely string my words together, for all the scoffing sounds choking me. "Oh—oh—this—this is something. That's rich. You've got some comment to make about my morals. Unbelievable. For your information—not that I need to defend myself— Skandar has been a friend for a few months. A *friend*. I went out with him tonight because he was going through some tough things, and that's what friends do. Just like he's been around the last few days helping me out of some tight spots."

This last bit of news checked Daniel in his anger. "What do you mean 'tight spots'?"

"Oh, your mother's sedan stalker put in an appearance. Yes! Turns out he wasn't after Angela Martin so much as me and Ned." Daniel made a quick movement toward me, which I evaded. I didn't want his sympathy. "It was Mike's dad. Skandar showed up once and ran him off, and another time he…kept me company…while Mr. Loftus and I had a little discussion about Mike."

"What did he say—Mike's dad? What did he want?"

The urgency in his voice caught me off guard. "What else? He wanted what Mike wants. He wants me to give up adopting Ned."

Daniel took a moment to absorb this. "You…must have been scared. With all of us gone."

"I was. I think it's okay now. All sorted out."

"Why didn't you call me? I know I was out of town, but I could have done something."

"You mean something more than you were already doing?" I demanded. Hot tears started behind my eyes, and I glared at the bookshelves until I had forced them back down.

"What are you talking about?"

"I'm talking about the fact that I *did* try to call you—and some woman answered! I wasn't the only one with my hands full this weekend. You were in something of a tight spot yourself, weren't you?"

Daniel exhaled as if I had punched him. Took a step back. Looked conscious. He opened his mouth to speak and then shut it again. A wave of something—anxiety? guilt? indecision?—washed over his face before I could read it. What was it?

Firmly, I took myself in hand.

It didn't matter what it was.

Because whatever it was, it wasn't good. Wasn't innocent surprise, I mean.

My heart sank at this silent confession.

I guess some tiny fraction of me had hoped against hope that I imagined it all. That there was a perfectly good explanation for why I should call his number and get some woman doing God-knows-what. That he had lost his phone, maybe—or that someone had stolen it—that he lent it to a prostitute—anything! Anything but that I had guessed right.

"You…called me?" he said at last. "Spoke to a woman?"

Until I could control my voice, I didn't dare answer. "If you could call it that."

"What did she say to you?"

I blinked at him, dumbfounded. "Why do you keep doing this? I tell you I tried to call you and got *some woman*! Don't you think I should be the one asking the questions? Like who she even was?" Did he honestly think he could give me some line-by-line explication of the moans and groans and pants and flops I overheard? *I was getting a massage, Cass.* Or, *it was the asthmatic chambermaid trying to flip the mattress.*

Spare me.

He had sunk into the armchair, breathing quickly, thinking hard. "Whatever she said—whatever you heard, Cass—it…wasn't what you thought it was."

It made me want to break something, listening to him choose his words so carefully.

I pressed my hands flat against my legs to keep them from trembling. "I'll ask you one more time, Daniel. Who was she?"

His grip on the armrests tightened. "I—I…can't say. It's a confidential matter. A…business matter."

"Confidential." I took a shaky breath. "A business matter. Isn't that convenient? All those trade secrets and nondisclosure agreements you lawyers deal with." My mind flew to the woman I discovered on his lap that day in his office, and then to Skandar and Katherine ripping off each other's clothing in the office conference room. I didn't care if this was the way the world worked. I didn't want this to be my world.

Daniel rose slowly and came toward me. "Cass. It was not what you think it was. Trust me." He said each word precisely, deliberately, not taking his eyes from me. I wondered if Jason had looked at Phyl this way, when he disavowed all wrongdoing. The eye contact was probably crucial to the Denial.

This was all I was going to get, it seemed. This preposterous, I've-been-sworn-to-secrecy line. If this were a movie, Daniel would at least have turned out to be an undercover CIA operative or an assassin or something—instead of just a dumb cheating lawyer who couldn't be bothered to come up with a better story!

I had two options: I could cling, weeping and raging to his lapels, making a bigger fool of myself than I already had, or I could make a clean break. Preserve my residual dignity. Let him know he was total rogue and even make him squirm a little.

"I see. So you and this…colleague or client…had weekend meetings that you can't talk about, for whatever reason. Okay. Well. I hope, since you didn't get the time off from…work, you at least got to go someplace exciting. Surely that's not confidential, is it?"

"You don't believe me."

I blew up. "Is it absolutely impossible for you to give me just one straight answer? One answer that you don't have to stall over and think about beforehand? Where the bloody hell were you last weekend?"

He grunted, and I was amazed to see that sweat had broken out on his forehead. He ran both hands through his hair, turning from me. "We—uh—did some golfing in Eastern Washington."

"Golfing."

For a minute I could only stare at him because the lie was so transparent. Not to mention so poorly delivered that I half expected him to try again.

He didn't, and the minute stretched into two.

Then three.

So be it.

I suppose it was golfing of a sort. Balls. Clubs. Holes-in-one. The particular form the lie took didn't interest me, nor did trying to expose it. It was enough that he did lie. For the second time, and right to my face.

Just when I needed it most, my rage evaporated—as swiftly as it had come—crowded out by hurt and exhaustion. I felt suddenly heavy, as if I were coming down with Joanie's ailment, and wanted nothing so much as to go to bed.

He was not going to tell me the truth. And I didn't have the energy to keep hammering him. What would be the use? Questioning would only force him to tell me more lies. Make me look more the fool.

No.

This had been a bad idea all around.

He might do this sort of thing every day, but I was out of my league. Way out.

Just leave it, Cass.

Daniel had been watching me closely, and the antagonism I no longer felt seemed to have transferred to him. Gone was any discomfiture. When he spoke again, his voice was cutting. "What? That's it? No more questions, your honor—the prosecution rests?"

"What does it matter?" I brushed off his aggression impatiently.

"Yes, what does it matter—you've already made up your mind about me, haven't you, Cass? What does it matter if I tell you that nothing went on this weekend? Nothing like you're thinking. It's always going to be my word against your paranoia—yes, your paranoia! Your eagerness to think I'm the biggest—"

"Paranoia?" I snapped, indignation breaking through my dumpiness. He lies to my face and then calls me paranoid? Apparently there were only so many fallbacks available to cheaters. Like Jason, Daniel had already covered Denial and was now moving on to Accusation. Would he bother with Assurance?

"No," I bit out. "Paranoia was Phyl overreacting to Darla. Any fool could see that Wayne is a man of integrity and would never cheat on her."

"Ahh…" his voice dropped dangerously. "Meaning, any fool could see, on the other hand, that I'm a man of no integrity who would never hesitate to cheat on you."

"You said it—not me."

"No, you said it."

"No, you did."

"I was saying what you were implying."

"Well, if the shoe fits!"

"Oh my God," Daniel groaned, slumping back into the armchair and putting his head in his hands. "What is happening here—we're starting to sound like a bad sitcom. Look, Cass. Let me try this again: I don't know what's going on between you and that guy, but for me it's only been about you. You have to trust me on this. You really think I would have gone off with some other woman, after I'd just gotten as close to you as I'd ever been?"

Ah-ha, I thought, feeling my resolve weakening. Here we have the Assurance. Come on, Phyl, you know you're my one and only.

"It seems to be your pattern," I responded stiffly, perching on the sofa armrest.

He was shaking his head. "No. You know what—you're not going to do this to me. Let me remind you that I wanted to *marry* you back in May, and it was you that turned me down. Don't talk to me about my pattern. If I dated a few women since then, it was because you ordered me to, and I'm an accommodating man."

"Yes," I agreed. "Quite the martyrdom."

"It was irresponsible of me, I see now, to take you at your word," he continued. "Had I not dated anyone, you would have said I couldn't know my mind. But having dated a few people, you call me unfaithful."

This stuck in my craw uncomfortably, it being too close to what I'd thought more than once before we got together. But that wasn't the problem! I had chalked Darla and Kristen up to my stupid requirements because they predated me, but I couldn't do that with this getaway weekend. This sleepover overlap.

"This isn't about Darla and Kristen," I declared. "Or the client on your lap, for that matter. It's only about this weekend, and you being secretive about it."

"If I'm being secretive, you ungrateful—"

"Ungrateful?" I cut him off. "*Ungrateful*? What do you mean by that? You think I'm not grateful that you agreed to shelter me and Ned? I've told you before that I am grateful—" holding up my hand to forestall his interruption— "or do you mean I'm supposed to be grateful that you, with women always falling all over you, actually stooped to notice someone like me?"

"I take that back. Scratch that word. I spoke out of turn."

"But that's what you meant, isn't it!" My voice rose to a squeak, but I clung to my resentment, lest I do something as humiliating as burst out crying. "'Out of the overflow of the heart, the mouth speaks'! If I want to be with you, not only should I overlook any of your questionable, smarmy, extracurricular activities, but I should be *grateful*—"

Daniel said something earthy then about what I could do with my gratitude, and the next thing I knew he had pulled me up by the shoulders and was aiming his mouth my way.

One uninvited kiss a night was about all I could stomach, however, and this one promised to be more torturous than pleasant, so I dodged away, shoving him so hard (and ineffectively) that I fell back with a thump onto the sofa. Scrambling up the next instant, I put the piece of furniture between us. "Keep your sleazy hands off of me, you—you—" Inspiration failed me here. "Just keep your hands to yourself from now on, okay?"

He gave me a long look. "You're really going to do this, then."

"Do what?"

"Tell yourself I'm an untrustworthy manslut and not worth the risk."

"I don't put you in the marriage bucket, at any rate," I said, trying to even out my breathing. "But I'm not worried about you. Anyone who can bluff his way through what you just tried—maybe your pride has been wounded, but I'm sure you'll—"

"I think we're through here."

Daniel apparently didn't care what I was sure of. His tone was final and his expression closed-off. "You should go now. Ned was a little fussy tonight. Gave Phyl some problems."

"Now you tell me!" I said faintly. His sudden emotional withdrawal took me by surprise. Just because I wasn't going to buy it didn't mean he shouldn't spend a teeny bit more time on Assurance.

Unless he, when it came to it, didn't find it worth the effort.

At the door I paused. "Umm…this discussion notwithstanding, I just wanted to say that I'll be as good as my word from now on. Meaning, I won't make things difficult around here." He didn't answer, forcing me to go on. "And I hope you'll be fine with…just going on. No reproaches or weird tensions. Ned and I will give you as little trouble as possible."

Still nothing. I cleared my throat. "I'm referring, of course, to our agreement. The—er—'pre-nup,' as it were."

At last he stirred. Came toward me. But only to open the door and indicate that I had better get myself through it, if I knew what was good for me. "Yes, I remember what you're referring to, and your opinion of my integrity *notwithstanding*, you'll also find me as good as my word."

With that he shut the door gently.

In my face.

CHAPTER 27

Thief

Is it still considered running away if the trip was scheduled?

Because that's what I felt like I was doing. Running away. From everything and everyone. If I was in Ohio, that meant that, for four days and three nights, I was free from looking over my shoulder to see if Mike's dad was following. Free from any new disturbing revelations he might have to impart. I was free from Skandar's company. Free from the muted, relentless pressure he exerted on my future. And if not precisely free from my own inward debate, I at least hoped to get a little distance and perspective on it.

But most of all, I was free from seeing Daniel.

It had been a dreadful time. Not on the surface of things. No, no—on the surface of things the Palace was running smoothly.

I had forbidden Joanie to meddle on pain of death. "We've hashed it out—kind of. So leave him alone. If we're going to have any peace around here, and if I'm going to be able to keep it together, you can't be yelling and throwing things."

"But I wanna know exactly what he was doing! How can you not want to know, Cass? And who answered that phone?"

"He says he was golfing. What would be the point of pressing him to make up something more elaborate? And he won't tell me the woman's name because it's 'top secret.' What do you need a name for anyhow? The guy's slept with enough women to publish his own baby name book—pick any one you like."

To relieve her feelings she railed at me a good long time, but apart from being rather huffy with her brother, she kept her promise. And Daniel and I kept ours.

In front of others, we were able to be more than civil. We followed normal routines. We participated in conversations. There was no dashing from the room, no coldness or barbs aimed at each other. I didn't spit in his food when I served it; he didn't pretend to gag when he ate it. All fine.

However.

Who knew how heavily I had grown to depend on him until I no longer could? How I had learned to take it for granted that he cared on some level—as a friend, if not as a lover. Even when he dated other women, there was still his presence in my life. His conversation, his company occasionally, his interest in what happened to me. Now I felt as if this were gone entirely. He wasn't smoldering behind my back, plotting revenge. I almost wish he were. Instead, he was absent. Indifferent. Elsewhere.

If other people weren't present, he would exchange the merest civilities with me before taking himself off. He remained friendly to Ned—pats on the head, extending a finger to be gripped, a few words here and there. I even once caught him in that classic interaction, pointing to himself and enunciating, "Daniel. Daniel." But to me—nothing.

I found my lingering anger ebbing away after a few days. So what if he was a cad and a traitor. I still missed him. Although he wasn't marriage material, I wished there were some way to broach the subject again, to ask if we could—cliché as it was—be friends. But, in those few moments when I caught him alone, his utter detachment shut me down. Had he been nursing anger, I might have found an open-ing. Maybe talked to him about forgiveness and letting bygones be bygones—but his blankness shut me down. How could I even bring it up, when he might turn a puzzled look on me and an "I'm sorry—what did you say your name was, again?"

And then, after a few more days, the opportunities to speak alone, such as they were, dried up. Because Violette Bellamy came back.

All that scary joy I had experienced for my few days was hers. She would arrive at the Palace nearly every evening, some potluck offer-ing in her hand, to greet Daniel with a tremulous smile. Who knows why they never went to her place. I suppose Daniel had always been something of a homebody with whoever he was dating, and Violette was no exception. But in this case, instead of his girlfriend joining us in the Palace kitchen, the two of them would always load up their plates and head for the Lean-To. I didn't know what to make of it.

"Do you think it's because they're sleeping together?" I asked Joanie, as we watched them go one evening.

She knew without my saying that I was pretty low and came to put her arm around me, resting her head against mine. "I dunno. They have to eat first anyhow. Or maybe they do kinky things with Phyl's organic mashed potatoes."

I nudged her with my elbow. "Stop."

"I could sneak over and peek in the window."

"No, no. Leave him alone. It's none of my business anymore. Re-member?"

"Yeah, I know. Nothing seems to turn out like we planned." She was silent a moment and then gave me a squeeze. "But hey—I know something that will cheer you up! Or at least distract you. Plus, you'll have the joy of doing something sacrificial for me."

"What..?" I asked, leery.

"That retail complex opening in October. There's going to be a fancy dinner at one of the restaurants and then a private grand-opening party on the top floor of the hotel. You absolutely have to come with Creep and me. All free—I'll even let you invite that Skandar."

I had already wriggled loose from her. "Aww, Joanie! Don't ask me. I'm so not in the mood. Can't Phyl and Wayne go with you guys?"

"Don't be a drag, Cass! I knew you would, which is why I already tried with Phyl, but her Mom is going to be visiting that weekend and Phyl wants to stay home with her. But that means she can watch Ned, and you can get out and forget about my idiot brother."

"Hmm."

"Please, please, pretty please, Cass!"

"Hmm."

"Promise you'll think about it, at least."

What was the point? I knew Joanie would wear me down eventually. She could be as stubborn as her brother. Except that her brother had given up on me.

I gave myself a shake. "Only if I can go stag. If I take Skandar he'll read so much into it that I'd probably find myself married to him by the end of the evening."

"Good point," agreed Joanie, glad to get her way so easily. "I'll get you two tickets, but you don't have to use them both. We can share Creep. He'd be thrilled to show up looking like he had two dates." She threw her arms around me again and kissed me hard on the cheek. "Thank you, Cass, ever so much! It might even border on fun for you—more fun anyhow than moping around here with Daniel and Virulent."

"Maybe it's them you should be inviting."

"Ha! No way. I don't want to look at *that* all night any more than you do."

· · ·

Mom was less eager about me getting away.

"You can catch all sorts of germs on those planes, and Ned is so young."

"I don't think anyone with SARS will be flying between Seattle and Cleveland, Mom. Besides—I read they recycle the air through HEPA filters, so it's actually cleaner than your average air."

"But those cramped seats! HEPA filters won't help if the sick person is jammed right next to you and sneezing all over."

"Well," I said with a touch of exasperation, "as we know, we all of us could go any minute. Really, Mom. I promised Nadina I would visit. Maybe I'll get lucky and the flight won't be too crowded. Then I can sit between Ned and the sickie and throw myself under the virus bus."

• • •

I did not get lucky.

The leg from Seattle to Houston was of course packed, but at least it was uneventful, and I straggled off with Ned eager to board the next plane. Because I myself had never seen any reason to go to Cleveland, I pictured an empty flight, where Ned and I rattled around, reclining across as many seats as we pleased while flight attendants solicitously offered extra beverages.

As it was, the flight was overbooked, forcing me to check Ned's car seat at the gate and carry him on my lap. The imagined aisle-to-myself dwindled to a window seat, blocked in by a kindly old couple who, upon buckling themselves, promptly fell asleep for the duration of the trip. Nothing roused them: not the beverage cart, not me wrangling the diaper bag in and out from under the seat in front of me, not Ned spitting up his bottle shortly after take-off and the grumpy attendant feeding me towels and napkins to clean up the mess. To make matters worse, the lady behind me *did* sound like she had SARS, or some similarly fatal upper respiratory disease. I swear she put her mouth right to the gap between the seats every time she succumbed to a coughing fit—I could almost feel the infected gusts blowing my hair.

Despite all, I managed to nod off, head leaning against the window and Ned tucked safely in my arm. As he put on weight he was only waking me once per night, but ironically I was sleeping worse than ever. It wasn't just the Daniel issue. Especially at night, when I could drop my behave-as-if-nothing-happened act. No. From the moment I went upstairs until whenever I managed to cross the line into unconsciousness, it was all Mike, Mike, Mike.

Mike the biological father.

Mike the reformed.

Mike the soon-to-be-paroled.

Mike the employable.

Mike the college student(!).

Mike the wanting-something-to-fight-for.

Mike the…brother in Christ?

If he was truly all those things—especially the last—could I justify my actions? Would Ned really be so much better off with me that I should press my cause?

If I gave Ned away now, he would be none the wiser. There would be no memories of me. No feelings of loss.

My loss, on the other hand…

I couldn't say when it happened—when Ned had slipped in and stolen my heart. With all the doubts about the adoption situation, I had been careful in my mind not to call him mine, not to indulge myself imagining our future together. But what can you do? If you care for someone day and night—feed him, bathe him, dress him, rock him, give things up for him like sleep and money and independence—how can you come out on the other end feeling something as mild as fondness? No—you either hate and resent him, or you love him with every last breath in your body. You love him like I loved Ned.

Loved him.

Did Mike?

How much of his battle was spite, and how much was a father's yearning to be reunited with the flesh of his flesh? If I had blown up my life and lost Min, the second I came to my senses, wouldn't I have fought with everything I had to get her back?

Added to my angst was the niggling awareness that I didn't want to pray about the situation. Not just didn't want to—I didn't. If God agreed with Dale Loftus—that Mike was a new man and as ready for fatherhood as I was for motherhood—I didn't want to know. Ned was mine! As good as promised to me. Promised, confirmed.

"Excuse me."

The twinge of strands of hair being yanked from my head woke me. TB Mary had risen to a crouch in the row behind me, her hand gripping my headrest for support. "Can I—" (hack hack) "—get out?" Please do!

I tried to shield Ned from the germs showering us, dismayed to find him sleeping with his mouth wide open. After a couple attempts to push it shut I gave up and leaned over him. Well, we would have to see how his immune system was working some time or another, and he'd already survived exposure to Joanie's miserable bug.

When the plane landed a couple hours later, I stumbled up the jetway somewhat the worse for wear. A protesting Ned had been wrestled into a clean outfit but Nadina would have to take me as-is.

A screech greeted me as I passed into the terminal from the concourse: "Ca-a-a-a-a-ass! Whoo hoo!" The girl almost hugged me in her excitement, but with Ned's car seat in the way she settled for thumping me on the back. "Dude—he's huge."

"You're here! I thought I wouldn't see you until tonight."

"Yeah, well, I begged out of the lab this afternoon and said I'd come tomorrow—so that way you can see the lab too. You rented a car, right? Because otherwise the trains'll be jam-packed and I'll have someone's face stuck in my armpit from Tower City to friggin' Shaker Square."

"Ooh. Lucky for you you'll be riding in style in my Hyundai Accent or equivalent economy car. You look wonderful, Nadina. No, I mean it."

"It's the uniform, right?" She fanned the navy plaid skirt for me.

"Clearly. You look like a shotputter from the Scottish Highlands."

A shotputter with an air of general well-being. Substance abuse was behind her; Mike was behind her; pregnancy was behind her; childbirth and separation were behind her. It was as if, at long last, the real Nadina finally had permission to come out.

. . .

"But I was going to take you and Aunt Sylvia out for dinner."

"Nah. She was already thawing the ground beef for the meatloaf. Maybe tomorrow night." Nadina gave my hotel bed an experimental bounce. "Dang—this place is *fantsay*. No wonder you didn't want to stay with us and sleep in the bed my great-grandma died in."

"I didn't pick it because it was 'fantsay'—I got a good deal online, and the only other choice nearby was some one-star motor court with bullet holes in the walls."

A knock on the door interrupted us. When I opened to let the bellhop wheel in a crib for Ned, I saw Nadina remove herself to the sofa where she draped against the armrest. The girl actually batted her eyelids at the pimpled youth, and he goggled back at her while I ransacked my purse for the first bill that came to hand.

"Hey—can you at least not get pregnant again before my very eyes?" I asked when he was gone.

"Dude. You don't know how starved you get for man flesh, when you go to an all-girls' school. The only guy I ever see is stupid Jean-Luc the frogmeister at the lab, and he's like 30 and somehow convinced some poor s-u-c-k-e-r to marry him. And bellhop-guy beats Mike, at least, right? I mean, he's *employed*."

Speaking of employed…I was silent for a minute. Nadina watched me assemble Ned's diaper accoutrements. While I used cloth and a service at home for Phyl's sake, on the road it was all about disposables.

"You know, Nadina…Mike's dad, in one of our conversations, mentioned that, when Mike gets out, he's been offered some kind of job and college credit program. Did you know anything about that?"

She snorted. "No. Remember how you kept nagging me to quit 'having contact' with Mike and Dale? I'm not the one all BFF with them now. But, God, if Mike's gonna be employed and going to college, plus going all sober and born-again, I'd think you'd be all over that, Cass. Telling me I should totally get back together with him."

"Hmm." I gathered Ned's plump ankles in one hand and hoisted him to slip the clean diaper underneath.

"'Hmm' what?" She came over and sat on the bed, careful not to jog Ned. "That was a joke. You think I should get back together with him?"

"No, I'm pretty sure that never crossed my mind."

"What then?"

I took a deep breath. "I guess I may as well say this now. I can't do it in front of Aunt Sylvia, and it's so much on my mind that I don't think I can wait."

"Ooh, scary! Say what now?"

Before I answered I focused on doing up Ned's onesie but got the snaps one off and had to start over. "Say that I'm kind of struggling with the whole adoption thing. I'm not totally positive that I'm doing the right thing."

"Whatever—that is not even funny, Cass."

She waited for me to laugh with her, but when I didn't, her mouth dropped open fractionally. Without thinking, she bounded off the bed, sending Ned rolling. "What the *hell*, Cass? You're not kidding me?"

I caught Ned up. Oh, cripe. I probably shouldn't have said anything. Too late now.

"What are you even talking about? You can't change your mind," she said, breathing fast. I thought for a second she might shove me. "—What—you don't like Ned now?"

"It isn't that at all. Don't look at me like that, Nadina! It isn't that. I haven't changed my mind—I love Ned. Love him! I want to be his mom forever. I'm just saying that lately part of me has this horrible, sinking feeling that I won't be."

She appeared slightly mollified but continued to gape at me, shaking her head. "Because why? Are you getting all freaked out about the fighting-Mike-in-court business again? Don't you think I'm too young for you to be always unloading on me?"

"Yes," I said. "Forgive me for that. And forgive me for this. But if I ever did have to…give him up…I could hardly do it without telling you."

"What—I don't—Cass, I don't know what you're talking about. Give him up? What for? You gotta be kidding me. Because Mike might get some dumb job? Gimme a break. Flipping burgers or whatever the hell job they find him is gonna be so lame—even your sorry-ass one would pay more, no joke. Don't go all weird on me like this. You promised."

Grabbing her arm to stop her pacing, I pulled her down next to me on the sofa. "It's not the job, Nadina, though that's part of it. I didn't ever expect Mike to be able to afford raising Ned. I can only do it because I'm dipping into my husband's insurance payout still. It's not the job. Or even him getting sober. It's the religion part."

"Aaagh." She pressed her fists against the sides of her head. "You're such a friggin' *freak*, Cass! Nobody besides you cares if Mike started going to Bible study. What does that have to do with anything? He probably went 'cause it looked good on his report or 'cause it gave him time off from other guys kicking his ass. It's got nothing to do with nothing."

"I don't expect you to understand. And I'm not saying I'm giving up. I'm just trying to tell you that I'm having a hard time. I don't feel peace with this. I know you think all the religion stuff is just crap—"

"I don't think that," she broke in. "I think God is awesome. I just don't think you always need to be living your life looking over your shoulder or thinking that you know what God wants and nobody else does. Religious people always think they're right and everyone else is wrong. That God's on their side and nobody else's."

"But that's what I'm trying to say, Nadina. I don't think I'm right, here. I don't think God is on my side with this adoption. For days I've had this awful suspicion he might be on Mike's, and I don't want to face up to it."

She groaned. "Why the frig would God be on Mike's side? I think you just want to be done, Cass. I dunno—you don't want to spend the money or have to go to court—"

"Mike is Ned's biological father. But, more importantly to me and to this discussion, if Mike 'got religion,' if he … found his way to Jesus … then—oh, Nadina—then he's my brother. I can't be hauling him to court trying to take something from him."

"Well, fuck me—" Nadina vaulted to her feet. "Mike reads himself a couple Bible verses and buddies up to some pastor, and now he's your friggin' 'brother'? What the hell does that make me? I fucking had the baby—carried that baby because you told me that my life mattered—and now, on second thought, since I'm not your fucking 'sister' you're gonna go back on what you said to me?"

"Shhhh…" I gave a nervous glance at the telephone, half expecting the front desk to ring and say, Could we please keep it down? "How many times have I told you that I love you, Nadina? And it's all still true—your life matters and carrying Ned and giving him a chance at life was a beautiful thing—"

"Oh yeah? So fucking beautiful that you're gonna throw it in the Dumpster and give him back to that lame-ass Mike. Way to stab me in the back, Cass. If that's your love for me, you can fucking keep it."

"I don't know what to do," I said through gritted teeth. "It's not like I'm enjoying this. I was just trying to tell you some of what's going on in my head. I love you because I love you. We've been through a lot together. I love Ned because I can't help it. I want him—I don't want to let go of him for any reason. If I say Mike might be a brother, I only mean I would be forced to love him out of sheer obedience—because God does and asks me to. And if I have to love Mike that way,

I shouldn't be…insisting on my own way at his expense."

Another shake of the head. "No. You'd be loving Mike at my expense. And Ned's."

My hand reached for her, but I knew she would fling it off in her current mood. "Listen, Nadina. If Mike really is a changed man, where would Ned lose? He would be provided for. He would be loved. He would have a father and a grandfather. Boys need fathers, especially."

"So get married," came her stubborn reply.

For Pete's sake—maybe I would, just to shut everyone up. "Come here, Nadina. Sit with me again. Tell me: if I let Mike have Ned—and I'm not saying I will—how would it hurt you?"

"Because—because—" she cleared her throat, blinking. "Because Mike was bad to me. He didn't give a damn about me. He didn't care how he trashed my life because his was already trashed. Drugs. Sex. Money. That's all he wanted from me. Why should I give him anything?"

Ah. I felt my own eyes well up. She knew she was precious now. Thank God.

I settled for giving her elbow a squeeze. "You're right, you know. *That* Mike didn't deserve anything from you. And I certainly wouldn't want to give him anything beyond a good knock to the head with a two-by-four."

"He's still that Mike! He still doesn't deserve anything. If you're gonna give up the fight, Cass, and go all soft on me, I'll just take Ned back from you and fight him myself."

"What—you already threw a couple years of your life away on Mike—now you want to sacrifice even more to spite?"

"If you won't."

"I won't."

I sighed. "But—and I mean this, Nadina—I will fight for however long it takes to get Ned what's best for him. Because I love him. Don't worry about that. I only wish I could be positive it was me."

CHAPTER 28:

All-Nighter

However much I relieved my conscience by 'fessing up to Nadina, it didn't make for the easiest visit. We didn't bring the topic up again, but in her silences and diffidence I felt the weight of her disapproval. What was the point of insisting that I wanted to keep Ned? That I longed to add Nadina's opinion to all the reasons I should press on, fight Mike to the death, brother in Christ or no?

She was sixteen. And she was right—I shouldn't have burdened her with my indecision. But if I somehow came out on the other side resigned to giving him up, I could hardly drop that bomb on her with no warning.

One thing was certain: I needn't worry about Nadina taking Ned back to pursue a draining, fruitless court battle of her own. Aunt Sylvia would sooner see her dead.

"Doesn't she look better now?" the tiny, angular, wispy-haired older woman demanded, almost before the introductions were finished. "Don't you be rolling your eyes, Miss! I'd like to see them lock up in that position. Any fool can see how well you are. Now that everything's behind you."

"She looks wonderful," I said. "I told her so."

Aunt Sylvia made a pleased sound. She ran a practiced eye over Ned. "Well done, there. He looks healthy. All Graham—that's our side of the family. None of that Loftus taint to suck him down."

"Yeah," agreed Nadina. She narrowed her eyes. "No Loftus taint."

Her great-aunt shot her a suspicious look. "What—not defending your hero today?"

"Not today. Smells good, Aunt Sylvia. When's dinner?"

"Do I look like the help to you? Dinner's when you set the table. Put that phone down! Don't be checking your messages when we've got a guest." And so on.

Around Aunt Sylvia you couldn't help but sit up straight and mind your manners, but I could understand how Nadina bore it with no resentment. Even with humor. She was learning with Solomon that, although the kisses of the enemy are profuse, faithful are the wounds of a friend.

And Aunt Sylvia was a friend. She plied Nadina with food. Asked after every detail of her day. Followed up on subjects from yesterday. Bragged to me about what Nadina's science teacher wrote on her test. Occasionally reached over to pat her great-niece's hand, ignoring any pretended irritation. And judging from the amount of information Aunt Sylvia already knew about me, this in-depth conversation was not unusual. No wonder Nadina considered hanging out with her "crabby aunt" at the end of the day a highlight.

When the girl rose to clear the table and do the dishes, Aunt Sylvia leaned in and fixed me beadily. "Even though it's done her a world of good to come out here, I appreciate you keeping an eye on Nadina like you did. She was too much for her mother." She sniffed. "Everything was too much for her mother. Didn't grow up till she was forty, and even then I have my doubts some days."

I only smiled, knowing better than to get in the middle of that.

Without asking if I wanted any, she poured me some coffee. Decaf, I hoped, since I would already have trouble getting to sleep with the time change.

"Had my doubts about you too, when Nadina told me she was going to have this baby."

"Do you think it's done her harm?"

Aunt Sylvia clicked her tongue against her teeth. "No, I'll give you that. Probably a good thing to realize her actions have consequences. Can't just go vacuuming something out because you've got a party to go to."

No ready response to this presented itself, but my companion didn't need one. "Not that I think you're much the wiser, mind you. Last time you tried to raise a child you had a husband and a house and a family income."

Chalk it up to fear—maybe I didn't want Aunt Sylvia, of all people, joining the hurry-up-and-get-married chorus—but I blurted, "I could say the same to you. Nadina's a handful."

Her eyes gleamed, and she gave a short bark of a laugh. "You're right. I'm an interfering old woman. But I never claimed to be a wise one. What can I say? Love makes fools of us all."

I took a sip of the coffee: black, bitter, and—I suspected—instant. "You can say that again."

• • •

The next day was a schizophrenic mix of sightseeing and shadowing Nadina. While she was at school, Ned and I slept in and then wandered the galleries of the Museum of Art. In the afternoon we met her at St. Helen's for the campus tour and caught the Red Line to the Case Western lab where she worked. To my disappointment the much-abused Jean-Luc was not around, and I had to settle for admiring his immaculate lab bench and the buckets of frogs.

Saturday morning Nadina had an unavoidable study group, so Ned and I revisited the university campus. It was chilly; the leaves were beginning to turn. Because of the cold, perhaps, it took him longer to fall asleep, but back and forth we strolled along the curved façade of the Kelvin Smith Library until Ned's eyelids drooped and I slipped inside to check my email.

October 1. As I anticipated, a message from Lori.

> Cass:
>
> Mike was granted parole and is slated for release November 2.
>
> L. Lincoln

November 2. Delightful. Three days before Phyl's wedding. I guess, unlike me, the parole board wasn't losing sleep over the authenticity of the New Mike. They bought it. Or it was real. Or it was real enough that they could think of better uses for his Coyote Ridge billet. Crap. There went my feeble hope that I could get my court date while he was still in prison.

Ned and I drew some curious stares as I wheeled his stroller through the reading room to a cluster of leather lounge chairs. I pulled out yesterday's art museum guidebook, but Fra Angelico's *Coronation of the Virgin* couldn't crowd Mike out. Too serene, considering she had to give her son up, too, and to worse people than Mike. Did the coronation make up for it? Or the thought that she participated in the whole Saving-the-World operation?

I gave up reading and sat staring out over the grassy oval. By now there was a soccer scrimmage going. It made me think of Bryson, of options. I pictured him all grown up in college. The flaming red hair streaking across the field. Skandar and me, graying and proud, there for Parents Weekend..?

Surely not. Never ever.

On the other hand, as Joanie pointed out, my own visions for life had a way of going up in smoke. Troy. Min. James. Daniel.

"Not Ned."

I might have said it out loud. My fists were clenched.

"Not Ned. Ned is mine."

My breath came fast. Was it this easy, making a decision? Why hadn't I thought of it before? There was no law saying I had to be the one going through life, riddled with doubt, while everyone else just did whatever they liked. Why not just—in the absence of clear direction—do what I wanted to do? And what I wanted to do was keep Ned.

I didn't care if Mike was elected the next Pope—I was sick of losing everyone, one after another. Whatever God might be doing in Mike's life he could do without my assistance. And certainly without Ned's. Because Mike couldn't love Ned like I did. If Mike was my brother in Christ—a huge *if*—then I was his sister, and who was to say he shouldn't give way to me, instead of insisting on his rights?

I wouldn't give him up. *I won't give him up!*

Heart pounding with the suddenness of my decision, I didn't notice my phone ringing until it reached full volume and the nearest Silence Nazi shot over to jab me in the shoulder. She pointed at the sign: "The KSL is a cell-phone free zone." Big red circle with a line through it.

The triumphant smile I bestowed on her made her pause, but she rallied and scowled at me until I had shut off my ringer. I could have kissed her. I could have kissed anyone.

When my boy and I were outside, I dialed Phyl back.

"Hey there. What's going on?"

"Wow. You sound excited. You must be having a good trip."

"A great trip! I've got Ned, after all."

"Oh," said Phyl, puzzled. "Well, how's Nadina? Are you enjoying your visit?"

"She's doing great." I filled her in on some of the details, leaving out the whole now-moot argument over Ned. "The only fly in the ointment is that Lori emailed me to say Mike gets paroled beginning of November. Not that it matters, ultimately."

"Ooh…I'm sorry to hear that, Cass. We hoped they'd keep him a little longer." She paused. "And I hate to add another bit of bad news, but that's why I called."

My breath caught. "What? Is it Daniel? Is he okay?"

I could picture her pitying expression and regretted my impulse of concern. "No, no. Nothing like that. But it is Daniel. Umm...he asked me yesterday to remind you that you haven't paid your October rent."

"I *what*? It's stinking October 1st and I'm in Cleveland! Of course I haven't paid the rent, but I'll be back in a couple days and pay it then."

"I know, I know," she said soothingly. "I said that."

"And what did he say? I've paid it a few days late before—what happened to the grace period?"

"He said it's due now. And that you should have thought of it before you left."

Words failed me. So this was how it was going to be now? Was he looking for an excuse to kick me out, since he'd been trapped by his verbal agreement to the pre-nup?

"Do you want me to cover for you, Cass? Things are tight, but I can do it."

"Oh, no, Phyl. I'll take care of it."

Not wanting to shoot the messenger, I pleaded Ned waking up and ended the call. Then I flipped over to my contact list for Daniel's number. If he got the message—great. If not, whoever he was having sex with at the moment could enjoy it. The man was lucky I was on such a high over Ned. Otherwise my message would have been scathing, rather than simply terse.

Snail mail or wire? Wire—need account + routing #.

The petty bastard. Not that I was positive I could wire money, even if desired. It was nearly lunchtime and the banks would close soon.

But he must have been hunched over his ledgers counting his pennies because the reply came back within three minutes.

Wire. Rout 325081403 Acct 192261461. If recd before 10/2 no late chg.

• • •

I woke up in the middle of the night, unsure where I was. Small wonder, after the day I had.

There was the mad scramble to find a bank, to get the cash advance, to pay for the wire. There was the curt message to Daniel when the deed was done:

Your pound of flesh en route.

There was the wrath to be swallowed on receiving his Shylock's reply:

The villainy you teach me, I will execute, and it shall go hard but I will better the instruction.

There were the reproaches from Nadina when Ned and I subsequently showed up late to the rendezvous at the Botanical Garden. There was the Garden itself to be wandered through. There was the swimming Nadina wanted to do back at my hotel. There was the dinner out with her and Aunt Sylvia, followed by the torturous teen movie Nadina chose while her great-aunt babysat. Then there were Ned's issues.

When we came in the door at ten we found Aunt Sylvia passed out in the recliner, snoring, Ned writhing around in his car seat, red-faced from screaming his head off. "That kid barely fell asleep—how can he be awake again?" Aunt Sylvia demanded, a touch defensive. "I don't blame him for waking up, though. Must be hungry. He wouldn't take his last bottle."

I was too amazed by this news to waste time reproving a 70+-year-old woman for nodding off. "Wouldn't take his bottle? Ned always takes his bottle."

His pale hair and fleece pajamas were wet through with sweat. Rocking and hushing him, I lay the back of my hand to his forehead. Hot as blazes—but from illness or being overwrought I didn't know. "I'll try to feed him now, before I go. You don't happen to have a thermometer, Aunt Sylvia—?"

She didn't. Or not one she could find, at least. Nor would Ned eat. He turned his head repeatedly from the bottle, crying more loudly each time.

"He must feel badly," I said. "Nadina—where's the closest drug store?" Back in the car we went to the Shaker Square CVS, where I loaded up on infant acetaminophen and a thermometer and humidifier.

"Dude," said Nadina, when I pulled up in their driveway again, "maybe you guys should just sleep here."

I pictured me lying in Great-Grandma Graham's deathbed while Ned's fussing kept everyone up all night. "No, I'll go on back to the hotel. He should be fine soon."

Ned's temperature was 99.6° when I cajoled him into sleep. I had changed him into dry pajamas and gotten the right dosage from my medical insurance hotline before wearing a groove into the hotel room carpet walking him up and down its length.

Only to be awakened now.

I rolled over to peer at the clock. 1:30 a.m. and Ned was crying again. Weakly, this time. Please, I thought, let it be hunger.

I knew before I reached for him that it wasn't. Had Ned been hungry, his cries would have been insistent, lusty. Not this faint, effortful puling. *Oh, God.*

100.9°—climbing, despite the medicine. Nor had enough time passed that I could dose him again. Off came his pajamas while I resumed pacing, trying to get the insurance people on the phone again. Graveyard shift Sunday morning—it could take half an hour. The hold music was a maddening, pointless piece: atonal scales, clashing instruments, no hint of melody.

102.1° —off came the diaper. I got a wet washcloth from the bathroom and started sponging Ned. "Shhhh…it's okay, my little darling. Shhh….Where are these damned nurses? Answer the phone, damn you—answer the phone!"

The curses died in my throat when a wave rippled through my baby, turning his plump little limbs in an instant to rock. "Ned?" Unheeded, my phone fell to the tile floor, battery cover flying somewhere behind the toilet. "Ned?" His blue eyes had disappeared, rolling back so only the whites showed, and his troubled breathing broke off.

"Oh, God! Oh, God ohGodohGod—" Slipping, almost going down, I stumbled out of the bathroom. 9-1-1. Screw the insurance hotline. Punching the numbers on the hotel phone got me nothing—silence— and still Ned held his breath, a baby carved from marble. Dial 9 to get out. 9 for an outside line, yes yes. Oh, God—but how would they ever find me up here? They would waste time prowling the hotel corridors looking for my room. Meet the paramedics in the lobby. Yes.

Tears ran down my face, but I didn't have time to dash them away. Raincoat. Blanket for Ned. I was halfway out the door before I remembered to run back for my purse and in the elevator before I thought of my phone. Never mind. Why didn't he move? What was happening? Laying my head to his stiffened chest I heard, rather than felt, him draw a slow, shallow breath. At least it was a breath—was it enough? Brain damage—I had read somewhere how many minutes the brain could go without oxygen before things started going wrong. Some desperately small number. Ned was going to be brain-damaged from fever and lack of oxygen. No—it was worse—he was going to die.

"Lady—Lady—slow down. Calm down," urged the drowsy clerk whom I summoned from God knows where with frantic banging on the desk bell.

"Am—ambulance. Please! Call the ambulance. My baby—the

baby—he's having a seizure. A convulsion. Something. Please—oh, God, hurry."

The young man straightened up. Scrambled out from behind the counter to look at Ned. "Has he done this before? Does he have a fever?"

"No! I mean yes!" I cried. "I mean, what would you know? You're wasting time! He'll die—call 9-1-1—"

"But, Lady—no—you've got to calm down and listen to me—there's no point in calling the ambulance. We're on the campus of the Cleveland Clinic. Their emergency room is a block away—I can run you down there in the hotel shuttle this second."

· · ·

There would never in all my life be another night like that one.

My mind has already begun to push the memory away, to wrap it up in wool and forgetfulness. It was so like the time I lost Troy and Min, in its nightmare quality, but so different in that, with them, I came along after the fact. They were already dead.

With Ned there was the horror that he would die before my eyes. In my arms. Die, while the triage nurses raced past, rolling in the heart attack, the gunshot wound, the stroke victim needing the miracle drug. I wasn't the only one weeping and screaming in my pajamas.

"Seizures? How long? Fever? Age of the baby? History of these?" The nurse completed her inventory. Held up a tired hand to silence my pleading. "We'll get to you as soon as we can." Handed me insurance paperwork. Sent me over to sit by the woman nursing her arm and a bleeding scalp.

The words on the page blurred. I managed to unearth my insurance card but got no further before I let the clipboard drop. Pointless. Who cared who paid for what, if he was going to die.

Protectively, I bent over my baby boy. Laid my cheek to his forehead. His muscles were relaxing inch by inch, but the fever raged on. Sometime in the last hour he had peed on me. Was that good or bad?

Peeing was good. A bodily function. Through my lips I tried to breathe cooling air on him as I prayed. I had been praying from the moment he seized, an inarticulate stream of desperation. But now I hunkered down. Withdrew into myself. Prostrated my soul.

My God.

My Father.

Hear me.

Don't leave me. I can't do this alone.

I can't do this again.

I tell you what you already know: Ned is yours. Not mine, not Mike's—yours.

I give him back to you.

I surrender.

• • •

A hand on my arm.

I raised my head, my eyes bleary. How long had I been crying and praying? The bashed-up woman next to me was gone. Poor thing. Well, she was in God's hands too.

"I'm Dr. Anita Jodha. Let's have a look at this baby, shall we?"

She was a young Indian woman. A resident, perhaps. The hand pulled me back gently.

"Ah—he's a young one, isn't he? I don't blame you for panicking."

Her voice and manner were so soothing that I let her take Ned without resistance. She slipped a plastic temperature strip under his arm, cradling him against her and humming while she ran through her checks: femoral pulse, hips, heart, lungs.

"Mm-hmm, that's high—you've probably already given him some medicine?"

I nodded. Told her every last detail on the night, my voice getting stronger as I absorbed her calm. "Dr. Jodha—is he going to die? Why did he seize up like that?"

She smiled. "I think he's going to live. Live to cause you other scares and sleepless nights."

"But what happened, then? Will he have brain damage?"

"No brain damage." She replaced him in my arms and helped me up. "Come with me. You say it lasted ten minutes or less? And that his whole body stiffened up? My guess is his system was responding to the sudden spike in temperature. Some babies do. Not many, but some. It's terribly scary for the parents."

I nodded inadequately. Found I was gripping her hand, the tears welling up now out of relief and splashing off her engagement ring. I let go. "Sorry."

Another smile. She flexed her mangled fingers. "If you gave him acetaminophen a few hours ago, we'll try some ibuprofen to bring the fever down."

"That's it?" I wobbled after her down the corridor. "Just a seizure caused by the fever? Will it happen again?"

"I don't think so, if we can lower his temperature. I'll dose him up and you go home and watch him closely for the next 24 hours. I suspect he'll just go into the next stages of whatever bug he's fighting."

"Go home—? Can't I stay here? I'm actually just in Cleveland on a trip—I'm at the Inter-Continental. I'd feel so much better if I could watch him here, Dr. Jodha."

"In the Emergency Department?" She emerged from rummaging through a cabinet to hand me a diaper. "I think you'll be much more comfortable in your room. And the Inter-Continental is practically part of the Clinic." Tilting her head, she measured the medicine in its dropper. "Look—he'll want to sleep soon. Wouldn't you rather sit in a nice, comfortable armchair where it's quiet? You don't need that craziness out there. Maybe get some sleep yourself, Mom. You've had a hard night."

"If he seizes up again—or if his temperature doesn't come down—"

"Then you come right back. We'll even call it the same visit." She winked at me.

The tears started again. "Thank you. Thank you so much."

"Shhh...you're welcome. Go on. Do your paperwork and go back to the hotel. If you hurry, no one will see you in your pajamas."

CHAPTER 29:

Getting Things Straight

My four day trip to Cleveland stretched into a week. After my reservation ended at the hotel, I moved after all to Aunt Sylvia's and found Great-Grandma's deathbed not so terrible. Ned's fever continued for another day, kept in check by the ibuprofen. Congestion followed. A cough. Fussiness. But his appetite returned and there were no more seizures. I sent Dr. Jodha roses.

And though the horrors of that night passed, my resolve remained. I remembered what I told God. What I learned.

"I'm bummed that you have to go back," said Nadina the night before we were scheduled to fly out. She was at the kitchen table with her homework while I cleaned up after dinner and Aunt Sylvia watched *Wheel of Fortune* with Ned. "I've gotten kind of used to having the little dude around with his snotty nose."

"You'll see him at Thanksgiving."

"Yeah, but then Mom is moving out, so when will I see him or you after that?"

"You will. Though, if I ever bring Ned out again, it's going to be in a plastic bubble."

"What do you mean 'if'?" The girl was too quick for me.

I cocked an ear toward the living room, not really wanting to have this discussion with Aunt Sylvia around. Hearing only "I'd like to buy a vowel," I joined Nadina at the table.

"You remember what we talked about when I came," I said. "This whole trip—that awful night when I had to take Ned to the ER—it's helped clarify things for me. Look, Nadina. I love Ned with my whole heart. I want to be his mother. I want to adopt him. But I need to hold that lightly right now."

Her lip trembled, and she bit it to keep it still. "Meaning what? Way to send me mixed messages, Cass."

"It means that, when I get back home, I'm going to meet with Lori Lincoln and tell her what I'm thinking—that I can't go full steam ahead." I let that sink in before continuing. "Not until I talk to Mike— see him for myself. That means I have to wait until November. But Nadina—if he really truly is a changed man—"

"You mean religious."

I swallowed. Nodded. "If he really truly found God now, he'll be changing. He won't be the same disastrous Mike. He and I—I hope we can meet together and have a genuine conversation about what would be best for Ned. If we agree it's me I'll be thrilled. If he's absolutely convinced that it would be him, I would need to get my mind around that. But I'm trying to want what God wants for Ned—whatever that might be—even if it's not me."

Groaning, Nadina laid her head across her arm. "Oh, God, Cass. I hoped that craziness at the hospital would make you think you didn't want to lose him."

I leaned over. Dropped a tentative kiss on her hair. "It did. But on top of that it made me realize what I should have known already—that he isn't mine to lose."

• • •

Skandar and Bryson picked me up at the airport. I would have asked Joanie or Phyl, only it was Thursday, and I knew they would be cooking for the open house. As I strapped in Ned's seat, Bryson unbuckled to give me the customary strangling hug, and when I straightened up, Skandar managed to land a kiss on my cheek.

"Good heavens! Reiner must have called."

"Cynic. I haven't heard a thing."

Bryson filled the drive with his easy chatter, and we were through Renton before Skandar spoke up again. "Shall we get dinner?"

"Oh, no. Thank you. Neddie's been sick, you know, and we're on Ohio time. I think we'll just stay in." I hesitated. "It is Thursday, though, if you two wanted to eat at the Palace." Our open houses had never before included children, but Ned was always there. And if Daniel didn't like it, he could lump it.

"Do you have a Wii?" asked Bryson.

"A Playstation, I think, but you're welcome to it after dinner. Speaking of which, if you're coming, let's stop off at the store and pick something up."

Good thing we did because the house was packed. Not just Joanie and Creep and Phyl and Wayne and Daniel and Violette, but—to my amazement—Perry and Darla.

After a week of not seeing Daniel, I was a little out of practice—didn't quite make eye contact, and my introductions sounded flustered. But I took refuge in accosting my brother. "Perry! I didn't know you were coming—I'm so glad."

"Well I've got to come, haven't I, if you're going to be absconding with my nephew and nearly killing him in the process," he said, taking Ned from me.

"Who told you I nearly killed him?" I felt the color draining from my face—not because of Perry teasing me but because I hadn't thought how dreadful it would be to tell him or my parents that I might hand Ned over. My mind, in fact, had gotten no further than worrying about my appointment with Lori the next day.

It was my brother's turn to look uneasy, and he threw a glance at Darla. "It was—uh—Joanie. She texted me. Just thought I should know."

Sure enough, Darla's habitually sunny features clouded over. "She sure likes to keep you in the loop. I should think if your own sister didn't think it was important enough to tell you, then Joanie didn't have to go out of *her* way." She crossed her arms over her chest, which served the dual purpose of expressing her displeasure and squashing her boobs together attractively. Perry seemed affected by neither.

He shrugged. "Joanie texted me, if you must know, because I texted her first. I wanted to know why Cass didn't call me back."

"I dropped my phone in the hotel bathroom," I said to Darla. "It took me a couple days to get back to him."

Darla's hands went to her hips. "Why should a couple days matter? I've known Perry to let a *whole week* go by before he bothers to return a call."

This fishwife Darla took me by surprise, since I had only seen the playful kitten before, but it was clearly not Perry's first encounter.

"We talked about that already, Darla, and I apologized. Give it a rest."

"Give it a rest like you'd like to give our relationship a rest, you naughty boy!" She turned on me. "Your brother says all kinds of things he doesn't mean—it must be the actor in him."

I bristled. "That's not a bit true. If Perry says he'll do something, he will. He might be a little late, but he'll do it. You can depend on him. Unlike some people. How would you have handled—?" Breaking off, I glanced involuntarily toward Daniel. He was feeding Violette something off his plate, and she responded with a grateful kiss.

Someone tugged on my arm. I looked down to see Bryson. "Princess—I found a ball in the garage. Can I take it in the backyard?"

"Of course." I blushed, pointing at the door. I hoped no one had heard the nickname.

"'Princess?'" bellowed Creep, stalking over, Joanie making

apologetic faces behind him. "Why does that kid call you Princess?"

"It's a long story."

"He calls her Princess because she's beautiful," said Joanie, putting her arm around my waist.

Darla took one look at Perry's softened expression and decided two could play at that game. "It's because her life reads like a fairy tale."

I stared. "Which fairy tale would that be?" Skandar appeared at my elbow with a drink for me, his eyes impassive. Indeed. If my life read like a fairy tale, his was from the same sorry book. "Actually, Darla," I said, "my life reads more like the first half of every fairy tale—you know—the part where everyone dies."

Darla gasped as if I had stabbed her, leaving me to stammer, "Oh my gosh—I was kidding. Really."

"Cass is at the part in the fairy tale right before everything turns around," said Skandar in his low voice. "Right before the happy ending." I shut my eyes. Please—dear God—I appreciate him trying to help, but now the idiot is going to tell this crowd we're engaged!

"That's too bad." It was Daniel. I suppose all Violette's kisses weren't loud enough to drown us out. "Because Cass has an aversion to happy endings."

My grip tightened on the stem of my glass. "It's not a happy ending if the princess ends up with the villain."

"Especially if she's such a bad read of character that she can't tell who the villain is," he said amiably. "Or if she really thinks she'd be happier living in her little tower the rest of her life, braiding her hair."

Joanie's arm tightened on my waist. I ignored the warning. "And what a pleasant tower it would be, if the villain weren't given to skulking about the place."

"Funny how owners like to do that—hang around, keep an eye on their property."

"Yes, but thank heavens that's not all the villain likes to keep an eye on." I heaved a mock sigh. "So many princesses, so little time."

At this point, Phyl—God bless her—what were we going to do when she was gone?—intervened. "I'm whipping up the soufflés now," she announced. "So I need a show of hands: how many for chocolate and how many for Grand Marnier?"

. . .

One hour, a bowl of goulash and a chocolate soufflé later, Bryson was frowning at the media cabinet. "What sports games are there, Daddy? There's no soccer. There's not even baseball."

"Hold your horses, I'm looking," said his father, running his finger down the cases. "If we can't find one, maybe Cass will let you play Grand Theft Auto."

"Very funny," I said.

"There's golf," came Daniel's voice behind me. I hoped he didn't notice me jump.

"I don't know how to play golf," said Bryson.

"It's easy. I could show you."

Daniel's fairy tale comments still rankled. "He certainly could," I said. "Mr. Martin knows all about golf. He never misses an opportunity to improve his game. To score, I mean."

Skandar raised an eyebrow at my tone, but Daniel said, "Well, you know what they say, Bryson—practice makes perfect."

I couldn't help myself. "Is that what they say? You must be world-class by now."

Every man has his limits.

He turned his level gaze on me. "May I speak with you?"

Oops.

Reluctantly I followed him to the entry way. Not wanting to meet his eyes, I found myself staring at his chest, which didn't help my self-possession. Shoulder? Ditto. Feet? Too submissive. And anywhere between his chest and knees was clearly off-limits. I trained my eyes on the safety glass lining the front door.

"Cass."

"What?"

"I see you're in the mood for insinuations."

"You see nothing. I wasn't the one who started in on the 'happy endings.'"

"It's the plain truth. You're the one starting in on the golf. I would advise you to say something straight out, if you want to accuse me."

Oh? Like it wasn't the plain truth that he cheated and called it a golf excursion?

"Whatever for?" I countered. "There's nothing to prevent you lying to my face." I traced my finger along one of the leaded diamonds in the window. "Besides, insinuations are so much more fun. We all know what a master you are of the *double entendre*."

He made an impatient movement. "For variety, then, let me make myself clear: you continue to assume I was unfaithful to you, and I continue to deny it. It's all water under the bridge at this point. I think you need to move on."

That got my attention. I glared at him. "I have moved on. I'm not crying into my pillow wishing you would induct me into your harem again, if that's what you're thinking."

"How odd, then, that your verbal potshots smack of dog-in-the-manger."

"Dog in the manger—you wish! You have my full permission—blessing, even—to hump anything in the whole stinking barnyard. Not that you wait for permission."

"Thank you. I may not need permission, but it does relieve my mind. If you're so agreeable about me 'humping anything in the whole stinking barnyard,' I wonder why you got upset in the first place."

I struck my fist on the wall, heedless of who heard me. "I got upset because I do happen to care when people cheat and lie and then try to pin it on me! Like you're trying to pin this on me! God knows I wouldn't take such pleasure in needling you if the feeling weren't mutual."

"Ah…that temper of yours. I hope Skandar knows what he's getting into."

I might say the same for Violette, but she would discover Daniel's true nature soon enough—they were running up against two weeks.

"Let's start this conversation over, Cass. If I'm not mistaken, I seem to recall our agreement required civility on both sides."

"That's right. But if *I* recall, it was you who fired the shot over the bow—when you set Phyl on me like a collection agent for the rent check!"

Something passed over his face. He looked away. "It was due," he said simply. "I do apologize for my inadvertent bad timing. Had I known Ned's health was worrying you, I would have given you a few days' grace."

How generous. For a petty man, I meant. After a moment I said, "In the interest of fairness, Ned wasn't sick yet. It was that night. When I went to three different banks and spoke to countless bank personnel trying to get you your money before they closed, he was the very picture of health."

"Good to hear." He rocked on his heels.

In the ensuing silence, happier sounds carried to us: cheers and applause from the PGA Golf Tour game, Joanie and Perry laughing about something in the kitchen, the clink of glasses and dishes as Phyl and Wayne cleaned up.

We were not going to be able to live like this.

Daniel was right. I needed to move on or move out. And since I might be about to lose Ned, I couldn't bear the thought of moving out. I had to forgive Daniel. Whatever his shortcomings as a Significant Other, for everyone's sake and household peace I had to remember his strengths as a friend. If he chose to harass me from time to time, I would just have to rise above it. Ignore it.

I tried to arrange my face into a smile. "I'm glad we could resolve that. Well. Anyways…how have you been? I hope things are going well at work."

There was no answering smile. Rather, a corner of his hard-set mouth turned down. He shook his head. "Please. Let's not bother. I was just looking for a cease-fire. A truce. We don't need anything more than that. I don't want anything more than that. Excuse me."

· · ·

"You didn't tell me it was your housemate you were in love with."

Bryson had gotten the hang of the golf game and agreed enthusiastically when Skandar offered to let him play both turns.

I considered denying it. But he'd probably heard enough to make that pointless. "Yes, well, what difference does it make?"

"I'd say, for one thing, it makes it harder for you to get over him."

"It'll happen." I kicked my slippers off and hugged my knees to my chest. "All his other girlfriends have managed."

Phyl and Wayne were getting out the Scrabble board in the dining room, Perry going to join them. How he managed to scrape off Darla was anyone's guess. At least Ned was still accounted for: Perry had him in the sling. "Cass?" Phyl jingled the bag of tiles. I shook my head.

Skandar moved closer to me so he wouldn't need to raise his voice. "I see how you might feel you wouldn't have other…living options."

"I'm not completely without options," I said, "even if I wanted to move. Perry said I could live with him. Or I could move back in with my parents, tail between my legs. Or, heck—I could marry Dale or Mike Loftus. How would that be for happily ever after? The problem would be choosing between them: would I want the freakish, stalker father or the freakish, felon son?"

He didn't laugh. Come to think of it, the man never laughed at my jokes. Daniel did—or used to. Daniel also slept around behind my back, but you couldn't have everything. Sigh. Either Skandar was depressed or I wasn't funny. Probably both.

"Well, Cass, I have an option for you. You could move in with Bryson and me. No, hang on a second. Hear me out. We've got plenty of room for you and Ned. It might help you see your way clear."

It might also help me feel like the second Mrs. de Winter, what with all the photographs of Katherine and the pescatorian décor. No way. "For Pete's sake—did you just think of this fifteen minutes ago, because Daniel and I were sniping at each other?"

"No. I thought of it that time you were alone and Mike's dad came by."

A few weeks ago, then. For Skandar and our relationship, that almost qualified as long-range planning. This had to stop.

"Skandar." I put my feet back on the floor. "I did see my way clear to some things while I was in Cleveland."

He bent his head to look sidelong at me. I wondered how many years it had taken him to grow that ponytail he had when I met him. Or how many years it would take him to grow it back. He was so set in his ways—so persistent. If I weren't ruthless now, this could drag on forever.

Bryson dinked a beautiful chip shot and we clapped.

"Skandar," I said as quietly as I could, "I figured out that I can't marry you. Not now and not ever. Not if we're friends for a hundred years. Not if I were to move in with you now. It just wouldn't work. We're not a fit." Ruthless enough?

He said nothing.

Bryson swung wildly this time, laughing. "That was you, Daddy. You're losing!"

"That's my final decision," I went on, Ming the Merciless. "You've been … a good friend to me and rescued me more than once, so I feel terrible saying this, but I would feel worse not saying it. I wish you the very best in life, you know that. But the very best for you isn't me."

A muscle worked in his jaw.

"Does this mean you want me gone?"

"Of course not—I just want to be absolutely clear. I like you. I care about what happens to you—both of you. I'm happy to keep being friends, as long as we understand each other." I leaned even closer. "The kissing has definitely got to stop. Maybe getting rid of me altogether would be best, for Bryson—or at least branching out, friend-wise."

"I'll think about it." He was such a hard read that I couldn't tell if he was hurt or furious or disappointed or blasé. "Hey, Bry. Let's wrap up the Tour. It's getting close to your bedtime."

"Aww, Daddy. I wanted to play Pebble Beach."

"Some other time."

At the door he gave me a long look and almost succeeded in smiling. "It's okay, Cass. I'm not going to drive off a cliff on the way home. You made yourself clear." He tousled his son's red hair and sent him off to unlock the Audi. "Bryson and I will pull through. I wish I could say the same for you."

So did I.

Skandar and I weren't the only ones who ended something that night. I barely got the door closed before Joanie pounced on me, squeezing the breath out of me. She was gloating. "Did you see? Perry broke up with Darla! She left when you and Skandar were in the backyard with Bryson."

"Oh! That's how he can play Scrabble with Phyl and Wayne."

"I wanted to hear what they were saying, but everyone was so noisy, all I caught was something like 'you just aren't man enough to tell me you want to end it'—but how can she blame him for not being man enough, when she was always calling him a naughty boy?" Joanie cackled.

"Lower your voice, goofball," I said. "Do you want the whole house to know you were eavesdropping and that you're actually in love with my brother instead of the man you're dating?"

"Like you're one to talk! I couldn't catch what you were saying, but you and Daniel were having a pretty heated discussion earlier, and he came back into the kitchen looking like he wanted to crack somebody's head open."

"He did?" He was so calm with me. Maddeningly so. It was some comfort to know I still had the power to aggravate.

"Yep. It took Virulent lots of petting him and soothing his brow to perk him up. She finally dragged him off to the Lean-To—I guess so we'd stop annoying him." She glanced around. "Speaking of sulky men, where'd Skandar go?"

"Home."

"What—what are you grinning about? No! You finally, finally told him he had to go cry on someone else from now on?"

"Stop it. He was fine today. He's fine 80% of the time, which sure beat my record in the first year. And isn't Bryson a nice boy?"

"Yeah, but you already got your own nice boy. You don't need another one."

I didn't answer, not wanting to get into it.

She tugged on my hand. "Well, come on back. I have a brilliant idea for the retail opening in a few weeks, now that you got rid of Skandar."

"What? I thought I was going stag."

"Uh-uh. Because you're my very bestest friend and you love me so dearly, you're going to ask Perry to come with us."

I shook her off. "What is wrong with you Martins? You're already dating someone! That means you're not supposed to be scheming to get someone else. If you want to go out with Perry, break up with Creep. Don't string him along."

"Oh, Cass! What would be the good of dumping Creep right before he's got this big shindig with all his friends and his parents' friends? Don't be so heartless. I promise you—cross my heart—that if Perry shows any signs of coming around, I'll dump Creep the second we're alone."

"Won't that be obvious? Won't Creep feel kind of used?"

Joanie waved this away. "I'll smooth it all over. 'It's not you, it's me' blah blah. I have a little more experience at this than you. Goll—look at the mess you made with Daniel. Both of you at each other and making everyone else uncomfortable."

"We've worked it out," I said. "We'll behave now. I'm going to try to rise above it when he baits me—not that he will anymore. Daniel said he just wants civility—just light, shallow chitchat when other people are around. He said he…doesn't want anything more than that."

That he meant it became more and more obvious as the weeks went by. Civility, silence, distance.

When we finally did talk again, it had to be on my initiative. And, if not for Mike, even that might never have happened.

CHAPTER 30:

The 180

My speech was practiced. *Lori, I want you to hold off on filing my petition to adopt. Before we file, I need to talk to Mike.*

Okay, so it probably didn't qualify as a speech. It was more like two sentences, and things got murky after that. I pictured my attorney's appraising stare and tented fingers and bobbed hair and got sort of queasy. Why did I feel like I spent so much of my life trying to defend superficially indefensible choices? Why I wanted to adopt a baby, why I didn't want to marry the unsuitable men who asked me, why I might not be justified in adopting the baby after all…

The elevator doors opened. I wanted to stay on, let them close again and ride up and down till I worked up some courage, but my fellow passenger stabbed the Hold button with her finger. "This is your floor, isn't it?"

It was.

I slogged off, took my seat in the reception area after waving at Dorothy. A crazy few months. No Skandar today. In fact, we had never crossed paths in Lori's office again. What random hairsbreadths separated different paths in life. Imagine if I made this appointment today to announce, Lo!—I was getting married as she advised, and to none other than the client I met in her office. Something told me Lori would receive that news unblinkingly, but this—

"Cass." She beckoned me.

There I sat in the leather armchair; there she sat opposite, hands folded on the blotter, vast desk between us.

I cleared my throat. At least I knew she loathed small talk. Nothing would distract me from my two sentences. I added a preamble: "You're probably wondering why I wanted to meet with you today."

"I don't imagine I'll be in suspense long. I presume you wanted to know what feedback, if any, Barbara Dobbs the social worker gave me regarding your post-birth follow-up visit."

Distraction #1. "Oh! I—uh—I didn't know you would hear anything for weeks and weeks—until she filed something. She gave you some feedback?"

Lori Lincoln's rosebud mouth pursed. After a moment of—I could only guess—internal debate, she said, "Nothing official. But I've known Ms. Dobbs for years and worked with her on more cases than you can imagine. She…tends to let me know her opinion of things before anything is made official."

I sat forward. "Oh, I see. And…she gave you her opinion on my situation?"

"She did." The rosebud mouth eked out slightly in either direction. I think I was meant to interpret it as an approving smile. "It appears that everything is on the up and up. She sees no delays in getting the necessary documents to me, and the moment I receive them I can file the petition to adopt with the court."

How I would have welcomed that news—exulted—only a couple weeks ago.

"Yes," I said. "About that petition…" My two sentences! What were my two sentences? "What about Mike?" I blurted, going off script. "He would file an objection, then, I think you said?"

The fractional smile widened. "Ordinarily."

My set speech was coming back to me. In any case, I wasn't interested in Lori's Cheshire Cat impression. "Lori—that's just it. I want to hold off on filing the petition to adopt. I need to talk to Mike."

"What?"

"Mike will be out in less than a month. I want to talk to him."

"About what? Barbara will meet with him, and that will be that. I think you should stay out of it."

Now I was the one mystified. "What? Why would the Dobbs—I mean Barbara Dobbs—why would she talk to him? That's not part of the home study."

"To get his consent to the adoption."

"Huh? You just said he would file an objection to the adoption."

"No, *you* just said he would file an objection. I'm telling you that I think he'll be giving his consent." Seeing my utter bewilderment, Lori permitted herself a laugh. She slapped a triumphant, impeccably-manicured hand on the blotter. "Yes, Cass, that's my news for you. If you hadn't set up this appointment, I would have been contacting you. Gary Lansing, the state-appointed public defender, called me—*quite disgruntled*—to say that, contrary to his advice, his client had decided to consent to the adoption. Mr. Lansing was headed to the court to file Mr. Loftus' Petition of Recission this very afternoon. There! What do you think of that?"

I didn't know what to think. My head spun with the news. But why? Why on earth would Mike give up? Where did this decision come from?

"I don't understand."

"Recission means he's rescinding his paternity affidavit."

"No, I mean I don't understand why Mike would consent. He's always been dead set. Every message he's ever given me is that he's dead set."

"Well, he's not anymore." Lori inspected the polish on her left pinky.

345

Frowned. "Of course, nothing is official until Barbara—Ms. Dobbs—gets that consent signed, which she tells me she will pursue upon his release and return to the area, but I consider the recission the next best thing. One can't be filing and un-filing week by week—I'm his father, I'm not his father—without making a poor impression on the court."

I couldn't stop shaking my head. "I don't understand. I need to speak with him."

Lori looked up. "Nonsense. You don't need reasons. Don't look a gift horse in the mouth. We'll get his consent and our court date and nail this down before he changes his mind."

"You think he'll change his mind? Did Mr. Lansing tell you why Mike gave up?"

"Absolutely not. And I didn't ask. It doesn't pertain. It's a gift, Cass. Just take it."

"But—"

Lori sat forward. Nailed me to my chair with narrowed eyes. "Don't tell me you've changed *your* mind."

"No! Oh, no. I want Ned with all my heart. It's just—"

"Well, then. Barring any new developments, I'll contact you again when I receive official notice of recission from the court and again when Ms. Dobbs schedules her meeting with Mr. Loftus. I needn't take up any more of your time today." She was already turning away and doing the straightening-the-papers-in-the-file-folder move.

"Wait, Lori—please. Would it be all right if I met with Mike after he gets out, too? I understand if you don't need to know his reasons, but it would really help me. I didn't get a chance to say it, but I was doubting I should go ahead with the adoption until after I spoke with him. This is all so sudden. I'm glad, of course, to hear he's not going to contest things, but with all the emotional energy I've been spending on this I just feel like … I would have more … peace or something, if I could know what was happening on his end."

Her grip tightened on my folder through the course of my speech, crumpling it, and, with an effort, she managed to lay it back on the desk. "Cass, if you hadn't changed your mind, why were you doubting you should go ahead with it?"

Where even to begin? With the end, I suppose. "I…heard…that Mike might have had something like a…spiritual awakening while he was at Coyote Ridge. If that really was the case, I didn't want to be wrangling with him in court. Not if we ultimately were on the same side."

With no folder in her hand, she was forced to clench her fists. Seeing my eyes follow the motion, she took a deep breath and uncurled her fingers. They were trembling. "Suffice to say, 'spiritual awakenings' that come under duress, when one is in prison, do not always produce saints. If you have any love for the child, you would hardly want to place him in the care of a convicted felon, spiritual awakening or no."

"Yes, I know that," I said, feeling my cheeks grow hot. For Pete's sake, you would think she was the one all along saying convicted felons shouldn't be allowed to adopt kids. "I didn't say I was just going to hand him over—just that I wanted to see Mike and judge for myself if he really was a changed person. It went without saying that, if I thought he was a…faker…an opportunist…I would fight him to the death before I'd give him Ned."

It also went without saying that Lori Lincoln thought I should leave character assessments to larger-brained folk like herself. She tented her fingers. Spoke in her best we're-all-reasonable-people-here tone. "Well. How fortunate that Mr. Loftus has made any such judgments on your part completely moot. Had he become Gandhi himself, he no longer wants the child. He doesn't want the child, and you do. Case closed."

"Then it wouldn't hurt, if I saw him?"

"I would not advise you to do anything of the kind."

"It wouldn't be illegal, would it?" I persisted. "Maybe—maybe you could come along to make sure it was all above board."

Lori inhaled so sharply that she choked. She had to wait for her coughs to subside before she could speak again. "That would not be at all appropriate. It might even strike Mr. Loftus as coercive and persuade him to retaliate. No. I'll have no part of it. If you choose to meet with him, it's against my advice. My recommendation is that you abandon the idea altogether. You have to make up your own mind, of course, but if you continue to insist on seeing him, at the bare minimum, wait until after the adoption is final."

But that would be months from now! Months and months.

I had already upset her enough for one afternoon, however, so I kept this protest to myself. Nodded. She probably thought Daniel owed her big time for saddling her with such a trying client.

I rose. "Thank you, Lori. Sorry to be so weird about it. This is, like you said, all great news."

"Hmm." She was smoothing the creases from my file. "Have a good day, Cass."

• • •

It was raining.

As part of my general foot-dragging that day, I had taken the bus, telling Louella that I might be gone several hours. ("Don't you worry about it," she said. "There's nothing I don't know about babies." Indeed. As a nurse married to a doctor for fifty-plus years, Louella even knew about the febrile seizures which had nearly finished me off in Cleveland. "Oh, dear, that must have given you a scare. Good thing Ned is such a little tank.")

A little tank, and the tank was mine. Ned was mine.

Or all but.

I didn't know why or how it came about. It had never occurred to me, in my moment of surrender, hunched over my loss in the Cleveland Clinic ER, that Mike on his end might also be reconsidering.

In my case I had released Ned into God's hands. Was that also what

Mike had done?

With the moisture outside and the damp heat within, the bus windows were fogged up. Using the end of my sleeve, I rubbed a circle clear and peered out. Gray, lowering skies. People striding the shining sidewalks, huddled against the wet. A few umbrellas.

We were all going somewhere.

Me, Mike.

I guess neither Mike nor I wanted our paths to run parallel for years, with occasional snarled knots where we confronted each other in court. And before I could try to cut him loose, he set himself free.

I was glad of it—grateful. And I would let him go, yes, after I got my chance to talk to him. I would tell no one—not friends, not family, and certainly not Lori—but I would talk to him. I would know why.

• • •

I waited until I knew school was out to call Nadina.

"Cass? Here I was thinking you probably weren't going to call me much anymore."

"Yeah—this is the last time. I just wanted to let you know I dropped Ned at the fire station because I really couldn't hack it anymore."

The line was silent. I could picture her by the frog buckets, mouth open.

Then I laughed. "I'm kidding, you dope!"

"Dude—what is wrong with you? No wonder you hardly ever crack jokes—you are so not funny at all."

"I know, I'm sorry. That one was in poor taste, wasn't it? But no, Nadina, I called you again because I have wonderful news!"

"You're getting married?"

My turn to be irritated. "No—with the men currently in my life, that wouldn't be wonderful news. But I saw Lori Lincoln today, and she said Mike's defender said Mike is withdrawing his paternity claim! He's not going to fight the adoption anymore! When he gets out in a few weeks, the social worker is going to meet with him to sign the consent to adopt—what do you think of all that?"

"No way."

"Way."

"No. Way."

"Yes. Way."

"Oh my God! Yay! Oh my God!" Hearing Nadina's excitement fired up my own. "You're sure?"

"Well, nothing's set in stone yet, but the defender was on his way to file the paper, so that one's in the bag. And Lori said that, even if Mike gets cold feet, it would look bad before the judge that he kept changing his mind. I still don't understand it all. I don't know why Mike would suddenly back down."

"Aw, Cass—who cares? Just so he does. Maybe he thought he didn't want to get home from being a fry cook and go change diapers. That is awesome. I've been trying to get used to the idea that you might give Ned up, but it wasn't going too well. I mean, I know you think you want what's best for him, but you're not the one who lived with Mike and all. The dude had issues, and I'm betting six months of being someone's bitch out at Coyote Ridge did not help."

"Thank you, mental health counselor."

"This is good, too, because, after you left, Aunt Sylvia got me to dish the dirt, and she was so hella pissed at you. You were gonna have to stay at the friggin' Intercontinental if you ever came out again because no way was she gonna offer my great-grandma's bed."

"Oh, no!" I shrunk at the thought of Aunt Sylvia's ire. "You think she'll calm down now?"

"I dunno. I mean, it's still you being willing to give up Ned—it just happens that Mike chickened out first. You don't get any credit for that. But she'll relax after a while. Maybe give you kinda the cold shoulder when you come out. But if you've got Ned, and it's official, she'll warm up. She got to liking him."

"Oh, I hope she'll forgive me," I said. "Because I got to liking her too."

"Yeah, yeah—oh, shit!"

"What?" I asked anxiously.

"Nothing—fucking frogs—" There was a clunk as she put the phone down, and I heard more cursing and clunking, along with some splashes.

"What eez happening here?" another voice demanded. "Thees water on the floor is dangerous."

"Duh! Then maybe don't walk in it, Jean-Luc," said Nadina. More shuffling and thumping followed before she picked up the phone again. "Gotta go, Cass. Froggamageddon. Call you later, 'kay?"

"Okay," I said. "Count to twenty, right?"

"You have no idea."

CHAPTER 31:

Ring Out the Old

I had no idea.

"Did you find something to write with, yet?" Joanie demanded. "This is crucial."

I hardly heard her, still staring as I was, at the midnight-blue velvet ring box in my hand. My phone had rung while I was cleaning the Lean-To—Joanie wanting me to write down her dry cleaning ticket number and help her out in a time crunch. Since I was upstairs making the bed with no pens or paper handy, I whipped open the nearest nightstand drawer and rummaged through it.

A ballpoint, a discarded gift card envelope, nail clippers, a watch, some stray batteries, a cell phone charger, and this. "Hang on, Joanie."

Setting my phone down, I perched on the bed's edge, the half-on, half-off fitted sheet crumpled beneath me, and gingerly opened the box.

An engagement ring winked up at me. No—winking didn't begin to describe the tiny beams of light thrown every which way by the facets of the diamond, a brilliant flanked by two smaller pear cuts, the stones glittering in their pavé setting. White gold? Platinum? Beautiful.

"Cass?" came Joanie's voice from the discarded phone. "Cass!"

I snapped the ring box shut. Replaced it in the very back of the drawer.

"What is it? What are you doing, Cass?"

"Cleaning the Lean-To," I said, my breath coming rapidly. I felt as if I had stumbled on something contraband—condoms, or a diary. "Joanie—Daniel has an engagement ring in the back of his nightstand drawer."

"Oh my gosh! He doesn't."

"I was looking right at it."

"He can't—I've never seen one, and I sometimes go through all his stuff when it's my turn to clean."

"You do? That is so wrong, Joanie. Except I guess I just did it, too. Do you go through my stuff?"

"Oh, on occasion. Yours is less exciting. I never read anything." She dismissed this. "But a ring—! I don't believe it. Is it pretty?"

"It's … the prettiest ring I've ever seen."

"Wow. I'm gonna have to check it out the next time he's not home."

"Maybe you won't have to sneak around," I said grimly. "I'm sure Violette would be happy to show it to you."

"Argh! It can't be, Cass. They've only been going out a month or so. I have no idea why he has that, but surely he doesn't have plans for it."

"They've been together five weeks—not that I'm counting," I corrected her. "Violette made it past the four-week hurdle. She's in the top 5%. So who knows? Besides, what man spends a few thousand on an engagement ring that he doesn't have plans for?"

"I don't know," she fretted. "Maybe he's had it ever since he asked you to marry him in May, and he just never bothered to return it. Humiliating, you know, for a guy to have to say he got turned down."

Well, Joanie's fiancés would know all about having to make humiliating engagement ring returns.

"But when's the last time you went through his stuff, Joanie? Are you saying you haven't done it since May?"

"Oh," she sighed, "I don't know…I guess I poked around a while back, and I didn't see any ring. Either he had it well hidden, or he bought the thing pretty recently. Crap. I don't want Violette for a sister! She's always, 'Yes, Daniel,' 'No, Daniel,' 'Daniel, darling, let me wait on you hand and foot'—like he needs any more of that in his life. You at least got pissed at him once in a while and pissed him off, too."

"Yeah. Unfortunately Daniel and I veered a little too much that direction." I slammed the drawer shut. "Okay. You know what? We don't have time to talk about your brother's love life if I need to run by the dry cleaner for you. Give me that ticket number."

• • •

"Where on earth did you get a tux? Did you actually shell out to rent one?" I asked my brother, coming to stand beside him in front of the dining room mirror.

He paused in his James Bond imitations. "Are you kidding? I'm already losing money taking this weekend off. I raided the theater's costume closet. This one's more *Private Lives* than *Casino Royale*, but it fit. Is that what you're wearing?"

I laughed. "Thanks a lot. Don't I look all right? It's Phyl's. They say it's a black-tie gala, but I really didn't want to wear some great golden gown, even if Phyl had one."

He scrutinized my cocktail dress. Red silk shantung with a Sabrina neckline. "You look like a bridesmaid."

"I *am* a bridesmaid," I said. "Or bridesmatron, if there is such a thing. Brideswidow? Or at least I will be in a couple weeks. Sheesh. You'd think by my age I'd be done with bridesmaid dresses, but I didn't count on some friends having a second round. I would've worn my bridesmaid dress to this thing, in fact—it looks better than this one—if I weren't afraid I'd spill something on it."

"Phyl may be on her second round, but you'll still have to do Joanie's first wedding." He fiddled with his bow tie. "You think she'll marry this Craig Sloane?"

Turning him to face me, I helped him with it. "Why would she? Joanie never marries anyone—not even the guys she gets engaged to."

"But this one's rich and good-looking and opens retail complexes."

Ah.

I gave the bow tie one last tweak. Clapped my brother on the shoulders. Well, why shouldn't everyone have a chance at love? Joanie might break his heart—no, Joanie would in all likelihood break his heart—but they might be very happy until that time. And odds were they'd last longer than Daniel and I did. Those three days, I mean. For Pete's sake. Strangers paired at random on the street could last longer than that.

"So what?" I smiled up at him. "Craig may be rich and good-looking and open retail complexes, but you're poor and not-as-good-looking and open in shows that no one goes to see."

To my surprise, he didn't give me the well-deserved punch in the arm I braced for. Instead, he sagged into one of the Duncan Phyfe dining chairs. "Yeah. That's me."

Ooh—he had it bad. I pulled out the chair next to him. "A pity party! Am I invited?"

"The more the mournful-er."

Nudging his knee with mine, I tried to get him to look at me. "You are so pathetic! And not very bright either, if you've gone this long without realizing that Joanie doesn't give one lick about Craig Sloane. Not him or any other guy. Because she's got the mistaken and probably extremely temporary idea that she would rather be with you."

My words effected an immediate transformation.

"Really? You mean it?" He ran an excited hand through his hair, undoing his careful grooming. "You're not just kidding me?"

"Why would I make something like that up? No, I'm not kidding. I think if you asked her for one dance tonight at this horrible thing, you would be guaranteed never to see Craig Sloane again in your life. I just hope she would wait till the end of the evening before she ditched him."

· · ·

Joanie did, but barely.

I would have felt sorry for Creep had he not been eyeballing a few women himself in their Luly Yang and Bottega Veneta frocks and high-heeled Christian Louboutins. (Joanie had to identify these items for me, this being my debut in what passed for high society.)

While not precisely underdressed, I was clearly out-classed. It certainly didn't help matters that, halfway through the evening, as I exited the mirrored bathroom, I noticed a spot of spit-up on my shoulder, presumably deposited by my dear son when I was whizzing around the house getting things in order for the sitter. Let's hope that explained why no one hit on me, leaving me to spend most of the event sampling items from the buffet or sitting on a pouf eavesdropping on other conversations.

This came of being single, I supposed. Single and surrounded by people in love. Perry and Joanie had eyes only for each other that evening—no way would spit-up on her shoulder have escaped his notice. And as for Violette and Daniel, who put in a brief appearance on their way to someone's Halloween party, the woman appeared to spend as much time grooming him as herself. Her hands were constantly on his clothing, in his hair, adjusting, stroking, arranging, picking, petting. If Daniel were ever to get lice, Violette would come in awfully handy.

On the plus side, since her hands were ever in view, I could always be on the lookout for sparkling new pieces of jewelry. No ring yet. Each time I checked there was always the moment of relief, followed by the pang of fear: maybe he would ask her tonight. In my disastrous "pre-nup," I hadn't planned for the eventuality of Daniel marrying. Would he and his bride live in the Lean-To? Or would they want the Palace, and all to themselves?

In any event, after that night Craig Sloane never again darkened the Palace door, and Joanie and Perry both had to upgrade their cell phone plans to cover their constant talking and texting.

• • •

"You're the classic case of someone who dispenses advice without taking it herself," said Skandar. Another week had passed, and we were doing the rounds, taking Bryson up and down neighborhood streets trick-or-treating. Bryson was dressed as a soccer pirate—his own invention—and they had even dug up an old felt pumpkin costume for Ned.

After I told him I could never marry him, I wondered for a while there if I would ever see or hear from Skandar again. As the days went by I swung between guilt and relief. Sometimes I wanted to pick up the phone and check in; other times I thought any pangs of missing them I should quash as pure selfishness.

The wait was worth it, however. The Sebaris returned. Skandar returned. But he had made some changes. He told me about co-workers he had gotten together with, and the one other fellow from the Grief Recovery class he had called up to grab a beer. All good signs. Good steps. Even better, my earlier cruelty took care of any lingering notions that we might rescue each other. We were at last, as we had never completely been to this point, friends.

Which is not to say Skandar was cured of his moodiness, or that our interactions didn't still lead to shaky emotional moments, but the question of us—the possibility of Us—no longer loomed overhead, our own personal sword of Damocles.

I didn't mind him being around when he was dumpy—I just didn't want him thinking I was going to fix things. As a result, Skandar took to dropping by the Palace when he felt like it, sometimes with Bryson, sometimes alone, sometimes cheerful, sometimes morose. It was what it was.

Bryson, too, seemed to be adjusting to the new world order. He continued to call me Princess, continued to hug me with unwonted enthusiasm whenever he saw me, but Skandar told me Bryson was now playing the field: "He's got a thing for the Art Specialist at his school—makes her pictures and cards, gives her treasures from his room. Thank God the woman is married, otherwise I would have to try for her next."

Bryson came tearing back to us where we stood in the street. "Look, Daddy! They gave out real-size candy bars! Let's go see what they have at that house with the spider webs all over it."

"Lead the way." Skandar waved him along with the flashlight.

I fell into step with him. "Okay, Mister. So what advice am I handing out and not taking?"

"The bit about giving up and moving on, branching out."

Ned's pumpkin-stem felt cap had slid over one eye. I straightened it. Rubbed his plump little legs to warm them.

"As far as I can tell," Skandar continued, seeing I wasn't going to respond, "you're still moping after that housemate of yours. The one who cheated on you and who's heavily involved with someone else."

"Do we have to talk about this? And I am not either 'moping.' I'm just neutral. I hardly even look at the guy. We barely say twenty words a day to each other."

"That's what I mean." He raised a hand in greeting to the occupants of the spider-web house, after they loaded Bryson down with two handfuls of candy. "I've been showing you everything's okay between us by acting normal. We talk, we hang out. I don't try to dodge you."

"I don't try to dodge Daniel," I said. "It's just—I would like to be friends—I…miss him—but he was the one who said he didn't want that. You can't be normal with someone who doesn't even want you around."

"If he's the one who cheated on you, why's he so angry at you?"

I mulled this over. "I guess he didn't like me questioning his integrity. And he thought I was a cheater, too, because I went out with you that one night, and you had to go and kiss me."

Bryson reappeared, his pirate patch askew and his plastic cutlass dragging. "Wow, Daddy. Feel how heavy my bag is getting! How many more houses can we do?"

"A couple. It's starting to rain."

"You aren't going to eat all that candy, are you Bryson?" I asked. "Your teeth will rot out."

"Cool!" he exclaimed. He detached his cutlass and handed it to Skandar before running backwards from us. "Then I'll really look like a pirate."

When he was out of earshot again, Skandar said, "Look—I'm sorry about the kiss. Would it help if I explained to him that you were just keeping me company on a tough day, and I took advantage of it?"

Ugh. "Oh, Skandar, I appreciate the offer, but I think it's too late for explanations. It would look really strange and desperate if I brought it all up again. Besides, what does it matter if I wasn't cheating on him? He still was on me."

"Well, but maybe then he wouldn't be so opposed to smoothing things over with you."

I shuddered. "No. No. Just leave it for now. The man forever has women wanting things from him. He's moved on. He told me to move on. He doesn't seem to be pining for friendship. I'll be fine. I just need some more time." Not to mention Daniel might never need another female friend, if he married Violette. I tried to shield Ned's face from the raindrops. "If Perry and Joanie end up getting hitched, then maybe I'll revisit it, for the sake of family peace. But otherwise…"

He shrugged. "Have it your way. You always do. Bryson—hey, Bry! Let's go, Bud. We're all getting soaked out here."

The entry way was full of boxes when I got home. Phyl had been packing all month, but with her wedding this very Saturday she really stepped things up. Threading my way through the towers of kitchen gear, books, linens, gardening tools, and clothing, I found her in the kitchen.

"Oh, Cass! What a mess everything is. I'm sorry about this. It's just that Wayne borrowed his friend's pick-up tonight, so we're trying to make as many trips as we can."

"Don't worry about it. Let me get Ned situated, and I'll help you."

"Was trick-or-treating fun? Ned is the darlingest pumpkin," said Phyl, coming over to kiss him. "I love his fat little hands."

For some reason I felt like crying. The Palace would be a much lonelier place when Phyl was gone, what with Joanie wrapped up in Perry and Daniel keeping a hostile distance. "I'll miss you so much Phyl. Not that I'm not happy for you, but we'll be lost without you. All the plants will die and everyone will fight and we'll even miss seeing Benny once in a while. And who will mix our drinks?"

"Aww, Cass. You're all wet, but I'll hug you anyhow. You forget that I started some of the fights these last few months. Don't worry—when Wayne and I come over for open houses I'll guest bartend. How could we stay away?"

"Did you…talk to Daniel? Does he still say you don't need to find someone to replace you?"

"That's what he still said, as of last weekend. Maybe he's leaving it up to Joanie, or maybe—" She broke off, suddenly getting very busy rooting in the lower drawer for her embroidered dish towels.

"Or maybe what?"

She made a face. "Or maybe he and Violette have plans for my room."

I clutched her hand. "Phyl!" I whispered. "Did you see her tonight? Did she have the ring on?"

She shook her head. Whispered back. "No ring yet. They're in the Lean-To, keeping out of the way." Among other activities, I imagined.

No ring yet. I felt the usual relief followed by anxiety.

"Okay." Get a grip, Cass. "I guess we'll just have to wait and see. Let me get Ned out of his wet pumpkin suit, and I'll be right back down."

"Actually, Cass, while you're up there, could you just take this box and dump all my summer clothes in it? I've got them thrown all over the bed. Stuff in anything you think I won't wear in the next week, okay?"

• • •

It was nearly midnight when I collapsed across my bed after a final check on Ned. The entry way was emptied of boxes; Phyl's room was skin and bones; the corner of the garage we called the wine cellar had been decimated. If Daniel wanted champagne to celebrate an engagement to his lady love, he would have to hit the liquor store first.

I wasn't sorry to be exhausted. Exhaustion meant I could tumble into sleep without dwelling on unpleasant things. Including, but not limited to: (1) tripping over bronze planter pots in the hallway, thus announcing my presence with a mighty clang while Daniel was kissing Violette good-night in the doorway (she looked distinctly disheveled but still—heaven be praised—ring-free); and, (2) having Daniel glance up, mid-smooch, notice me with no change in expression, and return to his devouring of her face. Since he historically wasn't given to public displays of affection, I could only gather that I did not count as another person. I was wallpaper. Or was that a wallflower?

But, far more importantly at this juncture, exhaustion spared me thinking about the text I received yesterday from Dale Loftus.

No, he wasn't stalking me again. This time I had initiated. Because, as Mike's release date drew nearer and nearer, my desire to speak with him face to face increased accordingly. I didn't want to write Mike at Coyote Ridge, even if I knew how to, so I fell back on contacting his father. Texting, because I wasn't up to calling him and knew that, if I asked Skandar to do it, I would face hours of are-you-crazy types of conversation.

I wondered if his reply to me was the first text message Dale Loftus ever sent.

> Yes. M will meet you for coffee Starbucks Lodge.
> Fri 11/4 9:00A.

CHAPTER 32:

Silent Partner

"Where the heck are you going? We've got brunch with Phyl and fam at 10:30."

"I know, I know," I told Joanie. "I'll be back before then. Ned's all fed and changed—he'll fall asleep in a minute, so be sure to put him in his car seat so that I can just grab him and go when I get back, okay?"

"But where are you going?"

"Tell you later."

I wanted to get to the coffee shop early, to make sure Mike and I had a place to sit for our conversation and that there would be no time spent in line together, ill at ease, not talking. My experiences with Skandar had at least taught me that. And just in case Mike had the same thought, I had to get there even earlier than he might.

He was late, it turned out. By quarter after, my tea was drained, I'd given up looking over the discarded newspaper and was starting to have to go to the bathroom. But I couldn't abandon our table now—what if he still planned on turning up? I debated calling Dale Loftus. Who knew—where Dale was concerned, he might even now be lurking just around the corner, watching events unfold.

At twenty past, I pulled out my phone. Scrolling through my "L" contacts, I saw in my peripheral vision someone drop into the leather armchair opposite. Mike.

How exactly I recognized him, when I had only met him once, nearly a year ago, I couldn't say. He didn't have an unforgettable face per se—I tried often in the intervening months to recall it—it was the impression he made on me that stuck. Still, focused, secret. The slight, self-contained figure held in check. The flat green gaze.

He wore ordinary oversized clothes, black and flannel and baggy. No loud orange jumpsuit, no parole officer handcuffed to him. The silver rings I remembered still adorned his bony fingers. His tow hair was cut short. But Coyote Ridge had left its mark. He had withdrawn even more deeply into himself. The shell had hardened.

I wondered how he managed to remember me. Maybe Dale had described me.

We looked at each other.

I scooted to the edge of my chair to angle myself forward.

"Hello…Mike. Thank you for meeting me."

Nothing.

"Can I get you some coffee?"

A shake of the head.

I was beginning to understand Lori's aversion to small talk. Mike was not the sort to be buttered up by perky remarks on how pleasant it must be to be free again, or how nice that he got out so early, or did his dad go pick him up. He didn't want to be here with me. My job was to find out what I came for and then release us both.

This time I was prepared, and I stole a glance at the index card in my hand. No set speeches there, but one bullet point: Why did you let go of Ned?

Because nothing else came to me, I said it just like that. "Why did you let go of Ned?"

It was bald. Abrupt. I bit my lip to prevent myself from filling the silence with words.

A minute went by, or two, or five. Mike studied his rings. I supposed they were confiscated when he was taken into custody and returned only Wednesday when he got out.

The silence stretched. I tried to fit the plastic lid back on my empty cup, but my fingers wouldn't cooperate.

Maybe Lori was right. I was not going to know why. It was a gift. I would have to make my peace with that.

"I got…" he said at last.

I looked up.

"I got to get on with my life."

Of course. Good. But what did that mean? Was it about money? The emotional tie? The religion? "You have a job, I hear, Mike. That's great."

His lip curled. "If you're looking for thanks, you can keep looking."

"Thanks?" I repeated. "Why on earth would I be looking for thanks?"

He paused. Trying to read my sincerity, I guessed. "Because I'm gonna be at the studio again."

"You are? Really? Oh! That's wonderful. I didn't know the state could arrange something like that—private sector, I mean. That's perfect for you. I'm so glad."

"It's not through the state."

"Oh." I analyzed this. "You mean you asked Ray Snow if he would take you back, and he said he would? He's a good guy."

"Naw. He came and asked me. He wanted me back."

I didn't know quite what to make of this. Ray Snow had gotten so fond of having a studio lackey in the four months Mike worked there that he found he couldn't do without him? "You must have done good work for him," I said, "if he went all the way out to Coyote Ridge to ask you back. How did he even know you were coming up for parole? Did you keep in contact?"

"Naw. The lawyer told him. The lawyer brought him."

Now I was truly at sea. "Wow. That's some public defender you have. Getting in contact with your old employer and—and—" and basically twisting his arm so that he would take you back, I wanted to say. Kudos to Gary Lansing. My taxpayer dollars at work.

"Not Lansing." Mike's voice sounded impatient now, although his expression remained flat. "Snow's lawyer."

"What?"

"Ray Snow's lawyer told him. Brought him."

I held very still.

"Explained to me about the job and if I wanted to get some college credit. Told me about how child support works. My guy—he's just wanting to get me out of prison, see. He doesn't really get all that adoption and child support stuff. Ray's guy did."

I must have been holding my breath because I exhaled in sharp relief. Not Daniel, then. Some other lawyer of Ray Snow. "It's complicated, isn't it? All that kid stuff. I've learned a lot from my lawyer, too."

"I got to get on with my life," Mike said again.

"A job you like. And college," I repeated. "Is the college part a state program?"

He looked suspicious. "Naw. It's part of the job deal. If I do good at work I can take a college class. If I pass that class, the next one is paid for, till I get my requirements done."

Good heavens. I knew Ray Snow was a generous man, but this did seem above and beyond the call of duty. Maybe he should have consulted his lawyer less and his accountant more. "Wonderful," I said.

We sat another minute, Mike's knee beginning to jiggle. My time was ticking. So, as far as I understood, Mike had let Ned go because Ray's lawyer painted a picture for him: a picture of what life could be, struggling under the financial burden of fighting for and raising a child, or else losing in court and possibly being stuck nevertheless with child support payments. In contrast, life could hold entirely different possibilities: a job working with music, as he loved, a chance at an education. A fresh start.

I frowned. It wasn't exactly like Esau selling his birthright for a bowl of red pottage, but it wasn't exactly unlike, either. Paternity affidavit as blank checkbook; rescind it and you get off scot free. So be it. I was only too grateful to have Ned and had no intention of suing Mike for money. As the proverb went, better a dry crust with peace and quiet than a house full of feasting, with strife.

Speaking of Bible verses. "May I ask you something?"

"I thought that's what you been doing."

"Your…father…mentioned that you…were meeting with a pastor fellow out there."

His face, never very open to begin with, closed off altogether. He shrugged one shoulder.

"A…good guy, I hope."

Another shrug. "Got to have things to do. I had a class on the five-paragraph essay, too."

He had no reason to confide in me, of course. And every reason not to. But still—

I gave myself a mental shake. Come on, Cass, what were you expecting? A tearful confession? Mike rising from the baptismal waters with glowing countenance and a testimony on his lips?

I made a last effort. "Well, I guess I was just wondering if that had anything to do with you letting Ned go. The religion, I mean." As opposed to the five-paragraph essay.

"That's my business."

"Yeah." I smiled inwardly. All my sleepless nights and hand-wringing led only to this. Whatever was between Mike and God was going to stay between Mike and God. Part of Mike's story, and not mine. A gift, as Lori said. A mystery.

I reached for my purse. I needed to be going anyway, before my absence freaked out Joanie and the bridal party.

"Wait." Mike pressed a hand on his jiggling knee to stop it. "What's he like?"

No need to ask who.

"He's...he's Ned. He eats a lot, sleeps a lot. He's cheerful and easy-going. He has blond hair and blue eyes and a big head. He's altogether big. And healthy, the doctor says." Even now, the memory of Ned's seizure sent a shiver through me. "He can smile now and reach for things. This morning he grabbed my hair and pulled it."

Mike nodded throughout this recital, not looking at me.

"I want you to know, Mike, that I'll take good care of him. The best I can. I love him with my whole heart."

A muscle flexed in his pale jaw, but he said nothing.

"And...I wish you all the best. And your dad, too. I know you—um—may not...feel like you like me, but I hope that won't always be the case."

"My dad took it real hard when I said I was gonna let you have the baby," said Mike, his gaze skating across me to the fire in the Lodge hearth. "He told me later that he chased you down on your bike and tried to convince you to give up."

"Oh, good heavens! That was a little scary," I said. That dreadful weekend when Daniel cheated and Skandar had to run Dale off and Joanie got sick and I biked all over town. "You didn't know about that, at the time? I guess I always figured you two were on the same page about the adoption."

Another shrug. "We were. Until that weekend. It wasn't till after Ray Snow and his lawyer come out to visit that I changed my mind. And then I told Dad first thing and he goes nuts. I told him it was lucky you didn't press charges and get us in worse trouble."

The car keys I had fished out of my purse slipped through my numb fingers. "It was *that* weekend that Ray Snow and his lawyer came?" My voice sounded unsteady, and I quickly bent down to retrieve my keys and hide my reddening cheeks.

"Yeah. They came and talked to me Saturday and let me go and think about it, and then they came back on Sunday to talk some more."

"Oh, my. You did decide fast." I cleared my throat. "That lawyer must have been pretty persuasive…I still don't understand how Ray Snow even knew an adoption lawyer."

"Naw, the guy wasn't an adoption lawyer. He did other stuff for Ray. But he had lots of notes." Mike's knee started its vibrating again. "He couldn't answer all my questions at first, but he figured stuff out before they came back Sunday."

I had to know.

He had called me *ungrateful*.

"Hmm…that's funny. Being a lawyer to a guy who knows all those rock stars. Did he have crazy glasses, like Ray Snow wears?"

Granted, it was a dumb ploy. Mike actually turned to look at me, puzzled. "Naw. He was just this big blond guy. Looked like a lawyer. What's it to you?"

Everything, unfortunately.

"Nothing, nothing," I said. I snapped my purse shut. "Thank you again for meeting me, Mike. Good luck in the future. If you need to get a hold of me, your dad has all my information." And then some.

Mike gave a final shrug. I considered offering to shake his hand but decided it would go over weird.

"Thanks," I said for the hundredth time, as I stood up. "Good-bye."

• • •

Sometimes when you're searching hard for something it's nowhere to be found. Like where you parked the car, or where you left your phone, or the reason why someone would decide, on second thought, that you did not have to rip his biological son from his cold, dead hands before he would give him up.

Sometimes things just come. Land in your lap.

Mike and his motivations were no more transparent to me than a month ago. And this might have troubled me more except that I couldn't spare it another thought.

After I left him, my steps led me automatically back to my car. I unlocked it, got in, drove home, greeted others, went to brunch. And everything just came to me. My body obeyed my brain's silent electrical commands. My mouth smiled at the right times. Appropriate words and laughter issued forth. I heated Ned's bottles, fed him, changed him, put him down for naps, made googooing sounds at him when he was awake.

And all the while my mind turned over and over Mike's accidental revelation.

Daniel was the one who convinced him to give Ned up.

Daniel.

So evasive about that trip—the mysterious things and people he needed to line up before he went. So conscious afterward, when I asked him where he was. He planned all along to try to help me but didn't want me to know.

Which meant that, in addition to being the unfaithful liar who broke my heart, he was also, and at the very same time, my secret ally.

It was just what I thought—Daniel's strengths lay in friendship and not in love. Too bad his acts of friendship made me love him. Whatever progress I had been making in the getting-over-him department was lost, at this point.

But if he and Ray Snow saw Mike on Saturday and again on Sunday—if they went out to Coyote Ridge for that express purpose—where did the woman come in? He couldn't have planned to meet her—even I didn't think him capable of scheduling infidelity smack in the middle of a mercy mission. Maybe his meeting with her was serendipitous. He ran across someone luscious at the Best Western and couldn't resist some anticipatory celebration sex. Or there was nothing on pay-per-view Saturday afternoon, so he resorted to seduction to pass the time. Then what about the roses he sent me, and the text message? It all didn't fit.

One thing I knew: I might settle for mystery where Mike was

concerned—just thank God Mike did change his mind, in fact, and count my blessings—but no way could I stand for that with Daniel. I wanted to know the truth. Needed to.

• • •

I saw him once that day, in passing, as Phyl's family and bridal party were loading up to head for the rehearsal and rehearsal dinner. Joanie sent me back in for Phyl's mock bouquet of gift bows, and Daniel must have emerged from the Lean-To when he thought the coast was clear.

It had been a long time since I glimpsed him alone and unguarded. He was at the sink, watching the finches chasing each other from the feeder. In profile, his face looked almost tired, meditative.

"Daniel." Like all my actions today, I spoke without forethought, coming forward to him, my hand outstretched.

Who knows what I might have said—I'm sure my autopilot would have gotten everything just right, as it had all day—but at the sound of my voice he stiffened. Whirled to face me, the guard going up again. "I thought you'd gone."

I waved the bow bouquet as explanation, shrinking back a little at his tone. We stood looking at each other a minute. It shouldn't have been hard to say, "I want to thank you for speaking to Mike and getting me my baby," but the words died in my throat. I don't think he was interested in my gratitude any longer.

"Go on," he said roughly, jerking his chin at the door. "They're waiting."

Sure enough, Joanie chose that moment to lay on the horn, startling me into motion.

"See you later," I blurted.

If he answered me, I didn't hear it. He was staring out the window again.

I shut the door softly behind me.

CHAPTER 33:

Phyl's Wedding

The morning and afternoon of Phyl's wedding day passed in a blur. Perry came by early, giving both Joanie and Ned resounding kisses and cheerfully listening to all my hurried babysitting instructions. The instructions were more for my sake than his. He already knew the basics of infant care, and if he could keep Ned alive and largely unharmed until I saw them at the wedding, that would do.

Meanwhile, we girls rushed off to our whirlwind of beautification: manicures, pedicures, massages, a long stint at the salon where our hair was shellacked into place. Stepping gingerly into our caramel-colored gowns, getting Phyl all squared away, shooing away Wayne, posing for countless photographs at the church.

Even while I primped and ironed and ate and chatted and helped Phyl with a thousand tiny tasks, my mind kept wandering to Daniel. I would not let another day pass. How could I get him alone—when could I get him alone—to thank him? To tell him how grateful I was. Whether he cared or not. The love part—well, that was too late. That ship had sailed, but I wanted him to know how much I appreciated all he had done for Ned and me. He had loved me, in his way, and I was thankful.

. . .

I easily picked out his bright hair among the seated guests. Even had he been bald I would have known him: his was the only face not turned in my direction as I came down the aisle. Look at me, stupid. It's probably all downhill from here, looks-wise, so don't miss it! He found me lovely enough last winter at his office party, but apparently that was then, this was now. Tacking on a fake smile for the photographer at the top of the aisle, I took my place on the left side. At least with my back to him, I wouldn't have to look at Daniel not looking at me for the whole ceremony.

Joanie was absolutely gorgeous, of course. I had as much fun watching Perry staring at her approach as I did watching her myself. Ned got a hold of Perry's tie and was sucking on it with a will, but my brother was oblivious, mesmerized.

Despite Joanie's glory, Phyl, on this day of days, managed to outshine her. As she floated toward us, her head crowned with lilies and her gentle smile wobbling but radiant, I thought Wayne might become one of those passer-outer grooms. He turned bright red and kept swallowing, and I saw his best man muttering in his ear, most likely reminding him not to lock his knees.

It was a quiet, heartfelt ceremony—no tearjerker songs or poems written by the wedding party. A ceremony I should have been able to get through dry-eyed and almost did. The singles pastor and congregational care pastor co-officiated for Phyl and Wayne, and my mind went back to my own wedding day, where Troy and I clutched each other's hands, and he tried to make me laugh only because he looked nervous enough to cry himself. Unknown joys and sorrows ahead. Min was a shared joy, but I had to do the sorrows alone.

I felt suddenly old, as if I'd put all possibility of marrying again behind me when I refused Skandar. If I wouldn't marry for convenience and couldn't marry for love, I should just put my head down and plow ahead. Raise Ned. Someday be the middle-aged lady in the front row on the right, weeping into a handkerchief at his wedding. It wouldn't make much of a romance novel, but it would be a good ride.

Peeking along my shoulder at Ned, I saw he had yakked a little on Perry's shirt and was now innocently sucking on his fist. Cutie Pie. My brother was just then accepting a Kleenex from the guest next to him and dabbing at the spot.

No, not a romance novel, but I wouldn't miss it for the world.

Without conscious thought, still smiling in amusement, I turned my head a few degrees more, to where Daniel sat. He was watching Wayne and Phyl light the unity candle, but perhaps feeling my gaze, his eyes flicked over to me. By his side was the ubiquitous Violette, blotting tears and leaning against him—still ringless, thank God—but that was par for the course, and I wasn't going to worry about it. Whatever coolness had been between Daniel and me for the last couple months, if it were to continue, it wouldn't be my doing. We had always been friends. We could be friends again. I would hound him, stalk him, Dale-Loftus style, until he broke down and agreed. I grinned at him now, almost laughing out loud when I saw his start of surprise. I even dropped a wink before turning my attention back to the bride and groom. Sometime today I would talk to him. I didn't care if Violette were there or the entire wedding party—I would talk to him.

And it seemed I would never be without the wedding party. There was the recessional after the ceremony where I was paired with Wayne's 19-year-old cousin, the 6'4" Drew—I suppose because our singleness, if not our heights and ages, made us compatible. Then forty minutes with the photographer to capture every possible portrait combination. By the time the wedding party began piling in the cars to head for the reception, I was more than a little nervous. What if Daniel only intended to make a cameo appearance there?

Joanie crammed in the back seat of Mary's car with me, landing smack on my bouquet and finishing it off. "Crap!" she muttered. "Did it leave a mark? That's all I need at the reception—grass stains on my butt. People will think I fell down."

"Just be happy people still try to look at your butt," I said.

"What's with you?" she mocked. "You've had three marriage proposals in one year—don't tell me no one's looking at your butt."

"Skandar doesn't count," I insisted. "He wasn't interested in any part of me, really, much less my butt. To him I just had good stepmother potential for Bryson."

Shrugging, Joanie said, "If you say so, Cass. It wasn't like it would've been a huge sacrifice for Mr. Morose to land a girl like you. But you'd better say yes to the next guy, or you'll get my reputation."

• • •

When Phyl originally chose the Salish Lodge for a November wedding, Joanie and I thought she was nuts. What was the point of a terrace view of Snoqualmie Falls if it would be cold and rainy and dark and everyone would have to huddle inside trying to peer out fogged-up windows? But, like magic, the rain abated mid-week, leaving the skies clear and cold and the Falls high.

When we pulled up, it was gathering dusk, and most of the guests were clustered in the firelit reception room, drinks and hors d'oeuvres plates in hand, while the live band tuned up in the corner. Phyl and Wayne's entrance provoked cheers and much fork-on-glass clinking, and when all eyes turned to watch them kiss, I cast furtive glances around for Daniel. Nowhere to be seen. Had he already come and gone? Or did he skip the reception altogether?

My heart pumping, I threw my mashed bouquet and tiny handbag down at the wedding party table and threaded through the crowd. Not at the bar, not by the dance floor or outside the bathroom. I pushed through one of the double doors leading out to the terrace.

It was nearly deserted outside, cold—the temperature dropping along with the sun—and the Falls were much louder on this side of the Lodge. Louder, but not loud enough to prevent Violette's voice carrying to my ears.

"I knew it," she murmured huskily, "but it didn't matter to me because I would take any part of you I could get." Sure enough, off to the left in the furthest corner of the terrace there was still enough daylight for me to make out Daniel's back and Violette's hands in his hair, pulling him close.

Ridiculous, really, how many times in the past few months I'd been an unwilling witness to his romantic interludes. Not just the past few months—with the exception of that space last winter and spring (and our pathetic Three Days) where he had been interested in me, my entire acquaintance with him could be measured and ticked off by the various women he'd taken up with, and the varying degrees of physical intimacy therewith.

I could have walked away then and tried to find a more private moment to talk to him, but with a guy like him, who knew if such a moment would ever come? Better just to have my say. Get it over with and leave him free to make out with Violette the rest of the night. As long as I wasn't interrupting an actual Proposal, they would just have to deal with it.

"Excuse me," I said, through my suddenly chattering teeth. Striding over, I tapped him on the shoulder.

Daniel spun around to stare at me, and I heard Violette's disgusted sniff. Ignoring him for the moment, I made an apologetic face at her. "I'm so sorry to butt in like this. This will just take a second, and then you can…can…carry on." Rubbing my arms for warmth and courage, I turned back to face that man I was hopelessly in love with. His face was set in grim lines—maybe he minded this break in the action more than I'd supposed.

"Daniel," I began hesitantly, "umm…I just wanted to say thank you. I spoke with Mike—Nadina's Mike—yesterday morning—" Daniel straightened, his gaze sharpening, and the rest of my speech came out in a rush. "He let slip that you actually went along with Ray Snow to see him when he was still at Coyote Ridge, and that your talk with him—both of you—that you really made sense to him and made him feel like he could let this battle go. I know Ray probably wouldn't have gone on his own or offered what he offered, if you hadn't convinced him—the job, the chance for college credit. It was generous of you. I just—like I said—I didn't know about that piece of it, and I just wanted to thank you for helping me and Ned. So—so—thank you— really. I know now why you slipped and called me ungrateful that day, and I'm sorry if I've seemed ungrateful. I wish I would have known. And—well—and that's all, so you two have a nice evening."

I gave Violette an encouraging push back toward Daniel, and before either one could respond, I fled.

$$\cdot \quad \cdot \quad \cdot$$

Perry was perched on one of the tables, Ned snoozing peacefully in the car seat beside him. I didn't care that you're never supposed to disturb a happy baby—I unbuckled and worked him out to hold him, bending over to hide the tears I felt welling up.

"Hey, hey," said Perry, putting an arm around me. "Didn't you threaten me on pain of death to let him sleep whenever he wanted? He just had a big bottle and a giant burp, and now he's down for the count." He was. I gave little Neddy a kiss on the forehead and one on the nose and then tucked him back into his seat. His little blond hairs were sticking up in bedhead tufts, reminding me momentarily of Nadina.

"I wish I could just sit with you and Ned during dinner," I said.

"C'mon, Cass," said Perry, "they're waiting for you at the wedding party table. Go make sure no one hits on Joanie and save me a lambada."

In spite of myself, I laughed. "You pervert."

Judging by the one empty seat, it looked like I was going to be between the 19-year-old cousin and Wayne's brother-in-law, so I gave Phyl a kiss on the cheek and Wayne a hug and took my place. Daniel and Violette were at Perry's table, and at least they spared us their hands-on demonstrations because I didn't see them touch each other the entire meal.

. . .

Four courses and seven toasts later, Phyl and Wayne took the dance floor, Phyl blushing and Wayne looking proud enough to bust. Wayne evidently belonged to the grip-her-hard-around-the-waist-and-turn-slowly-counterclockwise school of dancing (of which my late husband Troy was a card-carrying member), but Phyl didn't mind a bit.

"I don't really know how to do this," said 19-year-old Drew nervously, when the band summoned the wedding party to the dance floor a few minutes later. It being your standard waltz, I thought even I could handle this one.

Smiling encouragement, I put his hand on my waist and took his other damp one in mine. "Just take little steps," I said. "No one's looking at us anyhow, and everyone else will join us in about a minute."

A minute might be fifty seconds too late, I thought an instant afterward, when Drew mashed my foot for the second time. "Let me lead," I hissed. "1-2-3, 1-2-3…" He nodded, blushing, and I proceeded to push and pull and haul him around the dance floor like a dress form until we were both laughing.

"This isn't so bad," Drew declared. "At our formals we don't do a lot of slow dancing, but I'd be more up for it with a partner like you."

"Older women," I joked. "We're experienced."

"Not to mention strong," he added, when he made to go the wrong direction and I tugged on his shoulder.

"And fast!" I teased, whipping my foot away before it could be crushed a third time.

By the time the guests began joining the wedding party on the floor, Drew and I were having such fun kidding around that we didn't immediately decamp. He attempted to twirl me under his arm but only succeeded in catching my forehead in his armpit, and then he surprised me by throwing me back for a dip. When I came up, gasping and giggling, it was to find Daniel's hand on Drew's shoulder.

"I'll take it from here," Daniel said coolly.

"Oh!" Drew looked uncertain. "Well—hey, man, do you mind if we finish the dance?"

"I'll take it from here."

Drew frowned but reluctantly released me. "Okay…but, Cass, maybe I could catch you for another go later?"

"Sure," I agreed, shooting Daniel a dirty look that said, He's only nineteen—would you quit being so pushy?

"Unfortunately, Cass's card is full for the rest of the evening," said Daniel, putting his hand on the small of my back and scooting me toward him.

Irritated, I elbowed his arm away. It was nice that his lordship deigned to speak to me again, but he needn't be rude to Drew. "It isn't either, Drew. I'll come find you later." Before Drew could answer, Daniel grabbed me again and whirled me expertly away.

"Really, Cass—flirting with a boy half your age."

"Excuse me? Does Drew look 16½ to you?"

"No, but he looks like a college kid on the make," replied Daniel. "I'm going to strap Ned to you to scare him off."

"Not necessary, I guarantee you," I laughed. I wanted to sing for joy. He was teasing me! "I'm sure he thinks I'm ancient."

"Then he should respect his elders and not look at you like that."

Rolling my eyes, I started singing under my breath, "'How much for that doggy in the manger..?'"

He didn't respond, only pulling me the slightest bit closer, and I hoped he didn't feel my racing pulse. Dancing with me must mean I was forgiven. Thanks and apology accepted. We could talk again. Hang out. Be comfortable. Be friends.

Still, if only I had said yes to him when he first told me he loved me, months ago—maybe things might have gone differently. Or maybe not.

"Cass," he interrupted my remorseful thoughts, "can we talk?"

I raised my eyes to his, smiling faintly. "Where's Violette?"

"She had to go." His hand pressed more insistently on my back. "Let's talk."

"Shoot."

He shook his head, his brow furrowing. "No, not here. Come out on the terrace with me."

If it had been chilly out there earlier, it was freezing now. Wrapping my arms around myself I wandered over to the railing, where the waterfall could only be perceived as a dim, roaring glow. Sudden warmth as a jacket settled over my shoulders. Daniel's. When I turned, I could make out his button-down shirt blue-white in the darkness and his eyes on me. "Better?"

I nodded.

For a minute we just stared at each other. I thought he was the one who wanted to talk, but he looked at a loss where to begin. After weeks of stony silence or open hostility I didn't feel much better prepared.

Fine. I would go first.

"Tell me," I began, "was it when you were out of town that weekend in September that you went to see Mike?"

His eyes glittered. A brief nod.

The weekend he was with that woman. The pieces didn't fit together.

"Was it—was it just you and Ray Snow who went to see him?"

A pause. "It was just Ray and I who saw him."

That carefulness. That old evasiveness. At least he wasn't going in for another round of Denial, Accusation and Assurance, as Jason had with Phyl. Then again, maybe Daniel didn't care enough anymore.

Still, if we were going to put everything behind us, I needed to know what happened. And if he wasn't going to volunteer the information, I would have to ask. Once more.

"Daniel." I pulled his jacket more closely about my shoulders. "That was the weekend I called you, you know. When I spotted Mike's dad skulking around outside the Palace and freaked out. Before Skandar showed up." My mouth curved ruefully. "I wanted to hear your reassuring voice."

He barely nodded. "Yes."

The falls rushed past, invisible now. Someone opened the door onto the terrace—laughing and stumbling out—"Hey! It's way cooler out here—feels good!" The man pulled on his companion's arm, leading her away to an isolated corner.

"That—that woman answered," I persevered. "The one you…couldn't tell me about." Or wouldn't.

Silence.

"She sounded…out of breath. Like she was—you were—like she was—" There didn't seem a delicate way to put it. He would have to use his imagination.

Daniel said nothing.

I sighed. "So you were also—there was also a woman with you that weekend?" What was it—some kind of threesome? Unbidden, I envisioned Ray Snow wearing his crazy glasses and a pair of tighty-whities, going for broke in some sordid hotel room like an aging Jon Bon Jovi.

Still he hesitated. Then— "I know this is what got me in trouble before, but—but, like I told you then, I can't say more about it."

A snort escaped me. "Of course not. I'm not insisting—trying to make you break your precious word. It's fine. It doesn't matter. I just wanted to let you know that that was how I knew."

"Knew what?" His voice was hard.

"Knew you'd spent that weekend with a girlfriend," I said, as casually as I could, turning away to see what the laughing couple was up to. Making out, apparently.

Daniel's hand came up under my chin, jerking me around to look at him. "You don't know anything. You're wrong, Cass. You're dead wrong." His breathing was tight. Or maybe that was me. "I can't talk about it," Daniel went on. "Yes, there was a woman, but, for the hundredth time, she wasn't a girlfriend. God, I went away thinking that was it—we'd finally come to an understanding. That it was just a matter of how fast I could convince you to—" He shook his head in frustration. "You're the one—I come home to find you with that guy—"

I felt the old anger flare. He truly was the King of Double Standards. "Are we really going to go through this again?" I demanded, wrenching free. "Every time I turn around, you're lip-locked with someone or someone's hanging on you or sitting on your lap or—heck—even answering your *phone* while you're busy doing God knows what, and you somehow want to make this my issue?"

"I've told you, in every one of those instances, that nothing was going on," Daniel said. "Appearances are bad, I'll grant you—"

"How generous of you," I snapped. "Look, Daniel, we don't need to keep going over and over this. Let's just give it a rest." My shoulders sagged. For Pete's sake, this man exhausted all my emotions. "You know, I don't know how this keeps happening—all I wanted to do tonight was thank you for helping me. Thank you, Daniel, again. Thank you with no strings attached."

He said nothing, and after a minute I wondered if the conversation was at an end. I ought to go check on Ned anyhow. Perry probably wanted to ask Joanie to dance. When I opened my mouth to excuse myself, Daniel finally spoke. "I meant it to be a gift to you, 'no strings attached'—me helping you get Ned—nothing in it for me but treasure in heaven," he added wryly, "but it turns out I'm not that selfless."

In answer to my questioning look, he said in a low voice, "We've had a rough time of it, Cass. Maybe you can't stand to hear me on this subject anymore. God knows you've accused me of every fault attributable to a man for the past several months—you've attacked my character, my integrity, my constancy. I told myself there was no getting through to you. I told myself I was just going to leave it. Not that a...an untrusting...mind wouldn't have had grounds for thinking I was lying and hiding things from you, all occasions informing against me, as they were. But it hurt to think you didn't know me better by now—that no matter what I did, you weren't going to give me any credit, weren't going to trust me. No, wait—" he held up a hand to stop me from interrupting. "All I want to say is that, you know what, I've decided I don't give a damn if you trust me or not, or if you think I've been sleeping with anything that moves. You feel grateful toward me, you like me well enough, you find me attractive. It's enough for me. Marry me, Cass."

Daniel always had the element of surprise on his side—that was for sure. When I managed to stop gaping at him, I stammered, "Y-you just admitted you went away on some secret weekend with some mystery lady right after we got together, and then not two hours ago you were making out with Violette, Daniel! Why in creation can't you get it through your head that maybe you weren't made to be married?"

The long-familiar wicked gleam of his eyes. I felt, rather than saw, him loosen the jacket wrapped around me, that his hands could steal underneath and run up the length of my bare arms. When I shivered, the hands drew me closer. "I can't get it through my head because, for almost a year now, it's all I've wanted." He spoke this with his mouth almost touching mine, and I felt my resolve begin to leak away. "Violette was saying good-bye."

"In that case I'd hate to see 'Merry Christmas,'" I managed to breathe, feeling my stomach do a somersault when I heard his low chuckle.

Fine.

Whatever.

So be it.

He won.

Maybe Daniel's weekend activities in September were going to be another of the mysteries I would have to live with. Mike and God. Daniel and that woman. Whatever he had done, he didn't feel guilty about it, and the truth was he *had* helped me, *had* advocated for me. It would have to be enough. If I was going to trust him again, it would have to be enough.

All I knew was that I was through fighting him. Through fighting with him and through fighting my feelings for him. If I couldn't know everything about him, I knew as much as I needed. And if I couldn't have every piece of him, I wanted whatever he would give me. Violette's murmured words came back to me: "It didn't matter to me because I would take any part of you I could get."

Well said, Violette! I would take any part of Daniel that Violette or Mystery Woman or Darla or Kristen or whoever else didn't want. Come to think of it, those words did sound like good-bye. Score one for truth-telling?

He was kissing me now. Slowly, just brushing his lips over mine. I held my breath, grateful for his hands holding me up. "Marry me," he murmured against my mouth. "I love you like I've never loved anyone in my life, you misguided, obstinate woman."

Unable to manage more than an inarticulate sigh, I leaned against him. His lips on mine grew more urgent, and I wrapped my arms around his neck, kissing him back. Wow! Take that, other couple making out in the opposite corner of the terrace. With all the activity, the jacket slid off me to the deck, but I hardly noticed, pressed as I was full-length against him, his hands roaming over my back to where the caramel satin gave way to skin. Too soon, Daniel broke off and pulled away, ignoring my whimper of protest.

"Kiss me again," I ordered, tugging on him shamelessly.

"Not until you say you'll marry me."

Deep breath. Ragged sounding, considering I'd been panting a moment ago. "I'll marry you."

I tugged on him again, even standing on my tiptoes—if the mountain wouldn't come to Mohammed—or whatever the equivalent Christian expression might be—but Daniel didn't move. "Hey!" I said. "A deal's a deal."

He may as well have been carved out of marble, for all the results I was getting from pulling on him. Daniel swallowed. Cleared his throat. "You'll marry me?" Eager nod. "Even though you think I'm hiding something from you?"

"Uh-huh."

"Even though you declared me guilty of lying and cheating on you?"

"On appeal, the verdict might yet be overturned."

He considered. I ran my fingers up the nape of his neck.

"Even though I haven't been baptized in the waters of Jordan?"

"How close are you?"

"I've got a toe in."

"Works for me." I pulled on him again. He resisted.

"Tell me why."

Who could blame him for pressing his advantage, after my months of stonewalling him? But I didn't care anymore. Surrender had gotten me Ned—what else might it get me?

"Because I love you, you stupid man. I lo—"

That was as far as I got before Daniel was kissing me again.

CHAPTER 34:

Game, Set and Match

Just when I was happily glued again to him head-to-toe, twirling my fingers in the same hair Violette styled not two hours ago, Daniel pulled away once more.

"What now?" I demanded, unable to keep the grumpiness from my voice. "Is there a problem with my kissing?"

"'How poor are they who have not patience,'" he chided, "'We work by wit, and not by witchcraft; and wit depends on dilatory time.'"

"Richard III?" I guessed impatiently.

"Not even close." He bent down to retrieve his jacket and replaced it around my shoulders. "Iago. Though Richard III isn't a bad idea, considering I'm wooing a widow."

"Not to mention what a 'foul lump of deformity' you are."

Grinning, he tucked a lock of my hair behind my ear. "Don't be surly, darling." My heart thrilled at the endearment, and it must have shown on my face because he laughed softly. "I've waited long enough for you and devoted more thought than most men to what it would be like if I got you. When I start, I'm not going to stop." Daniel dropped a kiss on my forehead. "Do you want a big wedding like Phyl?"

"Huh? Do we have to talk about this now?"

"Yes."

Strange man. "Then, no," I said. "No, I don't want a big wedding like Phyl. I've—I've already done that—unless you want one...?"

He looked amused. "For you, Cass, I could be talked out of it." He took my hands in his and swung my arms lightly. "Would you say the religious part of the ceremony is more important to you, or the legal part?"

This line certainly fell in the dodgy category. I frowned at him. "Are you trying to pull a fast one on me? You don't have some nutty Mrs. Rochester in the Palace attic, do you?"

"Answer the question."

"I don't know. They're both important. I suppose maybe the religious part is more important to me—I don't really care at this point if we file joint taxes or if I get all your money when you die. What are you getting at?"

"Just trying to plan our evening." He led me back toward the doors. "Give me a few minutes. Now would be a convenient time for you to check on Ned and make good on your promise to that idiot college kid."

The next thing I knew, I was back on the dance floor with Drew, goofing off to some Black-Eyed Peas song. Neddy was being happily bounced by Phyl's great-aunt, and she shooed me away with a "you young people go have fun." If I was a "young person," Drew was positively infantile, but I got her point.

"What happened to Mr. Master of the Universe?" was Drew's first question. He was definitely more at home with the faster music, although our brief ballroom stint seemed to have inspired him, and he had both my hands in his grasp.

"What a perfect description for him," I laughed. "I think he's off working on the next stage in his plan for world domination."

"And that includes dominating you?"

"He's going to try his best. We're getting married."

This kind of talk was clearly out of a 19-year-old's league, and he didn't have much to say the rest of the dance. Add to that, one surprised look at Ned, who I took in my arms after being escorted back to Phyl's great-aunt, and that was the last I saw of Drew.

• • •

"Think he's too young to be a witness?" came Daniel's voice behind me, maybe twenty minutes later. One hand pulled me against him while the other ruffled Ned's hair. I could get used to this.

"Witness to what?"

"Our marriage." When I looked at him questioningly, he gave me a slow smile. "I managed to corner the congregational care pastor on her way out, and after some persuasion on my part, I've convinced her to stay a little longer at the reception. It took some time to explain that I understood this wouldn't be legally binding but wanted to do it anyway."

I should have known he wouldn't waste an instant, but this was beyond comprehension. "Have you lost your mind?" I yelped, twisting around to stare at him. "I'm not marrying you *tonight*! Especially in some half-baked, legally-meaningless sham ceremony!"

He just laughed. "The sham ceremony is only Stage One. I got a lecture from the pastor about how marriage is total union—two lives becoming one. You can't avoid filing taxes with me and getting my money when I die, I'm afraid. She absolutely refused to go along with it until I promised to have the legal documents in her office by Monday. So I thought we'd do the God part now and then transfer Ned's car seat to Joanie's Camry and head off for Reno—it's closer than Las Vegas—"

Reno! "And we are not stealing your sister's car and driving over the Siskyous and up into the Sierra Nevada in November, Daniel."

"You want to take your Civic, then?"

"I'm not driving anywhere!"

"All right—we'll fly. First thing tomorrow. You're right—a better plan. That'll leave tonight free for more pleasant activities, though I'm not sure you'll get as much rest."

"For Pete's sake, if I'd known what was going through your mind, I would never have encouraged you. What's wrong with waiting a few days? Going down to the county next week for a license and catching the pastor in his office one afternoon? Telling our families, for crying out loud?"

"I'm done being patient. If you like, we won't sleep together till we're legal, but I'm not giving you the chance to have second thoughts. We lost the last six months because I was stupid enough to listen to you in May, and this time we're doing it my way. If we had the first time, there would've been no adoption troubles, no Darla, no Mystery Woman, no Violette, no anything—"

"This is too fast!" I whined. "Just yesterday we were hardly on speaking terms and I thought you hated me, and now—now—"

"I did hate you yesterday, you little fool," he said. "Hated your guts. It hurt a damned sight less than loving you. My mantra the last couple months has been that you didn't want to be happy and deserved to go be miserable with that Grim Reaper you picked up. You wanted to believe the worst about me, so who was I to get in your way?"

I felt my mouth gather into a pout. "So, fine—you did hate me. Why are you in such a rush to marry me now?"

That amused look I knew so well. The one I had missed. Daniel leaned toward me and gently kissed each eyelid. "Because. It turned out my survival tactic only worked if you hated me back. Yesterday afternoon when I didn't know you were home, and you found me in the kitchen—you said my name and looked for all the world like we'd never fought a day in our lives. It pissed me off that you could blow a hole in my defenses that easily. And today—all you had to do was throw me that one smile during the wedding and the rest was shot to hell. When you actually *winked* at me, I seriously considered vaulting over the first five rows to grab you before your good mood passed."

We were otherwise occupied for some moments, but Ned's chubby hand yanking on one of my stiff ringlets recalled me to reality. "But Daniel! What about Ned? I'm a package deal, remember?"

"Hmm…" he said, against my ear, "do you think kissing his mother senseless falls in the category of 'Fathers, do not exasperate your children'?"

Pushing on his chest to give me some thinking room, I said, "That's what I mean: are you okay with being a father figure to Ned?"

A heavy pause. From the corner of my eye I saw Phyl smashing wedding cake into Wayne's face while onlookers cheered. Then, "If you don't mind that I don't know what the hell I'm doing and can barely remember having a father myself, I think—I think—I'd actually rather just be his father."

Wayne, always the gentleman, fed Phyl a dainty bite before reaching for a napkin to clean himself off.

When I didn't answer Daniel immediately, I saw him swallow. "Cass, we can cross that bridge later, if you'd rather—"

"What do you mean, 'be his father'?" I asked cautiously. "Do you mean, adopt him?"

Daniel nodded, not taking his eyes off me. "We don't have to decide now. You just wrested him away from Mike, after all…"

Still, I hesitated. It was one thing for me to decide I could live with some doubt where Daniel was concerned, but surely there was no need right away to make anything permanent with Ned. What if I found, a year from now, two years from now, that my doubts weren't wholly unjustified? That there was more to the mystery than he let on?

Lines appeared around his mouth as his jaw tightened. "Damn you for that thought."

Ignoring my indignant huff, he dug his cell phone from his pocket and handed it to me. "Before you make any vows to me tonight—" waving a hand impatiently to cut off my protests—"I want you to call

Lori Lincoln. Ask what we would need to do to have me adopt Ned."

"It's Saturday night!" I objected. "She won't be in her office, and I don't have her cell."

"I do," he said curtly, putting his phone to my ear.

Before I had time to do more than wonder if adoption lawyers charged emergency weekend rates like plumbers, I heard Lori's voice come on. "Yes, Daniel, I'll tell her."

"Oh!" I exclaimed. I thrust Ned at him so I could hold the phone myself. "It's not Daniel, Lori, it's Cass. Umm...I apologize for calling you on a Saturday night, but Daniel insisted. I—er—we just have a quick question." Really quick. Like less than ten dollars.

I pictured Lori putting her fingertips together precisely and pinning me with her beady eyes, but she exploded this image when she spoke again, her voice hesitant. "Well, then. Yes. All right. Ahem. Well, before you ask your question, Cass, Daniel has asked if I might make a brief confession."

Confession? My mouth popped open in surprise. "Confession?" I echoed. Confess what? And could confessions be billed to me? "Is everything okay with Mike and the adoption?" I demanded. "Everything above board?"

"Uh...yes," said Lori. My limited imagination couldn't envision her squirming around, but judging by her voice, that must be exactly what she was doing. "As it happens—what I need to tell you is that—that that weekend when Daniel and Ray Snow went to visit Mr. Loftus at Coyote Ridge, I was—I went in an advisory capacity."

"You saw Mike?" I gasped. "Is that even legal? You gave me such grief the other day in your office when I asked if *I* could see him—I didn't know it was because you wanted me to get in line!"

"I did not see Mi—Mr. Loftus," Lori said quickly. "It turns out I got the flu and had to stay in the hotel room, which is just as well because I wouldn't have gone in anyway. Not all the way in, at any rate. Not where Mr. Loftus would have seen me, I mean. Daniel just wanted me right at hand in case there was going to be any document signing or whatever. Or if he had any urgent legal question or nicety."

Mystified, I said, "Well, okay then. You didn't see Mike or do anything illegal, so why are you confessing to me?"

It seemed the Lori I knew too well returned to her body then because she replied in her long-suffering, how-low-is-your-IQ-today? tone. "I'm confessing because I swore Daniel to secrecy about that weekend. He tells me you think he was off with some mystery woman because some mystery woman answered when you called. It was me, of course. I'd forgotten my cell phone at work again, and he left his with me so they could reach me. Not that it helped. By the time *he* called I was fast asleep, and he had to ask me all his questions later. But *your* call—well, I was awake for that—barely. If I hadn't had a 103° fever and been halfway delirious, I never would have picked up, and you would have been none the wiser. As it is, my confusion seems to have made a royal mess of your personal lives."

Turning away from Daniel and hunching my shoulders protectively, I hissed, "That woman was you? You were panting—what was I supposed to think? It sounded like I'd interrupted some hot-and-heavy session."

"I was trying to breathe, for God's sake! Besides the fever, I was achy and congested, and if I had to talk, that meant I had to take time off from breathing. I defy anyone to find Sudafed in Franklin County—I suspect it's all being used for meth production."

"Why did you swear him to secrecy, then?" I persisted.

"For someone as bright as Daniel claims you are, you certainly can be thick, Cass," said Lori with her cool irritation. "I swore him to secrecy because I had no business being there. No business being anywhere near Mr. Loftus without his own lawyer present, especially to participate in behind-the-scenes wheeling and dealing. But there I was, because Daniel Martin is a hard man to say no to, as I think you know. I wouldn't even be coming clean now if I didn't feel confident about a positive outcome to your case. And just because I've let you in on the secret doesn't mean you have my permission to tell anyone else. Now, if I've satisfied your curiosity, I'd like to get back to my Saturday evening. I'm sure your own question can wait till the next business day..?"

"I'm sure it can," I said limply. She signed off, and a moment later I clicked Daniel's phone shut. Held it out to him. "Well. I didn't see that coming."

He only smiled.

A waiter approached us, bearing chocolate wedding cake in one hand and lemon in the other. Daniel waved him away, but I reached automatically for the lemon. I needed a moment to think. And besides, Joanie and Phyl and I spent a good portion of a weekend sampling cakes, and I was not going to admit to not having any.

Given my preoccupation, I might as well have been eating Styrofoam, but I ate it slowly and deliberately while he waited. When I finished, he took the plate from me and balanced it on the side table beside him.

"Cass?"

"Tell me I wasn't absolutely dead wrong about everything," I said woodenly. "Everything I accused you of, I mean. Calling you faithless and lacking in character and integrity. And maybe smarmy, too. I might have thrown that in."

"No, no," he assured me. "Not absolutely dead wrong. I am slightly smarmy. I did make out with Darla and Kristen and Violette more than once. It soothed my ego after your constant rejection and accusations. Not the client in the office, however—though I probably would have, after I saw you kissing Skandar. You were wrong to think I was unfaithful—I think it would be more accurate to call me jealous and vengeful."

"You're the worst! You admit it! Making out with people to console yourself and get back at me—what about their feelings?"

"I was always up front that I was just looking for entertainment.

Nothing serious."

I shook my head. "I ought to marry you just to spare other women your torments. Don't you know no woman buys that line? She always hopes she'll be the one who wins you over against your will."

Hesitantly, I laid a hand on his arm. "Will I always have to worry you're going to go make out with someone else whenever we get in a fight?"

"Doubtful. You look particularly inviting when you're angry," he said incorrigibly. "And I hear make-up sex is some of the best around."

Taking a seat on the cushioned bench, Daniel balanced Ned on one knee and pulled me, now blushing, onto the other.

"I was at least right in thinking you were petty," I said. "That was extremely small of you to bug me for the rent when I was in Cleveland."

Instead of looking sheepish, Daniel laughed outright. "You were gone, and I didn't know where you were, and I couldn't think of any other excuse to ask Phyl. You notice I didn't ask Joanie—she would have seen right through it and given me a good tongue-lashing."

I smiled back at him. "Why should you care where I was? I was your hated enemy."

He shrugged. "Keep your friends close and your enemies closer."

"You could at least have dropped the pretense when I offered to wire the money. That was the hugest hassle."

"Mmm...I liked to know you were thinking of me, even if it was just in anger. Plus, you're so miserly with your messages that it was a pleasure to work some out of you."

"Just as I thought. You *are* petty. Petty and vengeful and more than a little smarmy," I said, "and I'm misguided and obstinate. What a couple we'll make!"

"No worse than many others. Better than some."

I looked at him measuringly. "I know you're a heathen, but the Bible does say that, if your enemy is hungry you're supposed to feed her, not have revenge make-outs."

"It also mentions something about keeping no record of wrongs," he replied evenly. "Nor would there have been revenge make-outs in the first place, had you paid more attention to the bit about how love 'always trusts, always hopes, always perseveres.'"

I should've known, with a bookish mind like his, that after only a few months of reading the Bible he would already have pertinent quotes at his fingertips. Next time I'd have to argue from something more obscure. Beleaguer him with Leviticus, maybe. Nag him with Nehemiah.

"How long were you planning on keeping Margaret Russ waiting?" was his next question. Margaret Russ being the congregational care pastor.

Groaning, I covered my face with my hands. "And I can't have *her* marry us, Daniel. She led my Grief Recovery class after Troy and Min died. It would be so tacky to hit her up for an ad-hoc marriage ceremony 2 ½ years later."

"Nonsense. It would give her a nice sense of closure. She could check you off her list as Largely Recovered."

Was that what I was? I was certainly miles and miles emotionally from where I had been, just a couple years ago. And three years ago..! In a crazy way, I had come full circle. Lost a husband and a child, found a husband and a child. How exactly did this all come about?

Like Ned, Daniel reached for one of my shellacked ringlets, though he frowned when he felt how stiff with hairspray it was. "Is this actually your hair, or are you wearing something?"

"It's mine," I said defensively. "It's not extensions, if that's what you mean. They just used about half a can of product on it."

"Well, you'll have to have a shower before we go to bed; otherwise I'll feel like I'm sleeping with a blackberry bush." Before I could do more than sputter at his effrontery, he rose to his feet, hauling up me and Ned. "C'mon, you. It's better to marry than to burn."

· · ·

Reader, I married him.

Well, sort of.

We stood before Margaret Russ in an alcove of the lobby, with no witnesses save the desk clerk and my pre-verbal son. Daniel asked if I wanted to grab Joanie or Perry, but I could hardly believe I was going along with this. I was not going to make it even more egregious by stealing Phyl's limelight. Friends and family would have to wait for later. "After we're back from Las Vegas," Daniel said in my ear.

Margaret had done enough weddings in her tenure at the church that she could recite most of the ceremony from memory, though she had to catch herself at the crucial moment: "And now, by the power vested in me by God and by the State of Wash—by God, rather—I pronounce you man and wife. You may kiss your bride."

As if there hadn't been plenty of that already.

· · ·

"Your place or mine?" said my husband softly, a couple hours later. "Or neither?"

I insisted we stay until the very end of Phyl's reception to see the couple off, but we returned to the Palace to find Joanie and Perry still gone somewhere. It was only us in the entry way.

"You would wait?" I asked.

"I could. I behaved myself the rest of the reception, didn't I? Which is more than I can say for you." Laughing, he kissed away my indignant response. "It's up to you, Cass. I got you to marry me. You can't escape me anymore. That knowledge alone would hold me another year, much less 24 hours."

I blushed. Looked away. "Well, I—uh—I think I'd like to be with you tonight, if that's all right."

That gleam of amusement. "I can take one for the team. How long do you need?"

I thought of Ned, my hair, the disastrous state of my bedroom after this morning's rush—"Would we be…sleeping in my room, Daniel? It would be weird out in the Lean-To, with Perry right there in the guest room. At least in my room Joanie is at the other end of the hall."

"Who said anything about sleeping?"

"You're impossible."

"How long do you need?"

"A half hour. Maybe forty minutes. But you can't come up because my room is a total mess, and—and—" and I wanted to get myself just right.

He ran a hand along my hip, pulled me against him. "I have things I need to get done myself. Like booking our airline tickets so Margaret Russ doesn't excommunicate me. Come get me when you're ready."

If I didn't get away from him this instant, I was going to be ready right now.

I woke Ned to give him a bottle—with any luck he'd sleep through then until six in the morning. No need to turn the monitor on, if Daniel and I would be in the same room. Ay ay ay. Then I stashed things in drawers, threw scattered clothes in the hamper, aired and straightened the bed. Followed this with the quickest shower, grateful that all the morning's beautifications meant I didn't need to do any of that now.

What to wear was a problem. I didn't want Joanie and Perry coming home and catching me traipsing about in a cami and knickers. Even the kimono robe I fetched from the back of the closet would surely raise eyebrows, but I was too vain to don sweats for my wedding night.

I must have taken longer than I thought. Emerging onto the deck, I noted the lights were out in the Lean-To. Could he possibly have gone to sleep? But, no. When I padded barefoot past the chaise longue, I saw the flash of his arm in the darkness as he caught me.

"What are you doing out here?" I squeaked. "It's freezing."

He rose to wrap me in the blanket he had around him. I couldn't see his expression, but I heard the hitch in his voice. "I actually was…praying."

"You what?"

"Or reciting. I tend to get them mixed up. It was that verse:

When I look at the heavens, the work of your fingers,
The moon and the stars which you have established;
What is man that you are mindful of him,
And the son of man that you care for him?"

"Oh, that one."

"Yeah, that one. I feel…thankful tonight."

"Me too."

"And it's not just the moon and the stars that make me think that."
He lifted my chin to the light to consider me, tracing a finger along my
jaw. "God, you look beautiful."

"Ooh, I love it when you feed me lines."

This earned me a pinch. "Silence, wife. I won't let you ruin this moment. Here—hold the blanket." A small task, but it was hard to obey
when I was so close to him. I ran my free hand luxuriously over his chest,
annoyed even by the thin t-shirt that got in the way. Maybe if I snuck
my hand under it—he seized it. "Patience. Here, Cass—this is for you."

I felt him press something into my hand. A ring box. I recognized
its velvet cover. "Ah…"

"Open it."

My throat tightened as my eyes filled. "I already have."

"What?"

"I found it weeks ago—I was cleaning your place and Joanie called
and I had to write something down and needed a pen. It was in the
drawer. I thought all this time it was for Violette. I kept waiting for it
to appear on her finger."

He paused. Grinned at me. "Serves you right, then. I kept waiting
for you to make some hideous announcement that you were going to
marry Skandar. Of course it's for you. I bought it while I was on that

blasted trip. I figured three days was long enough for you to make up your mind—it was longer than I needed. The damned thing was burning a hole in my pocket. I almost asked you the second I came back, but you set me straight."

"Oh, don't remind me, Daniel."

"Put it on."

I slid it on, that beautiful ring. "It's a little loose. I'm afraid to wear it—I wouldn't want to lose it."

"You like it, then? We'll get it adjusted. I don't want anyone thinking you're still available."

"You're one to talk. I'm going to get you the giantest ring ever. It might just cover your whole left hand."

"Whatever you say. I'm yours, after all."

He held my hand up so we could admire the sparkle, and that ring did sparkle. "It's like the stars, Daniel, the ones you were praying about." Just like them. We looked upward again.

I've always been lame at astronomy—at gunpoint I might have been able to spot the Big Dipper—but tonight the twinkles and flecks of light may as well have been my own wedding fireworks. Celestial confetti raining down on us from a rejoicing Father in heaven.

Who was man, indeed? Who was I? Just another of the hopeful, the faithful. Above all of us the same stars, lighting our way down the centuries. The same watchful care.

Thank you, Father.
For Daniel.
For Ned.
My gifts.
My blessings.

"Ready, love?"

"Ready."

Reading Group Guide

1. What expectations of the plot and characters did you have coming into *The Littlest Doubts* after having read *Mourning Becomes Cassandra*? How did *Doubts* meet or upset those expectations?

2. What problems and obstacles does Cass face over the course of the novel? Which ones result from her own choices, and which are beyond her control?

3. In Chapter 3, Lori Lincoln tells Cass, "It is a serious matter to take children from their biological parents, especially if the biological parents are eager to take them and prove their fitness." What is Cass's initial reaction to this? How do her feelings change as the story unfolds? How fit do you consider Mike Loftus as a father? Does your opinion change?

4. In Chapter 7, Cass hears the familiar story of Abraham in church and sees parallels to her own situation. (The Abraham story is found mainly in Genesis 12-22.) What are these parallels? In what ways do Cass's experiences with Ned continue to follow Abraham's with Isaac?

5. Consider the title. What are some of the things Cass doubts, and why? How do you distinguish between justifiable doubts and

irrational ones born of fear? Do you believe she was justified in doubting Daniel? Why or why not?

6. What does Skandar represent to Cass? How does his situation and temperament both draw her to him and repel her? What do you think she represents to him?

7. With both the adoption and with Daniel, Cass chooses to surrender her own wishes and live with a little doubt. Do you think she makes the right decision in either case? Would you have made the same choices, under those circumstances?

8. Would you say *The Littlest Doubts* ties up more neatly than *Mourning Becomes Cassandra*, or were there still some things you wondered about, as a reader?